One Last Wish

One last Wish

ELLA HARPER

CANELO

First published in the United Kingdom in 2017 by Canelo

This edition published in 2019 by

Canelo Digital Publishing Limited
57 Shepherds Lane
Beaconsfield, Bucks HP9 2DU
United Kingdom

A CIP catalogue record for this book is available from the British Library.

Print ISBN 978 1 78863 375 8
Ebook ISBN 978 1 911420 45 3

Look for more great books at www.canelo.co

Printed and bound in Great Britain by Clays Ltd, Elcograf S.p.A.

2012

'There is no easy way to say this. I'm afraid your daughter has terminal cancer.'

Rosie's breath caught in her throat. No. Something had just shifted. In the way things did when they were terrifying and irreversible.

Rosie squeezed Nate's hand. Harder than he had squeezed hers when she had given birth to Emmie. Because this was far, far worse. The surgical consultant in charge of Emmie had just said terminal cancer. Cancer. That was terminal. Terminal meant… it meant…

Barely aware of anything else but the heavy weight of those horrific words, Rosie realised she didn't quite know what to do with herself. Apart from screaming. Rosie knew she felt the urge to scream, at the very top of her voice. Like a banshee. Until her throat bled and until no more noise came out. It was either that or she might have to pummel the surgeon's chest. Slap him hard around the face. Hurt him. Because even though it wasn't his fault, Mr Hobbs had just told them that Emmie was going to die.

Nate cleared his throat and squeezed Rosie's hand equally hard.

'I'm so sorry, Mr Hobbs. Forgive me, but I don't understand what has happened here.'

Rosie stole a glance at Nate. His expression was earnest and Rosie's heart twisted torturously because she knew exactly how he felt. Nate wanted to have hope. He wanted to believe there might be a tiny shred of optimism that might take them out of this hideous reality.

Nate carried on, clearly struggling to form his words. 'Emmie has had chemo. Chemo, at her age. She's only five, Mr Hobbs. Five years old. She was sick day and night and all her beautiful hair fell out.' Nate's voice cracked. 'She's had radiotherapy. You operated on her. On her brain. You cut her head open and… and…'

Feeling desperate, Rosie helped Nate out. 'It's just that our daughter has endured more than most adults could cope with, Mr Hobbs. And now this. You're telling us…'

'That it's terminal. Yes. I'm so terribly sorry. I'd give anything to be telling you different news.' Mr Hobbs looked regretful. Sympathetic. Agonised.

Nate stared at him, only seeing an impassive face. Did Mr Hobbs have children? Did he know what it was like to go through something like this? To watch the most precious thing in your life endure pain and distress and ghastly treatments that had so many side-effects they had barely been able to keep up with them? And now… this? Nate felt impotent with rage. He felt weak and helpless and so full of fury, he could barely choke it down. In the distance, he heard Rosie yelp and Nate realised he'd been clutching her hand so hard he had nearly crushed it.

'Sorry,' he whispered, letting go and putting his arm around her shoulders instead. He held her fiercely and turned back to Mr Hobbs. 'Are you saying we have to sit our daughter down and tell her she's not going to make it? That at some point, that massive tumour could grow and squash her brain and… and kill her?'

Mr Hobbs looked pained. 'I'm afraid so.' He pointed to the scan on the wall behind him. 'Emmie's mass is a malignant primary tumour, as you know. We're dealing with what's called a medulloblastoma here. It has developed at the back of the brain. And unfortunately, this type may spread to other parts of the brain and into the spinal cord. The position of it...' Mr Hobbs tailed off, regretfully. 'It's too large and it's too dangerous. We could sever the spinal cord... damage Emmie's brain beyond repair. It's highly probable, not just a possibility. I'm so sorry. There is nothing more we can do in terms of surgery.'

Rosie swallowed. No more surgery sounded like a good thing. But it wasn't. She knew that it wasn't. Because no more surgery meant that the tumour was too large and couldn't be taken away.

'More chemo?' Nate suggested. 'More radiotherapy?'

'Emmie could have more chemo but she will need breaks from it,' Mr Hobbs said gently. 'Think about the quality of life Emmie has had during chemo. Ultimately we're talking about prolonging her life, not saving it. I'm incredibly sorry.'

'Jesus.' Nate slumped in his chair. He didn't know what else to say. There was nothing else to say.

'Are there any other tests we can do?' Rosie said. She knew the answer. But she had to try. Because otherwise she was literally giving in and accepting that there was no hope whatsoever.

Mr Hobbs reached for Emmie's file. 'I'm absolutely certain we have covered everything with the tests we've done. MRIs, brain angiograms, lumbar punctures. Blood tests, biopsies. There isn't much else we can do now because we know what we're dealing with and we know that we have tried everything possible to cure or remove this huge tumour.'

Rosie's lip trembled.

Mr Hobbs closed the file. 'We have counsellors who can help. You're not alone...'

Rosie felt the tears blocking her throat. She had never felt so helpless in her life. This couldn't be happening. It couldn't be. Emmie was their world, she was everything. Rosie finally broke down completely and she turned into Nate's shoulder, sobbing uncontrollably. Nothing had made them happier than when Emmie had arrived. They had been so lucky to have each other, so lucky. The feelings they had for one another, the relationship that was so full of magic. And Emmie had completed that; she had completed them. They couldn't lose her. It was unthinkable.

Nate clutched Rosie to him. 'She's a baby, she's just a baby…' he said wretchedly. Nate worked hard to get control of himself and after a few minutes, he dug deep and kissed Rosie's tears away, his hands shaking as he held her face. 'It's OK, darling,' he was saying, not even sure what words he was uttering. 'It's OK. We'll be OK. Emmie will be OK… She can't die. She won't. OK?'

Rosie shook her head silently. She didn't want Nate to be in denial. She understood it, but they had to face this. Together, they had to face this.

'We have a very good counselling team here,' Mr Hobbs began. 'They can help you come to terms with this…'

'We don't need anyone,' Nate shouted at him, still holding onto Rosie. 'We don't need any more counselling. All we've done is speak to counsellors. For the past three years.'

Mr Hobbs took a breath. 'I understand, Mr Johnson, I really do. But this is a huge thing to come to terms with.'

Nate let go of Rosie and stood up. 'Is it? Is it a huge thing to come to terms with? How do you even know?'

Rosie stared at Nate, devastated. Nate – six foot five, a giant of a man. Tall, dark and handsome. Everyone said so; it wasn't just that she was biased. But somehow he seemed diminished by this news. Crippled. He was a shadow of himself, cowed by the

4

horror he'd been confronted with. Rosie fished in her bag for a tissue. She was a mother; where were all her tissues? Surely she hadn't used them all up. She found one and wiped her face with it.

Rosie screwed up the tissue. God. Emmie. Their beautiful daughter. She had brought joy and love and happiness into their lives from the second she had arrived. Of course she had slept badly and had been a finicky eater, but they hadn't minded that. The terrible twos had passed unnoticed by and large because Emmie had been in and out of hospital, but three had been a troublesome year. But it wasn't that; it was Emmie's temperament. She had just been lovely from day one – a happy baby and a mischievous but delightful toddler.

Rosie paused in her reverie. But they had known something was wrong, she and Nate. Emmie's balance was off; she was sick a lot. She clutched her head as though it were about to explode and she had seemed overly tired and sleepy for no reason. And then she had started having fits and they had taken action and there were tests and scans and then life had suddenly imploded. Doctors, specialists, consultants, surgeons, hospitals, treatment, pain. There had been rounds and rounds of all of these things, with highs and lows and things none of them – Rosie, Nate or Emmie – had been equipped to experience.

Rosie sobbed silently into her tissue, feeling as though she was suffocating. She had thought that the worst possible pain a parent could go through was to see her child suffering. Hooked up to a chemo drip, her hair falling out in clumps. Holding her whilst sickness wracked her little body, even when there was nothing more inside her to release. But that was nothing compared to hearing that Emmie could die at any point. That the tumour that rested on her brain – in a place that was too dangerous to operate on – could just decide to expand and take her life at some point.

'I can't bear this,' Nate was saying, pacing like a caged panther. 'I can't bloody bear it. I want to punch the wall, I want to hurt someone, anyone. I can't bear it! This can't be happening to my baby, it can't be…'

'Nate…' Rosie pleaded, hating the way he was reacting but wanting to do the same. His distress and frustration were palpable. 'Nate, please.'

Nate stopped and looked at Rosie's tear-streaked face. He immediately dropped to his knees next to her. 'I'm sorry, babe. I'm so sorry. I'm here. Hold onto me and we'll get through this together. We'll get through it together, I promise…'

Rosie met his eyes, feeling a punch to her stomach. There was a hateful mass killing their daughter and they were utterly powerless to stop it.

'H-how long?' she said abruptly, voicing the horror that neither of them really wanted to confront. She heard Nate gasp, but she held Mr Hobbs' gaze.

Mr Hobbs took a breath. 'It could be years. It could be less, but the tumour hasn't changed significantly in the past six months. It's a difficult one to call, but I hope Emmie has years left, not months. I really do hope so, anyway. But I cannot call it – I must state that.'

Nate and Rosie stared at one another, not even able to speak now.

'Shall I bring Emmie in?' Mr Hobbs asked as kindly as he could. 'We can talk to her together. Or we can sit with this news for a little longer if you like. There is no hurry.'

Rosie let out an inhuman howl and put her arms around Nate's neck so tight her knuckles turned white.

Nate raised eyes, swimming with tears, to Mr Hobbs. 'W-what do we say?' he managed. 'How do we possibly tell her that she's dying?' As soon as he said the words out loud, Nate started to cry, weeping into Rosie's hair, holding her body close and hard against his as if he might keel over without her.

'With the utmost care,' Mr Hobbs said, getting to his feet to squeeze Nate's shoulder. 'We tell her with the utmost care and we are all as brave as we can possibly be.'

Rosie shook her head, blindly putting out a hand to stop him from moving towards the door. 'Stop. Wait. I don't think I can do it. I really don't think I can do it.' She tried to breathe and couldn't, not without her whole body jerking and pulsing. 'She's my baby... my life...'

'I understand.' Mr Hobbs paused. 'I'm so sorry. We can wait. Emmie is playing happily in the other room.'

Nate wiped a hand across his face and let out a shuddering sigh. 'We have to do this, Rose. We have to be brave.'

Rosie wasn't sure she could dig deep enough. How was she supposed to do this? She wasn't prepared; she didn't know what to do. She looked at Nate and put her face against his.

'I love you,' she said, close to his ear.

'And I love you,' he said, pulling back and looping her hair behind her ear. 'And the only thing we both love more than each other is Emmie. So we have to do this.'

Rosie took a breath and looked at Mr Hobbs. 'OK.'

Rosie and Nate stood up shakily. Nate reached for Rosie's hand and she slipped hers into his. As Emmie came into the room, they squeezed each other's hands as hard as they could. And somehow, they made themselves brave.

Five Years Later

Rosie

'Imagine you're pushing fifty tons of mud,' Rosie called out to her class, bending her leg at the knee before flexing it out again gracefully. 'And use… your… breath…'

The class dutifully copied Rosie as she counted the reps, even Maisie, who was in her sixties but more flexible than some of the youngsters who were lined up in the front in matching black and neon Lycra. Who also found it hilarious whenever Rosie mentioned their pelvic floors.

Rosie moved on to some inner thigh exercises. Aah, these girls. They were only in their early twenties! They had no concept of the horrors childbirth could wreak on such areas of the body, the way Rosie had now that she was in her mid-thirties. And they would have long forgotten their Pilates class by the time their babies came along, let alone the instructor who cracked them up by mentioning 'rude stuff' when they were content to tit about in Lycra looking all bendy and hot.

Rosie paused for a second. There it was. That emotive, inner twitch that reminded her that as hard as she tried, even the powerful focus of exercise couldn't completely obliterate the fears that kept her awake at night. It was like an extreme form of panic… a terror that rushed up without warning and caught in her throat. *Emmie.* Rosie's head swivelled to the phone sitting next to her iPod. It wasn't flashing or beeping. Everything was fine. Emmie was fine.

Rosie forced herself back to the present and glanced at the three men in her class. *They* didn't bat an eyelid whenever she mentioned pelvic floors, but actually they should. She wondered if she should advise them that they should, if *their* pelvic floors were working as they should do, be able to hold a wet towel up with their... umm... parts.

Er, no. Maybe not, Rosie decided, checking her watch discreetly. A sensitive subject at the best of times. And one of the dudes was in his fifties and looked as though he might keel over if the word 'parts' was mentioned, let alone anything else.

Rosie stood up, feeling back in control. 'Legs in table top, please,' she called, watching her class move onto their backs and position their legs in the air at a ninety degree angle. 'Touch those toes down to the floor one at a time... on a count of eight, seven, six...' She moved around the studio checking posture, reminding students to breathe. Not just *when* to breathe... to *actually* breathe. Some students totally forgot to breathe when they were exercising. Rosie often found them turning puce in the face and sucking their cheeks in as they concentrated so hard on perfecting a position, they forgot that air entering and leaving the body was rather more important.

'And another eight... seven... six...' Rosie said, enjoying the view of her class working in unison to the music. They looked like a pop video when they were in full flow. 'And... *another* eight!' she called, feeling collective waves of mock loathing emanating from her class.

Rosie shrugged it off. They always did this when she went a bit hard-core. It was her job to push her class at times.

Rosie took a breath and joined in at the front again so she didn't look too bossy. Then as part of the cool down, she demonstrated the mermaid stretch. 'And here is the one my mentor used to call the porn star... Give it your best, ladies... and gents... and... you're done.' Her class gasped at the final effort of exertion and then clapped themselves cheerfully.

Rosie quickly gave them some motivating feedback from the front of the room, smiling at her class as they rolled their mats up and chatted to one another. Rosie switched her music off, still in the zone for the moment. She loved the way exercise made her feel; all the endorphins rushing around her body, knowing she had done something amazing for herself – and for all the men and women in her class as well, which was the best part of her job. Teaching had been an absolute godsend for her; pure escapism. Her saviour, in fact.

The familiar dread shot to the surface and Rosie caught her breath. *Stop, stop, stop*, she told herself. It was OK. Emmie was at Lily's house. And Rosie trusted Lily with her own life, let alone Emmie's. Emmie was with her cousins. Everything was fine. No news was good news. Nothing had happened in the hour and fifteen minutes she had been away.

Release the guilt, Rosie intoned inwardly, echoing a sentiment that she and Nate had been taught in therapy. It was actually quite effective. For a person who spent around ninety percent of her life feeling responsible and as if she should constantly be doing more and solving the issue that had been thrown at them like a hand grenade, releasing the guilt to… wherever… felt cathartic.

Rosie checked her phone again and looked up as her boss Anna came into the studio.

'Hey. Everything OK?'

'Kind of.' Anna frowned. 'I mean, yes. But no. At least… I have news.'

'What's wrong?' Rosie was concerned. Anna was a combat fitness instructor. Zero body fat, a lean, mean power machine. No nonsense. Not much ruffled her feathers, yet right now, she looked seriously disturbed.

Anna took Rosie to one side. 'I've been offered a job. Abroad.'

'Abroad?'

'Yes. In Crete. Working at some swanky resort.'

Rosie pulled her sweatshirt over her head. 'That's amazing!'

'I know.' Anna was clearly feeling troubled. 'Except for the fact that they want me to start next week.'

'Blimey. That's quick.'

'Yes. And I really want to take it.' Anna nodded. 'I'm going to take it. I'm actually going to do it.'

'Wow. Er… what does that mean?'

Rosie frowned. Anna had been acting weirdly for the past few months because even though she wasn't a person who talked about her personal business much, recently, she had seemed really distant. They got on well and had a good rapport, but it was all about work with them. Which suited Rosie down to the ground. When she was at work, she wanted to be focused on work and nothing else. It had got her through some hard times. It didn't completely take her away from Emmie's diagnosis but it had its moments.

Anna eyed her caustically. 'It means you just got a promotion, Rosie. You're going to be the new boss. I'm appointing you, I'm training you at high speed and then... I'm off.'

Rosie put her hands to her mouth. This was incredible! She'd been waiting for an opportunity like this for the past few years, but the timing hadn't ever seemed to be right. Not with everything else that had been going on. Rosie pushed the thought aside with a smoothness that had come with practise and time. It was a twisted form of denial, but it worked. Sometimes.

'Do you mean it, Anna?'

'I mean it. I actually can't think of any other way it's going to work out. So we're doing it.' Anna moved restlessly from trainer-clad foot to trainer-clad foot. 'I have this boyfriend, you see.'

Rosie paused whilst packing her bag and glanced at Anna. Her boss had always seemed rather... sexless, if that wasn't too harsh an assessment. Work-focused, anally-retentive, machine-like. Anna hadn't, in the entire fifteen months they had worked together, ever mentioned boyfriends or men or dates or anything remotely pointing to the opposite sex. And now, she apparently had a boyfriend. One who presumably had something to do with the abrupt about-turn Anna was experiencing.

'He's gorgeous, hot, beautiful.' Anna appeared to have opened the floodgates on her personal life all of sudden. She actually sounded rather girly and gushy. Her eyes were shining. 'He's Cypriot, if you haven't guessed.'

'Right. I see. That makes sense.' Rosie's phone pinged. She hurriedly removed it from her bag and eyed the screen fearfully.

'Who's that? Your sexy husband?'

Rosie raised an eyebrow. Since when had Anna thought Nate was sexy? Rosie glanced at the small, pear-shaped diamond on her left hand. What had happened to them? Rosie refused to blame Emmie because it wasn't her fault. She suddenly shook her head by way of a response, realising Anna was still staring at her.

'It's my sister, Lily.' Rosie said, relaxing and reading the message again. 'It's OK. Everything is OK.'

Anna nodded. 'She's your twin, right? That would drive me insane, having a twin.' She grabbed the back of her foot and held it against the back of her thigh, clearly enjoying the stretch. 'Kind of like looking in a mirror all the time. And seeing yourself at your worst sometimes.'

Rosie shrugged. Her feelings towards her twin sister Lily were strong, but they were nothing close to the idea Anna was outlining. Not remotely.

'Anyhoo. I'd better be off.' Anna checked her watch. 'I have a class in two minutes and I need to warm up. And you probably need to dash off and pick your kid up, right?'

'Right.'

Anna made for the door. 'Glad we had that chat, Rosie. I'll deal with everything and it's all going to be great, I promise!'

'Fantastic. Thank you.'

Rosie watched Anna skip happily off to her class and, by contrast, felt herself thud back down to earth again. Pilates… exercise in general, had become her sanctuary, her place of healing. When she was working out or teaching a class, Rosie had developed a way of discon-necting from her racing mind, of putting the petrifying thoughts that periodically paralysed her into her body and into her teaching. But those thoughts always returned. They had to. Because the thoughts Rosie worked so hard to distance herself from weren't just her thoughts. They were her reality. Her life. It was just the way it was now. It had been that way for five years now.

Rosie shouldered her bag and headed out. The thing was, so much of her life was awesome. Tons of it. Her job was amazing and she loved it. She'd just got a promotion! But more important than anything else, Emmie was the best kid in the world. The best. And she always would be. Rosie was also very lucky, she reminded herself, because she had a good marriage.

Rosie stepped outside the gym and took a gulp of fresh air. OK. So something needed correcting in that statement she'd just made. Her marriage wasn't good. It used to be good. In fact, it used to be exciting, romantic, fun, sexy and strong. Off the scale wonderful. The way she had always thought marriage should be when two people got it incredibly right. Whereas now, it was merely... passable. At best.

Rosie felt her chest tighten, and not just because of the sharp March air. Admitting that truth about her marriage, even in her head, had just jolted her heart. Knocked it sideways. Nate. *Nate*.

Rosie leant her head against the wall, shaking her head slightly as if to dispel the image. What else had been wrong with the jaunty list she had mentally trotted out? Oh yes, Emmie. Well. Emmie *was* the best kid in the world. That much was true. Emmie brought light and sparkle and giddy giggles to everything she touched and to everyone around her and although Rosie knew that as Emmie's mum she was totally biased, that fact was also indisputable.

No, the part that had jarred was the part where Rosie had unconsciously inserted the phrase 'and she always would be'. Emmie would *always* be the best kid in the world.

Rosie headed over to her car, feeling the thick, familiar sensation of a thousand balled-up tears lodging in her throat. Because the truth of the matter was that Emmie would never 'always' be the best – or indeed, the worst – kid in the world. Because Emmie was dying. And that, Rosie thought as she yanked her car door open furiously, was at the root of everything in her life that was cloudy and sad and angry and desperately, dreadfully, horribly, *fucking* unfair.

Rosie slid into her car and hurled her gym bag onto the passenger seat. And that feeling about Emmie threatened to overpower Rosie and overwhelm every living, breathing second that it flooded into her mind, body and heart. This was the cold, hard truth of the matter. Emmie was going to die. Before either of her parents. And it could happen any day, at any time.

Rosie put her face in her hands, feeling wretched. She couldn't wait to see Emmie because she cherished every second of time she had with her daughter. But right in this moment, what she could do with, what she really needed right now, was Nate. Nate. The old version of him. The guy who had always been there for her, always there to put his arms around her and make her feel amazing and safe and protected. Even when nothing in Rosie's life felt remotely safe, Nate had somehow been able to make her feel better.

Rosie took a deep breath and put her hands on the steering wheel. And willed Nate to come home early. To talk to her. To be there for her. To hold her. To want to be with her again, the way he always had in the past. Because the only thing that had ever made Emmie's situation even vaguely bearable had been Nate. Their hearts had been broken by the terrible pain they had gone through, but Rosie's heart had fresh splinters now, ones caused by the breakdown of her marriage. But maybe those splinters could be mended. Maybe Nate would come home early and would want to spend time with her, when Emmie had gone to bed.

Rosie started the car, feeling her heart contract. Nate and Emmie. Her entire world. She couldn't think of a life without them in it.

Nate

Nate stared at his computer screen and sighed. He couldn't stand filing reports. And sitting at his computer for hours on end made him feel restless. He was a police officer; a Sergeant, well on his way to being promoted to Inspector. Nate liked being out on the streets. Driving to emergencies. Helping people. Keeping everything under control. Filing reports was a necessary evil but it bored the hell out of all but the most anally retentive types.

Nate frowned and hit the backspace key a few times. Most of his colleagues wrote their reports by hand but he always typed them – with two fingers, like some sort of hapless chimpanzee. And he only typed them because he had shit handwriting that not even his own mother could read. His partner Gill said it was because he had 'some French in him', because presumably that meant it was a given that his handwriting would be terrible.

Right on cue, Gill appeared over his shoulder. 'Oh dear, Johnson. Chimp typing again. You know why that is, don't you?'

'You know you're xenophobic, right?'

'Oh stop speaking French to me, haha,' Gill said, laughing, as she perched on the edge of Nate's desk. She flapped a folder in his face.

Nate leaned back in his seat, smiling. He and Gill had been partners for the past four years and they got on famously. Gill was a straight-talking Essex girl who seemingly wore the same grey trouser suit to work every day. Nate assumed she must have five of the same, however, since Gill was super-clean and tidy to the point of OCD. She did at least vary the colour of her shirt, but clothes weren't really Gill's concern. She was dedicated to the job with a focus that even Nate, known for his fierce intensity, found impressive. And they somehow managed to find fresh banter to amuse each other with most days. Which made the job a whole lot easier.

Nate abandoned his report and took the folder Gill was brandishing out of her hand. He was very fond of his partner. She was like a mouthy little pit bull with a great sense of humour thrown in and she took great delight in winding Nate up about anything she could think of: his 'posh' background (Nate was from South West London – not exactly Chelsea, but Gill glossed over that), his 'funny' accent and, of course, his looks. Gill was completely immune to Nate's charms, being happily loved up with a giant of a man she called 'Sexy Kev', a heavy-set man with a fluffy beard and hoop earrings. Nate enjoyed this aspect of their relationship because Gill spoke to him in a way many women didn't and he welcomed it.

'The Peabody case?' Nate raised his eyebrows.

'Oh yes. We're playing with the big boys now, Johnson. It's about time.'

And it was. He and Gill had been after a juicy case for months and now one had dropped right into their laps. The Peabodys were a sinister little family set up who, as clichéd as it sounded, lived on a council estate on the outskirts of Essex. They – three brothers close in age and a menacing father who reportedly ruled them with a rod of iron – were mostly involved in petty crime and intimidation, but of late, there were whispers that they might have evolved, progressing into more serious crime. Crime involving guns and robbery and extreme violence.

Nate scanned the file. He was doing his best to process his low-key reaction to having such a gem of a case land right in his and Gill's laps. Gill was right; they'd both been waiting for such a case for months now, having tired of small-time, local crime which yes, was all very productive in terms of keeping the streets safe, but it was hardly the kind of stuff to set the world on fire.

'You're not exactly doing an Irish jig around the office, Nate,' Gill huffed, nudging his chair with the toe of her brogue. 'This is great news.'

'You're not doing a jig either,' Nate pointed out reasonably.

'Ah, but I can...' Gill jumped off the desk and started hopping from one foot to the other, much to the amusement of the mostly male office.

Nate rolled his eyes. 'Sit down, Potts. You're making a big, old fool of yourself right there.' He grinned. Gill amused him greatly and it made his day go quicker.

Gill shrugged and sat down again. 'So what? I'd rather react like that than act all cool like you. What's got into you?'

Nate regarded her, feeling a familiar rush of anger rush to the surface. But he let the fury slip away when he saw compassion in Gill's eyes. She knew what had got into him. They spent more time together than they spent with their actual real-life partners; there wasn't much they didn't know about each other. Much to his occasional discomfort, Nate had become more intimately acquainted with Gill's periods, smear tests and general 'women's issues' than he might have wanted, but at the same time, he liked how open she was because it made him respond in kind.

'Anything new to report?' Gill asked in an undertone.

'No.' Nate shook his head. 'Same old, same old.'

'Bloody stressful, though, innit? Even same old, same old.'

'Yep.'

As ever, Nate appreciated Gill's talent for understatement. She knew he detested people asking him how Emmie was, because it was like Groundhog day. Emmie was… how Emmie was. She was dying. She could go at any second, which was the horrible, horrible thing about it. That was the problem with inoperable brain tumours; they just sat there, mocking everyone, doing their thing, and they got to choose when they grew and expanded. Nate felt his eyes fill with tears. Wow. The way it hit him like this! It came out of the blue… sometimes when he was thinking about it, sometimes when he was focused on something completely different.

Now and again, almost as if to break the monotony, Emmie's symptoms flared up and then it was like being on high police alert; nerve-wracking, traumatic and puke-inducing. But aside from that, it was just the same thing. It was like trying to relax and watch TV with a ticking time bomb in the corner of the room. One you loved with all your heart and couldn't contemplate being without. And Nate had run out of ways to describe that state of being because it was pretty much indefinable.

Nate checked his watch. It was late, but Emmie was at Lily's, so she was perfectly safe. Rosie's sister knew the drill. The slightest change in Emmie's behaviour or symptoms would initiate a phone call to both himself and Rosie. His phone was silent. Everything was OK. Rosie was teaching a late class, unusually; normally she was with Emmie as soon as she came out of school but Lily had assured her that she would keep an eye on Emmie.

Nate let out a breath. 'I want to spend every second with her, you know? Sometimes I just want to leave this job and lie in bed cuddling her.'

Gill nodded.

Nate held up his hand then dropped it uselessly. 'Take her to Legoland again because she loved it so much. Disneyland, the park, the cinema... anywhere she wants to go.'

'But Emmie just wants a normal life,' Gill said, gently. 'She wants to go to school and hang out with her friends. Be as normal as possible.'

It was true. And Nate didn't blame Emmie for that. She had been through such a hard time. Chemo, radiotherapy. She'd lost all her hair. It had broken Nate's heart. And now that there was nothing to be done, ironically, but live, that's exactly what Emmie wanted to do.

Gill gave him a sympathetic smile. 'You used to love this job, Nate. I mean, even when you found out about Emmie. It seemed to keep you going, fire you up. But something's changed over the past few months. You've lost your appetite a tad.'

'I know. I'm sorry.'

Nate rubbed a hand over his eyes tiredly. He worked long hours but his exhaustion was caused by such a multitude of worries, they overlapped one another like crashing waves and blurred into one. Emmie… Rosie… Emmie… *Emmie*…

'Never apologise,' Gill told him, pulling her stern face. 'You're under a huge amount of pressure. Every single day. This job is actually the least of your worries.' She paused. 'It's just a shame because you used to see this as your escape, right? Your place to come and temporarily let go of stuff. But lately…'

'I know. I don't know what's happened.' Nate put the file down onto his desk and dug deep. 'It's not like anything is different with Emmie. I don't know if it's just… the strain of this ongoing thing. Me and Rosie…'

Gill jerked her head to indicate that they should go to the coffee area. Leading the way, she waited until a few colleagues were out of earshot and keyed in Nate's coffee order.

'What about you and Rosie?'

Nate folded his arms and leant against the machine. 'We're just… I don't know. Something is very wrong. I mean, I know I already told you that. But it's actually getting worse.'

'Worse? In what way?'

Nate shrugged. 'We're not talking much. The…' He glanced at Gill then remembered how she delighted in telling him about her sex life. 'The passion has pretty much gone between us.'

Gill pondered. 'Hmm. OK. That's a tough one. I mean, on the one hand, it's totally understandable, isn't it? You're dealing with Emmie. It's a passion killer, unfortunately, that kind of thing. I mean, I don't know that first-hand obviously; I don't have kids. But on the other hand, that was a real feature of your relationship, wasn't it? Not just in the early days, but the whole time. Even after you'd had Emmie.'

Nate sipped his coffee. It was true. He and Rosie had always had something special. It wasn't just about the passion, because that made it sound shallow. It was about the intimacy and the closeness. The affection and the tenderness. Just looking at Rosie could do it for him at times. At least, that's how it always had been.

But things had been rough for a while. Quite a while. Not just rough, but really quite grim.

'Did things change after Emmie's diagnosis?' Gill asking, punching her numbers into the drinks machine. 'In that area, I mean.'

'No. Not for ages actually.'

Nate stared into his coffee sullenly. When had it all shifted in the wrong direction? He couldn't exactly pinpoint the moment he and Rosie seemed to have drifted apart. But it wasn't when they received Emmie's horrific diagnosis. If anything, the trauma had pushed him and Rosie even closer together. They had clung to one another like limpets to a rock, with their arms wrapped around each other, their foreheads touching and their limbs entwined. In every way possible. The only thing that had given them solace in their darkest moments had been one another.

No. It had been more of a gradual thing, Nate realised. A slow slide away from one another that he hadn't noticed until recently. And he couldn't believe that was the case. Was he just some preoccupied moron who hadn't noticed that what used to be a fantastic marriage was suddenly in a very bad way? No, he wasn't. Because it hadn't been sudden; it had been gradual. A feeling of unease that had descended into a huge sense of discomfort and despondency over a period of time. Set off by an event or events that Nate couldn't pinpoint.

He swallowed, unaware of Gill watching him with concern in her eyes. What was that thing he and Rosie had read when they were first dealing with Emmie's diagnosis? Something about it being a known fact that when two parents were dealing with a verdict that was as appalling and shocking as theirs, either or both could implode emotionally. That what parents needed to do was support one another – get each other through the host of different emotions that exploded to the surface. Guilt, sadness, fear, anger, grief, uncertainty.

Nate and Rosie knew this. They knew it. It wasn't a secret – they weren't unfamiliar with this concept. Nate hurled his unfinished coffee into the bin. Why weren't they holding it together? Why was their marriage cracking and falling apart? They knew how hard this stuff was, both of them. They'd had counselling, for heaven's sakes! They knew better than most people that they had to stick together in a situation like theirs. That appointing blame, and even worse, not communicating were the worst things to do.

'Nate.' Gill put her hand on his arm. 'It's OK.'

'It's actually not, Gill. It's really not.'

Nate frowned. He didn't feel like himself at all right now. He knew he was a grumpy son of a bitch at times, but he soon snapped out of it normally. This felt different. This feeling was affecting Nate's work; his entire approach to life.

'I'm worried about you, Nate.'

Nate shook his head. He was worried about himself. He struggled to get through his days at the moment, because he was consumed by anxiety about Emmie. About getting an unspeakable phone call. About facing his greatest fear. At night, his subconscious seemed to go into overdrive, tormenting him with the most awful thoughts and projections. And there was nothing he could do about it.

Nate felt angry. And impotent. Impotent with rage at the position he and Rosie had been put in. He felt utter fury at the way their lives had changed from heavenly to horrifying. And there was nothing Nate could do with those feelings, nothing. They were pointless and he knew it, but he couldn't seem to get a handle on them. He didn't know how to get rid of them, cope with them, process them… whatever the hell he was supposed to do with such things.

He should know; he had had enough therapy. He and Rosie had gone through individual therapy, couple's therapy, family therapy. They had both had so much counselling, they had grown sick of the predictable speech patterns, but at the same time they should have been well-versed enough to be able to cope with what had happened to them. Especially since they had been warned of the effect Emmie's diagnosis could have on their relationship and, ultimately, their marriage.

Nate frowned. Emmie had mentioned something about a new counsellor she had been assigned. He only hoped this one was better than the other ones she had seen. Emmie was an incredible kid; old beyond her years. She needed a special kind of person to get through to her; to be able to understand the way she was tackling her terminal diagnosis.

Nate rubbed his eyes. Rosie had always been his person. The person he turned to when he felt petrified. When it felt as though the unease and angst in his mind was more than he could cope with. And now it felt as though she was no longer there for him. Well, it was more that she didn't want him around. God, he spoke to Gill more than he spoke to Rosie – even after work hours were over!

As if she had read his mind, Gill made a suggestion. 'How about a drink after work tonight?'

Nate went to say no. He should say no. He should go home. He should be with Rosie and they should talk. Emmie would be in bed by the time he finished work anyway and Nate should want to spend time with Rosie because she was his wife and he loved her. The thing was, Nate wasn't sure Rosie still loved him. And being around her made him feel like a failure at the moment. He felt that he couldn't support her or be who she wanted him to be.

Nate hated himself. He just wanted to be there for Rosie. But he just didn't know how to find his way back. Still. There were worse things he could be doing, Nate thought to himself. He nodded at Gill.

'OK. One drink. Just one.'

Gill smiled. 'Great. We can relax and have a chat about everything.'

'Nah.' Nate jerked his head in the direction of his desk. 'There's nothing to talk about.'

'We can talk about food and cooking if you want,' Gill said, pulling a face. 'You love talking about food. It's the other love of your life.'

Nate shrugged. 'Maybe. I need to get on with my reports.'

'OK, Johnson.' Gill left him to it.

Back at his desk, Nate was shocked to find tears pricking at his eyes yet again. What was happening to him? He had to get his shit together. He simply had to. He'd be no use to Emmie if he carried on like this. And whatever was happening with Rosie and however much she didn't seem to want him around, Nate was resolute about one thing. He would never ever let his daughter down, not ever. Because she was the most important person in his world to him.

Nate quickly wiped his eyes and started punching his keyboard like a chimpanzee again.

Emmie

'So.' Dr Tom regarded Emmie. 'How are you feeling?'

Emmie pushed her fringe out of her eyes, but only because it was irritating her; not because she wanted to see her counsellor better. Dr Tom. Her new counsellor. She had been assigned counsellors from around the age of eight, so she could talk about her feelings. Her feelings about dying, mostly.

She chewed her lip. She was always nervous when she met a new counsellor. Her last one had been lovely, but Emmie wasn't sure she had 'opened up' much. Dr Zara had been assigned another case and now she had Dr Tom. Emmie liked the way the Dr's used their first names as part of their title.

She swallowed. 'I, umm… never really know how to answer that question.'

'Why not?'

'Because…' Emmie paused and pulled at a loose thread on the ugly, grey chair she was curled up in. 'I don't know if you're asking me about my diagnosis or if you're actually asking about me.'

Dr Tom smiled. 'I'm asking about you, of course. I know about your diagnosis.' He held up his folder. 'I have all that info in here. And as fascinating as it is, it's not who you are, Emmie. I'm interested in you. In what's going on in your brain, rather than the tumour that's squashing it.'

Surprised, Emmie met Dr Tom's eyes. 'You said tumour.'

'Yes. Yes, I did. Is that taboo?'

'No.' Emmie looked down. 'But people usually avoid saying that word in front of me. Apart from when I'm actually in hospital for tests and stuff.'

'Well.' Dr Tom smiled. 'I'm not "people". Also, you're ten. "People" probably think you can't deal with hearing the word "tumour". But that's because they don't know you well enough to know how well you're coping with being told your brain could get crushed at any time. Make allowances for them; not everyone is as brave and pragmatic as you. I don't know you very well either... yet. But I'm already impressed that you're so together.'

He glanced at her file again. 'So you've had chemo.'

'Yes.' Emmie's eyes welled up at the memory. Chemo had been the most horrible experience of her life. The drip itself had been fairly gentle, but the stuff that happened afterwards had been awful. She had been so sick and tired all the time. Her skin had turned flaky and red. And she had lost nearly all of her hair. That had been the most embarrassing thing of all. Emmie had hated being bald. She smiled for a second, remembering the bright pink wig her mum had bought her to wear. It was a bob with a blunt fringe. Not remotely like her own hair, but fun. And a bit itchy. But very cool.

'Radiotherapy?'

Emmie nodded. 'And surgery. That's when they realised there was nothing they could do.'

'Yes. I saw that. That's all very scary for a person your age.' Dr Tom closed the file. 'So. They decided that the tumour was inoperable. Too large to remove.'

Emmie let out a breath. 'Yes.' She remembered the moment her parents had told her about her diagnosis very clearly. It was imprinted on her mind and she could recall the way a terrifying coldness had spread through her body. Her stomach had churned as if she had eaten something bad and she had almost been sick on the spot. Her parents had been very brave about it but she knew they had felt as petrified as she was.

Dr Tom rubbed his fingers on his trousers. 'That's a tough thing to hear.'

'It was really bad,' she agreed. 'But it was five years ago. I still hate it but I'm used to it.'

'Are you? That's a huge thing to get used to.'

Emmie wasn't sure she was being truthful about that. Was she used to the idea that she was going to die at some point? That the massive tumour in her head that gave her headaches, made her feel nauseous and affected her balance and her eyes was at some point going to make everything stop working? Not really. She wondered if she should talk to Dr Tom more about that.

'Emmie is a nice name,' Dr Tom commented whilst he waited for her to digest her thoughts.

'Thank you. It's short for Emmeline. Which is like Emily, but French.'

'Fancy.' He smiled to show that he was joking.

'I have a French grandmother.' Emmie chewed on her fingernail then stopped. Her fingernails looked terrible with all the gnawing she did. 'Which means my dad is a quarter French. Which means that I'm…'

'Veering off the subject.' Dr Tom raised his eyebrows at her, indicating that he meant business. 'So. How are you, Emmie?'

Emmie took a second to study Dr Tom properly. He was probably quite handsome, in an *old* kind of a way. He had brown hair that stuck up in tufts and... brown? Yes, brown eyes that matched his hair nicely. And glasses. The geeky kind with black rims that looked cool. On the right person. Dr Tom looked cool.

Dr Tom was probably around *thirty*, Emmie surmised. Not old for a counsellor, as they all tended to be like lovely grannies, in Emmie's experience. But he was almost as old as her parents, in fact. That thought made her brow crease slightly. Her parents. They were a whole other issue. An issue that bothered her more than anything else. Even her tumour.

'I'm OK.' Emmie flexed her legs out as she finally answered Dr Tom's question. She was actually getting cramp. 'These chairs are really uncomfortable.'

'And they are also very ugly,' Dr Tom agreed, shifting in his. 'To be honest, they're totally pants. I should get some new ones. What do you reckon?'

Emmie threw him a smile, mostly because of the words he was coming out with. Pants. Dr Tom was funny.

'Maybe. You should get some beanbags. Pink ones.'

'I don't know about that. Pink?' Dr Tom mock-shuddered then picked up his file again. 'Let's talk about your homework.'

'OK.' Emmie's stomach dropped a bit. She had found the homework really hard to do. She had been as honest as possible, but she didn't know how Dr Tom was going to react to it.

'I asked you to write about your greatest fear.' Dr Tom picked up the diary he had bought for Emmie to note her thoughts in. It was purple with silver swirls on it and it had a small lock on the edge, presumably to keep it secret and safe. 'Interestingly, your greatest fear isn't dying.'

Emmie felt a sob bubbling up in her throat. She wasn't sure she could talk about this stuff. Even with Dr Tom.

Dr Tom paused then gestured to his bookcase. It was in a small alcove beyond his office. 'Do you want to have a look at anything there? I have some Harry Potter, I think. You can borrow anything you like.'

'OK.'

Emmie got up awkwardly and went over to the alcove so she could get to the bookcase. It was a cute little space – like one of those en-suite bathroom things, but with bookcases instead of a shower and toilet. Emmie scrutinised the books. She had all the Harry Potter novels; had read them several times over, but she didn't want to offend Dr Tom, because he was being really nice.

'You have lots of medical books.' She raised her voice so he could hear her from the alcove. It echoed a bit.

'Yes. I'm a bit geeky like that.' Dr Tom raised his voice too and scratched his head. 'But I like fiction as well. Do you read much?'

'All the time.' Emmie pulled a book out. It was old and tatty but it looked interesting. 'It takes me away from everything a bit. I can… lose myself for a while.'

'Reading is brilliant for that.'

'My mum reads a lot. And my dad lies in bed and we read together.'

Dr Tom waved his pen at her from his office. 'No way! My dad did that too. In fact, my dad gave me that book you have in your hand. No, no... borrow it. It's a really great book. It's about a singing cake.'

Emmie smiled. 'Thanks.' She sniffed it. It smelt really old.

'Why aren't you scared of dying, Emmie?'

Emmie faltered, even though Dr Tom's tone was gentle. She turned to find him standing in the doorway. 'I don't know. I mean... it's not so much that I'm not scared of dying. It's just that... other things scare me more.' She felt a tremor in her chest and she turned away so she was facing the bookcase again. She pulled out a big medical book on the shelf in front of her.

'Oh don't borrow that one,' Dr Tom warned, leaning against the door frame. 'It's *so* boring. Put it back quickly, otherwise your tumour will be the least of your worries.'

Emmie glanced at him and before she could stop herself, she laughed. 'You said tumour again. You're a bit obsessed, aren't you?' She slotted the book back into place. 'I'd love to be a writer.'

'You write very well. I really like how honest you are in your diary.'

How did Dr Tom even know she was being honest? Emmie scraped her dark hair into a ponytail then let it go so it draped around her neck again. Ever since her hair had grown back, she couldn't stop touching it. It was coarser than before, not as glossy, but Emmie didn't care. It was hair and she looked normal and that was all that mattered.

'Of course, you could just be highly inventive,' Dr Tom said, as if reading her mind. 'You might be trying to impress me. Or distract me from the real issues.' He gestured for her to sit down again as he returned to his seat. 'But somehow, I think you're being truthful in this diary. These words come from the heart.'

Emmie felt hers tighten. Dr Tom seemed to have a weird way of understanding her. She liked it, but she didn't really get how he had managed to get in her head the way he had.

'For the record, it's always best to be honest with me,' Dr Tom said in a kindly tone. 'Otherwise we're going to have some really random conversations in this room. And then I'll get bored and make you read that massive medical journal instead.'

Emmie curled up in the horrible, grey chair again. 'OK. I don't want to read the big medical book. But I am being truthful,' she added, remembering what she'd written. It made her feel all breathless again and she didn't like it.

Dr Tom adjusted his geeky glasses. 'So. You make a good point. Of course we are all going to die. You make a good point there. But you… You could die before… me. Before your parents. And yet you seem reasonably unconcerned about that.'

Emmie shook her head. She had this huge lump in her throat and she didn't want it to turn into huge tears. She didn't cry often but she could feel it rising. And she didn't know Dr Tom well enough yet to cry in front of him. Doctors, even therapists, sometimes reacted very strangely to sobbing. Emmie had experienced everything from silence followed by the feel of a box of tissues being thrust into her hands, to the sound of whomever she had blubbed in front of joining in.

'It's not… I'm really scared. I don't want to die. But I don't have any choice. That's been made really clear to me.'

'OK.'

'I just… It's just… There are other things…'

'What you are really concerned about,' Dr Tom said, smoothly interjecting – 'your greatest fear, in fact, is your parents. Your parents not making it. As in, them splitting up. Getting divorced, maybe.'

Emmie wrapped her arms around her knees.

'May I?' Dr Tom gestured to the diary.

Emmie hesitated. She wasn't sure she wanted her words read out loud but could she even say that?

'*This situation is killing my parents,*' Dr Tom read. '*Even more than my brain tumour is killing me. I know I'm not going to make it but I'm scared they're not going to make it either. And…*'

'Stop.' Emmie tightened her grip on her knees and felt the sob in her throat spill out into her mouth. She felt sick. 'Sorry.'

'No need to say sorry in this ugly little room,' Dr Tom said, giving her a nice smile. 'Ever.'

Emmie gave him a watery smile in return but she felt a rush of gratitude. She felt safe with Dr Tom. Emmie was fairly certain he wasn't about to dissolve into tears any time soon. Which was good. It was great, in fact. The one thing Emmie hated was grown-ups crying about her diagnosis. She didn't cry about it that often, so why should they?

'That was hard for you. Hearing that out loud.' Dr Tom's was soft, but probing.

'I'm… I'm not sure I wanted you to read it out loud.'

'Then you should have said that, Emmie! I'm really not like other counsellors. Trust me. You can say whatever you like in here. Whatever you like.' Dr Tom handed her diary over. 'But for the record, I can be extraordinarily prudish about swearing.'

'I'm ten,' Emmie protested. 'I'm not allowed to… Ahhh, you're trying to make me laugh.'

Dr Tom rolled his eyes. 'I'm so obvious. I can see you're going to keep me on my toes, Emmie. But back to your parents. You think their relationship is over?'

Emmie leant her head back against the chair. 'I don't know. All I know is that they used to be happy. I remember it. And I've seen photos.' She rubbed her nose. 'They always used to smile and laugh together. They were in love. And now they're not. Not happy, I mean. And maybe not in love anymore. That makes me really sad.' She felt hopeless saying all of that out loud. It wasn't something she talked about, not even to her best friend.

Dr Tom sat up. 'You know that's not your fault, right?'

Emmie felt herself wobble inside. 'But it *is* my fault, Dr Tom. It really is.'

Dr Tom laced his fingers together across his knees. He was wearing jeans, Emmie noticed. With rips in them. Surely that was against the rules?

'You think your illness has torn them apart.'

It was a statement rather than a question. Emmie appreciated that. 'I know it has. They were happy. I overheard my Auntie Lily saying it once. More than once. She and my Uncle Jamie talk about it quite a lot… when they think I'm not listening. And then I came along. It was fine when I was fine but then they got my diagnosis and they fell to pieces.' Emmie heard the crack in her voice and she halted, sure she could get control of herself again. But as it turned out, she couldn't. 'I hate it. They were happy and then my cancer ruined everything.' Emmie burst into tears, immediately covering her face with her hands.

'Oh, Emmie.'

Emmie felt Dr Tom's hand touch her shoulder briefly, professionally. She lifted her hands from her face to find Dr Tom crouching down next to her.

'Aren't you going to ask me about my feelings?' she gulped. 'And where is the box of tissues?'

'On my desk over there. I'll get them in a minute.' Dr Tom sat back on his heels. 'I don't need to ask you about your feelings, Emmie. You're sobbing your heart out. I know you're feeling horrendously guilty and responsible because you feel that your tumour has driven a wedge between your parents. I said tumour again. That's three times in one session – maybe more; you're right; I'm obsessed. God knows why; that only scores an eight in Scrabble.'

'You weren't lying about the geeky thing,' Emmie said. She sniffed and flushed, embarrassed to be dripping with snot in front of Dr Tom for some reason.

'Yes,' Dr Tom agreed amiably. 'I really am a geek.' He stood up and reached for his tissues. 'There you go. I'll make sure I put those in a more prominent place next time.'

'Please don't. I don't cry very often. This is just a bit of a bad day.'

Dr Tom regarded her seriously as she rubbed her face with a tissue. 'But this thing with your parents. I want to work on it.'

'You want me to write about it more?' Emmie felt her heart sink.

'Not unless you want to.' Dr Tom took his glasses off and cleaned them on the front of his checked shirt. 'No. I meant that we should do what we can to address that situation.'

'My parents falling apart?'

'Yes, that. If we can.'

'How can we?' Emmie felt a buzz of excitement. She hadn't ever had a counsellor who actually wanted to help her with anything. Well, that wasn't exactly true. They all wanted to 'help' her, but mostly with her feelings, not with practical stuff. Which was kind of what she really needed.

'I don't know yet.' Dr Tom put his glasses back on.

Emmie decided he was nicer-looking with the specs.

'But let's work on it, shall we? See what we can come up with together? Your head, my head… Together we must be able to find a solution.'

Emmie thought she might want to kiss Dr Tom. Or hug him, at very least. But she knew that wasn't appropriate. Instead, she said 'Thank you,' as nicely as she could. It didn't seem enough but she didn't know what else to say.

'You're very welcome,' Dr Tom smiled. 'It's just… looking at your file, it seems that other counsellors have talked through everything you're going through. Repeatedly. I'm happy to do that with you anytime you want, OK? But the reason I asked you to write a diary is because I wanted to understand what's actually on your mind right now. What will make your life easier. And you seem very upset about your parents.'

'I am. I'm so worried about them.' Emmie went to bite her thumbnail again and stopped herself.

'OK. So. Homework for next time… find out about your parents. Pre-Emmie.' Dr Tom handed her diary back. 'Can you do that?'

Pre-Emmie. Emmie smiled. 'I think I can do that.'

'Because then maybe we can have a think about what might have happened to drive this wedge between them. I know you think it's you, but maybe it isn't. Is that worth looking at?'

'Yes.' Emmie nodded and rubbed her face. 'Do I look as though I've been crying?'

'No way.'

'OK, good.' She opened the door. 'Although my mum sometimes buys me an ice cream if I look really upset after counselling. Or if I don't, actually.'

'Ice cream? It's March.'

Emmie couldn't help rolling her eyes. 'That doesn't make any difference when it comes to eating ice cream. Trust me.'

'I'll see you next week,' Dr Tom called as she left. 'I might even have some pink beanbags by then.'

Emmie smiled. It had to be said; Dr Tom wasn't remotely pants. Quite the opposite, in fact. 'What's he like?' Rosie asked as she jumped up from her chair. She tossed aside the magazine she'd been sort of reading.

'He's really nice,' Emmie said. 'And a bit geeky. Quite handsome.'

'Oh well. Handsome indeed.' Rosie smiled. 'He sounds great.'

'He lent me this book.' Emmie held it up.

'*The Singing Cake*,' Rosie read, pulling a face as she held it closer. 'Pooh, it smells a bit.'

'I like it.'

'What's the other book?'

'It's a diary.' Emmie tucked it under her arm defensively. She didn't want her mum to know she'd been writing personal stuff about her and her dad.

Rosie grabbed her handbag. 'Rightio. No need to clutch it like that. I had a diary once. I'd have gone bonkers if my mum had read it.'

'It's kind of private, that's all.'

'Of course it is. Aah, there's your dad.' Rosie's mouth tightened as she caught sight of Nate striding towards them.

'Hey. How did it go?'

'Dr Tom wears jeans,' Emmie informed him. 'With rips in them.'

'Good lord.' Nate glanced at Rosie quickly then put his arm around Emmie. 'Who's up for an ice cream?'

'I was just about to suggest that,' Rosie said.

'Great minds,' Nate responded, frowning slightly.

'Yes please,' Emmie said quickly, sensing the tension between them. 'Can I have a Magnum?'

Nate nodded. 'Whatever you want, Ems. I might join you. But not the white chocolate one. Eugh.'

'Come on, mum,' Emmie said. Why had her dad said that? He knew the white chocolate one was her mum's favourite.

Looking uptight, Rosie took Emmie's hand. 'Nothing wrong with white chocolate,' she said snippily as they walked outside.

'Didn't say there was,' Nate answered. 'Well, I did, but I didn't mean anything weird…'

'Of course not,' Rosie snapped.

Emmie suddenly felt like crying. And it was nothing to do with her tumour. It was because it felt like something else was dying right in front of her and she was powerless to stop it.

2011

'She looks so happy, Nate. Even when she's asleep. How can that be? With everything that's going on in her life, how can she radiate happiness when she's not even awake?'

Rosie reached out and gently stroked Emmie's hair. It spilled out across the pillow like a dark cloud. Emmie stirred slightly, but remained asleep, snuggling more deeply into her duvet. Her hands were wrapped around a dog-eared teddy she had had since birth, imaginatively named 'Bear-Bear', but she looked contented... unperturbed. As though the whirlwind that was her life was in fact serene and problem-free.

Rosie removed her hand from Emmie's head. The last thing she wanted to do was wake Emmie up. She needed her sleep. She was having chemotherapy, for heaven's sake.

Rosie wasn't sure when she and Nate would feel comfortable enough to give up the night-time vigil they had adopted since Emmie's diagnosis, but for now, they were going with it. They had moved two chairs into Emmie's room that sat side by side by her bed just like the ones in the hospital and they watched over now the way they had when she fell asleep after her treatment.

Nate rubbed his chin, knowing that Rosie's question was rhetorical but feeling the need to answer nonetheless.

'I don't know why she manages the happy thing like that, Rose. I think... because she's a kid. Because she doesn't under-stand what's happening to her.' Nate smiled, but it was brief and tinged with sadness. 'But honestly? I think Emmie radiates happiness because she's absolutely ace and nothing whatsoever fazes her.'

Rosie sat back and squeezed Nate's knee. It was true. Emmie was just this amazing kid who let everything wash over her. She wasn't perfect; not by a long stretch. In fact, as babies went, Emmie had been something of a challenge. Eating habits that verged on fanatical from breast to bottle through to solids and some three-year-old tantrums post hospital visits that registered as epic, inducing health visitors to produce laminated star charts to try and curb Emmie's 'spirited' behaviour.

And god, the issues with sleep early on! Rosie could still recall with weary accuracy the months they had endured trying to get Emmie to sleep through the night. Other parents waxed lyrical about how they'd 'cracked it' after a mere eight weeks, smugly certain they had the magic formula as a parent, sure they had skills other parents didn't possess as they had achieved what every other parent was desperate to when it came to the sleep regime. Maybe they had, maybe they were just lucky – who knew? Rosie's twin sister Lily had had one fabulous sleeper (smugly waxing lyrical) and one terrible sleeper (reeling, shocked and perplexed by such a thing). Either way, Emmie still took an age to settle at times, still woke two to three times a night and was still prone to arising early and letting the whole house know about it.

'Man, do you remember how terrible she used to be at sleeping?' Nate said, putting his hand over Rosie's. He looked down and linked his fingers through hers.

'I was just thinking that. Christ, we tried everything.' Rosie shook her head. 'Controlled crying, sternness, kindness.'

'Strict routines, flexible routines,' Nate agreed ruefully. 'We felt like the most crappy parents in the world. Especially when

Jason and Chrissy used to go on and on about how their two wouldn't dare get out of bed before seven thirty a.m.'

'God yes. I used to want to slap Chrissy really hard when she said that. I just didn't have the bloody energy.'

Nate let out a short laugh. 'Me neither. Sleep deprivation renders you completely powerless to fight back. I was like a zombie for the first two years. We both were.'

He glanced at Emmie. He didn't care about the lack of sleep in the early days. He yearned for the early days. At the time, they had felt challenging, but Nate now realised that those difficulties had been nothing compared to what they were dealing with now. The early days, at very least, had been free from the threat they were now all forced to live under every single day. Sleep deprivation was nothing in the face of chemotherapy; it simply crumbled by comparison.

Nate stared at his daughter. She was so beautiful. Even without being biased, Nate knew it was true. She was a pretty girl, with lovely manners (hammered into her with parrot-fashion repetition that had threatened to send both him and Rosie utterly insane), who didn't deserve what had happened to her. Not that anyone deserved cancer. No one did. But Emmie was just a kid. And a good one at that.

Nate shook himself out of that headspace. It wasn't helpful and it made fury rise inside him like a raging storm. Life sucked sometimes. Everyone knew that. And it wasn't worth dwelling on. The main thing Nate tended to dwell on was why life had chosen Emmie for this 'journey' or whatever they called it. Why she had been chosen and not him. Nate could have dealt with this and he would take it from Emmie in a heartbeat.

'Our baby is having chemotherapy,' Rosie said suddenly.

'Yes.' Nate tightened his grip on her hand. 'Yes she is. And she's sailing through it.'

Rosie bit her lip. She was. Emmie was stoically going through her treatment in a way that seemed fairly normal for many kids, according to the team of doctors in charge of her case. Apparently kids endured their treatment in a way that adults didn't; seeing it simply as something they had to go through, that didn't require over-thinking.

Rosie found this fact comforting. At least Emmie viewed her treatment as a tick-list of moments to get over and move on from. Rosie wished she could say the same, but it was something at least that Emmie had a black and white view of it.

'I wish I could be as chilled about all of this as Emmie is,' she commented, turning to Nate. 'I wish I could empty my head of all the horrible thoughts I have.'

That was the beauty of being a child, perhaps, Nate mused to himself. They weren't prone to over-thinking. Their minds tended to be like butterflies; alighting on one topic whilst simultaneously registering another that was equally fascinating and all-consuming.

If only, Nate thought ruefully. He'd give anything to be so easily distracted from the worry that constantly occupied his mind. To be taken away from the intense anxiety over losing Emmie. But he also accepted that it was the way it had to be. Being a parent changed everything, distorted the overall view of life... especially in these kinds of situations. Nate had even found himself offering a number of deals to God since Emmie's diagnosis. Or the Universe. Or whoever might be listening. Not her, me. Take that tumour out of her head and stick it in mine. I can take it, I matter less. It's not that I'm stronger, it's that I'm an adult. Not a child. A child, for Christ's sakes.

Nate clenched his fists. Sometimes he wanted to take the Universe and give it a massive, great...

'Oh god.' Rosie's voice held a sob in it.

'What?' Nate unclenched his fists and sat up. 'What?'

Rosie turned to him, clutching something in her hand. 'It's her hair,' she whispered shakily. 'Emmie is losing her hair.'

Nate started at the wisps of dark hair in Rosie's hand, utterly stricken. They knew this was coming. They had been warned about this. Emmie had been warned about this. They had discussed wigs and scarves and funky hats. Rosie had already invested in a bright pink wig she thought Emmie might think was cool and a selection of hats ranging from caps and boaters to a cute pork pie effort.

But seeing Emmie's hair in Rosie's hand like that… Nate couldn't bear it.

Rosie scrunched the hair up in her hands, bent over and wept. Silent, wracking sobs.

Nate put his arm around her and held her tightly. His lip trembled with the effort of not losing his shit. Emmie's hair. Her beautiful, beautiful hair. He stared at his daughter. This was horrible. She was going to go bald. Well. Patchy first, apparently, then they would probably shave it off and she would be bald. No kid should have to go through any of this… the pain, the humiliation.

Emmie stirred and turned in her sleep. There was more hair on her pillow. Quite a lot of it. Wisps and the odd hunk. A sob caught in Nate's throat.

'I've been putting off brushing her hair,' Rosie whispered, looking at Emmie's pillow in horror. 'I've been terrified to do it because of this. Every time I go to brush it, every time I go to wash it, I think oh God, is it going to happen now?'

'The docs said it would go far sooner,' Nate said, hating how reasonable he sounded. Should he add 'every cloud and all that' and sound truly cavalier?

'They did.' Rosie nodded. 'They said within the first month as this kind of chemo is so aggressive.'

Something suddenly occurred to Nate and he was galvanised into action.

'Rosie, let's go.' Nate stood up and took Rosie's hand. 'Come on.'

Rosie stole another glance at Emmie and allowed Nate to lead her out of the bedroom. He took her to the bathroom and started rummaging around in the cupboard under the sink.

'What are you looking for?'

'The clippers.' Nate pulled a box out then shoved it back in again.

Rosie gasped. 'You can't… you can't shave her hair off, Nate. Not yet.'

'Eh?' Nate carried on searching.

Rosie was appalled. What on earth was Nate playing at? Emmie losing her hair was shocking. Horrific. How could Nate possibly think of getting rid of what little she already had left?

Nate emerged, triumphant. 'Here they are.' He opened the box and removed the clippers.

'Y-you can't…'

'I want to.' Nate fired the clippers up and turned to the mirror.

Rosie grabbed his arm. 'No.'

Nate turned. 'Rosie. I want to shave my hair off. So Emmie doesn't feel alone.'

Rosie blinked. 'Your hair?'

'Well, who else's?' Nate shook his head. 'You thought I was going to shave Emmie's hair off? Why on earth would I do that?' He gazed at her. 'I mean, maybe later if it goes all patchy and she wants us to do it, but not yet.'

'I don't know. I'm not thinking straight. I'm upset.' Rosie put the toilet seat down and slumped down onto it.

Nate knelt down in front of her and put the clippers on the floor.

'Rose. Rose, look at me.' He grasped her knees. 'Babe, it's OK. Emmie... losing her hair is horrible. We knew it was coming, but it's shit and shocking and honestly, it's making me want to punch a wall.' He squeezed her knees. 'But I'm not going to. And you're not going to fall apart either. We're going to do what we do best. We're going to pull ourselves together and we're going to be strong for her. Right?'

Rosie bit her lip. She could see tears in Nate's eyes and it made her heart lurch. She knew Nate felt as much pain as she did when Emmie was suffering. They were always on the same page. And she loved Nate for that. Loved him deeply. Because no one else understood.

How would life be without this terrible burden, Rosie wondered? Would they have had another child, maybe? They had talked about it once, before Emmie's diagnosis. But it hadn't ever been mentioned again. Because apart from the fact that Emmie needed their full attention and support, Rosie and Nate both knew they couldn't risk their hearts by having another baby. Even though the odds of another baby getting cancer were seriously remote, they couldn't take that chance. This anguish was intolerable. Double the anguish would, quite simply, break them.

Rosie wiped her eyes. 'OK. So let's do this.' She sniffed and grabbed some toilet roll.

'You're so, so brave. So beautiful and so brave. Thank God Emmie takes after you.' Nate gathered Rosie up and kissed her forehead tenderly. She fell against him and slid her arms around his waist.

This was a strange journey they were on, he and Rosie, Nate thought with a flash of anger. It wasn't how they had imagined their lives to be. It wasn't what any couple would choose to go through when they had a child.

Nate took a deep breath and let go of Rosie. He turned to face the mirror again. He took a deep breath. He wasn't a vain man, but he had a good head of hair and it was going to be strange without it. He held the clippers up and got started.

Rosie watched as Nate focused on the task in hand and made neat lines over his head. The bathroom floor was soon littered with dark hair. Rosie had never seen Nate without hair. His hair had always been a bit of a 'thing'. He had a kind of quiff going on that really suited him and he used it to show his moods… Sticky-up meant relaxed, gel and parting meant ready for work. And now suddenly, it was gone.

Nate put the clippers down finally and stared at his reflection. 'Oh man. Was that a massive mistake? I look… really weird.'

'You don't.' Rosie ran a hand over the stubble. 'You look… hot.' She gave him a rueful smile. 'Who knew? Almost-bald makes you even sexier.'

'Almost-bald.' Nate peered at his reflection. 'God. I don't even look like myself. But at least I had a choice, right? Em's going to just have to go through this whether she likes it or not. But hey. Solidarity and all that.'

Rosie stared past Nate's reflection and looked at her own. If Nate could do it, so could she. She picked the clippers up and with a shaking hand, she switched them on and put them to the side of her head.

'What are you doing!' Nate jerked her hand away.

'Solidarity. You just said it. That's what I'm doing.' Rosie pulled the clippers back and managed to shave a tiny area before Nate yanked them out of her hand.

'Rosie!' Nate held the clippers behind his back. 'There is no way on earth I'm letting you do that.'

'Why the hell not?' Rosie turned on him furiously. Why the hell did Nate get to tell her what to do? 'Why do you get to do solidarity and I don't?'

'Because you're normality,' Nate answered calmly. 'Do you see? I'm solidarity in this instance. But Emmie needs normality too. That's you. You need to look normal. Like her mum. You're like... you're like school. Pre-school. Whatever.'

Rosie's eyes blazed. 'Maybe I don't want to be "school", Nate. Maybe I want to be...'

'Bald?' Nate raised his eyebrows. 'OK. Listen. I get it. And you'd do it; I know you would, because you're brave and feisty and you'd do anything for her. And I love you for that.' His voice softened. 'But you're her mum, Rosie. You have to still look like her mum. I'm her dad; it's different.'

Rosie breathed. And stopped being angry with Nate. He was right. Emmie did need normality as well as support. And what was to be achieved by the pair of them being bald? Emmie might hate it.

They both turned as the door opened.

Emmie came in, holding out a handful of wispy hair. 'My... my hair is falling out.'

Rosie's heart caught in her chest at the sight of Emmie in her cute Peppa Pig nightie. Emmie looked sleepy and tearful and far too young to be dealing with the effects of chemo. She glanced at the floor. 'Daddy, your hair is falling out too. What happened?'

Nate scooped her up. 'I shaved it off because I want to look just like you.'

Emmie ran her hand over his head. 'It feels all spiky! Is that what mine will feel like?'

Nate put his fingers to a small, bare spot on Emmie's head. His heart squeezed painfully but he forced a smile onto his face. 'No. Yours is lovely. It's all soft. Rosie... feel.'

Rosie reached a hand out and felt Emmie's head. She met Nate's eyes in agony, then grinned at Emmie. 'It is! How cool. Not all spiky like Daddy's!'

Rosie felt panic rising in her chest. She had to get out of the bathroom. She couldn't stand it anymore. 'Hang on,' she managed. 'Back in a sec.'

Rushing to the bedroom, she sat on the bed abruptly. Christ. The support team at the hospital at warned them this bit would be tough, but Rosie had no idea it was going to feel like this. She could feel a gigantic sob rising inside. It felt like a giant snowball wanting to burst out of her throat. She squashed it down. Not yet. Later for that. Always later for that.

Remembering something, Rosie opened her wardrobe door and fished around until she found what she wanted. Taking a breath, she headed back to the bathroom.

'Ta da!' She held up the pink bobbed wig she had found for Emmie online.

'Cool!' Emmie made Nate put her down and grabbed the wig. 'Can I wear it in bed?'

Rosie hesitated then shrugged. Cancer put everything in perspective. All the rules went out of the window. 'Sure. Why not?'

Emmie whooped and, distracted from her trauma, set about pulling the pink wig on in a lopsided fashion and padding over to the nearest mirror.

'There's this place we can go to that sells wigs like Disney princesses,' Rosie said. 'They... they're made of real hair.' She swallowed. She wasn't sure she liked that idea. 'But anyway, you could have hair like Elsa from Frozen. Or... like Belle, maybe.'

'No thanks.' Emmie tugged at the pink wig. 'This is so cool.'

Nate looked at Rosie over Emmie's head. 'You're awesome,' he mouthed.

Rosie shook her head. She wasn't awesome. All she'd done was bought a cute wig. Nate had shaved his head.

'I'm tired, mummy,' Emmie mumbled, looking through the pink acrylic fringe.

'Me too.' Rosie lifted her up and smiled as she felt Emmie's little legs around her waist. 'Cuddle in bed?'

Emmie nodded and dropped her head to Rosie's shoulder. Rosie shot Nate a trembling glance and left the bathroom.

Nate gripped the edge of the sink. And not for the first time wondered at his heart's astonishing ability to withstand such intensely explosive bursts of love, rage and pain simultaneously. Every time he thought he couldn't push his emotions any further beyond the limits they had already endured, there was still a more extreme level to experience.

Forgetting the mix of Emmie's hair and his hair littered all over the bathroom floor, Nate tiredly sloped off to Emmie's bedroom to watch over the only two things in his life that truly mattered.

Rosie

'So. How is all your Pilates shizzle going?'

Rosie raised her eyebrows. She and Lily might be twins but they practically spoke a different language. 'Pilates... shizzle?'

Lily shrugged and waved a hand good-naturedly. 'Stuff. Malarky. Shizzle. You know what I mean. How's it all going?'

Rosie regarded her sister. They weren't identical so it wasn't one of those freaky things where she felt as though she was looking in a mirror, as such. It was more odd, if anything, because Rosie often felt as if she was watching a different version of herself. Herself in an alternate universe. There were physical similarities, of course – she and Lily had the same dark hair, Lily sporting a more stylised version of Rosie's wild and untamed mass, and the same nose. The same blue eyes but Lily's were wide, whereas Rosie's were cat-like. But their lives were poles apart.

'Well?' Lily frowned.

'Pretty well.' Rosie scooped some coffee foam up onto her spoon, smiling at Lily's impatience. It always reminded her of Lily when they were kids. 'I got a promotion the other day. Mostly because Anna is leaving.'

'Anna.' Lily's brow furrowed. It cleared momentarily. 'Aah, I know. Slightly scary-looking boss lady. Machine-like. So into exercise, she makes everyone feel as though they should be in detention for not doing star jumps whilst waiting for coffee.' Lilly shuddered to illustrate her distaste for people like Anna.

Rosie grinned. Lily had attended a Pilates class once – just once – when Rosie had first started out. She had puffed and panted comically all the way through it, doing her best to put on a show of solidarity by making an appearance, but obviously finding it anathema. She had exited the gym like a bat out of hell after Anna had enthusiastically extolled the virtues of regular exercise and hadn't returned since.

'I always thought Anna might struggle to get a boyfriend,' Lily went on. 'She's so FULL ON.'

'Well, that's where you're wrong. She's jetting off to Cyprus to be with the love of her life, who is apparently a hot Adonis.' Rosie sipped her coffee gingerly. This café always served the coffee so hot, it often caused lip singeing. 'Hence the job vacancy.'

Lily blinked a few times. 'Well I never. She's the last person I would have thought would rush off into the sunset with some love god.'

'She also said Nate was sexy.' Rosie looked up, feeling someone's eyes on her. It was Jonny, one of the young guys who made coffees. One of the 'baristas', she supposed she should call him. She felt herself blush slightly and, feeling ridiculous, she looked away.

'Well. Nate *is* sexy,' Lily said reasonably, breaking the corner off a salted caramel muffin. 'What's wrong with her saying that? Apart from the fact that it's Anna and I thought she was a bit... asexual.' She grimaced. 'Salted caramel, I ask you. How poncy. Can't beat a blueberry muffin in my view.'

'You think Nate is sexy too?' Rosie regarded her twin. Lily had never said anything of the sort before now.

'Everyone thinks Nate is sexy, Rosie. Jamie has even said it once or twice and he's a dude. He's got that whole French thing going on, hasn't he? That certain... whatever that French phrase is.'

'*Je ne sais quoi*. That certain *je ne sais quoi*.'

'Yes. That thing. Nate has it.'

Rosie felt a jolt. It was true. Nate did have something about him, always had. It wasn't just his looks; it was the way he was... A way he had about him.

Rosie picked her coffee cup up and cradled it in her hands. She supposed she hadn't noticed that about Nate for a while. Nate seemed to irritate the hell out of her in a number of ways, which didn't sit right at all.

He never used to annoy her, Rosie mused. Not remotely. Nate had his own quirks as all men did, but she wasn't one of those women who sat with others character-assassinating her husband about his pants being strewn all over the floor, forgetting her birthday or never pushing the vacuum cleaner around. Far from it. In fact, Rosie had always found those conversations rather embarrassing as Nate was very tidy, never forgot a special date and he might not vacuum, but he cooked – he adored cooking, which was an incredibly attractive trait in a man, in Rosie's opinion – and he didn't need angry lists of outstanding DIY jobs to get things done.

But somehow, these days, Nate seemed to drive her to distraction. And Rosie had forgotten that Nate was extremely attractive and capable of turning her insides to liquid with just a glance.

Rosie was rather taken aback by this realisation. She sensed distance between them but she was also supremely frustrated with Nate. She couldn't stand the way he retreated into work the way he did. Rosie understood that it was a classic, male reaction in some ways, but it drove her nuts. Work distracted her too; of course it did. But she didn't bury herself in it the way Nate did. It was avoidance at its worst, surely?

Lily nibbled at the muffin absentmindedly as she checked her phone.

'Oh man! Why didn't I notice that George has a school trip tomorrow? He needs a packed lunch, "healthy snacks" and wellie boots… Bit of a problem as he's grown out of his and my shopping order isn't coming until Saturday.' She rolled her eyes at herself. 'Mummy fail once again. Oh well. I'm sure we can sort something out for him. Even if he has to go in looking a bit weird wearing Maya's pink wellies. With… a sausage roll and a Kit Kat in his rucksack.'

Rosie battled with herself, but felt her stomach tighten involuntarily. Lily seemed to breeze through life without a care in the world and it made Rosie feel desperately, hideously jealous. The way Lily talked about her kids… as though the only things she needed to worry about were whether or not she'd be judged if her snacks didn't promote healthy living and if George's wellies pinched his toes or he looked like a girl in pink ones.

If only she could think about Emmie that way. With a carelessness about food and clothes and school and all the other stuff most people associated with children.

Rosie glanced down at her coffee, amazed that tears could spring into her eyes with such rapidity from a single, odious, envious thought. But when it came to Emmie, emotions gushed forth like a flood from a burst river bed, often out of the blue and with an intensity that bewildered Rosie. And the worst thing was, she knew she was being unfair. Lily couldn't help that her life was straight-forward. That her life revolved around her genial husband Jamie and her two lovely, rather eccentric kids. And why shouldn't it? Lily's life was normal, like most people's. She and Jamie argued occasionally about money or the dreaded list of DIY jobs and Jamie periodically moaned about them not having sex at 2am or in the open air anymore.

Because essentially, that was all Lily and Jamie had to worry about. And there was nothing wrong with that. Moreover, there were times when Rosie was grateful for the normality her twin's life provided. It grounded her and kept her sane. Sometimes, she needed to quieten the rush of fear and anxiety that occupied her head when she thought about Emmie and talking to Lily about how middle class muffin flavours had become was the only way to catch her breath and realise that there were other things in life to consider that didn't involve hospitals and tests and a terrible, bleak diagnosis.

'It's alright,' Lily said gently, putting her hand out to touch Rosie's. 'I know. And you know I'm so deeply sorry about Emmie.'

'Yes.' Rosie felt the word choke in her throat. 'And the thing is, I love how normal your life is, Lils. I need your life to be normal, you know? I crave it and I need to hear about it and I need to just soak it up and allow it to wash over me. I hate that you see jealousy in my eyes sometimes. I honestly wish I didn't feel that way.'

'You're my twin.' Lily squeezed Rosie's hand briefly. 'It's not so much that I see it; it's that I feel it. But I understand. I really do. Never apologise. It's me who should be doing that.'

'No need. I told you. I need the normality. I *want* to talk about George's gender confusion when he's forced to wear pink wellies.'

'Poor George,' Lily mused stoically and without sympathy. 'The things I put that poor boy through. Still. It's what they call character building, right?'

Rosie laughed. 'Something like that.'

'So anyway.' Lily pushed the muffin across the table with the contempt it deserved. 'Fill your boots with that. Anything new with Emmie?'

'Actually yes. She has a different counsellor. Some guy called Dr Tom.'

'Dr Tom. How very modern. Have you met him yet?'

'Not yet. But I think we're due to soon.' Rosie peered at the muffin. 'Emmie came out of her session gushing about him wearing jeans. With rips in them. And she described him as "geeky" and "handsome".'

'Gosh. I fancy him already.' Lily sat back in her chair. 'How inappropriate would that be? Fancying one's child's counsellor?'

Rosie broke a piece of muffin off. 'Stop it. Anyway, he's given her this diary to write in. She was all secretive about it.'

'Maya has a diary as well.' Lily pulled a face. 'Honestly. You'd think she was writing Harry Potter the sequel or something, the reverence she gives it. Be prepared for Emmie to go properly secret squirrel on you over that.'

'OK. I agree with you about the salted caramel thing. Eugh.' Rosie pondered Dr Tom. 'I think it's good for Emmie to have someone to talk to, though. Someone who isn't involved. Someone she can confide in. None of the others have been that great, have they?'

'I suppose not. Too old, perhaps? But anyway, I think it's lovely. Especially if he's hot and wears ripped jeans.'

Rosie shook her head. 'Pack it in. He's my daughter's counsellor, you weirdo.'

'Haha, just messing.' Lily checked her watch. 'Oh dear. It's nearly time for the school run. So not only will it chuck it down with rain in a minute, but we also have to collect the children and amuse them until bedtime. I need the loo.' Letting out a dramatic sigh, Lily got up and left the table.

Rosie smiled to herself. She might have the odd pang of jealousy about Lily's life, but her twin made her laugh a lot. She was a good person to be around; fun, light and totally inappropriate.

Rosie drained her coffee, wincing when she realised it was stone cold now. She and Lily hadn't been that close as kids – mostly because they had been so different. Rosie was the first-born: a high achiever, tall, serious, studious and, according to Nate, the more attractive twin, but he was obviously extremely biased. Rosie had worked as a legal secretary in a high profile firm before abandoning that career to become a Pilates instructor. She needed something to keep her mind off Emmie's diagnosis and her fitness classes could be more easily slotted around Emmie's hospital appointments and medical commitments.

Lily, by contrast, was mischievous, laid back, a bit on the short side and fairly average as a student because she had been far too busy having fun to care overly about her studies. Lily had also been a real daddy's girl, something that had driven a slight wedge between the sisters. Rosie had never really understood why she hadn't connected with her father the way Lily had. It hurt her even now and he was no longer with them, so unfortunately Rosie had no way of making peace over that issue.

Which is why she always tried to resolve any issues Emmie had. Because her tumour was like a ticking time bomb; none of them knew when it might decide to grow and destroy her. Rosie felt tears creeping up on her and it made her furious with herself. She literally couldn't control herself when it came to Emmie.

'You didn't like the muffin?'

Rosie jumped and turned to find the cute barista next to her.

'We weren't fans, no. I mean, I'm sure other people love that flavour but…'

'Nah. It's just trendy, isn't it? I'm more of a blueberry kind of guy myself.' He smiled as he started to clear the coffees away. 'I'm Jonny, by the way.'

'Oh.' Rosie felt his eyes on her. 'Hi Jonny. I'm Rosie.'

'Rosie. Nice. I like that.' Jonny held her gaze for a second, then ran a careless hand through his rather long, dark hair. 'Would you like any more coffees? A different muffin, maybe?'

'Er no. We have to leave shortly. School run,' Rosie added. That should do it. Jonny was being quite flirty, but he could only be twenty-six, at most. The idea of children would be abhorrent to him, no doubt, and his mini-flirtation would be over in seconds.

'Oh, you have kids? I love kids.'

Rosie checked his eyes, but he actually looked as if he meant it.

'What age?'

Rosie felt flustered. 'I just have the one. She's ten.' She felt wrong-footed. And she suddenly didn't want to talk about Emmie anymore.

'I have two,' Lily said, joining in as she returned to the table. 'Ten and seven.' She glanced at Jonny with some amusement. 'Are you after some babysitting money? Or might you be interested in adopting? We could negotiate a price either way.'

Jonny laughed. 'Neither, thanks. I just like kids.'

Lily started to collect up her paraphernalia, shrugging her arms into an army-style jacket as she stuffed her phone and wallet into her handbag. 'That's because you don't have to sort out their packed lunches... Jonny...' she said, eying his name badge. 'Make them dinner. Every. Single. Night. Buy them endless pairs of wellies. You wouldn't be saying you love them then, trust me. No siree.'

'Maybe not,' Jonny smiled, catching Rosie's eye. 'You're making it sound quite stressful.'

'Well, it *is* stressful,' Lily said sternly. 'Having children is a serious business, Jonny. Rather like making muffins in flavours people enjoy.'

'Yes. Blueberry all the way.'

Lily sniffed. 'Well. You've redeemed yourself with that. We're going to need boxes full of blueberry muffins next time we come in. Will that be alright?'

'I'll arrange it myself.' Jonny smiled at Rosie again. 'You have a good day. Hope your ten-year-old doesn't need any new wellies.'

Rosie let out a short laugh. 'No, I think she's fine on that front.'

'Let's go,' Lily said, marching to the door.

'Bye Jonny,' Rosie said, hurrying after her. She didn't turn back to look at him, but she could feel his eyes watching her as she left. It felt oddly exciting and Rosie was cross with herself. She was married. To an extremely lovely, handsome man. Well. She wasn't sure Nate was lovely anymore. But he was probably still handsome. She hadn't checked recently. Maybe she should. Rosie swallowed. She definitely should. She and Nate were in quite a bad way. A very bad way.

'How are things with Nate?' Lily said as they walked to her car.

Rosie had given up wondering at the telepathic bond between them and at Lily's innate ability to read her mind at the most inconvenient of times.

'Not great,' Rosie replied. She held her hand up. 'You were right about the rain.'

'Well, it's almost April,' Lily stated. She stopped Rosie. 'And what are you going to do about that? About you and Nate not being great.'

Rosie pulled the edges of her jacket closer. 'I don't know.' She felt the familiar feeling of frustration and irritation coil itself around her again. She realised she should say something to Lily. 'We're so caught up with Emmie most of the time. Maybe we've lost ourselves a bit.'

'Find yourselves again,' Lily urged. 'Rose, I mean it. Find yourselves. You and Nate have something special… That thing that most people don't ever find.'

'You and Jamie have it.'

'No. We don't.' Lily took out her car keys matter-of-factly. 'And I'm not upset about that. Some women might be, but I'm not. Me and Jamie… we're OK. We get on. We're well-suited. But it's not like you and Nate. That's different. You have true love. Passion. Intensity. You have the real deal. Don't lose it. Because… because… the thing is, Rosie…'

Lily met Rosie's eye and halted.

Because one day, Nate was all she was going to have. Rosie sensed Lily's words; she didn't need to hear them spoken out loud. Because one day, they were going to lose Emmie. And all they would have was each other. And even though there had been a time when Nate had been more than enough – the only thing Rosie ever needed – now, the thought of being without Emmie was truly terrifying. Because somehow, they had lost their way. As the heartache of Emmie's diagnosis had played out, she and Nate had drifted.

But the true love Lily spoke of. That had to be there still. Surely? Rosie felt a rush of panic. But was it? Was it still there? She had no idea anymore.

Rosie got in Lily's car and made a pact with herself. She had to reconnect with Nate. Despite what was going on with Emmie, Lily was right. She and Nate had something special. Something other people didn't have. That love thing people spoke about in books and films. And it was worth salvaging. Not just because Emmie might not be there in the future – Rosie felt a blow to her stomach like a physical punch – but because Nate mattered. She and Nate mattered. And Rosie was going to make sure Nate knew that too.

Nate

'Hey. I know you're disappointed. But it's not the end of the world.'

Gill's tone was conciliatory.

Nate hurled his rucksack into the back of his car. 'Of course it's not. My view of what represents the "end of the world" is very far removed from most people's, Gill.'

Gill gave him a look and leant against the car.

Nate sighed. 'Sorry. I know you know that.' He ran a hand over the back of his head, the gesture irritable and jerky. 'It's just... this promotion. It would have been a really positive thing for me. Good news I could have gone home with. Something that made us feel as though we were on the up.'

'I know. It's a shitter. You really deserved it too.' Gill scuffed the toe of her shoe on the ground. 'With any luck, Robson will make a right mess of it and they'll draft you in like they should have done in the first place.'

Nate shook his head. 'Not the point. If they wanted me, they would have chosen me. It's as simple as that.' He shut the car door and took up a position next to Gill, their body language unconsciously mirroring. 'Listen, I get it. If I look at it the way our bosses are going to, I would think that I've been distracted. That I've had a bit too much time off work.'

'Because your kid has a tumour!'

'Doesn't matter.' Nate shrugged. 'This is the police force. We all need to be committed.'

'You *are* committed,' Gill said hotly.

Nate threw her a smile. He and Gill were equally defensive of one another. 'I love how loyal you are. You know I feel the same way back, right?'

'Always.' Gill chewed her lip. 'It just makes me so angry. You're great at your job, Nate. And I'm gutted for you.'

'Thanks.' Nate put his arm around Gill and gave her shoulder a squeeze. 'You're the best partner. Shame you're not the one in charge of the big decisions.'

'Yeah.'

'Jeez. First the Peabody case, now this.'

'I know.' Gill patted Nate's hand. 'It's been a rough ride for both of us. You more than me, natch. But you know I can't trump you on the personal stuff.'

'True enough. Cancer more or less out-trumps every-thing.' Nate removed his arm and smiled at Gill. 'Right. I should get home.'

'Will you tell Rosie about the promotion thing?'

Nate's expression shut down slightly. 'I don't know. I never know what I'm walking into these days when I go home. I sometimes feel a bit left out, you know? Which will sound dumb. And martyrish. Bloody hell.' He paused, feeling irritated with himself. 'I work such long hours and Rosie and Emmie spend so much time together. I sometimes feel as though I don't know what might have happened during the day while I've been chained to my desk here. Or charging around with you, saving lives and all that kind of thing.' He gave Gill a lop-sided smile. 'I mean, Rosie sends me texts if anything major occurs, but apart from that, I'm clueless.'

Gill let out an impatient sound. 'I hear what you're saying, but isn't that the case for most working parents? Male or female? Whoever goes to work – in some cases, both, if money is tight – that person really doesn't have much to do with home life after breakfast and before dinner. I mean, soz and all that as you know I'm always on your side, but if you're pulling that card, I'm going to have to call bullshit on you.'

Nate burst out laughing. 'Haha! God, I'm so lucky to have you, Gill. You're just what I need when I get all maudlin and start feeling sorry for myself. You're so right. I *am* just like any other parent.'

'Well.' Gill opened Nate's car door for him. 'You're not exactly like any other parent, dude. Not all parents are dealing with the kind of thing you face daily. But when it comes to the feeling a bit left out vibe – you're definitely not alone there.'

'You're brilliant.' Nate smiled. 'Life is all about perspective. Rosie is always telling me that.'

'Go home. Go tell Rosie about those tossers in there getting it *spectacularly* wrong.'

'I will. Thanks, partner.'

Nate got into his car. He watched Gill tug her phone out of her pocket as she strolled to her car, presumably to give Sexy Kev a call.

Nate sighed. He envied Gill the ease of her relationship. Not in a jealous way – it was more of nostalgic thing. Because this was exactly how Nate and Rosie had been in the early days. Inseparable. The first point of contact when something awful happened. When something fantastic happened. The first text of the day... the last text of the day if not together. And if not together, FaceTiming until they both fell asleep.

These days, the only contact they tended to have related to Emmie. Emmie's appointments, Emmie's test results, Emmie reacting to something illness-related.

Which was understandable, Nate reasoned as he headed home. He and Rosie needed to discuss Emmie; she was their priority. And since her diagnosis, life had literally been a rollercoaster – up one minute, down the next. They had reached something of a plateau now in terms of Emmie's condition because there was nothing anyone could do. It was simply a case of... waiting. Existing. Coping.

Nate sat in some traffic for a while, but instead of cursing it, he welcomed the thinking time. Drumming his fingers on the steering wheel, he thought about the way things used to be and he couldn't help missing Rosie's other texts. Ones that simply said: 'Morning, handsome!' or 'Can't wait for you to come home... counting the minutes.'

Those were the text messages that kept Nate afloat during tough work days. They used to make him feel alive, give him a buzz and cause a soppy grin to appear on his face pretty much all day long. Not that Nate blamed Rosie for not messaging him as such. She had a lot on her plate and a great deal on her mind. So did he. Such pleasantries had gone out of the window. Nate just missed the texts. He missed the way they made him feel and most of all, he missed Rosie.

Pulling up onto the driveway, Nate sat in his car for a moment. He needed to be different. He needed to go in with a different mindset so he could mend some bridges between himself and Rosie. Because Nate knew he often rocked up at the house feeling weird and apprehensive and awkward and instead of communicating that in some way, he would wade right in like some moody idiot, hell-bent on destruction.

Nate took a breath. Right. *Do things differently*, he told himself as he put his key in the lock. He heard voices coming from the kitchen and headed that way. Rosie and Emmie were sitting at the scrubbed, white wooden table they used for pretty much everything from eating to doing homework. The table was covered in books and various pencils, pens and rubbers so Nate guessed food wasn't the issue right now. Which was a shame because all he had eaten since 8am was a sausage roll because he had been absurdly busy and hadn't been anywhere near the canteen.

Nate knew better than to bring up the issue of dinner, however. He had done that on the odd occasion without even thinking and had got short shrift from Rosie, who had always had a genuinely superb excuse in that either something had happened to Emmie or – far less likely – work had got in the way. And as much as he missed walking into the house and inhaling the delicious, mouth-watering aroma of homemade spaghetti Bolognese, Nate wouldn't dream of bringing it up. And quite frankly, making himself a sandwich now and again was the least of his worries.

Maybe he would offer to cook. Yes, good plan. Nate loved cooking and Rosie would be happy that he had taken control of a mundane task.

'Hey,' Rosie said, looking up from Emmie's home-work.

'Hey.'

'Dad.' Emmie pulled a face and held up a book. 'Maths.'

Nate pulled a face back. 'Oh man. Maths is the work of the devil.'

Rosie frowned. 'Oh good one, Nate. Now it will be even harder to get her to do her homework.' Her expression then softened slightly, as though she realised she might have sounded snippy.

'It *is* the work of the devil,' Emmie agreed, winking at Nate.

Nate was fairly sure Emmie didn't really understand what the expression meant but he grinned anyway. Then said sorry to Rosie.

Rosie shrugged off his apology, which put Nate's back up a tad, but he said nothing and took a seat next to Emmie.

'So. What's so taxing about the maths homework?'

As Emmie talked Nate through some mind-boggling multiplications, he tried to catch Rosie's eye. She seemed nervous, as though she had things she needed to say. Perhaps they could talk later.

'How about a nice bottle of wine later?' Nate suggested after pointing Emmie in the right direction with her homework.

'May-be,' Rosie said, with what sounded like reluctance in her voice.

Nate felt disheartened. He was reaching out to her, for heaven's sakes! It was only a bottle of wine. And it wasn't even about the bottle of wine. It was about the chat and the connection and the opportunity to talk about what had happened today.

Nate glanced at Emmie. As far as he could tell, Emmie was fine today. As fine as she could be with a ticking time bomb in her head, of course, but still. So why was Rosie so reluctant to sit down with him and chat over a bloody bottle of wine?

'Shall I cook something?' he said.

'No, it's OK,' Rosie said, looking distracted.

Nate frowned. He had been looking forward to cooking something. He had decided to make Emmie her favourite pasta with ham and three cheese sauce and for himself and Rosie, crab linguine. He'd need to pop out and grab a few bits, but it wouldn't be a hassle.

'Crab linguine?'

Rosie shrugged.

'Shall I order us a pizza?' he said, getting to his feet. He wanted to cook, but maybe Rosie just wanted life to be simple.

'Yes!' Emmie cried, looking ecstatic.

'Er, no,' Rosie said, looking anything but ecstatic.

'Is this some healthy eating issue?' Nate said, suddenly feeling incredibly weary.

'No, it's not,' Rosie snapped. 'It's because I have a pizza in the fridge already, Nate.'

'Oh right. Sorry.'

Nate sighed. It was like they spoke different languages these days. He spoke Japanese and Rosie spoke... German, for argument's sake. Or they might as well, the way they communicated. Even about wine and pizzas.

'Have you had a bad day, Dad?' Emmie asked, looking up from her calculations.

Nate glanced at her. Emmie's eyes were wide and troubled and Nate could tell that she was upset, that she was picking up on the friction between her parents.

Nate felt a rush of guilt. What on earth was wrong with him and Rosie? Why couldn't they make this work? Why, when their daughter was living with the most horrible fear known to man, could they not just get along like normal people?

Because they were no longer normal people, Nate realised. Because life and its twists and turns had turned everything upside down. But normal was what Emmie deserved and Nate was furious with himself that he couldn't seem to make that happen for her.

'Dad.' Emmie was still staring at him worriedly. 'Did you have a bad day at work?'

Nate decided he might as well open up about not getting his promotion. As Emmie had asked him directly.

Rosie abruptly got up and took a pizza and some garlic bread out of the fridge. Turning her back on Nate, she busied herself with dinner preparations, tugging out trays and tearing off sheets of aluminium foil.

Nate felt shut out. And insignificant. Like his troubles didn't matter. Rosie clearly wasn't interested in finding out if he had had a bad day or not.

'No, Ems. I didn't have a bad day,' Nate lied, the disappointment of losing out on his big promotion hitting him hard. He dug deep and pushed it to one side, because it didn't matter. Not really. He gave Emmie a hug.

'Thank you for asking, gorgeous, but I'm absolutely fine.'

'You look sad,' Emmie mumbled into his shoulder. 'I hate it when you look sad.'

Nate swallowed, suddenly finding a huge lump in his throat. 'I'm not sad, baby. I'm really not. I'm… going to get changed, OK?' He pulled back and felt Rosie's eyes on him. He couldn't look at her. He wanted to, just in case there was a glimmer of sympathy or concern in the eyes he had always got lost in, but just in case there wasn't, he'd rather not take the risk.

'Pizza will be ready in twenty minutes,' Rosie said as he turned away.

'Great. I promise I won't get us a nice bottle of wine to go with it.'

Nate shut the kitchen door behind him, mentally kicking himself. What had he said that for? Now he sounded petulant and moody, instead of disillusioned and wretched and heartbroken. Which, let's face it, was exactly how he felt inside.

Berating himself for the unexpected, hot tears that were threatening to fall, Nate did his best to man up as he headed upstairs to get changed. Not getting his promotion was nothing compared to seeing himself and Rosie disintegrating as though there had never been enough glue holding them together in the first place.

Emmie

'So what do you think is going on with your dad, then?'

Emmie flung herself onto her best friend Cara's bed. 'Don't know. He's just acting weird. They're both acting weird.'

Cara sat down at her dressing table and studied her reflection in the mirror. 'Why is your mum acting weird?'

'I can't really explain it. They're both just... odd.'

Emmie sighed. She couldn't even put her finger on what was going on with her parents. It just felt as though something had changed. They didn't communicate anymore. Conversation was about food and doctors and boring stuff.

'They don't laugh anymore,' she said out loud, trying to convey her thoughts.

'I'm not sure my parents laugh *that* much,' Cara commented, scooping her blond hair into a messy up-do. 'It might not mean anything. That's just grown ups, isn't it? None of our friends' parents seem to like each other that much.'

Emmie checked her split ends. 'Well mine used to. Laugh a lot. I mean, I was really young when I got my diagnosis, but I'm sure I remember seeing them laughing and smiling back then. And I've seen lots of photos and videos of them doing it.'

'They might just not like each other anymore,' Cara suggested helpfully as she examined her hair from a different angle. 'It might not be anything to do with your cancer thing.'

'You say cancer almost as many times as my new therapist.' Emmie grinned briefly but felt it fading as the guilt over her illness crept in and consumed her. It was a familiar, but uncomfortable feeling, and she had had it for as long as she could remember. Guilt, guilt, guilt. It's all she seemed to feel when it came to her cancer. 'Actually, he says "tumour" rather than "cancer", but you know...'

Cara gave her a half-smile.

Emmie sat up and clasped her knees. 'And of course it's to do with my cancer thing. I don't like it but that's what it is.'

Cara dropped her hair and turned around with an earnest expression. 'Yes, but you always think that, Em. Whatever happens. And it's not always that. Not really.'

Emmie chewed her lip. It was nice of Cara to say that, but most things seemed to be about her tumour when it came down to it. Her entire life revolved around it and so did her parents'. It was just the way it was. And it felt really horrible.

Cara threw herself onto the bed next to Emmie. 'So go on. What happened? Why are you all upset about this?'

Emmie shuffled up a bit to make more room. 'It's just that... last night, my dad came in and he looked all sad about something.'

'K...' Cara shrugged. 'Sad about what?'

'I don't know. He didn't say. Then he tried to pretend nothing was wrong.'

'So you're just guessing.'

Emmie started biting her fingernails. 'And then he offered to get a pizza and mum got all cross because I think she thought he was making a dig about her not making dinner yet.'

'Was he? Stop doing that. Your nails will look terrible.'

'I don't think so.' Emmie sat on her hands. 'And then my mum got all stroppy because she already had a pizza and my dad just went really quiet.'

'So basically they had a row about a pizza.' Cara looked unruffled as she leant against the wall. 'My parents row about stuff like that all the time. Putting the bins out. Yogurt pots left on the work top. Boxer shorts on the floor. Money. Those are just some of the things I've heard them moaning about.'

Emmie nodded. 'I know. I know all about that stuff. Everyone does that. This is different. This is because of me.'

'Ems, I really don't think this is going to make you feel any better.' Cara looked rather exasperated. 'You keep blaming yourself for stuff and you don't even know if it's you. Your cancer thing can't be responsible for everything horrible in your life.'

Emmie stared out of the window moodily. Cara meant well; of course she did. And she did have a point. Emmie realised that all grown-ups rowed about silly stuff like pizzas and rubbish bins and clothes all over the place. And she knew that her parents were no different to other parents in that way. It was more that all they did was talk about mundane stuff or row about mundane stuff. And there was no way they had always been that way.

Emmie had seen photos from the early days, all the way through to the present day. Her mum was a keen amateur photographer and she was always taking photos and presenting them in special books and collages on the wall.

Emmie had assumed at first that it was only her life that had been recorded in amazing detail (she had a stack of beautifully bound books in her bedroom detailing every single moment from her time in her mum's tummy through to any major incident that had occurred ever since, scary hospital stuff notwithstanding), but she had since discovered tons of other books depicting her parents' relationship. The bar they had met at, various dates, their engagement, their wedding, birthday parties, an anniversary that seemed to be very special. Some of the photos of them had been taken by other people, obviously, but as time had progressed, more of the 'selfie' type photos had crept in.

But in all of them, her parents had been laughing. Happy. Carefree. They looked as though they were in love. They seemed to be into one another, besotted, full of passion and laughter.

And then she had come along, Emmie thought to herself. Cara said that grown-ups went crazy when babies arrived, because Cara's parents had lost it completely when her younger brother Ollie was born. Apparently they went crazy from all the crying and the fact that Ollie refused point blank to sleep for the first two years of his life.

Emmie had been told she wasn't a difficult baby in that way, but that aside, early pictures she had seen had been full of delighted smiles and wonder. Post birth in a teeny baby-grow with hearts all over it. Snuggled up in a car seat. Playing with a brightly-coloured toy on a play mat. Emmie smiled. She had been cute back then. And subsequent photos had shown equally idyllic scenes: her asleep on her dad's tanned chest in Majorca or somewhere as he slept under a huge parasol, his hand clasped protectively around her back. Her mum creased up with laughter at the sight of Emmie plopping a bowl of hummus on her head. Her dad whooping with joy as he watched Emmie toddling away from him. That one had been a video and Emmie had been in raptures when she first watched it... so strange to see herself as a baby!

It had only been as she had got slightly older that she had noticed the contrast in those photos and video clips. The difference between then and now. The smiles that had faded, the joy that was noticeably absent. The serious expressions, the furrowed brows, the forced smiles. And Emmie knew exactly why that was. And whatever Cara said — and Emmie loved her for being such a great friend — it was because of her. It *was*. And it made her feel heartbroken. And helpless. Emmie just didn't know what to do about it.

'So what's this new counsellor of yours like?' Cara said, maybe because she realised Emmie had gone really quiet.

Emmie turned back, welcoming the change of subject. 'Dr Tom? He's cool.'

'Dr Tom? He lets you call him that?'

'He asked me to call him that. He's very chilled.'

'Sounds it. Is he... you know...?' Cara wrinkled her nose.

Emmie scrunched her face up. 'What... hot? He's... handsome, yes. And he wears ripped jeans.'

'Ripped jeans...' Cara looked impressed. 'He sounds ace.'

'He's OK.' Emmie reached down and took a book out of her school bag. 'He lent me a book to read. And he gave me this as well.' She had forgotten about the diary Dr Tom had given her.

'What's that?'

'It's a diary.'

'I already have a diary. So do you. Why would you need another one?'

Cara jerked her head towards the special place she hid her diary, which wasn't that original because it was in the special, mirrored box her grandmother had given her that she kept under her bed.

'I do, but this one is different.' Emmie held it up. 'It's for me to write down stuff about how I'm feeling about my illness. Things like that.'

'Surely you don't need an extra diary for that? You told me you write stuff down in your diary about your cancer thing.' Cara got up and started rummaging through the box on her dressing table which was full of neon nail polishes.

'I do, but this is…'

Emmie didn't bother finishing her sentence. There were some things Cara didn't understand, even though she was Emmie's very best friend in the world. But Dr Tom's diary was different. Dr Tom's diary was for her to write down the stuff about her parents and why she was feeling so guilty and unhappy about the way they were with each other.

Emmie realised she hadn't done that yet, but she often felt that she lacked privacy at home. Her parents would often check on her when she had gone upstairs. Not without knocking on her bedroom door or anything, and

Emmie knew why they did it; they were worried about her. But it made her feel edgy about writing about them and knowing she could do it without being interrupted. But she was sleeping over at Cara's tonight; she would write in it later. She might have to do it with her torch under the covers when Cara was asleep, but that was OK.

'My parents are coming to meet Dr Tom soon,' Emmie said, remembering the meeting. 'He suggested it at our last session.'

Cara started taking her nail polish off with some pungent-smelling remover. 'Why would he want to meet your parents?'

Emmie shrugged. 'I don't know. I think he said it might help all of us.' She felt rather doubtful about that, but she did trust Dr Tom.

'My mum is calling you,' Cara said, nudging Emmie.

Emmie jumped up. 'That will be my mum checking I haven't, you know...'

'I know,' Cara said. She pulled an agonised face.

'Sorry.'

Emmie felt yet another flash of guilt. Cara couldn't cope with the thought of her dying either. Emmie sometimes thought her diagnosis was harder on everyone else than it was on her. It was a horrible thing to live with, but there was nothing she could do about it. It was everyone else who would be left without her, as they had all accidentally said to her at one time or another.

'Shall I paint your nails when you get back?' Cara said, holding up a bottle containing a super-bright pink polish.

'Yes please. I love that colour.'

Emmie did her best to smile as she left the room. It wasn't anyone's fault that she had a tumour. It wasn't even her fault she had a tumour. But it had such a huge effect on everyone around her, she couldn't help feeling terrible about it. Maybe she would feel better when she saw Dr Tom again, Emmie thought to herself.

'Thanks,' she said, taking the phone from Cara's mum. 'Hi Mum. Yes, I'm fine… nothing has happened. I'm still…' She paused, not wanting to say 'alive' because that sounded bad and it would make her mum wince. 'I mean, I'm OK. Nothing to worry about. Cara's is going to paint my nails in a minute.'

Emmie finished the call and handed the phone back to Cara's mum, who looked anxious before visibly relaxing when Emmie reassured her that she was OK.

Emmie paused with one foot on the stairs. Reassuring others was something she had got used to, especially over the past few years. She wished she could take everyone's focus away from the possibility of her dying at any given point, but it seemed she wasn't able to make that happen.

Maybe Dr Tom can help with that as well, Emmie thought optimistically as she headed upstairs. He was a counsellor rather than a miracle worker but he was also her only hope.

2014

Nate tried to unfocus his gaze, but found that he couldn't. It was as though his eyes were fixed on various points in the room but in way that was blank and vague. And the worst thing was that it seemed to be beyond his control. A cleaner moved in front of Nate's view and abruptly, he blinked and sat up.

When Emmie had undergone her first bout of chemo, he and Rosie had been struck by how glazed the parents who sat with their children looked. The beds on the ambulatory ward faced one another and parents seemed to stare hard at whatever was in front of them. Rosie had found it extremely rude and exposing; rude because there was no attempt to curb the staring and exposing, because it felt rather like being in a fish bowl. As though every move was being silently observed.

Further down the line, Nate and Rosie now realised that it was simply a result of sitting inactive for six to eight hours at a time. Of finding that reading or watching programmes on an iPad didn't sufficiently absorb the mind. That however gung ho one felt at the beginning of the process, that sense waned as the weeks passed. And as the after-effects of the chemo taking hold of the child experiencing it manifested themselves in technicolour horror. The violent vomiting that sometimes caused pulled muscles and horrendous stomach pains. The screaming – not just crying, but actual, involuntary screaming – that would accompany it on occasion. The stomach pains, the loss of appetite, the hair loss.

Nate snapped himself out of the thought. He didn't like to dwell on the terrible things Emmie had to go through. Living with the reality was harsh enough. The point was that after around three sessions of chemo – this last one having been suggested by a different consultant, after Mr Hobbs had left, who felt that one more go might be beneficial – he and Rosie had realised that they were acting the same way those other parents had acted when they had first arrived. That life inside the unimaginatively titled 'Chemo Room' became like a TV. That watching nurses moving around the room checking equipment and clearing up was like a rather mundane series on BBC2. Witnessing other families swapping beds as one chemo session finished and another began became the minutiae that occupied the mind and the eyes. The whole ward was like an ongoing reality show, albeit a tedious one. Nate had amazed himself by noticing even the tiniest of details about families when they arrived and settled themselves down. Body language, coping mechanisms, distraction techniques. The resilience of the children involved in this extremely unpleasant but necessary evil. Family dynamics, relationship tensions, quirky dress sense, bizarre food habits. It was all laid bare, for everyone to see.

Nate would never have predicted that he would find such commonplace details remotely interesting. But there was literally nothing else to do. Rosie would sometimes find herself dozing off, but that was because she slept far less than Nate in general. Nate laid awake at night worrying himself stupid over Emmie, but he was also a heavy sleeper under normal circumstances, so invariably, when he managed to drop off, he would go into a veritable coma. Rosie was such a light sleeper that even when she managed to actually fall asleep, she would often jerk awake again seconds later.

'Would you like a coffee?'

Nate sat up, realising the mother of the child in the bed next to Emmie was talking to him. Parents in the Chemo Room often became close but this woman was new and had arrived with her daughter for the first time today. She hadn't taken on the vacant staring thing just yet.

'Coffee. Do you fancy one?' The woman repeated her question politely. 'I can get one for you or you could remind me where the machine is?'

'Er...' Nate glanced at Emmie.

She managed a weak smile. 'I'm OK, Daddy. You can go.'

'Are you sure?' Nate didn't like leaving Emmie on her own while she was hooked up to the chemo bank. She looked horribly vulnerable and even though she was unbelievably brave, Nate knew she hated it.

Emmie nodded. 'I'm fine. I'm watching this show where kids make cakes and stuff.'

Nate stood up and kissed her forehead. 'Cool. Be back in a sec. It's this way,' he said to the woman, leading the way.

'I'm Jo,' the woman said, following him. 'My husband is coming along in a few hours' time and he's bringing some food and drinks but I'm not sure I can last that long.'

'Nate,' he replied. It was only a short walk to the drinks machine. 'We could go to the cafeteria, but I don't like being away from Emmie for too long.'

'I know what you mean. This is only our second session and it's absolutely terrifying.'

'Totally,' Nate agreed.

Jo got her purse out and smiled when Nate waved her money away. 'OK. I'll buy next time,' she said.

Nate got two coffees and handed one to Jo. 'So. You're new.' He studied her. 'Your second session, you say? I must have seen you before then.'

'I think maybe your wife was here last time.'

'Aah right.'

Jo cradled the coffee. 'Tell me... is it normal that people, umm...'

'Stare? Yes, I'm afraid so. Me and my wife Rosie found it bizarre at first, but now we do it as well.'

'Right.' Jo looked puzzled.

'It's hard to explain,' Nate said. He tried to to, all the same. 'It's weird, but you'll probably find that you can't really relax when they're having chemo. It lasts for ages and ages and you do all these things to try and keep busy but it's actually really hard to concentrate.'

'I see. Yes, I guess that makes sense.'

Nate sipped his coffee and grimaced. 'God, this stuff is crappy. I mean, I tried to work here once. I brought some paperwork in and tried to go through it, but for some reason, I couldn't keep my mind on it. I don't know if it's because it's Emmie in the bed next to me and I find it unbearable or what.' Nate stopped abruptly, realising that his voice had broken slightly.

'But anyway, you just end up staring, I'm afraid,' he added apologetically. 'It's like that room is a TV. None of us means to do it, but chemo is a tiring business.'

Jo nodded. 'My daughter Hazel has this tumour in her stomach and they thought they wouldn't be able to operate. But they think they can now so they're shrinking it with some chemo first and then she can have the op. And then we can hopefully get back to normal. And thank God, is all I can say. It's a horrible journey this, isn't it?'

Nate felt a flash of envy. Just a flash and then it passed. And the envy wasn't born of Jo's optimism, because he wouldn't want anyone to lose that feeling, but because he and Rosie were in a very different situation. Emmie wasn't ever going to get better.

The chemo was an attempt to shrink her brain tumour, but it was so large, it was inoperable and it wouldn't ever go away.

'What about you?' Jo asked. 'What's happening with your daughter?'

Nate bit his lip. It wasn't Jo's fault. She didn't know. But she had asked the question and he guessed he had no choice but to answer it.

'My daughter… Emmie, has an inoperable brain tumour,' he managed.

'Oh no.' Jo put her hand to her mouth. 'Does that mean…'

'It means that there isn't an end in sight. Or rather,' Nate let out a jerky breath, 'Rather that there is… existence like this, or… or a horrible end.'

'Oh my God.'

Nate could tell that Jo was mortified. People generally were.

'No, no. It's OK. Don't feel bad. It's just… it's just one of those terrible things that happens sometimes.'

Nate was aware how trite and empty his rehearsed speech sounded, but he had learnt through bitter experience that more emotionally honest comments tended to reduce him to a sobbing, snot-ridden mess. And they sure as hell made everyone else feel uncomfortable in a way that was hard to step out of.

'And here am I banging on about how glad I'll be to get back to normal,' Jo said. Her cheeks immediately flushed. 'I'm so sorry.'

Nate shook his head and sipped his terrible coffee. He had encountered this before; parents who bravely outlined the proposed schedule for their child's chemo, expressing earnestly resolute feelings about the 'end in sight', swiftly followed by intense shame and embarrassment when Nate or Rosie had to offer up the truth about Emmie: that there was no happy ending in their case. The trouble was, it was a fact. It was the truth. And there was no way of sugar-coating it in their lives – or anyone else's. Emmie's diagnosis – and her tumour – were a ticking time bomb.

And Nate understood the reaction of parents who had been given a clear, confident schedule of recovery. He yearned to feel what they must feel; as though they were building up to the biggest celebration ever at the end of the treatment. He knew that getting through this would be easier if the end result was worth it.

'I find it so frustrating that doctors and consultants don't like using percentages, don't you?' Nate said chattily. He knew the only way forward with this conversation was to chat and be normal and to gloss over the unpalatable truth.

'Yes, definitely,' Jo said quickly. She sipped her coffee and appeared to relax a little. 'I guess as parents, we want some sort of benchmark, don't we? Something we can measure this illness by.'

'I think that's very normal,' Nate said, leading the way back to the Chemo Room. 'We're only human and we work in stats and figures and something concrete we can use to understand what's going on here.'

'Yes.' Jo looked upset.

Nate knew why. He changed the subject slightly. 'The other thing to warn you about is that it can become quite expensive, this whole chemo thing. The travel. The food, in particular. Kids hate the food here,' he said, lowering his voice. 'You'll end up bringing your own most of the time.'

'OK, thanks.' Jo put her hand on Nate's arm before they went back into the room. 'I'm truly so terribly sorry.'

Unexpectedly, Nate felt tears pricking at his eyelids. Gosh. How ridiculous. He had had this conversation so many times before with any number of different parents. Maybe it was the kindly look in Jo's eyes. Maybe it was because Emmie was on yet another, hopeless round of treatment. Maybe it was basic envy that Jo appeared to have a more straight-forward journey ahead of her. Life had dealt her a cruel blow, but not one that was impossible to recover from, hopefully.

Nate dismissed that last thought. He no longer felt envy because he had somehow developed (apart from the odd, momentary flash or lapse) a level of compassion for other parents who weren't facing such a despairing journey. Nate knew exactly how he would feel if he were in Jo's shoes. He would feel impatient about reaching the end of the treatment, but the impatience would be underpinned by ecstasy. The thought that there could be a step by step process leading to the best possible outcome.

Nate turned to Jo. 'Just… keep chatting to us. Please? I get that it's hard to talk about, but my wife and I… we've found a way to cope with it.'

'Then you're braver than I could ever be,' Jo managed, sounding choked up. 'But of course. I wouldn't dream of blanking you, just because you're dealing with that.'

'Thank you.'

Nate believed Jo. He paused in the doorway for a second. He didn't mind if people stopped talking to him, but Rosie minded terribly. She found such things incredibly hurtful. Neighbours hurrying across the road to avoid her when she was out with Emmie looking especially sick. Emmie's friends' mums cancelling playdates for outlandish reasons, when they all knew the real reasons. Parents in the Chemo Room chatting away until they heard the reality then melting into the background because they didn't want to express euphoria at their own situations coming to an end when others would never experience that bliss.

This experience, mused Nate, separated the men from the boys, as his father always used to say. In the same way a divorce weeded out the naysayers and the disloyal, so did cancer.

'Emmie, would you like to have a go on Hazel's Nintendo?'

Nate turned to see Jo offering Emmie a pink machine and Jo's daughter Hazel leaning over to grin at Emmie. Emmie exclaimed happily as she took the machine and Nate threw Jo a grateful smile.

Cancer definitely separated the men from the boys, Nate decided as he sat on the bed. Or in this case, those who could cope with hearing the worst about someone and yet could move past it and be kind.

Life had the most ironic way of providing a heart-warming moment, but whatever form it took, Nate would happily embrace it.

Rosie

Rosie quickly checked the time again. She needed to finish her class and pick Emmie up from school so they could head over to Dr Tom's office. Rosie hoped to God Nate wasn't going to be late. His hours were erratic at the moment and this was such an important meeting.

'Let's move on to the clam,' Rosie called above the music. 'Move onto your side and let's get that alignment in place; ankles, knees and hips stacked...'

As she went into autopilot with her Pilates teaching cues, Rosie thought about Nate. Things had been so incredibly tense between them lately that she wasn't sure how this meeting with Dr Tom would go. Rosie felt as though they were on trial, as though Dr Tom might be assessing them in some way. She hoped not; she and Nate were not at their best right now. They hadn't been at their best for years, of course, but not many people knew that. Lily and Jamie, obviously, but they put quite a front on for everyone else.

But Dr Tom was a therapist. Emmie's therapist. Rosie was pretty sure there would be nowhere to hide. She refocused her mind on her class.

'So keeping those ankles together, let's lift that leg and *squeeze*... on a count of eight... with me, class...'

Rosie stood up and re-adjusted someone's posture. She felt rather exposed. Or rather, she felt like she and Nate would be… exposed. As frauds. As two people masquerading as a couple but whose relationship had actually fallen by the wayside a long time ago.

Switching her class onto their opposite sides to finish the clam sequence, Rosie berated herself. Hadn't she been all set to tell Nate that she loved him a few weeks back? Hadn't she been feeling as though she needed to let him know how much he meant to her after that coffee with Lily? And yet, when he came in the other night looking all hangdog, she had bitten his head off about a pizza. All because she thought he was making a dig about dinner.

Bringing her class smoothly into a stretch and relaxation phase, Rosie tried to let go of her tension. She and Nate had to start making an effort. They had to do it for Emmie. It was important that Emmie had two parents who supported her.

And who still loved one another, Rosie thought to herself painfully. She just didn't know if they actually still did. No, they did. She really hoped they did. She hated this horrible feeling of doubt that kept consuming her. But she genuinely didn't know if she and Nate still loved one another. They weren't behaving like two people who loved each other – the opposite, if anything.

'Thank you, class, and well done,' Rosie called, standing up to roll her mat up. Feeling her stomach churn with nerves, she made small talk with her clients as they packed up and left the gym.

Jumping into her car, Rosie dashed to Emmie's school. Within a few minutes, Emmie yanked the door open.

'Hey, Mum.' Emmie slid into the front seat.

'Hey. Good day?'

'It was OK.' Emmie put her seat belt on. 'Are you looking forward to meeting Dr Tom?'

'Yes, of course.' Rosie pulled away.

'No, you're not.'

'What do you mean?' Rosie glanced at Emmie.

Emmie smiled. 'You're all nervous. You always do that chewing your lip thing when you're stressed out.'

Rosie raised her eyebrows. Emmie was highly observant for a kid. Nothing went under her radar. Rosie sometimes thought Emmie knew her better than Nate did.

'Do I now?'

'Yes. You do.'

Rosie could hear a hint of laughter in Emmie's voice and she let out a short laugh herself.

'You don't need to worry,' Emmie said. 'About Dr Tom, I mean.'

'I'm not worried.' Rosie hoped she sounded convincing.

'Right. OK. But he's honestly really nice. He just wants to meet you and Dad. He's not going to interrogate you or anything.' Emmie giggled. 'He saves that stuff for me.'

'He interrogates you?'

'Well, you know. He's a therapist. It's his job.'

Rosie glanced at Emmie and frowned, but Emmie looked unperturbed. 'I'm not sure I like the idea of him interrogating you.'

Emmie sighed. 'I was joking. He just asks me questions and stuff. I don't mind. I like talking to him.'

Rosie took a turning, realising they were almost there. 'What does he ask you questions about?'

There was a pause. 'Just... how I'm feeling. Stuff like that. Nothing scary.'

Emmie sounded evasive. But Rosie didn't press her. Emmie was allowed to have secrets. Or at very least, she was allowed to have a safe place she could go to so she could talk about things she might not want to talk about with anyone else.

Rosie felt a pang. It pained her that there might be things Emmie didn't share with her, but she accepted that in the circumstances, Emmie — more than other kids her age — might have thoughts and feelings she couldn't possibly discuss with her parents. Because those thoughts and feelings might be too powerful for those closest to her to hear.

'Lead the way,' Rosie told Emmie, even though she knew the way. She stole a glance at her watch. Where the hell was Nate? He should be here by now.

If he didn't turn up... Rosie felt anger rising inside her stealthily.

Emmie walked confidently through the corridors, greeting members of staff like old friends.

Which to be fair, they probably were, based on the amount of time Emmie spent here, Rosie thought to herself. As they reached the door of Dr Tom's office, he opened it.

'Aah. Great timing.' He smiled at Emmie then dazzled Rosie with the same full beam. 'Mrs Johnson. Lovely to meet you.'

Rosie shook his hand. Good lord. Dr Tom was so *young*! Was he even thirty? He was wearing the ripped jeans Emmie had made reference to. It was rather unnerving. Like a school teacher sporting tattoos and earrings. It wasn't wrong at all, but it was unexpected.

Rosie relaxed. Dr Tom looked harmless. If ridiculously young.

'Do come in.' Dr Tom stood aside to allow them into his office. 'Take a seat. What do you think of the new beanbags, Emmie?'

Emmie threw herself into one. 'They're cool. They're not pink though. I think I said pink.'

'You did. But I decided navy might be better for my image. Even if they don't go with my horrible grey chairs.'

'Nothing would go with those chairs,' Emmie agreed, shuffling around happily in the beanbag to get comfy.

'You hate them. I know.' Dr Tom gestured to one of the normal chairs. 'Don't feel obliged, Mrs Johnson. The beanbags aren't aimed at the adults. I haven't seen an adult emerge from one with a shred of dignity.'

'Thank goodness.' Rosie sat down on a grey chair and grimaced. Lordy. The beanbag was probably actually the better option. 'I'm so sorry my husband isn't here yet. He must be stuck at work.'

'Does that happen a lot?' Dr Tom took a seat and angled it slightly, presumably to include Emmie in his eye-line.

'Nate being stuck at work?' Rosie shifted in her seat and not only because it was one of the most uncomfortable seats she had ever sat in. 'I guess so. I'd like to think he'd make the effort to come to this meeting, though.' She could feel her lips tightening but she was feeling extremely angry right now. Nate was late and this meeting was important. If he didn't turn up…

'Well. Hopefully I'll get to meet him shortly.' Dr Tom consulted his notes. 'Emmie, I was planning to ask your mum some questions about you. Is that OK or would you rather leave the room?'

Emmie shrugged. 'People always talk about me as though I'm not here. I'm used to it.'

Dr Tom laughed. 'Ouch! I didn't mean that. I meant that we could all discuss some stuff together. After I've talked about you as though you weren't actually here.'

Emmie grinned. 'I was only messing as well. You're funny, Dr Tom.'

'Thanks.' Dr Tom threw Rosie a rueful smile. 'She's a smart girl.'

'You're telling me.'

'I enjoy it. Keeps me on my toes.' Dr Tom shot Emmie a glance. 'Talking about you, not to you there by the way.'

'I know. But... shall I look at your books for a while?'

Dr Tom threw an arm out flamboyantly. 'Go for it. I got some new ones actually, just for you. Seeing as Harry Potter didn't impress. At the end there, by the boring medical journals.'

'Cool.' Emmie went into the alcove that contained all Dr Tom's books and, with a tact far beyond her years, shut the door softly behind her.

'So. How do you think Emmie is in herself, Mrs Johnson?' Dr Tom focused his attention on Rosie.

'Please call me Rosie. Mrs Johnson is so formal.' Rosie glanced over her shoulder at the alcove door. The book area was handy; she was fairly certain Emmie couldn't hear her. She retuned her gaze to Dr Tom. Just how young was he, anyway? It was rather strange being interviewed by someone who looked as though he might like the same music as Emmie.

'I think she's doing really well. She's a strong girl. And unfailingly upbeat.' Rosie swallowed. She didn't know where Emmie found the strength. She struggled most days and she wasn't the one who was sick.

'Rosie it is. And… yes, she is. Both strong and perennially upbeat.' Dr Tom met Rosie's eyes. 'Have you noticed her seeming… down at all recently?'

Rosie's brow knitted. 'No. Down? Not really. No, not at all. God.' She felt a shiver of panic. Her stomach did horrible flip flops whenever she thought about Emmie hurting in any way. 'Is something wrong? She's not… having pains she's not telling me about, is she?'

Dr Tom held up a hand. 'No, no. Please don't worry. Physically, from what I understand, Emmie is doing exceptionally well right now. As well…'

'As can be expected,' Rosie finished automatically. 'OK.' She calmed her breathing from erratic to normal. 'So you mean emotionally, maybe?'

'Yes. I leave the medical stuff to the experts. I'm all about the well-being aspect.' Dr Tom gave Rosie a genial smile. 'I'm just asking how you feel Emmie is at present. Emotionally. In herself.'

Rosie checked her watch again. Where the hell was Nate? God, this was so aggravating. He should be here! She shouldn't be doing this alone; they should be a team when it came to these things. Rosie hoped Nate wasn't doing anything stupid. She wasn't sure why she had suddenly thought of that; it had been years since she hadn't trusted Nate. And she was sure he hadn't been near a casino in years. But where the hell was he?

Just as she had suspected, Rosie felt exposed talking to Dr Tom. As if... there was something going on with Emmie that she was unaware of. Rosie knew that she and Emmie were extremely close but she reminded herself that Emmie was allowed a safe place, or whatever they called it, to come and say things she might not be able to say to her mum.

'OK.' Rosie took a breath. 'I think Emmie is fine. Maybe a little sad at times, but apart from that, I think she's in a good place.'

'A little sad.' Dr Tom nodded. 'Yes, I agree. What do you think is behind that? Apart from the obvious – although actually, in Emmie's case, it's not really about the obvious. As I'm sure you know.'

Rosie regarded Dr Tom caustically. How did he keep that lovely smile in place all the time? Even if his words sounded loaded, his expression suggested otherwise. 'If you mean that Emmie isn't focused on her diagnosis or the fact that she will die at some point, then no. I agree with you. As astonishing as it is, that amazing girl in there doesn't seem fazed by such a gigantic thing. I wish I felt the same.'

Rosie felt her face crumple and she quickly looked down at her hands. They looked pale sitting motionless in her lap but they were tightly twisted together, revealing her anguish.

God. Rosie hated crying in front of people all the time. It hardly mattered any more, of course; she had resigned herself to the fact that she regularly disgraced herself on the sobbing front. In pretty much every situation she could think of. At the hospital on countless occasions (this, was of course, a more excusable example) but also... at the cheese counter in Tesco's. Mostly because Emmie and Nate devoured French cheeses by the truckload. In a busy street because a beautiful Rolls Royce with pink ribbons had swept past and Rosie had been hit by the realisation that Emmie might never have a wedding day. At the cinema, buying cupcakes, picking up dry cleaning. There was a whole host of situations that could initiate a fresh bout of crying and the unfortunate thing was, there was no way of second-guessing any of them.

And although Rosie had been apprehensive about seeing Dr Tom today, she hadn't expected to cry. And not like this. This was one of those rare occasions, where the tears could be most acutely felt in her chest. It felt constricted, as though someone had a firm hand wrapped around it. There were actual tears but they were sparse and minimal. Most of the emotion was contained inside, it seemed. Rosie's eyes were wet but her cheeks weren't soaked. And nor were her clothes. So it was a contained release, rather than an outright burst.

Rosie often wondered if this was some bizarre strategy her body had developed for when Emmie was around, a form of crying without losing complete control of her faculties. Because the tears that fell when Emmie were absent were plump and plentiful. An uncontrollable torrent, no less. The tears fell unbidden, often accompanied by the most terrifyingly loud sobs, animal-like in their wildness. Rosie was deeply ashamed of those outbursts, even though they were beyond her control at the time. But afterwards, she felt guilty. Uncomfortable. Because her crazed howls were incredibly intimate but they had been released into normal society without warning. Unleashed into society like that elephant in the room no one wanted to look at or talk about.

Today's tears were caused by a mixture of emotions; Rosie knew that. Her heart felt battered from watching her child in torment, but Rosie also felt white-hot rage at Nate's absence.

How could he? How could he be so late for a meeting that could help Emmie? Rosie wanted to yell and scream. Perhaps strike poor Dr Tom, just because he was there. But of course she couldn't. She felt Dr Tom's hand on her arm and she looked up. He was proffering a box of tissues.

'I thought I'd put those in a really prominent place as well. Emmie said that I should because people do often need tissues in this office.'

'Thank you.' Rosie plucked a handful of tissues from the box, wondering if Emmie was OK behind the closed door. She was grateful for Emmie not being able to witness her crying, however. The parent should always be stronger than the child, right? Right.

Rosie dabbed at her eyes. 'I apologise. I don't know where it comes from half the time.'

'Totally natural.' Dr Tom nodded towards the alcove door. 'I'll just check on Emmie.' He put his head in and Rosie could hear muffled voices.

'She's fine,' he said strolling back to his chair. 'She's deeply engrossed in a Nancy Drew box set I found at the charity shop.'

'Oh I used to love those.'

'I think there are quite a few books in the series. You're onto a winner.' Dr Tom leant forward so he was leaning his elbows on his ripped jeans.

Rosie took a deep breath. 'In answer to your question, Dr Tom, I don't know what's behind Emmie's sadness. I could describe fairly eloquently what is behind mine, but in the absence of the obvious, as you put it, I really couldn't say. But I would love to know why you think Emmie is feeling sad.'

Dr Tom closed his file. 'I don't know if you're familiar with counsellors at all, Rosie, but we are really very annoying in many ways.'

Rosie scrunched up her tissue. 'How so?'

'We don't provide answers, is probably the easiest way to describe it.'

'Oh yes.' Rosie sniffed. 'You'll want me to… look inward and somehow figure out why Emmie is sad all on my own.'

Dr Tom looked past her to the door leading to his book alcove. 'We should rescue Emmie in a moment; even my new books aren't *that* interesting. But yes.' He returned his kindly eyes to Rosie. 'Can you think of any reason Emmie might be feeling sad?'

Rosie sighed. There could be any number of reasons Emmie might be sad, especially at a deeper level. Even though she seemed not to fear dying, did she wonder about falling in love? Going on a girly holiday? If she would ever forge a career? Rosie had no idea because Emmie had never mentioned those things. And in some ways, Rosie was glad, because it gave her hope that Emmie was ignorant of some of the joys that living to a certain age might afford her. Presumably, she couldn't miss what she wasn't aware of.

Rosie had experienced these things so she knew. She knew about the utter joy some of these things could cause. But Emmie most likely didn't. Perhaps her sadness stemmed from things that were more imminent. A school disco. A sleepover. A trip into London. But Rosie didn't know for sure.

'I don't know,' Rosie said eventually. 'I just don't know.' She felt stupid. She should know. She should know why her daughter was sad. Why didn't she?

'That's OK,' Dr Tom said.

Rosie could hear apology in his voice.

'I didn't intend to make you feel bad about this. And I'm not trying to worry you either. Emmie is fine and well in herself. We're just examining all sorts of things in her life at the moment, in an effort to clear her head and make sure she's as calm as possible.' Dr Tom adjusted his glasses. 'But please don't worry. We're just tossing some ideas around at the moment. Nothing serious.'

Rosie sat back in the chair and flexed her back. She felt tired. Weary to the bones. And where the hell was Nate? Rosie straightened.

'I can't understand why Nate isn't here. I'm so sorry.'

'That's OK,' Dr Tom said again. 'I'm sure he has a very good reason.'

'Are you?'

Rosie wasn't. She understood that Dr Tom had a duty to be polite, but he really was way off mark. Why was he sure Nate had a very good reason for missing Emmie's session? Rosie wasn't. She thought it likely Nate had got caught up at work as usual. That he had forgotten. She fumed inwardly. It was just downright rude. And inconsiderate. In fact, it was unforgivable.

Aware that she had gone off on a rather extreme tangent, Rosie nonetheless struggled to pull herself back into line. But she wasn't actually sure Nate deserved the effort it was taking.

'Let's get Emmie,' Dr Tom said. He called her. 'Do you want to join us?'

Emmie emerged clutching a book. 'This is ace. Can I borrow it please?'

'You may.'

'No Dad?' Emmie put her hand on Rosie's shoulder.

Rosie shook her head. 'No. Sorry, Emmie.'

Emmie face fell for a second. 'It's alright. Probably just work.'

Rosie felt Dr Tom's eyes on her. 'Yes,' she said brightly. 'Maybe you can meet Nate another time, Dr Tom.'

'Of course.' Dr Tom grinned at Emmie. 'Shall we have a quick chat alone? Rosie – is that OK?'

Rosie got up. 'No problem. I need a coffee anyway.' She dropped a kiss onto Emmie's head and, wrapping an arm around her shoulders, held her. Too long, probably. But Rosie couldn't bear the thought of her being sad.

She left the room and dropped her bag to the floor near the row of lined up chairs. Sitting down, she pulled out her phone. No messages from Nate. Not a single one.

How could he? How could he not turn up and not even message? Rosie felt angry tears coming again, but she refused to let them spill out. Because clearly, Nate simply wasn't worth it.

Nate

'I need to make a move.' Nate looked at his watch worriedly.

Gill checked hers. 'Right. You have that appointment for Emmie. What is it again?'

'Meeting her new counsellor. Dr Tom. Emmie thinks he's a hero.'

'Dr Tom...'

Nate nudged her then laughed as Gill nearly fell off his desk. 'Sorry, I forgot you don't weigh anything, woman. But yes, I know, I know. Dr Tom. He's about twelve and likes to be known by his first name. He wears ripped jeans and everything.'

'Wowzers.' Gill shook her head. 'It's all a bit too trendy-sounding for me. First names and ripped jeans. No wonder Emmie thinks he's some kind of god.'

'Yeah.' Nate tapped his teeth with his pen. 'I actually had a sad moment where I got all annoyed at the thought of Emmie hero-worshipping someone other than her dad, you know?'

Gill straightened the already-pristine collar on her shirt. 'That's different. No one is going to be better than you, dude. He's only her counsellor. And she knows she can be rude to him if she wants to. You're the person Emmie talks to about the stuff she really cares about.'

'Hmm.' Nate shrugged. He knew he was being an idiot about Emmie's counsellor. It was just that he had such an amazing relationship with Emmie, he couldn't help feeling weird about his daughter having someone else to talk to. Someone she might talk to about stuff she didn't feel she could talk to her dad about.

Nate sat up. Christ, was he jealous of his kid's counsellor? It was ridiculous. Emmie had had a few counsellors in recent years, but he suspected that there was something different about Dr Tom. He seemed to have connected with Emmie in a way that no other counsellor had.

Which was exactly why there was no way on earth Nate was going to miss this appointment this afternoon. About to head off, he frowned as Gill abruptly got off his desk and tugged at her suit jacket.

Without even looking, Nate knew that their boss had made an appearance. DCI Nicolls was a force to be reckoned with. And he only ever ventured out of his office to deliver special information.

Nate turned his chair and sat up, already on alert. And in a panic about the time.

'Relax.' DCI Nicolls nodded at both of them. 'For now.' He glanced at his watch. 'I'm aware that it's almost knocking off time, but we've had a tip-off.'

'A tip-off?' Gill said eagerly.

'Yep.' DCI Nicolls glanced over his shoulder. 'It's not the Peabody family themselves, but a family linked to them. We've had a tip-off about them meeting up tonight. On one of the estates. Doesn't meant anything will kick off but if it gets us closer, it can only be a good thing.'

'How firm is the tip-off?' Nate glanced at Gill. If the tip-off was legit, they were going to have to get to this meeting point somehow. But Nate also needed to be at the hospital.

'Oh it's definitely legit,' DCI Nicolls confirmed. 'It's from one of our best contacts. A horrible little snake, but he's usually spot on.'

'When and where?' Gill asked, grabbing a notepad from Nate's desk. She scribbled the details down as DCI Nicolls fired them off at breakneck speed.

'If anything kicks off, call for backup, OK? But it should just be observational at this stage.' DCI Nicolls glanced at Nate. 'You're looking stressed. Do I need to get someone else to do this?'

Nate hesitated. He couldn't bear the thought of letting Emmie and Rosie down. But this was critical. This was a minor way of him clawing back a little bit of respect at work, but it was going to have an impact elsewhere.

Story of my life, Nate thought furiously. He couldn't seem to do anything without messing up somewhere else, but this was no time for martyrdom.

'Purely observational?' he asked.

'Yes,' DCI Nicolls stated firmly. 'I don't want any nonsense tonight. I just need some eyes on this meeting.'

'We're the ones for the job,' Gill said, staring at Nate. 'A quick in and out, we'll report back and then head home.'

DCI Nicolls smiled briefly. 'Good. Well done. I'll be here for the next hour or so, which should be all you need. Let me know what happens.'

Nate watched his boss stalk back to his office and glanced at his watch again. 'Shit. This is going to be really tight for me time-wise.'

'We can do it,' Gill said confidently, turning to her desk to get her things together. 'In and out quickly and then you can make your meeting.'

'I'd better,' Nate muttered as they left. He had a bad feeling about this 'observational visit', but he didn't want to let his boss or his partner down. He just hoped to God he didn't let Rosie and Emmie down instead.

'I promise I'll make sure you get to your meeting,' Gill said as Nate headed towards the address they'd been given. 'But we have to show willing, right?'

'Right.'

Putting his misgivings to one side, Nate pulled up in what he hoped was a discreet location.

Gill sat up. 'Blimey. Look. Isn't that Peabody Senior over there?'

Nate followed Gill's finger. 'Yep. That's him. Mean-looking bastard isn't he?'

'Horrible,' Gill shuddered. 'He literally looks as though he could kill someone with his bare hands.'

'Yeah, about that…'

'I know.' Gill threw Nate a look. 'I know he's supposed to have done that. So hang on, is that other guy he's talking to someone from this other family?' She pulled Nate's notepad out of her handbag. 'The Kennedy family.'

'The Kennedy family?' Nate shook his head. 'Delusions of grandeur.' He checked his watch again. 'What are we actually looking for here? What are we observing as such?'

'God knows.' Gill scribbled in the notepad. 'I think Nicolls just wants to use us as his pet monkeys at the moment. We're bottom of the class, aren't we? Could do better and all that. D minus.'

Nate slumped moodily into his jacket. Gill was right, but it was a shame considering how amazing his career had been to date. Both of their careers, in fact.

'Stop sulking,' Gill said. 'I'm not even looking at you and I can feel you seething from here.'

'Whatevs, as Emmie would say,' Nate said, delving deep for some humour.

'Ha. Oh shit.'

Nate glanced at Gill. 'What's wrong?'

'I think they've seen us.'

'What?' Nate sat up.

'They've seen us. Peabody Senior is pointing at our car.'

'Fuck.' Nate turned to Gill. 'Kiss me.'

'What the actual…?'

'Just do it.' Nate put his hand on Gill's neck and pulled her closer.

Gill's eyes were wide as Nate planted his mouth on hers.

'Christ,' Nate said, as he pulled back slightly.

'I know. What the actual… and that, that was like kissing my bloody *brother*.'

'Yes, yes.' Nate knew exactly what Gill meant. 'But couldn't you have pretended just for a second? I mean, it's not like I'm not head over heels in love with my…' He turned. His car door was being opened.

'You… out.' Peabody Senior was leaning in. Some of his minions were standing back and watching, but it was bad enough that Peabody was so close.

Nate swallowed and got out of the car. 'Something wrong?'

Peabody stared at him. 'You tell me.'

'No crime against having a cheeky snog is there?'

Nate could feel adrenalin firing in his veins. Standing in front of him was a man who had not only killed people with his bare hands, if rumours were to be believed, but was also the mastermind behind several violent criminal incidents in the area. Catching him would be the biggest coup of both his and Gill's careers and the world would definitely be a safer place.

Close up, Peabody looked alarming. He was a big guy, with huge shoulders and a neck like a tree trunk. Nate knew him to be in his sixties, but he was well-preserved. Solid and packed full of muscle, like an aged Rottweiler that had never stopped standing to attention. His skin was rugged and weather-beaten, but it was his eyes that were giving Nate the creeps. There was something about those eyes that was sending chills down Nate's spine.

Peabody leered. 'A cheeky snog. Is that what this is? You expect me to believe that?'

'Why not?' Gill got out of the car and sidled up to Nate. 'Look at him! He's gorgeous.' She reached a hand out and squeezed Nate's bum.

Nate shot her a startled look but managed to grin at Peabody. 'See. Can't keep her hands off me.'

'Is that so?' Peabody eyed Gill. 'I like a keen woman.'

Nate felt Gill shiver next to him. He put his arm around her.

'Feel like sharing?'

Peabody turned and flapped a hand at his minions. They melted away obediently. Peabody returned his gaze to Nate.

'Sorry?'

'Sharing. Your lady friend.'

Nate felt sick. They needed to call for backup. But how the hell was he going to do that without blowing their cover? Even without his minions hanging around, Peabody was extremely intimidating. He had a reckless air, as though he was capable of anything. Intimidation, murder, rape…

'Er, not really, dude. She's pretty special.'

Nate tightened his grip on Gill. He could feel her squaring her shoulders. She was a brave little sod, but he didn't want her doing anything daft.

'I like special.' Peabody licked his lips. 'Come on, baby. Give me some sugar.'

'Give you some sugar?' Gill's tone was incredulous.

Nate felt his stomach slide. OK, so not many people said stuff like that in real life, but still. Gill had probably just made Peabody mad.

'You've got a smart mouth,' Peabody snapped, taking a step forward.

Yep. Peabody was mad. Nate held a hand up.

'She didn't mean anything by that. She's just crazy about me. She doesn't want anyone else. What can I say? You know how it is, right? Right?'

Peabody wasn't even looking at him. He had his mean eyes fixed on Gill like a missile on a target. 'You need pulling into line, little lady,' he snarled.

'I can do that,' Nate said jokingly, trying to keep his tone light. 'Seriously, if anyone can pull this lady into line, it's…'

'Shut up.' Peabody beckoned for Gill to step forward.

She swallowed and put her chin in the air. She went to step forward but Nate put a hand out. 'Gill. No.'

Peabody smirked, his eyes darkening.

Nate stared at him. He'd seen the look in Peabody's eyes before. It was the moment before the moment. The moment when a grown man lost his shit completely and turned violent. And Nate had this feeling that hitting a woman wasn't beneath Peabody. He had always trusted his gut in the past and he was about to do it now.

Just as Peabody's fist came out of nowhere, Nate shoved Gill hard and stepped into the space she left. Seconds later, he felt the full force of Peabody's fist in his face. Nate staggered backwards and felt blood gush through his fingers as he grabbed his nose.

He opened his eyes and turned his head to see if Gill was alright. She was sprawled on the floor holding her arm and Nate panicked. Christ, had he broken her arm? He regretted taking his eye off Peabody as he got another couple of punches in. In fact, he was raining blows, was that the expression? Nate could hold his own, but Peabody was in a frenzy. He lost count of the times Peabody's fist smashed into his face and then Nate actually saw stars. And red. Lots and lots of red. He fell to the ground, smashing the side of his face against the wheel of the car.

'Stay away from here,' Peabody sneered when he finally withdrew. 'Wankers,' he added for good measure as he stalked off, flicking blood from his fists.

'Oh God,' Gill said, as she struggled to get up.

'Did I break your arm?' Nate mumbled through his fingers. He'd forgotten how gross blood tasted. It was seeping into his mouth and down the back of his nose. Was that a tooth on the ground? Maybe not. A bit of his nose perhaps?

Nate had a sudden urge to vomit.

'I don't care if you did break my arm.' Gill got to her feet and gingerly took Nate's hand away from his face. 'OK. It's OK.' Her voice was shaky. 'You're still beautiful. Your face is more or less intact.' She gave him a rueful smile and started to cry. 'Bloody hell. That was so awful.'

'Don't cry.' Nate forced his lunch down again. No one likes seeing a tuna mayo sandwich the second time around.

Gill wiped her eyes. 'Give me some sugar. Why did I react to "give me some sugar", for God's sakes?'

'Because it's offensive. But yes.' Nate squinted at her. 'You could have let that one slide, to be fair.' He coughed and spat some blood out. 'Are you sure my face is OK?' He started laughing. As if he cared about that.

Gill took his chin in her hands. 'It's good. I actually won't be able to keep my hands off you for real.'

'Ha ha. Yeah. Sorry about that. Had to say something.' Nate cupped his nose again. 'Is my nose broken? And my head. Is my head in one piece? I'm in bits. It feels as though I was just whacked with a baseball bat.' He struggled into a sitting position with difficulty.

'You were. Just the human equivalent. I don't know what's broken.' Gill bent down and picked something up. 'Oh man. But I know that this definitely is.'

'Fuck. My phone.' Nate leant against the car in frustration, accidentally taking his hand away from his nose. 'That's all I need. Aah crap, and now I've bled all over myself. What's that quote from Macbeth? Something about having so much blood? That... that...'

'You sound a bit delirious.'

Gill was starting to sound panicked. And that made Nate panic. He gazed at her. Were there two of her? No, he was being silly. Gill's voice was starting to sound muffled to Nate. He shook his head in an attempt to clear his ears.

'I have Rosie's number,' Gill was saying. 'Nate, can you hear me? I'll call Rosie when we get to the hospital, OK? Because that is where we're going. Right now.'

Nate was absolutely sure Gill was speaking into her hand. Or she had moved far away from him because he couldn't hear her. 'Hospital? No. No way. At least, not unless it's the one Dr Tim works at. Tom. Dr Tom. Jeans. He wears funny jeans.' Nate tried to smile but it hurt too much. 'Funny jeans!'

'I know. Oh God, Nate. You're worse than I thought.' Gill started to pull Nate around to the passenger side of the car. 'But no can do, fella. You need A&E.'

'Rosie is going to kill me...'

'She won't. I'll tell her what a hero you were.' Gill stopped Nate before he ducked into the car. 'Because all the sexist chat aside, which obviously made me want to batter you, you were a bloody great hero just then, partner.'

'Stop it. He was going to hit you. What else was I going to do?' Nate's head was really starting to ache now. And he felt rather sick. Had he even got a punch in anywhere?

Gill grabbed his hand. 'I don't know, but you did the equivalent of taking a bullet for me today. He's messed your pretty face up a lot but if that had been my face his fist had connected with, I'm fairly certain I'd be a piece of pulp right now.' She squeezed his hand. 'Thank you, Nate. Thank you. I love you for that. And Sexy Kev will need to kiss you as well later.'

'Nooooo.' Nate slid into the passenger seat. 'There is definitely no need for that.' Was he speaking funny? He was speaking funny. And he'd gone a bit deaf. His ear was throbbing. 'God, that man was built like a brick shithouse.'

'He certainly was.' Gill started the car. 'What a nasty piece of work. He terrified the living shit out of me.'

'Did I say that out loud? And am I lisping? Am I speaking with a lisp?'

'Yes, you are, my friend.' Gill grimly turned the car around. 'Because you have a lip the size of Africa and your nose is hanging off your face.'

'You said I was still beautiful…'

'I lied. You look like shit. And you might never look the same again. And you saved my life, most likely, and you didn't blow our cover. And that's all Nicolls will care about.' Gill speed-dialled their boss.

'Ring Rosie. Sod Nicolls. Ring Rose…' Nate felt himself slipping into unconsciousness. He struggled to sit upright. 'Dr Tom. You'll need to call Dr Tom.'

'Alright, Nate. I'll call everyone. Just… just don't die or anything, will you?'

'Die? Don't be daft. Die?'

Nate was confused. He wasn't dying. His daughter was dying. And that was a hideous, heart-breaking fact. One thing Nate did know was that he had done something really bad today. Messed up. Let people down. Which was the last thing he had wanted to do – the opposite of what he wanted to do.

But he knew he wouldn't be able to explain it. That he wouldn't be able to excuse himself. Because it would look as though he had chosen his job over his child. And Nate would never do that. Never. But he couldn't lose his job.

'My job,' he said out loud.

'What's that?' Gill took a roundabout at breakneck speed and glanced at him briefly.

'My job. Can't lose it. Because that would be terrible.' Nate swallowed and winced. 'But I love Emmie. I love Rosie. All I care about. Emmie, Rosie.'

Gill nodded. 'I know, Nate. I know.'

With that, Nate promptly passed out.

Emmie

Emmie sat on the floor cross-legged and closed the Nancy Drew novel. The alcove attached to Dr Tom's office was surprisingly cosy. And it gave people space to talk. So her mum could talk openly about anything she wanted to, the way Emmie did when she saw Dr Tom.

Emmie sighed. Where was her dad? He'd promised he'd be at the meeting today. He had devoutly promised. Not just a pinkie promise – a real one. Emmie knew her dad's work could be demanding, but she had really hoped he would turn up today. Dr Tom had really wanted to meet both her parents properly and the meeting had been booked in for a good few weeks now. Emmie knew her mum would be really angry about it too. Her stomach churned uneasily, the way it always did when she thought about how bad things were between her mum and dad.

She looked up, realising Dr Tom was calling her.

'Do you want to join us?'

Emmie got up and went into Dr Tom's office. 'May I borrow this?' She gestured to the Nancy Drew novel she was holding.

'Of course,' Dr Tom nodded.

'No Dad?' Emmie asked, putting her hand on her mum's shoulder.

'No. Sorry, Emmie.'

Emmie felt her face fall, but she did her best to compose herself. 'It must be work,' she said, even though it sounded lame.

Dr Tom cleared his throat. 'Yes, perhaps. Shall we have a chat on our own, Emmie?' Rosie left and Emmie threw herself back into the encompassing comfort of the beanbag.

'Great,' she muttered.

'You're saying that because your dad didn't turn up?'

'Yeah. That.'

Dr Tom gingerly sat on the beanbag next to Emmie's. 'Ooh! OK. These really are difficult to sit on. Wow.'

Emmie giggled at his girlish outburst. 'There's a knack. Just don't move around too much.'

'Right. I'm not moving. But I'm already dreading getting up again. Whose idea was it to get beanbags?' Dr Tom settled his shoulders into the beanbag and pushed his glasses into place. 'OK. I'm ready. So. Your dad. It was a shame not to meet him.'

'Yep.' Emmie turned the Nancy Drew novel over in her hands. 'It will be because of work. It's the only thing that ever makes him late for anything.'

'Does that bother you?'

Emmie shrugged and put the book down. 'Not really. I mean – I wanted him to come today. To meet you and stuff. But the rest of the time, it's OK. He's a good dad. The best.'

Dr Tom nodded. 'In what way?'

'In what way what?'

'In what way is your dad a good dad?'

Emmie regarded Dr Tom.

'OK. So.' Dr Tom put out a hand to steady himself as he shifted slightly. 'Holy moly. This is like sitting in quicksand. Anyway. What I'm getting at is that children see their parents in different ways. And define them uniquely. So what you perceive to be the characteristics that make your dad a good dad could differ wildly from the next child I might see. I'm interested in your opinion.'

Emmie was struggling to resist the urge to laugh out loud about 'holy moly'. 'Umm, I don't know. He's just a great dad.'

'Because...' Dr Tom prompted.

'Because... he's always there for me,' Emmie said. 'He takes me places. Drives me and my friends around. He... cuddles me a lot. Spends time with me. We read together. He makes me laugh.'

Dr Tom picked up his notepad and scribbled. 'That's cool.'

'Yes, but it's more than that.'

Dr Tom waited.

'It's...' Emmie struggled. 'It's about... the nights he spent lying with me in hospital. It's... him shaving his head when my hair fell out. It's... him not caring when I've puked on him after the chemo. Like, all over him. Loads of times.'

'Ha. Yes. That's the measure of a man, that is.'

Emmie giggled. 'He was so great about it.' Her smile faded. 'So that's what I mean. He's a good dad. A great dad. And I have a great mum. I've put my parents through so much with my illness. I feel like I... owe them. Does that sound funny?'

Dr Tom smiled. 'You don't owe them anything. It doesn't work that way. But they both seem like great people. And from what you say, wonderful parents.' He paused. 'How do you think your mum felt about your dad not turning up today?'

Emmie picked at the beanbag. 'Angry. Disappointed, probably.'

'Right.'

'It's because the slightest thing sets either of them off.' Emmie dropped her eyes. 'I hate seeing my mum this way. She didn't used to be like this. She used to be happy; I know she did.'

Dr Tom laced his fingers. 'It's hard to watch someone you love hurting.'

Emmie blinked at him. This was what her parents went through every day, she realised with a jolt. Every day, they watched her hurting. Speaking of which, her stomach was starting to hurt now. Not just tighten.

'Are you OK, Emmie?' Dr Tom looked concerned. He sat forward on his beanbag and nearly slipped sideways. 'Oops. I'm not liking the beanbags. Do you have pains?'

Emmie let out a jerky breath. 'It's just my stomach. It's cramping up a bit.'

'I see. I'll mention that to someone and see if they can check you over.'

Emmie lay back on the beanbag. She was so sick of being checked over. Her stomach was hurting because she was wound up and worried about her parents, that was all.

'The cancer hasn't spread,' she said out loud.

'Didn't think it had,' Dr Tom replied briskly. 'I think it's possible your anxiety is affecting your digestive system a little. So. Did you manage to do your homework? I asked you to find out about your parents.'

'Kind of.' Emmie fished her diary out of her bag. 'You might want to have a read through this. I made some notes. And put some photos in there.'

'Cool.' Dr Tom took it and spent a few minutes reading. 'Loving the photos. They make a good–looking couple.'

'Yes. And they look happy… right?'

'They do.'

'And then they start not looking so happy. Look at those other photos. The ones of them in the South of France. I think I was really sick then.'

Dr Tom held one up. 'This? Emmie, it's perfectly acceptable for parents to look anxious when their kid is sick. That's normal human behaviour.'

Emmie nodded, feeling earnest. 'I know. But look at the difference in those photos, Dr Tom. They used to be so, so happy before it all went wrong. Before I went wrong.' She started to cry and bent her head.

'Oh Emmie. You didn't go wrong.'

Dr Tom radiated compassion. Emmie could feel it enveloping her with warmth even though she wasn't looking at him.

'Nothing about you is wrong,' Dr Tom continued. 'This is just a horrible thing that has happened to all of you.'

Emmie scrunched her fists into her eyes. She could feel Dr Tom staring at her, but she couldn't look at him.

'And you mustn't confuse the natural sadness of two people not wanting to see their baby in pain with a sign that you are responsible for any deeper issues today.'

'Dr Tom.' Emmie wiped a hand over her face.

'Yes?'

'You said you wanted to help me.'

'I do.' Dr Tom looked solemn behind his geeky glasses.

'Then please stop trying to convince me that this isn't my fault.' Emmie eased herself out of the beanbag expertly. She held a hand out to Dr Tom.

He took it and clumsily allowed her to pull him up. 'Heavens above. That's a one-off, if I may say so. I'll stick to my horrible, grey chairs in future.'

'Good idea.' Emmie made sure she had Dr Tom's attention. 'But if you want to help me, you have to drop this whole thing. OK?'

Dt Tom gave her one of his best smiles. 'OK. I'm just doing my job with this stuff, Emmie. I don't want you to feel bad about yourself. I'm not into blame.'

'I can't help the way I feel,' Emmie said reasonably. 'So it's probably better if we drop all of that. And do something.'

Dr Tom pretended to roll up his shirt sleeves. 'You want to get practical. Noted. So, what's the plan, Stan?'

'You crack me up.' Emmie bent down and packed her book and diary in her bag. 'I don't know what the plan is. I thought you were the ideas guy?' She straightened up. Her stomach still felt dodgy.

'Fair enough. So. You've given me some background on your parents. They do look very in love. As though they have something special.' Dr Tom pondered. 'What about putting together a timeline?'

'What's a timeline?'

Dr Tom grabbed a sheet of paper from the printer by his desk. 'You would try and find out when your parents met. How they met. Their first date. The kind of places they hung out when they were dating. When your dad proposed. All that stuff.'

'Wow.' Emmie felt excited. 'How do I do that?' She held up a hand. 'No. It's OK. I need to channel Nancy Drew. I'm going to treat this like a mystery that I need to get to the bottom of.'

'Brilliant.' Dr Tom drew a line on the piece of paper. 'This,' he pointed to one end of the line, 'is where they met. And this,' he pointed to the opposite end, 'is today. We need to go all Nancy Drew and figure out how they fell in love and why.' He scribbled some notes down on it. 'How about something like this?' He pointed to the page.

Emmie grinned. How fantastic Dr Tom was. What a perfect idea. She was thrilled already. Surely such a cool plan would work?

'Can we pull this off?' she asked.

'I think so,' Dr Tom said confidently. 'We're going to need all the right information and we're going to need some spies.'

'Spies?' Emmie wanted to giggle.

'Absolutely. Every good plan needs spies.' Dr Tom regarded her seriously. 'We need to get a little team of helpers together if we're going to make this work, Emmie. This is going to be like a military operation. We need some inside information and only spies can get us that kind of stuff. Think about who we can use... who we can trust.'

'Wowzers. I love it.' Emmie carefully folded the piece of paper and put it into her bag. 'Leave it with me.'

'Same time next week?'

'That doesn't leave me long, not if we're planning something excellent like that,' Emmie said, beaming. This was so exciting! 'But I do enjoy a challenge.'

'Me too.' Dr Tom glared at the beanbag. 'I might practice on that. See if I can get on it and off of it again without looking like a complete numpty.'

'Good luck with that,' Emmie said, pulling his door open. 'That's going to take you far longer than my home-work.'

'Hmmm, you could be right.' Dr Tom fixed the beanbag with a stare. 'But in my opinion, it's all about mind over matter...'

'Holy moly,' Emmie said solemnly. She left him to it, her mind already whirring with what she needed to do.

2015

'Rosie, are you sure you're not taking on too much?'

Rosie glanced at Lily irritably but saw only deep concern and love etched across her face. They were in a gorgeous little boutique dress shop Lily had dragged her to for some retail therapy and the last thing Rosie needed was to feel criticised or judged.

'Yes, I'm sure,' she said firmly. 'It will be mostly home study which I can do in the evenings and I've found a place nearby which runs the course. It's five minutes away so I don't have to stay there overnight and I can get home immediately if anything… if…'

'Right,' Lily said quickly. She stopped and placed her hand on Rosie's arm. 'It's not even that — not how far you'll be from Emmie. You're never far from Emmie. It's more that I'm worried you're doing too much. Your rigid exercise regime, the clean eating, re-training to become a Pilates instructor.'

Rosie tried a floppy, black hat on and caught Lily's eye in the mirror. 'OK. So, when we received Emmie's diagnosis, me and Nate — we knew we needed to be strong for her.'

'Of course. I think any parent would understand that.' Lily smiled. 'That hat suits you, by the way.'

'I'm not really a hat kind of girl. You suit hats, not me.' Rosie took it off and put it back. She ran her hand down the sleeve of a silk shirt hanging nearby. 'So you get that we had to be strong for Emmie — we have to be strong even now. Emotionally. As you say, it's what any parents would do for their child. But there's more to it.'

Lily picked up a black bodycon dress and held it against her body.

Rosie appreciated Lily's ability to read her. So many people just talked and talked and talked when there was a gap in conversations like these. When there was an obvious place to ask questions. Lily just waited, allowing Rosie to collect her thoughts.

'It's about… it's about being strong in every way there is to be strong,' Rosie explained. 'As in… eating clean and making sure that Emmie's diet is full of good, natural foods. Running daily. Because it clears my mind and it allows me to breathe. And I feel strong when I do it. As if I can handle what's going on in my life more easily because of it.'

Lily assumed a vague expression which meant that she didn't understand what Rosie was on about. She faced the mirror and held the dress up again, but Rosie could tell that Lily was processing what she was hearing.

Rosie sighed and pretended to look at the clothes. She and Lily were so different. Lily was allergic to exercise. Keeping fit was anathema to her, so it was going to be hard to convince her twin that physical fitness was good for the mind, the soul – and the body. That keeping her body fit and strong made Rosie feel as though she could do anything, cope with whatever life kept throwing at her. Cope better, at any rate. The ache in her muscles, the rush of breath in her lungs – all of it made her feel alive, strong and more capable.

Exercising made her feel more in control, Rosie realised as she picked up a cute halter-neck she knew Nate would approve of. The self-discipline involved. The endurance. The effect it had on her body. And in a life which was full of events that were beyond anyone's control, to the point of screaming frustration, any element of control was addictive. Essential, even. A regular exercise regime made the confusion and injustice of the situation seem more manageable somehow.

'The Pilates instructor thing will be good for me,' Rosie said out loud. 'It's a job with some flexibility and it pays well. And it will keep my mind occupied and my body strong.'

Lily hung the dress over her arm. 'I sort of get what you're saying,' she said. 'But I'm still worried you're doing too much. Taking on something that might be more than you can handle. Not because you're not Superwoman, because you are,' Lily added hurriedly. 'You know I think you are the most incredible person I know. Well, you and Nate combined. I'm just worried about you, that's all.'

Rosie nodded. She knew how much Lily worried about her. And she understood. She would feel the same about Lily if, God forbid, Lily ever found herself in a similar situation. But one of the many things Rosie had learnt from this experience with Emmie was that she had to almost disregard the anxiety of others. And also, that being selfish was of great importance, because it was critical to her well-being. Doing whatever made her feel good and capable and strong – that was how Rosie knew she had to live her life right now, to be the best support to Emmie.

'Are you sleeping?' Lily asked. She gestured to the top Rosie was holding. 'You should get that. It's sexy.'

'Where would I wear it?'

'Oh stop saying things like that! You're a young, beautiful woman.' Lily held her hands up. 'You don't need to remind me of what you're going through, Rosie. I know. I just don't want you thinking you're never going to wear a sexy top ever again.'

Rosie rolled her eyes and picked the top up again. This was a 'choose your battles' moment. And she couldn't be bothered to explain herself anymore today.

'Sleep. Are you getting some?' Lily repeated.

'Sleep?' Rosie surveyed some bejewelled clutch bags. 'Yeah. I'm getting some sleep. Plenty, in fact.'

Sleep could be elusive as a ghost to some parents dealing with a child who had cancer. Rosie knew this from chatting to other parents at the hospital and at a few support groups she had attended for a while. Some would restlessly pace the room all night long because of the intense fear and apprehension they were experiencing. Some simply lay in bed staring at the ceiling, fixating on a particular spot on a ceiling or doing anything they possibly could to avoid dwelling on the reality that awaited them in the lighter hours. Rosie – and Nate, as it happened – both fell into another camp: that of the parents who fell into bed and practically passed out. In their case, their energy levels were so depleted from living in a state of high stress and anxiety, when it came to lying down and stepping away from it, their bodies almost shut down – overcome from the exhaustion of dealing with the deadening weight of hopelessness.

Rosie was grateful for the respite, however. She had felt guilty at times, hearing other parents describing their insomnia and the subsequent side effects, but she had let go of that now. Her and Nate's experience with Emmie was different to most other parents and whatever form the respite came in was welcomed with open arms. The worst thing was waking up again; that initial, beautiful moment of calm and peace, which was instantly wiped out when reality hit and grief and pain descended.

'Well, that's good then,' Lily said. 'That you're getting some sleep. That must help with the feeling strong thing.'

Rosie glanced at Lily. So she did understand.

'If it was me, going through what you're going through, I think I would want to escape.' Lily stopped looking at clothes and turned to Rosie.

Rosie swallowed and said nothing.

'I would want to pack a few things in a rucksack and I would want to leave. Get away. Sit on a beach and just… watch the waves. Contemplate. Let my mind stop racing.'

Rosie bit her lip and nodded. That was exactly how she felt. Like escaping. Every single day, she would think about how it might feel to be free. Not of Emmie, God no. But free of this heavy, excruciating pain. Of not knowing how long Emmie had. If she would ever fall in love. Have a career. Travel. And every once in a while, Rosie would open her wardrobe door and look at an old denim rucksack she had and she would wonder how it would feel to stuff some underwear and some clothes into it, grab her passport and head to the airport. Just to get away. Just to be alone and get her head together. To feel warm sand between her toes, waves lapping at her feet. To stand at the edge of an ocean and just watch the ebb and flow of water.

But of course she couldn't do that. Rosie couldn't possibly do that. She had Emmie to think about. And what about Nate? How would he feel if she suddenly decided she needed to get away? Nate must feel the same. They hadn't ever had the conversation, but Nate was only human; Rosie was sure he must have similar feelings about absconding. Not because he was a bad person, but because, for any normal person, this was an impossible burden to endure.

Rosie faced Lily. 'That's exactly how I feel. Every day, Lily. Every single day.' The words caught in her throat suddenly.

'Oh Rosie.'

Lily immediately put down the clothes she was holding on a nearby cash desk and put her arms around Rosie. 'I'm so sorry,' Lily said. 'I'm so sorry, Rosie.'

Rosie burst into tears and clung onto Lily. She didn't do this. She really didn't do this. Not in public, at any rate. She cried in the shower, she cried in bed. And she cried alone on the walks she went on to get pints of milk she didn't need.

'I ask myself why you were picked for this and not me,' Lily mumbled, still holding onto Rosie. 'Why one twin was picked and not the other. And I don't know the answer. But I feel so bad for you. I hate that you're going through this, Rosie. I hate it. I wish I could take your pain away. I wish I could take Emmie's pain away.'

Rosie couldn't speak so she just nodded. She wouldn't wish this on her worst enemy, let alone her twin sister. She didn't ever wish anyone else was going through this. Rosie just often wished she and Nate weren't. And that Emmie was just a carefree, happy girl who had nothing more to worry about in her life than what to wear to the school disco and whether or not she could get her homework in on time.

'Right.' Lily pulled back finally. She put her thumbs under Rosie's eyes then wiped her own eyes. 'We look like shit, but whatever. So now we're going to shop. We're going to buy whatever we want, even if we don't know when we might be wearing it. OK?'

Rosie smiled weakly. 'OK.'

'And I can totally see you as a Pilates instructor,' Lily added as she gathered her pile of clothes up again.

'You can?'

'Defo. Actually, shall we find some tight Lycra for you to practice leaping around in?'

Rosie started to laugh. 'Yes. Yes, we could do that.'

'Good. Let's get you kitted out.' Lily led the way towards the small workout section in the boutique. 'Probably cost you an arm and a leg in here, but you'll look shit-hot.'

'That's the main thing,' Rosie agreed. She paused for a second, feeling stricken. It was a way a life for her now, feeling *that way, but occasionally it stopped her in her tracks. But life had to move forward somehow. Pilates. A way to move forward. From the way she felt about Emmie's diagnosis and from the frustration she felt about Nate and what had happened to their marriage.*

It wouldn't change anything dramatically in the scheme of things; Rosie knew that. But it felt good. And anything that felt good had to be worth it right now.

Rosie

'So have you spoken to Nate about not meeting Dr Tom?' Lily handed Rosie another margarita and slid onto a nearby bar stool.

Rosie held the stem of the glass. 'Nope. Nothing much to talk about, is there?'

Lily frowned. 'Well. I mean, he had a good reason to miss the appointment, didn't he? From what Jamie told me, he was defending his partner… what's her name again? Jeni, no, Gill.' Lily sipped her margarita. 'He was defending Gill from getting an absolute pasting from some horrible criminal dude. That's not his fault, Rosie. And at least he's on babysitting duty tonight so you can have a break.'

'God, whose side are you on, Lily?'

Rosie felt a flash of irritation. What was wrong with her sister? Come out for a chilled-out drink, she had said. Meet some of my mum friends and forget about everything, she had said. And here she was, talking about Nate and winding Rosie up about whose fault it was that yet again, Nate hadn't turned up for something important.

'You know you don't even need to ask that question,' Lily replied stoically. 'I love Nate, but he's not you. He's not my sister.'

'Your *twin*,' Rosie added, knowing that out-trumped pretty much everything.

'Right. So don't be daft asking me about my allegiance. It's a no-brainer.'

Rosie smiled. Of course it was. 'Sorry, Lils.'

Lily waved a hand. 'It's OK. But stop with all that, alright? We're on a night out and you need a break from all this. Nate should have come to the appointment but he was getting his head bashed in in the line of duty. Shit happens.'

'It certainly does,' Rosie agreed ruefully.

Lord, but she was tetchy right now! She hated herself for it, but she was so incredibly tired of it all. She just wanted life to be easy again, but that wasn't about to happen, so Rosie knew she had to sort herself out. She was out for the night! She should try and put everything out of her mind.

Rosie drank some more. It felt good. It took her away from reality when the edges were blurred a bit. She was also glad for the thumping music. Thumping music she could cope with. Anything more soulful or sensitive had her in pieces. Rosie hadn't realised how evocative music was until Emmie's diagnosis. Since then, there were many moments that felt like that opening scene in the Bridget Jones movie. In the same way that sad songs or a poignant lyric made a person who had just suffered a relation-ship break-up crumble, Rosie could literally find herself sobbing within seconds at something on the radio or on the TV. And she wasn't even a ridiculously emotional person. It was having a secret, inner despair that seemed to trigger thefloodgate effect. Card shops did the same thing. Seeing cards with 'Daughter' emblazoned across the front seemed to reduce Rosie to a dribbling wreck. She couldn't ever have predicted such a thing, but there it was.

Lily tore her concerned eyes away from Rosie's unconsciously troubled face. 'Aah, here are my friends.'

Forcing a smile onto her face, Rosie allowed Lily to introduce her to her friends as they all piled up at the bar. They were a lively bunch, clearly excited about being able to come out and have a drink together and one of them enthusiastically ordered a round of drinks for everyone.

Allowing the happy chatter to wash over her, Rosie fell silent for a moment and sat down on a bar stool next to one of Lily's friends. She knew it wasn't Nate's fault that he'd missed the meeting with Dr Tom. She knew he had a good reason for not being there. Rosie knew that Nate had most likely been a gent; a hero, even. She knew he had a fractured cheekbone and concussion from the altercation. He looked terrible. Gorgeous still, of course – but compared to normal, Nate looked terrible. He had been badly beaten and he had taken the pasting because he had been protecting Gill. Like any good partner, Nate had stepped up and done the right thing.

Gill had sent Rosie several texts about it as well. They had had a brief phone call. And Rosie believed Gill. She trusted her. Gill had been a fantastic partner to Nate for years now and Rosie knew Gill wouldn't lie to her, not even for Nate. But Rosie couldn't help feeling angry with Nate. She couldn't help it. Because once again, it felt as though he'd put his job first. Once again, she felt let down. Once again, Rosie felt furious on Emmie's behalf that her dad hadn't turned up again.

The thing was, it had all reached the point where it no longer seemed to matter what Nate's reasons were, or what a good guy he was being elsewhere. As far as Rosie was concerned, it was about Nate not being there for her. For Emmie. It was about Rosie feeling alone, when she shouldn't ever feel that way. It was about feeling horribly let-down.

Nate was her husband. Her partner. They were going through a nightmarish situation and they should be a team. They had always been such a strong, incredible team. Yet, lately, it just didn't feel that way anymore. It felt as though Nate was doing his own thing and leaving Rosie to pick up the pieces and explain things to Emmie. Even if that wasn't quite the case, Rosie couldn't seem to shrug that feeling off.

'So I hear your husband is in the police force?'

Rosie started and turned to find one of Lily's friends had sidled up next to her. The friend was wearing a tight, silver bustier top with equally tight jeans and skyscraper heels. She wore a determined expression that Rosie recognised and her heart sank.

'I'm Susie,' Susie said, holding up her cocktail glass by way of a greeting. 'Lily says your husband is the police force. I was about to offer my sympathies. My husband is a surgeon. I hardly see him either. Annoying, isn't it?'

'Can be,' Rosie shrugged, reluctant to enter into a huge discussion about it. She regularly used Lily as a sounding board but she wasn't the type to moan to someone she barely knew.

'God, it drives me *insane*,' Susie stated enthusiastically. 'I feel like a widow, you know? Those women who whine on about being a golf widow – that's nothing! Being married to a surgeon, or a policeman? Well. That's serious neglect, that is. I'm left alone constantly. Don't you just want to scream at him all the time?'

Rosie regarded Susie. Many things made her want to scream, but Nate's work hours weren't exactly top of the list. It was only when he missed something important that it bothered her.

'Not really, no,' she replied eventually.

'Well, I do. I want to batter him!' Susie passed her another drink. 'Come on, you look like you need this. But seriously, I just find my husband's work hours really aggravating. This issue is the bane of my life.'

Rosie almost drained her drink in one. She really didn't want to talk about this. Hadn't she come out tonight to not focus on all this stuff?

'Lily says you have a sick daughter?'

Susie clearly wasn't letting up. Dear God. Hadn't Lily given her a list of topics to avoid? Rosie glanced at Lily who gave her a bright smile from the bar.

Rosie put her drink down, knowing she was being unfair. 'Yes. I have a sick daughter.'

'Is is…' Susie lowered her voice. 'Cancer?'

'You don't need to whisper,' Rosie commented, half-amused. 'It doesn't make it sound any better.'

'Right.' Susie frowned as one of the other women rocked up with a tray of glasses. 'Oh look, we have a shot now. A Jammy Dodger… my favourite. Let's have this and then you can tell me all about it.'

Rosie downed the shot swiftly. She needed it.

'So what kind of cancer is it?' Susie couldn't help it; her voice dipped again on the key word.

Rosie sighed inwardly, but did her best to be patient. It wasn't Susie's fault. 'It's an inoperable brain tumour.'

Susie gasped and clapped a hand over her mouth. 'No way. Oh my God. That's horrendous. How do you cope with that?'

'By drinking lots,' Rosie said, picking her cocktail up. She drank it then put the glass down again.

'I don't blame you,' Susie said fervently. 'My little Toby has a terrible cough, you know. Do you think I should get it checked out? I mean, I thought it was nothing, but talking to you... well, it makes you think, doesn't it? I've been telling him to shut up for keeping me awake at night, but now I'm thinking, bloody hell – what if it's something way more...'

'Why would you think that?' Rosie shook her head. 'Does he have any other symptoms? Is he coughing up blood? Does he have trouble breathing? Is he losing weight or something?'

Susie looked appalled. 'Good lord. I don't know. None of those things, no. It's not... it's more this persistent cough thing...'

'OK, but why would you now think it's something more serious?' Rosie knew she was being unfair, but she couldn't seem to help herself.

'I don't know. I mean, I'm not sure I even really thought anything of it.' Susie started chewing her lip. 'But now I'm in a blind panic...'

'Don't be.' Rosie felt the fire in her chest subside. 'I'm sure you're worrying over nothing. Cancer...' she said the word deliberately and firmly... 'Cancer is actually very rare. Especially in children. Please don't start thinking the worst.'

Susie yanked her tight bustier down a fraction. 'It's very rare, you say? OK, well that makes me feel better.' She let out an audible sigh. 'I suppose you must get this a lot? People meeting you and immediately thinking everyone they know has… erm…'

'Cancer? Not so much, no. Surprisingly.' Rosie glared at Lily, who shot her a bewildered look and started to make her way over.

'Maybe I'll get Toby checked out anyway,' Susie said, returning to her self-absorbed thoughts. 'It's probably for the best, right? I mean, in your experience, would you recommend…'

'Do excuse me,' Rosie said, turning away and heading for the toilets. She knew Lily wanted to check on her, but she just wanted to be alone. Once inside the toilet cubicle, Rosie sank down onto the closed lid and put her head in her hands.

What was wrong with people? Why would Susie compare her son's cough to Emmie's inoperable brain tumour? Rosie had experienced every reaction on the spectrum when it came to Emmie's illness… or so she had thought. Previously kindly neighbours had crossed the street to avoid talking to Rosie when she had been walking home with Emmie. Friends had completely avoided the topic, purely out of fear of saying the wrong thing, but creating an 'elephant in the room' vibe that merely made everyone feel awkward. One friend had earnestly talked about it non-stop at one coffee meetup, clearly thinking that the way forward was non-avoidance and showing an in-depth interest.

Rosie sat up and realised she was quite drunk. She didn't know what the right answer was. Mention it, don't mention it. She just knew that crossing the street to avoid someone was heinous and so was comparing a kid's cough to an inoperable brain tumour.

Rosie got up and went out to the mirror. She looked dishevelled. Her hair was a mess and her eyeliner was all smudged. She looked tired and stressed out. She sighed, stroked her hair into place, and ran a finger beneath her eyes.

Outside the toilets, Rosie glanced over at Lily and her friends and decided she needed some air. Heading to a side door, she headed outside and gulped in some fresh air. She leaned against a wall and let her head tip back against it.

'Rosie?'

She started and pulled away from the wall. 'Er yes?' She squinted into the darkness. There was a young guy in front of her. He looked vaguely familiar.

'Jonny,' he said, stepping forward. 'From the coffee shop?'

'Oh yes.' As the light fell across his face, Rosie recognised him properly. 'What are you doing here?' She looked around with a smile. 'No coffee here.'

Jonny laughed and ran a hand through his dark hair. 'I know. I work here part time as well. Behind the bar. Getting drinks from the cellar, that type of thing.'

'Keeps you out of mischief,' Rosie commented irreverently. What on earth was she talking about? God, she was drunk.

'Well. Not always,' Jonny grinned at her. 'Nothing keeps me out of mischief completely.'

'Is that so?' Rosie couldn't help laughing. 'That's a bit worrying. I didn't see you in there.'

Jonny leant against the wall and turned his head to look at her. 'I've finished for the night. I've had a few drinks as well. So what are you doing out here all alone then?'

Rosie let out a noisy breath. 'Well. Firstly, I'm drunk and I needed some air.'

'Fair enough. And secondly?'

'And secondly…' Rosie stopped, confused. Secondly? Too many cocktails. 'Oh yes. One of my sister's friends was banging on about how her son might have cancer. Just because my daughter has it.'

Jonny pulled a face. 'What, like it's catching because she's talking to you? That's insane.'

'Yeah.' Rosie nodded. 'It's insane.'

'Were you rude to her?'

'Not really. Maybe. I'm not sure.' Rosie breathed some more fresh air in. She felt as though she had cotton wool in her mouth. 'I just know that since this whole thing kicked off in my life, I've become super-intolerant. And I really mean that. I have zero tolerance for people who are self-absorbed, who make out that their lives are tough because they've run out of balsamic in Waitrose. Do you know what I mean?'

'I do.' Jonny let out a short laugh. 'Balsamic in Waitrose. That's funny.' He reached out and flicked her hair from her face. 'But I get that it must be easy to let go of people – or maybe just to walk away when they start talking like that. With what you're going through.'

Rosie picked a piece of cement off the wall. 'Yes. It is actually. I used to be so tolerant of people, so understanding. These days, I'm just like – you're just using up my energy in a really bad way and I don't want to be around that.'

139

'Cigarette?' Jonny proffered a packet.

'I don't – oh go on then.' Rosie took one. She had no idea why, but it felt right to be doing it.

Jonny lit it for her and Rosie took a nervous drag. It had been a while since she had smoked, but it felt oddly good.

'Thanks,' she said. 'At least you're not acting like a weirdo around me.'

'No reason to. I like you.'

Rosie took a too-deep drag and started coughing like a novice.

'Are you OK?' Jonny patted her on the back. 'I only said I liked you. It wasn't a marriage proposal.'

'I know.' Rosie threw the cigarette on the ground. 'I'm just rubbish at smoking.'

'What's your surname?'

'What?'

Jonny raised his eyebrows. 'Your surname. What is it?'

'It's Johnson.' Rosie wasn't sure why Jonny wanted to know such a thing.

Jonny took his phone out and moved his fingers over the screen rapidly. 'Aah. Here you are.' He held his phone up and showed Rosie. 'I sent you a friend request.'

Rosie frowned. It was her page on a social networking site. 'Yes, that's me. We were on holiday in Thailand when that picture was taken. I burnt my feet on the first day. Who does that?'

She took her phone out. There it was. Jonny's friend request. Starting drunkenly at the screen, she hesitated. Was it wrong to accept someone's friend request? Nothing was going to happen with Jonny, was it? It was just an innocent friendship.

Rosie touched the accept button and tucked her phone away.

'Your feet? You actually burnt your feet. Ouch.' Jonny bent over and looked more closely at her feet. 'I would have kissed them better.'

'My feet?' Rosie pulled a face. 'Eugh. I'm not into that.'

'I didn't say I'd suck your toes! I said I'd kiss your feet. It's different.' Jonny straightened up.

Rosie stared at Jonny. She didn't know what to say to that.

'I bet you're good at kissing.' Jonny turned to face her properly.

'W-what?' Rosie's stomach shifted. What on earth was he on about?

'Kissing. You look like you'd be amazing at kissing.' Jonny leant in suddenly and placed his mouth on hers. He kept his there briefly, gave her a brief tongue flick then withdrew. 'I was right. You are.'

Rosie swallowed. What had just happened? Had she kissed Jonny? Or had she just allowed him to kiss her? She wasn't sure. It had felt good. Strange, but good. But also very, very wrong.

Rosie pulled herself up. She was married. She was married to Nate.

'I need to go,' she muttered.

'Do you?' Jonny put a hand on her arm. 'I'd love to do that again.'

Rosie stared at him. He was quite beautiful. He had lovely eyes – wide set and blue. A great mouth and a boyish smile. He had a boyish smile, because he was a boy. And he was out of bounds because she was married.

She went to leave and before she could even think, Jonny had pinned her up against the wall and his hands were in her hair.

'Tell me to stop,' he whispered.

Rosie found herself transfixed. By Jonny's intense gaze and by his mouth. She tried to speak but nothing was coming out.

Jonny bent his head and kissed her again. His mouth lingered on hers and he pressed his body against hers.

Rosie felt herself sinking against him. Just for a second. It felt delicious. It was making her stomach squirm. But it was also wrong. It was just – Rosie allowed herself to luxuriate in the kiss. Just for a few moments longer. Not because it was Jonny. But because she missed this. She missed the incredible way it made her feel, being kissed by someone. The closeness, the headiness. The taste of someone else's saliva on her lips. The sheer delight of being desired by someone.

God, she missed Nate, Rosie thought to herself. She missed him so badly it hurt. When had they last done this? Up against a wall outside – God, years ago. But in bed even? In the kitchen? A kiss. On the mouth. With tongues. They hadn't done it in ages.

Rosie put a hand out and stopped Jonny. 'Stop. Please.'

'Do you mean that?' He looked at her longingly.

'I mean it.' Rosie untangled herself. 'I have to go.' She walked past him and headed back inside the bar.

'There you are!' Lily grabbed her. 'Where have you been?' She leant in and sniffed. 'Have you been smoking?'

Rosie shrugged. 'Maybe. Can we go home now, please?'

'Go home? But it's so early...' Lily looked at Rosie searchingly and then nodded. 'OK. Let's go home, hun. I'll go get our coats.'

'Thank you.'

Rosie turned as Jonny walked past her and felt sure she must be blushing as he met her eyes. God almighty, what was wrong with her? She was married and Jonny was a child, for goodness' sakes. Rosie hated herself. She was an idiot. An absolute idiot. Making a fool of herself like that.

'Here you go,' Lily said, handing Rosie her coat. 'I told my friends that I thought I was about to have the squits. You so owe me...'

Rosie took Lily's arm. 'You *are* my twin after all.'

'I am. And I took one for the team because I suspect Susie was truly awful to you.'

'She was.' Rosie held onto Lily's arm. She was extremely drunk but nothing excused kissing Jonny earlier. Nothing. And it was Emmie's birthday soon – why on earth wasn't she thinking about that? Why was she thinking about herself and being completely selfish?

With a sense of shock at the realisation that she wasn't the person she had thought she was, Rosie clung to Lily as they left the bar. She hadn't ever thought herself capable of cheating. Nate had always been everything she had ever wanted. It had always been Nate. Rosie had never wanted anything more. And now she had snogged some kid around the back of a bar without even thinking about it.

Rosie felt a rush of tears hit the back of her throat. What on earth had happened to her? How could she have become this person?

'I do love Nate,' Rosie said, stopping abruptly in the middle of a road. 'I do. I just can't reach him. I don't know who he is anymore.' She started to weep with shame and embarrassment. And sheer hopelessness about Nate. And Emmie.

Lily put an arm around Rosie's shoulders, pulling her out of the road. 'I know, darling,' she said comfortingly. 'I know. It's going to be OK, I promise.'

But it wasn't, Rosie thought to herself despairingly. It wasn't. It felt as though everything was slipping through her fingers and she was powerless to stop it. She was suddenly poleaxed by a longing for Nate that she knew had been lying dormant for years. Rosie didn't want Jonny; she wanted Nate. She wanted Nate so badly it hurt.

But Nate was lost to her. And it felt as though it was too late for them.

Hiding the hysteria that was threatening to erupt, Rosie clung to Lily gratefully, glad that someone was here to take her home.

Nate

'No thanks, Jamie. I really need to get home.'

Nate rubbed the front of his head irritably. He'd sustained a scar on his forehead from a ring Peabody had been wearing that had effectively left a dent. The surgeon who had worked on him and patched his face up had told him it would fade in time but Nate didn't care about the mark on his face so much as the fact that it was incredibly itchy. Even now that the dressing had come off.

'Rosie has said she'll babysit and she's fine about it,' Jamie was saying, speaking loudly as if he was outside somewhere. 'Lily told me. And that, my friend, is *carte blanche* for us to go out and get absolutely rat-arsed.'

'I don't think so,' Nate said, leaning back in his chair.

He was sorely tempted, however. Work was on the quiet side at the moment after the incident with Peabody and Nate could do with a drink. Not several – he needed a hangover like the proverbial hole in the head he had literally suffered – but a couple would do nicely. His body still felt bruised all over but that wasn't what was tipping him over the edge. It was the way Rosie was being with him, how distant she seemed to be.

And Jamie was good fun. Nate hadn't bargained on having a brother-in-law who was also a good mate, but he had landed on his feet in that sense.

'Come on,' Jamie wheedled at the other end of the phone. 'We've been given a free pass. Let's go out and chew the fat. We haven't had a night out in ages. We could get a dirty burger afterwards. And the ladies went out the other night, didn't they?'

'You drive a hard bargain.'

Nate made a decision. Yes, the tension at home was unbearable. The way Rosie was avoiding him was soul-destroying. He could do with a drink – badly – and Jamie was great fun and a good listener. But Nate was already in the dog house. And he didn't need to be in any more trouble.

'I'm going to have to take a rain check.'

'No way!' Jamie made his disappointment obvious. 'That sucks, man.'

Nate smiled. 'Sorry, dude. Another time, for sure. But I'm really not sure staying out tonight is a good idea.'

'Alright then.' Jamie's voice was full of regret. 'But I'll hold you to another time, alright?'

'You're on.'

Nate put the phone down. He already wished he'd said yes. What was wrong with him? Rosie probably couldn't be any angrier with him than she already was and sharing the same space when things were so tense and difficult between them was the hardest thing in the world.

The second hardest thing in the world, Nate correctly himself swiftly. Living with Emmie's diagnosis beat every-thing hands down.

'You off?' Gill said, strolling over.

'Yeah.' Nate stood up and shrugged his arms into his jacket.

'Good. You look like crap again.'

Nate gave her a lopsided smile. 'Wow, thanks, partner. I actually thought I was healing pretty nicely.'

'The outside looks fine.' Gill grabbed his chin and turned his face one way and then the other. 'Those scars are fading. It's you I'm worried about. You on the inside.'

'Aah, don't go all therapist on me,' Nate complained. 'I'm fine.'

'Right.' Gill looked sceptical. 'Still, you need some time off. A break. I know you won't do it, but I know you just want to jump on a plane and get the hell out of here every now and again.'

'I'd settle for a beer, to be honest,' Nate said breezily, needing to shut Gill down. She knew him so well, she could cut straight to the heart of his feelings in a few seconds. The way Rosie used to, in fact. Not that he wanted to jump on a plane, exactly. There was another way Nate could replicate that sensation – but he didn't dare think about it.

'Go for a beer then. Shall I phone Sexy Kev and let him know I'll be late?' Gill already had her phone halfway out of her pocket.

Nate scooped his keys up. 'Jamie just asked me out actually, but I said no. Wasn't sure it was a good idea after, you know, taking a bollard in the head instead of going to Emmie's counsellor appointment.'

'Silly sod,' Gill tutted. 'That's exactly what you could do with. Listen.' She stopped him by putting a hand on his arm briefly. 'I've done my best to sort things out with Rosie. I've sent her messages… we've chatted on the phone.'

'That's really sweet of you. Thanks, Gill.'

Nate was fairly certain Rosie hadn't taken a blind bit of notice of Gill's earnest ramblings about the Peabody incident, but as ever, he appreciated her support.

'I don't know if it did any good,' Gill said gruffly, her eyes seeming troubled. 'But I did my best. I feel so fricking responsible, Nate. I'm so sorry. That was all you needed and I feel crap about it.'

'Aah, stop it.' Nate patted her shoulder. 'Don't beat yourself up about it anymore. I'm sure we both made mistakes. I can't really remember all the details, because after the first blow I turned into a bit of a punch bag, but I'm sure I was just as much to blame as you were.'

'You really weren't,' Gill said, shaking her head.

'Gill. In the words of the great Disney classic, let it go. Please. It's done. And apart from wishing we hadn't gone on that job and that I had been able to laugh at Dr Tom's silly jeans, I don't think we could have handled it any better than we did that night.'

Nate simply had to get out of the office. He thought the world of Gill, but he had enough going on right now. He couldn't handle her self-reproach on top of his own.

'OK. I hear you.' Gill stepped back. 'Phone Jamie up. Go for that drink.'

'Yeah maybe. Catch you tomorrow, partner.'

Nate headed outside and stopped as he took in some air. God, but he was struggling with the idea of going home. He could feel that itchiness flaring up inside him, that deep-rooted desire for escape. For some people, a visit to the beach might suffice. Maybe a trek up a mountain. For Nate, nothing would make him happier right now than ducking inside a casino and mindlessly frittering away several hundred pounds. It would be a brief, blessed release and he craved it.

Nate remembered how he used to want to jump on a plane, exactly the way Gill had just described. When Emmie had been diagnosed, Nate had felt a sudden, desperate urge to leave the country. To let something take him away from the awful reality that had replaced the beautiful one he had been living with before that moment. Nate knew he couldn't do it – wouldn't dream of doing it – but he had wanted to. He had wanted to so badly he could barely squash the feeling down and bury it. The thought of packing a bag and just getting the hell away was so tantalising for various different reasons, Nate hadn't been able to work out for a while how to stop thinking about it. He had eventually found a way, but he wasn't entirely sure it was much better.

'Jesus!'

Nearly jumping out of his skin, Nate found Jamie standing in front of him.

'Hey.' Jamie grinned. He was wearing a crumpled but expensive-looking suit and he'd removed his tie already.

'What are you doing here?' Nate shook Jamie's hand, feeling a sense of relief rushing over him at being able to avoid going home for a while. He immediately felt guilty about even thinking that.

'I've come to take you out of course,' Jamie said grandly, throwing his arms wide. 'I'm your little ray of sunshine and I'm here to make you feel all happy again.'

'You've been at the sherbets already, haven't you?' Nate said, giving Jamie a shove.

'Maybe a little,' Jamie said with an amiable grin. 'I took the afternoon off work to go to the dentist's and get my hair cut and… have a few sherbets and you're part two.'

Nate sighed. He had no idea what Rosie would think about him going out tonight, but he couldn't very well tell Jamie to go home now he'd made the journey halfway across London.

'Come on. I'm not taking no for an answer.' Jamie confidently led the way then stopped with a sheepish over the shoulder grimace. 'But you might need to show me the way to the nearest pub, seeing as you work here and I don't have a Scooby where I am…'

Nate smiled. Ten minutes later, they were safely ensconced in The Duke of York, which was unimaginatively named, but had a decent beer garden and a good selection of beers.

'So. I'm glad you agreed to come out for beers – finally.' Jamie raised his pint.

'I didn't, but since when have you ever let the truth get in the way of a good story?' Nate clinked his pint against Jamie's.

'True, true.' Jamie squinted in the late April sunshine. 'What a delightful day. I'm so glad I chose today to bunk off work.'

'What is it you actually *do* anyway?' Nate asked, glibly referring to the standard family joke they all brought up on occasion.

Jamie deliberately adopted the vague expression he used to bamboozle people. 'Financial stuff,' he said loftily. 'Very important financial stuff, my friend. Involving numbers and shit. Big numbers. And spreadsheets with lots of columns.' Jamie chuckled at his own nonsense.

'Listen, mate – no one really knows what I do. Not even me!'

'Good way to make yourself niche,' Nate said, taking out his shades and slipping them on.

'That's better,' Jamie commented cheerfully. 'Your ugly mug was making me feel a bit queasy there.'

'Soz. I've looked better, to be fair.'

'*Nate's so good-looking*,' Jamie grinned as he adopted a whiny voice. '*Nate's such a hunk*. That's what everyone is always saying. And now look at you. What. A. Bloody. State.'

Nate sarcastically flipped him the finger. Jamie was an average-looking guy with mousy brown hair and slightly protruding ears. He made up for it with 'banter' as he put it, but that didn't stop him ribbing Nate for being the 'best-looking son-in-law'. Jamie was also a tad rosy-cheeked today, but a few pints would account for that, Nate guessed.

'Best-looking guy in the family now,' Nate said, raising his glass. 'Enjoy that.'

'Loving every minute of it,' Jamie said, catching the eye of a pretty waitress in a rather short black skirt. 'Can I order from that lovely young lady? I can? Wowzers, what great service. Same again please, miss?' Jamie turned back to Nate. 'But seriously, you're a mess, fella. I heard you took an absolute hammering and now I can see the evidence. Big dude, I'm assuming?'

'Fairly large, yes.'

'What a hero you are then.'

'Yeah, yeah.'

Jamie leaned forward. 'Your duties as policeman of the year aside, because it's all too nauseating for words, onto the serious stuff. How are things with you and Rosie?'

'That's not the serious stuff,' Nate replied, dodging the question. 'The serious stuff is Emmie.'

'Well, of course. But that's always the serious stuff,' Jamie said matter-of-factly. 'That's not up for debate. Lily told me that things are pretty rough between you and Rosie right now so that's why I'm asking.'

Against his better judgement, Nate felt fire rising in his belly. He loved Lily to pieces, always had done. She and Rosie were like chalk and cheese in so many ways, but Nate had a good relationship with Lily. But there were times – only in recent years if he was honest, since things had truly fallen apart with Rosie – when Nate resented Lily. For the natural bond she had with Rosie. For the sibling closeness that made Lily the person to turn to when things weren't right with the world. Or with Nate. And that hurt Nate immeasurably.

He and Jamie were good mates, granted. They went out for beers now and again, they sniggered together like children at family parties and they talked a fair amount for two guys who were related by marriage and who were not friends of their own volition. Inasmuch as two guys ever talked, of course. Heart-to-hearts were not the order of the day by any means, but Nate and Jamie were at least frank when indulging in manly brevity.

But nothing could rival the bond between two sisters, Nate ruminated. Twin sisters, at that. And Nate hated himself for feeling jealous, for the envy he had for suspecting that Lily knew more about what was going on in Rosie's head these days than he did. But he couldn't help it. He and Rosie had always been so connected in the past, this gulf between them was agonising.

'Stop being so cagey,' Jamie said, interrupting Nate's thoughts. 'Why are things so crappy with Rosie?'

Nate sighed. 'I don't know, to be honest. We've been through so much together, there shouldn't be any reason why things have suddenly gone wrong.'

'Have they "suddenly" gone wrong? Or do you think things have been slowly going a bit Pete Tong for a while?' Jamie asked, looking up as the waitress arrived with their beers. He watched her watching Nate and sighed. 'Thank you. Can we start up a tab? Because I think we're gonna need one.' He waited for the waitress to leave. 'Even when you look like Quasimodo's uglier brother you're pulling the birds.'

'Shut up. She's young enough to be my… something highly inappropriate.' Nate threw Jamie a look.

Nate drank far too much of his pint in one go and collected himself. He couldn't very well start moaning to Jamie about Lily, could he? Aside from being Jamie's wife, it wasn't her fault that she knew more than Nate did about his own marriage. That was simply because things had broken down to such a degree between himself and Rosie that Rosie had resurrected Lily as her main confidante in life. Lily had preceded Nate and she was clearly picking up the slack now.

'Bit of a shitter when they know more about us than we know ourselves, right?' Jamie's rare moment of astuteness clearly astonished him because he looked rather perplexed afterwards. 'Bloody hell. Where did that come from?'

'Fuck knows.' Nate started laughing. 'Big girl's blouse.'

'I know. Maybe I have my period or something.'

'Ha. Maybe.'

They both fell silent. After a few moments, Nate sipped from his pint again. 'But anyway. You're right, as it happens. It is a bit of a shitter that Lily knows more about Rosie than I do. And more about my marriage being, you know. In the shitter.'

Jamie nodded. 'Yeah. Sorry about that, mate. I can't really slag my own wife off for that, but I do know that it can't feel great for you.'

Nate swallowed down the acrid annoyance he felt and moved on. 'But in answer to your original question… actually I can't even remember what that was. My marriage isn't good right now and with the whole Pete Tong thing… yeah, I reckon it's been a slow death, if I think about it.'

'Death? Sounds a bit drastic. Do you think they do pork scratchings here?' Jamie checked his mobile. 'God, I thought that was work chasing me up.'

'I'm sure they do pork scratchings. I'll ask when I go to the gents in a minute.' Nate felt impatient. Talking to Jamie was like talking to a child; his attention span was horrendous. But he was here and he was asking questions and Nate suddenly felt ready to talk. In fact, he kind of felt as though he might explode if he didn't.

'But if you want me to sum it up for you, Jamie, it's pretty desolate in my house at the moment. We really only talk about Emmie. We don't have any normal conversations anymore. There's this… distance between us that I can't seem to bridge.' Nate took a breath. 'We don't kiss. Or cuddle. We sleep on the edges of the bed with a gigantic gap between us. We're like two people who are frozen in our own sadness and aside from Emmie, there seems to be nothing else bonding us together.'

'Oh man.' Jamie slowly removed his suit jacket.

Probably to buy himself a moment to think, Nate decided. God, what was he doing, unburdening himself to a dude who couldn't take anything much seriously? Madness.

'OK.' Jamie pulled his collar up as if he meant business. 'So. That's pretty major.'

'Yep.'

'I mean, the sex thing surprises me. Like, the sleeping on the edges of the bed, which I assume means there's an issue with the whole… sex thing.'

Nate stared at Jamie. Was he really going to focus on that part? That part was… important, but it wasn't really the crux of the matter.

'Hear me out.' Jamie held a hand up. 'It's just that you and Rosie have always been so… I mean, that is really not how I thought you'd end up. You have such amazing chemistry. And I know that this whole thing with Emmie has been awful for you. Horrendous.' Jamie toyed with his glass. 'But you've always pulled through. You've always had that connection, that special…'

'That's just it though,' Nate interrupted. 'I agree with you. But somehow, somewhere along the line, that seems to have fallen by the wayside.' He rubbed his chin, realising he was mostly talking to himself. 'I love her. The same way I've always loved her. I want her. I want to hold her and talk to her and be with her. I just can't seem to reach her. I don't know what to do.'

Jamie fell silent. Nate didn't blame him. What on earth could anyone say to him? He removed his sunglasses and put his hands over his eyes.

'I'll get you some pork scratchings,' he said, getting to his feet.

'Good stuff,' Jamie said. He gave Nate a sympathetic glance. 'I wish I knew what to say to you, dude. I'm crap at this stuff. But I'm on your side. And I really want you and Rosie to work things out.'

'It's OK,' Nate replied, meaning it. 'I probably wouldn't know what to say to you if you were me either.'

Wearily, he made his way through the beer garden and ducked inside the pub. After a trip to the gents, Nate bought a couple more beers and some pork scratchings. He had the vague impression the girl behind the bar who'd served them earlier might be flirting with him, but he wasn't paying enough attention to know or care.

After a few more beers, Jamie suggested heading to another bar.

'I'm not sure,' Nate said, glancing at his watch. 'I've checked in with Rosie a few times and Emmie seems fine, but we probably should be heading home now.'

Jamie pouted. 'One more drink, Nate. One more. Come on...'

Knowing there was no such thing as 'one more drink', Nate led the way to a nearby bar. They had several more beers and Nate started to feel increasingly claustrophobic. He could feel a familiar craving rising inside him, like a starving man longing for a freshly-cooked pizza and a slice of chocolate cake swimming in cream. An alcoholic gazing at an ice-cold beer on a sunlit balcony.

He pushed it down. Hard. No. No. That wasn't the answer.

Hold it together, Nate told himself. Don't end up there. He noticed the time on a huge, decorative clock behind the bar they were in. It was late. They'd missed their last trains.

Brilliant, Nate thought.

'I think we should go for more beers,' Jamie shouted over the loud music in the bar, barely able to get his words out in the right order. 'And we need a strip club.'

'No, no, no,' Nate said firmly.

'No? No?' Jamie looked affronted. 'I'm saying more beers, dude. BEERS. And naked ladies. NAKED.'

'I heard you. And you're way past your limit and close to puking.' Nate half-carried Jamie to a main road and motioned for a cab.

'I am NOT.' Jamie shook Nate's arm off.

'Charlie big bollocks,' Nate told him. 'You can't possible cope with even one more pint. And definitely not naked ladies.'

'Awww. You're such a killjoy.'

'Yeah. That's me.' Nate felt relieved when a cab pulled over. He told the driver Jamie's address and assured him that Jamie was fine and wouldn't be sick. Even though he thought it was highly likely.

'How are you getting home?' Jamie slurred, holding onto Nate.

'Don't worry about me,' Nate said, opening the cab door and helping Jamie in. He shut the door and stepped back. Watching the cab pull away, he shoved his hands into his pockets.

Get another cab, he told himself. Get in a cab and go home. To Rosie. To a cold, half-empty bed. To feeling hollow and broken.

Nate started to stroll down the street he was on. He hated himself for feeling so sorry for himself. He wasn't like that as a person, he was sure he wasn't. Yet it was how he seemed to have ended up.

Pausing, Nate realised he was outside a casino. Had he walked here on purpose? Maybe. He had been here before. It was one of the flashier ones; it had bright lights and a plush-looking entrance.

Don't do it, he told himself. Don't do it. It's pointless. It's like… draining a pint when you know you shouldn't drink one. It was easy relief, guaranteed to induce self-hatred seconds later.

Nate held himself together for as long as he could. And then he went inside. He sat down at a roulette table, ordered himself a scotch and changed up some cash. Then he placed a bet, put a pile of plastic disks on red. And won.

Nate exhaled deeply. It felt good. It was relief. It was release. It was liberating. And he wanted more. He motioned to the waitress to bring him another drink and discreetly asked about credit. Then he gambled again. Nate put everything out of his mind and focused on red and on black. Again and again and again. And for a while, he found blessed oblivion. He moved from the roulette table to a poker table. And he played over and over again. Until he suddenly couldn't do it anymore. Like a food addict gorging himself on a pile of donuts, Nate felt sick. As though he'd over-indulged to the point of vomiting.

And he'd lost some money. Quite a bit of money. A stupid amount, in fact – the kind of money he wouldn't normally dream of squandering, because these days, he knew better. At least, he thought he did.

Nate abruptly left the poker table and went outside into the cool, night air. Covering his hands with his face, he slid down the wall and sat on his heels. He assumed that this was what rock bottom must feel like, because he wasn't sure he could sink much lower.

What would Rosie say when he walked through the door later? Nate thought to himself. Well, actually, he knew exactly what she would say. He grimaced. And that was without telling her about the gambling. That would send her into a frenzy. Understandably, because he'd had a bad gambling habit when they met and when things turned serious between them, he had promised her it would never happen again.

Nate got to his feet. He had to get home. He felt immeasurably sad that going home no longer made him feel as safe and happy as it used to, but he had to get back.

Rosie, he suddenly thought, utterly stricken. How can we go on like this? What the hell has happened to us? Stumbling away from the wall, Nate tucked his bruised heart out of sight and focused on getting home.

Emmie

'Oh wow.' Cara held a photo up. 'Your dad has hair here!'

'My dad has hair anyway.' Emmie laughed. 'He shaved it all off when my hair fell out and my mum told him she likes him better that way.'

Cara scrutinised the photo. 'Yeah. He looks a bit weird with hair actually. So anyway, how do we go about getting this timeline thing sorted?'

Emmie sat back on her heels. Her parents were both at work and her Aunt Lily was downstairs cooking some dinner for her and Cara. She had also promised to be on hand to fill in any gaps they might find in her parents' timeline.

'Well. Luckily for us, my mum is super-organised. She dates everything and she loves taking photos, so we have records of everything.'

'Yes, but we need *their* timeline, not your birthday parties and all that stuff,' Cara frowned.

'Hmmm. Aunt Lily said she'd help us if we need it, but I know quite a few of them because my mum has told me about meeting my dad loads of times.' Emmie tugged a photo album towards her. 'Look. This is a photo of the bar my dad worked in years ago. That's how they met.'

'Cool.' Cara peered at it. 'So what's the plan with this? We start from the point when they first met and try and work out the big stuff that meant something to them? How will we figure that out?'

'I don't know.'

Emmie felt impatient. Cara was asking too many questions and she didn't have all the answers. Somehow, they had to figure out the important stuff so they could get some sort of plan together.

'Did they have selfie sticks in those days?' Cara asked. She showed Emmie a photo of her parents grinning at the camera.

'I don't think so. They had to hold the camera up like this…' Emmie demonstrated with her hands. 'Because they didn't take pictures on their phones back then. And my mum loves using a camera, anyway. So they would get someone else to take a photo I think. Like, someone standing around near them or whatever.'

Cara pulled a face. 'Really? What if the person ran off with the camera?'

'Not sure. I just know that's how they used to do it. My mum told me.' Emmie was beginning to wonder if Cara was the right person to help her with this project. It was going to take forever if she was going to ask questions every five minutes.

'OK.' Cara finally seemed satisfied. She inspected the spread of photographs. 'I reckon we should put the one where they met by my door and then go through like that. Maybe we should put you coming along right here…' she placed a photograph at the end of the bed, 'and then we know that we need to fill all the gaps in between.'

Emmie smiled inwardly. She kind of knew all of that already, but it didn't matter. At least Cara was getting involved now and not wanting to know stuff Emmie didn't know the answers to.

'You're my very best spy,' she told Cara.

'I'm your only spy,' Cara corrected her with a grin. 'But that's OK. I'm loving being a spy. It's totally cool.'

Emmie nodded. 'Right.' She placed the photo of her dad's bar by the door. 'So. This is the point where they met. My mum went into the Lone Wolf bar with her friends in May...' She checked the back of the photo, 'no, October 2003 and she met my dad.'

'The Lone Wolf bar. Where is that?'

'I think it's in London somewhere. My dad lived there at the time, I think.'

'OK. What if it's not there anymore?'

Emmie felt poleaxed. She hadn't even thought of that.

'You were born in 2007 like me,' Cara said. 'So we have four years of dating to find? Holy moly.'

Emmie grinned. Cara found Dr Tom's little phrases as funny as she did. 'We can do it. Because my mum told me that the first real date my dad took her on was to this burger place he was obsessed with. So we're still in 2003 and that's... that photo album there. The one I found the photo of the Lone Wolf bar in.' She pointed at an album covered in cream silk.

'A burger place.' Cara opened the album. 'Is that... romantic?'

Emmie shrugged. 'I don't think my mum minded where the date was. And my dad loves a burger. He told me he couldn't ever eat a burger properly in front of her.'

'Why not?' Cara looked confused as she turned a page.

'Because he takes a bite and he squirts mayonnaise over it. And then he puts salt on it. Then he eats that bit and does it all again.'

'Eugh.' Cara looked disgusted. 'That's so gross!'

'I know.' Emmie shrugged. 'I think it's cute though. That he didn't want to eat like that in front of her. That's it!' She put out a hand and stopped Cara turning the pages. 'That's the burger place.'

'Awww, look. Someone took a photo of them together in there too.' Cara tugged the photograph out of the plastic sleeve and glanced at the back. 'The Lucky Burger Joint,' she read. 'They look really loved up.'

'Yep. And we need to include it, because that's when my dad told her he thought he was falling for her.'

Cara looked shocked. 'I don't think I'd like it if a boy said that so early on.'

Emmie screwed up her nose. 'My mum says that when you know, you know.'

'Lucky he didn't eat his salt and mayo burger in front of her then.'

'Yes.' Emmie pressed a hand to her forehead for a moment.

'Are you OK?' Cara sounded concerned.

'Yeah.' Emmie took her hand away and forced a smile onto her face. 'I'm fine. I just feel bad, you know? About my mum and dad. They were so happy and then…'

'Don't do that,' Cara said. 'It's stupid.'

'OK.' It was hard, but Emmie set those thoughts aside as best she could.

'So do you know all of their dates in order?'

Emmie thought for a second. 'Not exactly, but I don't think we need to do every single one of them. The idea is to try and replicate the big ones. Or the ones that meant something. That's what Dr Tom and I have discussed. I think about a month after they first met, they went to the cinema. Look.' She held up some small pieces of lilac paper.

'What's that?'

'The cinema tickets. They went to see *Love Actually*.'

Cara grinned. 'I love that film.'

'Me too. Anyway, they went to see that and they had a big snog afterwards in the rain.'

'Why do people always want to snog in the rain?' Cara asked, looking perplexed. 'Surely you just get really wet?'

Emmie rolled her eyes. 'How would I know?'

There was a knock at the door.

'Come in,' Emmie called.

Aunt Lily put her head around the door. 'How's it going?' She surveyed the mess on the floor. 'Wow. Make sure you have this all tucked away by the time your mum gets home, Ems.'

'I will.' Emmie got to her feet. 'So at this end here, you have mum and dad meeting. And this – this is me turning up.'

'You have them meeting at the Lone Wolf,' Lily said, crouching down. 'Spot on. And the burger place. OK. And... what's this? The cinema? Lovely. That was a big moment for them. Rosie said she knew she was in love with Nate by then.' Lily smiled. 'She wouldn't stop talking about him. It was nauseating.' She pulled a funny face. 'I'm joking. But she was so incredibly happy, I couldn't get annoyed with her.'

Emmie gestured to the photographs. 'What's next? When dad proposed?'

Lily glanced at some of the photographs and flipped an album open. 'I don't think you should miss out the zoo.'

'The zoo?' Cara said. 'Who goes to the zoo on a date?'

Lily shuffled some photos around. 'When you're with the right person, it doesn't matter where you go. But it was when they talked about something important. Having you.' She turned to Emmie and winked at her.

Emmie stared at her Aunt Lily. Her parents had talked about having kids that early on? That was so odd. Why would grown ups talk about having babies before they'd even decided to get married? She didn't get it.

'Well, I don't think they were talking about having me, exactly,' Emmie ventured. 'They wouldn't have chosen to have…'

'Stop it.' Lily straightened and handed her a photograph. 'They love you to pieces. They wanted you because you're you. And because you're utterly perfect to them.' She touched Emmie's cheek.

Emmie felt like she had a big lump in her throat. She wanted to cry. That couldn't be true. Who on earth would want a child like her? She had caused them endless heartache from the age of two. They had dealt with horrible news. They had watched her undergo countless surgeries and have procedures done that had made her body fall apart. They had watched her scream in pain and cry non-stop after chemo. Vomit so hard, she had sustained injuries to her stomach. Who would want a child like that? If they could choose, Emmie knew her parents wouldn't put themselves through this ever again.

'Emmie.' Lily put her arm around her. 'I can't tell you how much you are loved, sweetheart. None of this is your fault.'

Cara got to her feet as well. 'I don't like seeing you get upset,' she said, her lip trembling slightly. 'Maybe we shouldn't do this thing with your parents.'

'No!' Emmie realised she had shouted a bit. 'Sorry. I really want to do this. I want to help them remember who they were before me. It's… it's really important to me.'

'I know.' Lily turned back to the timeline mapped out on the floor. 'Right. So it's the zoo next. Then it's the proposal. Do you have all the info for that? Check in that box over there. Your mum keeps all sorts of memorabilia. Used to drive me nuts when we shared a room as kids.' She sighed dramatically. 'And then it's the wedding. And you have to include their first wedding anniversary. It was…' She paused and went a bit pink. 'Very – special, according to your mum.'

Emmie didn't know why her aunt had gone red in the face but she'd have a think about it later. She wrote the details down carefully in the diary Dr Tom had given her, making sure her dates were correct.

'And then there's the lovely dinner they had at that lovely little place in Chelsea that your dad thought was poncy. Posh. Er… up itself. Let's just say it wasn't his cup of tea.'

Cara giggled.

'But anyway. I think after that, you might have, ahem, been more than a twinkle in your dad's eye.' Lily started laughing and put her hand over her mouth. 'Haha, I can't believe I'm talking to ten-year-olds about naughty stuff!'

'She means *sex*,' Cara told Emmie pointedly.

'I know that.' Emmie rolled her eyes.

'Spaghetti Bolognese in ten minutes,' Aunt Lily said cheerfully, leaving them to it.

'She's nice,' Cara commented when they were alone again.

Emmie nodded. 'Shall we get all the wedding stuff together? There's loads of it. I need to work out how we can recreate it. I mean, how do we get them to sort of relive it? We can't pay for another wedding.'

'Send them to the venue?' Cara suggested. 'I don't know. Let's see what we can find. Your mum keeps *everything*,' she said, pulling a large box towards her.

'Lucky for us,' Emmie mused distractedly. Her vision had gone funny for a second. Just for a second. And now it was back to normal again. She felt a rush of relief. It was nothing. If it happened again, she'd tell someone about it. Right now, she was more worried about her parents.

2015

'Just need to check Emmie's obs again,' a nurse said cheerily, wheeling a noisy machine into the room.

Rosie lifted her head and wearily checked her watch. What time was it? Christ, it was 3 a.m.

'Must you do that now?' she asked.

The nurse nodded. 'I'm afraid so. I'll be very quick, I promise.'

Rosie bit her lip. They always said that. That they'd be quick. But they rarely were. They were thorough, but 'quick' wasn't an adjective Rosie would use to describe the actions carried out by the stream of kindly, excellent nurses who appeared in Emmie's room with aggravating regularity.

'Mummy?' Emmie sounded disorientated.

'I'm here,' Rosie said, rushing to her side. She grasped Emmie's little hand. 'It's OK, baby. They're just checking your obs again.'

'Again?' Emmie had a sob in her throat.

'Sorry, angel,' the nurse apologised as she checked her chart. 'But it has to be done.'

With difficulty, Rosie said nothing and watched the nurse carry out her duties. Emmie wept and held onto Rosie's hand until it was over. Rosie waited until the nurse left the room.

'Sweetheart, I'm so sorry,' she said, stroking Emmie's cheek. 'But they have to check on you.'

'What's going to happen to me in here?' Emmie cried wretchedly. ' I just want to sleep, mummy.'

'I know, baby.'

Emmie struggled into a seated position and threw her arms around Rosie's neck. 'I want to sleep, mummy. Please tell them to let me sleep!'

Rosie felt her heart constrict. Emmie sounded hysterical and that wasn't like her. When Rosie pulled Emmie away from her so she could look at her eyes, they were dazed and rimmed with red. She was pale, paler than normal and she looked spent.

'I'm so tired, mummy,' Emmie murmured in Rosie's ear. 'Just so…' She started to fall asleep again, not even able to finish her sentence.

Stricken, Rosie held Emmie's exhausted little body until she drifted off to sleep. She laid Emmie back down against the pillows, listening to her frantic breathing. Rosie knew Emmie's observations had been normal because the nurse had flipped her the thumbs up as she left the room. But Emmie seemed stressed out and not like herself at all. And Rosie knew exactly why.

Sleep deprivation was the worst thing. Even as a child, it caused horrible side effects, namely irritability and crankiness. In Emmie's case, she became emotional and teary and Rosie hated seeing her that way. She knew the nurses would probably write it off as being part and parcel of having chemo, all very natural, but Rosie couldn't bear it. They blamed hysteria on the medication Emmie was being given. The stress of chemo. But Rosie knew her own child and Emmie had been through worse than this. It was sleep deprivation, pure and simple.

And it wasn't just the checking of the obs which was causing the sleep deprivation. If it wasn't well-meaning nurses coming in to check Emmie's blood or some other level, it was cleaners coming in with one of those big floor cleaners – moving them around the floor in agonisingly slow circles, knocking the bed and the medical equipment. Sweeping, spritzing surfaces, straightening bed sheets. Then it was another person coming in to change towels or blankets. Then it was another person proffering an unappealing menu. Then observations again.

And it wasn't just that. It was the constant chatter outside the door, the phone ringing repeatedly. It was the sound of a poor child crying out in pain or screaming for a parent in an adjacent room. It was the sound of hands being slapped together after sanitary foam had been applied. It was the sound of china plates being stacked, of cutlery being sorted. And every sound was heightened. All of the sounds and noises were understandable and acceptable but even Rosie had reached a stage where each sound was like a smack around the head, jerking her awake and messing with her equilibrium.

The overnight visits were tough, Rosie thought, leaning over and tiredly placing her head sideways on the bed. Emmie was having to stay over because she was undergoing yet another bout of aggressive chemo. Towards the end of her last bout, Emmie was allowed to stay in a nearby hospital hotel with a cute rucksack that she could carry around with her – to walk around, even go to a restaurant if she felt well enough, and then to back to the hospital hotel. But during intensive courses, Emmie was required to stay in the hospital itself for two to three nights at a time. The rooms were nice, but it was the noise and the constant interruptions that were driving Rosie insane. She could feel the parental lioness in her rising to the surface. She fought it for a second, then gave into it, deciding that she really didn't care anymore. All that mattered was Emmie.

Rosie made sure Emmie was settled and went out to the nearby reception desk. Asking for some paper and a pen, she rapidly wrote out a notice that said 'No Interruptions'. She asked *for sellotape and she taped the notice to Emmie's door. Then she set herself up like a sergeant by the door.*

'No thank you,' she said firmly, as one of the cleaners approached with her big floor cleaner.

'But I…'

'No, sorry. I'm not allowing you in. My daughter needs to sleep.' Rosie gave the cleaner a smile and folded her arms.

The cleaner looked uncomfortable but she shrugged and moved away with her machine.

Rosie straightened in her seat, determined to stay awake. If she fell asleep, it would defeat the object. She spotted a nurse approaching with her menu.

'No thank you,' Rosie said.

'What do you mean, "no thank you"?' the nurse asked with a frown.

'I mean no thank you. Emmie will have something later.'

'But I need to know what Emmie will want to eat later,' the nurse said, trying to move past Rosie.

Rosie shook her head. 'It's OK. I'll text my husband and get him bring Emmie something when he comes in later on. She said she fancied a fondant fancy earlier. But she might have been delirious.'

The nurse looked affronted. 'But this is free,' she advised. 'Why pay to bring some food in when you don't need to?'

'Because my kid needs to sleep.' Rosie met the nurse's eyes unflinchingly. 'And she's not acting like herself and it's because she hasn't slept properly in hours.'

The nurse hesitated. Then relaxed. 'OK,' she said. 'For now. But I'll be back with my menu another time.'

'I'm sure you will,' Rosie murmured under her breath. She turned and glanced over her shoulder through the crack in the door. Emmie was out for the count. Rosie went to check on her,

paranoid as ever that something might be wrong. But Emmie was fine. She was in a deep sleep and her breathing was regular and measured.

Rosie returned to her post. Just in time, as another nurse was at the door, wanting to come in and swap some towels over. Emmie hadn't even used her towels, but Rosie silently handed them over and pointed to the sign on the door. This particular nurse reacted with a good-natured smile, but Rosie was sure that not all of them were going to be as accommodating. And she was sure that she would be thought of as stroppy. Irrational. Unreasonable. Over-protective. And many more unflattering descriptions that she cared little about. What did it matter what the hospital staff thought of her?

Around an hour later, another nurse appeared in the doorway with a file in her hand. Rosie braced herself.

'What's this?' The nurse pointed to the sign on the door.

'It's a sign saying "No Interruptions",' Rosie answered. She realised that sounded belligerent but she was fairly close to suffering from sleep deprivation herself.

'Yes, I can see that.' The nurse eyed Rosie beadily. 'But you can't do that. I need to check her obs.'

'Do you though?' Rosie got to her feet and met the nurse's gaze pleadingly. 'She's fine, nurse. Sarah,' she added, checking the nurse's name badge. 'She had her obs checked two hours ago and they were normal.'

The nurse let out an impatient sound. 'Yes, I know that. But I need to check them again. And I need to check them now.'

'OK.' Rosie took a different tack. 'Listen. I know my child, alright? She's hysterical. And it's not the drugs or the stress of the chemo. Emmie has been through all of this before. It's sleep deprivation.'

The nurse looked sceptical. 'We wake them for a second and then they drop off again straight away.'

'Well, Emmie doesn't,' Rosie insisted. 'She isn't dropping off again. Or if she is, it's because she's so totally exhausted, she can't do anything else but pass out. But she's not herself. She needs three to four hours sleep. Three to four hours uninterrupted sleep. Please. Please.'

The nurse sighed. 'OK. Three to four hours and no more. And you call me if anything changes, OK? You get someone immediately.'

'Yes, yes.' Rosie smiled gratefully. 'I promise I will. And I'm sorry for being a bitch, but I just want my kid to get some sleep and then she'll be back to normal again. And she'll cope better with this horrible chemo.'

The nurse patted her arm. 'I'm surprised more mums don't do this, to be honest,' she confided. 'Let's just not tell them. Because otherwise, I'll have anarchy in here.'

Rosie nodded. She felt deeply relieved and oddly triumphant. It was such a tiny victory. All she had done was keep some nurses and some cleaners away from Emmie and she had allowed her daughter to have a few hours' sleep. Much-needed sleep of course, but it was just sleep. In the scheme of things, nothing major.

She took a deep breath and assumed her position by Emmie's door. Her eyes unfocused every so often but she jerked herself awake. One of the times she did it, she found Nate kneeling in front of her.

'Hey,' he said softly, holding her knees. 'Are you OK?'

Rosie put her arms around his neck and rested for a moment. 'I'm OK.'

'I heard you were holding some kind of protest,' Nate said with a grin. 'I said, my wife? Protesting? Standing up for her child? As if.'

Rosie just about managed a smile. 'They think I'm a bolshie little sod, don't they?'

Nate laughed. 'Hell yeah. But they admire for it too, I can tell. And so do I,' he said, leaning in to kiss her forehead. 'You're bloody awesome.'

'I don't feel it,' Rosie said, getting to her feet. She stretched her arms above her head. 'I feel absolutely terrible.'

'Well. I'm here now.' Nate picked up a bag he had brought with him and ushered Rosie into Emmie's room. He lowered his voice. 'Go curl up on that bed they've put next to Emmie. Get some sleep. I'm on sergeant duty now.'

'Oh god, can I?' Rosie said, looking at the bed longingly. It wasn't that comfortable, but right now, it looked like a pair of warm, fluffy angel wings.

'Yep.' Nate walked to Emmie and very gently stroked her hair, the way he had learnt to when Emmie was going through hardcore chemo. 'Bless her. She needs this sleep, Rose. Good for you.'

Rosie gave him a weak smile. Oddly, now that Nate had turned up, all the fight had gone out of her. She was suddenly too exhausted to formulate a sentence.

'And I bought French Fancies for all of us,' Nate said, holding up the bag. 'And an apple pie from that shop you like for you.'

'You're the best.' Rosie laid down on the bed next to Emmie's. 'But I don't have the energy to eat right now.'

Nate nodded. 'I get that. I'll get them to heat it up for you later, gorgeous. Go to sleep. I'm taking over now.'

'Partner in crime,' Rosie mumbled as she curled up into a ball.

'Always,' Nate said, watching her. He had these moments where he was completely in awe of his wife. The way she dealt with Emmie, the courage she showed when really up against it.

There was this quiet, determined quality Nate had never known Rosie possessed until they had received Emmie's diagnosis. And since that day, she had surprised him in so many ways. The thing was, Nate had thought Rosie was amazing when he first met her, but the way she was now was something else.

Nate wondered if he told Rosie enough that he was proud of her. But he had this fear of sounding patronising, this worry that he wouldn't come across as sincere. Because telling Rosie he loved her was one thing, but feeling and communicating pride seemed more complicated for some reason.

Nate had a sudden urge to wake Rosie up and tell her what he was thinking. Surely there was a way he could tell her he was in awe of her without it sounding ridiculous? Nate went to wake Rosie, then stopped himself. Rosie needed her sleep too. She was strong and she was resilient, but she deserved to catch up on some rest.

Still keeping his eye on Rosie and Emmie, Nate took up residence on the chair by the door. He made a note to tell Rosie he was proud of her. Because he really was. He loved her now in ways he had never imagined, ways he had never expected to. Emmie's illness, as hideous as it was, had brought out different qualities of both of them. Nate had no idea if the qualities he was demonstrating were anything to write home about, however.

He looked up as a nurse poked her head around the door.

'I've heard about your wife's protest,' she said, looking stern.

'Amazing, isn't she?' Nate grinned, folding his arms.

The nurse started to smile. 'They both are,' she said with a wink. She craned her neck to catch a glimpse of Emmie. 'She looks fine at the moment, but I will need to check her obs in about an hour, OK?'

Nate hesitated, then went with his gut. 'OK. That means she'll have had around three to four hours sleep. That will make all the difference to her well-being, I can promise you.'

'Good.' The nurse nodded and withdrew.

Nate glanced over his shoulder. Emmie and Rosie were sound asleep, but at least he was here to pick up where Rosie had left off. He wondered how many mums would have the balls to do what she had done today. To disregard the rules for the sake of her child's well-being. Nate was sure many parents might want to take the stance Rosie had, but maybe they didn't want to rock the boat. Maybe Rosie had just reached a point where it no longer mattered to her what anyone else thought.

Nate wasn't sure. He just knew that the way he felt about his family made his heart feel as though it might explode in his chest at times. Which was as blissful as the pain that had brought that feeling about in the first place.

'Daddy?'

Nate turned. Emmie was sitting up in bed. Nate went to her.

'I don't want to do this anymore.'

Nate felt an icy trickle down his spine. 'What, sweetheart? What don't you want to do anymore?'

'This.' Emmie gestured to the machines. And the room. And to her head. 'I don't want any more treatment, Dad. I just want to be left alone.'

'Well, I guess we'd probably have to discuss that with your…'

A tear trickled down Emmie's flushed cheek. 'No, please. No more. I can't do it anymore, Daddy.'

Nate put his arms around her. 'OK, baby. OK. I hear you. If… if you want to stop, we can stop.'

'Please,' Emmie mumbled into his shoulder.

Nate held Emmie tightly. His poor baby. He didn't blame her. She had been through so much, so many treatments. So much *pain. He could understand why she wanted to stop now. But what might that mean for the future? Emmie's tumour was inoperable. The chemo hadn't shrunk it and none of the medication had helped. It hadn't grown, but it was still there. Huge, pressing, threatening to expand at any second.*

Nate gulped and glanced at Rosie, curled up asleep on the nearby bed. How on earth would she take this news, that Emmie wanted to put an end to her treatment?

Nate closed his eyes. He knew what Rosie would say. She would say the same as him. The same as Emmie. No more. Just... no more.

Rosie

'Lovely day,' Lily said, shielding her eyes from the sun.

'Amazing,' Rosie agreed.

'Great to see the kids playing so nicely together.'

'Absolutely.'

Lily cleared her throat. 'Not enjoying the small talk?'

'Not remotely,' Rosie answered dryly. 'Don't do it, Lil. It's as bad as going to one of Emmie's friend's houses for a playdate and the parents not having a clue what to talk about because they're so busy not talking about Emmie's tumour.'

Lily sat back in her garden chair and removed her sunglasses. 'Sorry. It's just really...'

'Awkward. I know.' Rosie took a seat next to her at the garden table, wincing as the hot wrought iron from the chair connected with the skin below her shorts. 'Maybe we should have cancelled.'

'No way. It's Emmie's birthday.' Lily nodded towards the kids who were shrieking as they bounced on a trampoline together. 'They're having a whale of a time.'

'At least someone is,' Rosie said gloomily.

Nate was inside cooking a huge roast dinner – in his element, in other words. Not necessarily the best thing to cook on such a gloriously hot day, but Emmie had requested roast pork. And she was the birthday girl, so roast pork it was. Jamie was keeping him company, which was code for 'drinking beer whilst Nate cooked up a storm' and the two of them were locked away in the kitchen as though very important business was going on.

Rosie was glad of the respite. Things were so highly-charged between herself and Nate right now, it felt as though a bomb might explode in their faces at any second. They weren't talking and they could barely look at one another. Their bed truly did feel as though a boat could be driven between the pair of them right now.

They had decorated the house in silence last night, putting up streamers and sparkly decorations. Nate had blown up a pile of metallic purple balloons without saying so much as one word and Rosie had iced a rather lopsided cake alone in the kitchen. She had always made her own cakes for family parties and had one made for the parties Emmie used to have for her friends. Nate was the expert cook and baker, but Rosie insisted on making Emmie's birthday cakes, even if they were rather homemade-looking. In the old days, Nate would have been in the kitchen with her, dabbing his fingers in the icing, making jokes about her weird sponges. This year had been signif-icantly different. Very quiet and very lonely.

Feeling empty and lost, Rosie remembered wondering how she hadn't actually heard the poignant sound of her heart splintering, because it felt very much like it was happening so loudly inside her body it might ricochet around the house.

Lily sipped her iced water, unaware of what was running through Rosie's mind. 'God, I wish that was wine, but it's my turn to drive. I've – I've never seen you two like this. Not… like this.'

'I know.'

Rosie felt despondent. Something had happened to her and Nate. Something really bad. Things had been sliding in the wrong direction between them for a long time, but now it felt different somehow.

Rosie watched Emmie on the trampoline. No one would ever know something was wrong with her when she was like this. Her hair had grown back since they had stopped the chemo, obviously, but it wasn't just that. Emmie looked happy and healthy. She had colour in her cheeks, she was all gangly legs as she bounced and cried out as one of her cousins playfully shoved her. Emmie looked the best she had in a long time.

Which was ironic, considering things with Nate were such an all-time low, Rosie sighed to herself. And epic fail, one might say. Rosie wondered what was going on with Nate. Other than the usual, obviously. Both of them had long ago accepted Emmie's condition as part of their day-to-day existence and of course, it affected both of them. But something had shifted.

Rosie felt a stab of guilt. She knew what had shifted in her world. She had drunk too much and she had been incredibly stupid. She had been weak and she had allowed some young boy to charm her and talk her into a kiss that she deeply regretted.

Rosie gripped the stem of her wine glass. How could she have done such an idiotic thing? She hadn't ever been tempted to cheat on Nate. He was her best friend and she adored him. And fancied him. Guilt washed over her again and her white wine threatened to make a reappearance.

'I kissed someone,' she blurted out suddenly.

'What?' Lily sat up and nearly knocked her wine over. She glanced over her shoulder at the French windows, which were firmly shut. 'When?'

Rosie took a gulp of wine. What was she doing? If no one knew, it couldn't explode in her face. But this was Lily. And the weight and feel of the acrid guilt was killing her.

'That night we went out with your friends.'

'God.' Lily looked deeply shocked. 'Who was it?'

Rosie bit her lip. 'That boy from the coffee shop. Jonny.'

'Jonny?' Lily looked perplexed, then her brow cleared. 'The one who went on about blueberry muffins that time? Lordy. Isn't he about twelve?'

Rosie rubbed her forehead. 'Don't,' she shuddered. 'It's bad enough as it is.'

Lily leant forward. 'OK. So what happened? You kissed. Anything else?'

'No!' Rosie met Lily's eyes. 'No, Lily. Nothing else. Just a stupid, drunken kiss.'

'You were very drunk that night,' Lily said defensively. 'Because that is not like you, Rosie. Not like you at all.'

'I know.'

Rosie felt sick again. Lily was her twin and therefore her most devout and loyal friend. And even she looked horrified.

'Should I tell Nate?'

'Absolutely not,' Lily said emphatically.

'Really?' Rosie frowned. 'I don't know. Maybe I should just tell him. He must know something is wrong between us. I mean, more wrong than it was before.'

Lily briskly sipped her water. 'Rosie. The only reason you want to confess is so that you can feel relief from the shitty burden you're carrying. And you know I normally advocate honesty. But things are so... tense between you and Nate right now. How will this help him, knowing that you had a stupid kiss with some kid you wouldn't look twice at if you weren't so desperately unhappy?'

Rosie felt tears approaching. She didn't deserve Lily's kindness. She was a terrible person. She was a cheat. And a liar, for not owning up to it. But actually, Lily had one thing wrong. She didn't want to confess to Nate to lighten the burden she was carrying. It was just that she was used to being honest around Nate. She pretty much told him everything – awful or not – and even though this would be the most awful thing she had ever discussed with him, Rosie felt strange not telling Nate something like this. Years ago, they had agreed that they would discuss any indiscretion with each other – granted, because they didn't ever think there would be one. And even though Rosie was aware that there were probably many things she hadn't confided in Nate over the past few years, namely her extremely sad feelings about the way things had deteriorated between them, she wasn't used to hiding actual information from him.

'I feel horrible,' she choked. 'Horrible about Nate. I love him. I haven't even looked at another man the whole time we've been together. I know things are really crappy between us, but he doesn't deserve that.'

Lily grabbed her hand and squeezed it. 'I know. But it was just a silly mistake. Don't mention it and find a way to move forward from this.' She hesitated as if about to say something, then paused.

'What?' Rosie wiped her tears away.

'Nothing.' Lily looked vague. 'So. Is there any evidence you need to get rid of? Any… text messages? Voicemails?'

'God no.' It was Rosie's turn to look shocked. 'Lily, how do you even know to ask those questions?! Have you…'

'Don't be daft,' Lily scoffed. 'I just watch a lot of TV when I'm ironing. And people in the world of celebs are always banging on about finding incriminating text messages.'

Rosie looked into her empty wine glass. 'No. There isn't anything like that. It was just a kiss. We haven't spoken since and I've avoided the coffee shop like the plague.'

'Good.' Lily jumped guiltily as the French windows were opened.

'Dinner will be in ten minutes,' Nate said. He glanced at Rosie, then ducked back inside.

Rosie put her head in her hands. God, things were dire at the moment. It was like living in a pressure cooker. She only hoped Emmie hadn't noticed what was going on.

'Mum!' Emmie rushed up to her, her cheeks flushed. 'Is lunch nearly ready?'

'Ten minutes, apparently,' Rosie told her. She hugged her and inhaled the smell of Emmie's hair. She loved doing that and had only realised how much she had missed it when Emmie's hair had fallen out.

'You smell delicious. Go and wash your hands, hun. You too,' she told George and Maya, who looked like extras from the musical *Oliver* at the best of times. And after two hours in the garden bouncing around and climbing, they were positively filthy.

Lily stood up when the children had gone inside. 'Are you OK?'

'Yes.' Rosie nodded and tidied the chairs up. 'And thank you. Thank you for not judging me.'

'Who said I wasn't judging you?' Lily replied airily. 'I'm thinking all sorts of things. I'm just not saying them out loud.'

Rosie smiled. That was one of the best things about having a twin. Lily understood her and knew exactly how to be in any given situation. Rosie felt yet another flash of guilt that she'd ever resented Lily. It was hardly her fault she had an easier life with Jamie and her kids. And she was pretty sure Lily wasn't judging her. She might think Rosie was an idiot, but Rosie was sure her sister understood.

'This looks amazing,' Rosie told Nate as he and Jamie started bringing plates of steaming food out.

'Thanks,' Jamie said with a grin. 'I worked long and hard to make this lovely birthday lunch for Emmie.'

'Ignore him.' Lily started putting serving spoons in the food. 'He always likes to take credit for things he hasn't done.'

Jamie stuck his tongue out childishly and Rosie watched them enviously. Lily and Jamie had such an easy, laid-back relationship. The banter, the fun, the little digs they made. Rosie would kill to be like that with Nate again.

'I was talking to Nate, anyway,' she said, as Nate came back in with the roast pork. 'Amazing job.'

'Thanks,' he said, averting his eyes.

Rosie felt hurt. She was trying. Why wasn't he trying?

'Wow.' Emmie sat down at the table, salivating when she saw all the food. 'Look at the crackling.'

'I saved a special bit for the birthday girl,' Nate grinned, picking up a large, juicy-looking piece.

'Oooh!' said Emmie. 'Thanks, Dad.' She bit into it, making them all laugh when crumbs went all over her pretty birthday top.

Rosie watched her, thinking that in different circumstances, she might be telling Emmie off for possibly ruining her clothes. Whereas now, such things didn't really register on her radar, because life really did seem too short for such things.

'Cracking roasties,' Lily said, helping herself to a large heap.

'Get her to do some Pilates after dinner, Rosie,' Jamie pleaded, clutching his head. 'She'll be moaning that her PJs are tight later.'

'Shut up,' Lily said good-naturedly. 'You love my tummy.'

'True,' Jamie sighed. 'Lucky though, eh? Otherwise your potato addiction would be a real issue.'

Rosie met Nate's eyes and felt a fresh rush of agony. They used to be like this. Actually, she and Nate used to be better than this. They used to muck about and tease one another constantly. Nate would wind her up, saying she was easy to rile and she would bite every time, even though she was trying to prove him wrong. They had always laughed non-stop, she and Nate. It had been one of Rosie's favourite things about their relationship. Seeing Nate looking so serious and miserable – so unlike himself – was awful.

God. Rosie wasn't sure she had ever felt so sad in her life. Not about Nate, at any rate.

'Thanks for my presents,' Emmie said, glancing at the pile of gifts she had excitedly opened earlier. 'The best one is from Aunt Lily.'

'Just from Aunt Lily?' Jamie pouted. 'I'll have you know that I had a lot to do with your...' He craned his neck. 'Your lovely stationery set.'

Emmie giggled. 'You bought me the makeup.'

Jamie frowned as he helped himself to some carrots. 'Makeup. Eugh. How girly.'

Maya smacked him on the arm. 'Can I have some makeup please?'

'No,' said Jamie amiably. 'Ask me another.'

The banter continued as the bowls of delicious food were passed around. Rosie collected her dodgy-looking cake from the kitchen and Nate lit the candles and did the honours with the camera on his phone as they sang happy birthday to Emmie. Rosie bumped into Nate in the kitchen as they cleared the table together while everyone else played silly games in the lounge and it was excruciating. Rosie wanted to hug him, kiss him maybe. Just talk. Anything to make this terrible atmosphere go away.

Nate seemed to be busy with some paperwork by the kettle. He was sifting through it quickly as though he was looking for something.

'Nate,' Rosie said, stopping him with her hand.

'Yes?' He looked at her and his eyes softened.

'I – I...' Rosie stared at him. What did she want to say? That she missed him? Wanted him? Wished he would just grab her and kiss her the way he used to, the way that left her legs trembling and her lips throbbing? That she would be happy with just a lovely hug from him?

'Rose…' Nate stared at her, seemingly about to say something. He put his hand on her hip.

Rosie swallowed. It was just the same. The feeling was the same. Nate only needed to put his hand on her for her to melt.

They both jumped as the doorbell rang, springing apart.

'Did you invite someone else?' Nate said, surprised.

'No. Did you?'

Nate shook his head.

Emmie rushed into the kitchen. 'I think it's Dr Tom,' she said. 'I told him it was my birthday and you said the other day that I could ask him over. Do you remember?'

'Er… yes,' Rosie said, glancing at Nate. She didn't remember saying that, but what else could she say? 'Go and answer the door then, Emmie.' She wiped her hands on a tea towel.

'Is that normal? That a counsellor pops over to a client's house?' Nate asked irritably.

'I don't know,' sighed Rosie. 'Emmie seemed keen for him to do it and I didn't see why it would be a problem. He's a really nice guy.'

Nate rubbed a hand over his head. 'I'm sure he is.'

'Well, at least you get to meet him now,' Rosie shrugged. Seeing his face tighten, Rosie instantly regretted her comment. 'I didn't mean that,' she started.

'Of course you didn't,' Nate snapped.

Rosie felt annoyed. She hadn't meant anything by her comment. She just meant that it was a nice opportunity for Nate to meet Dr Tom after all. It wasn't a dig at him for not turning up, but she guessed it might have sounded that way.

'Hello, Dr Tom,' she called as he strode past the kitchen. He waved and smiled and followed Emmie into the lounge.

'I'll go and say hello, shall I?' Nate said crossly. 'Seeing as you're such good pals with him already.'

Rosie was gutted. A few seconds ago, it had felt as though something good might happen between them. It had been a 'moment'. A moment that had felt significant and healing. And then, just as quickly, it had gone.

'I'm… sorry,' she said eventually.

'Yeah. Me too,' Nate replied. 'I'll go and say hello to him. Apologise to him as well.'

'I'll put the kettle on,' Rosie said, turning away. And there it was again. That nasty, heavy feeling in her chest. Not the one she carried around in her heart for Emmie, but the one in her chest that made her want to turn back time and go back to the time when she and Nate had been happy.

Rosie slowly took mugs out of the cupboard, wondering where her teapot was. Noticing that Nate had left the pile of paperwork in a mess, she started gathering it up. Placing it back in the cupboard, she accidentally knocked over the cracked, green pot Nate always threw his loose change into. Emmie had made the pot at a playgroup she had attended as a child and it was hideous, but Nate had declared it 'gorgeous' and had said that he wanted it for his 'pocket treasures', which had delighted Emmie at the time.

Gathering the loose change and scraps of paper up, Rosie's hand closed around something. Her stomach tightened. It was a poker chip. She didn't want to open her hand, but she was sure it was a poker chip. She uncurled her fingers and forced herself to look into her palm.

It was a poker chip. Nate was gambling again. Oh dear God. Rosie felt sick. No wonder he was acting strangely; he was as guilty as she was. She had kissed someone else and Nate had somehow ended up in a casino, after swearing blind that he would never, ever gamble again for as long as he lived.

Rosie wanted to run. She wanted to fling the back door open and run. Down through the garden and out of the back gate. She wanted to run as far away from Nate as she possibly could. Because now they really were broken. Nate's gambling had been the one thing she hadn't liked about him when they had first met. But he had got help and he had sworn he wouldn't do it again.

Rosie furiously hurled the poker chip into the bin. They were screwed. She and Nate were completely screwed. There was no way on earth they could come back from this. Not now. She placed her hands on the kitchen work top and took a deep breath. Somehow, she had to find a way to put this to one side so she could go into the lounge, greet Dr Tom as though nothing had happened and act towards Nate as if she didn't know he was gambling again, even though Rosie wanted to shove his face in her crappy birthday cake.

Because it was Emmie's birthday. And that was more important than Nate and what he had done. Rosie wasn't being hypocritical. She knew she was in the wrong as well. It was just that she had always trusted Nate with the whole gambling thing. In fact, she had never doubted him. But now, Rosie felt foolish. And hurt. And like something had just died for real.

She picked up the tea tray and went into the lounge.

'Anyone for tea?' Rosie said brightly. She shot Nate a livid glance then turned to Dr Tom. 'Cake for you? It's probably a bit burnt and eggy but it's all yours if you want it.'

'Way to go on the sales front, Rosie,' Jamie said, exchanging a glance with Lily. 'You made that sound really appealing.'

'I would love some burnt cake,' Dr Tom smiled. 'And for the record, I love eggs.'

Rosie could have hugged him for being so sweet. She hacked into the cake, shovelled a slice onto a plate and handed it to Dr Tom.

'There you go. Lily, could you pour some tea out please? I just need to nip to the loo.' Rosie dashed out of the room and ran upstairs. Safely inside the bathroom, she sat down heavily on the toilet seat. And sobbed her heart out. As far as Nate was concerned, Rosie had no more fight left in her.

Nate

Nate was so wound up he didn't know what to do with himself. It had been a difficult few days. The tension between himself and Rosie was nigh on unbearable. Blowing balloons up the night before whilst Rosie had decorated one of her adorably wonky cakes had been a real low point.

In the old days, Rosie's unpredictable cakes had been a source of great amusement and piss-taking between them. But not this time. Nate didn't feel as though he could make any jokes around Rosie at the moment. He had no idea how she would take any attempts at humour and deep down, Nate knew he wouldn't be able to pull it off. He didn't exactly feel like laughing and he knew that his connection with Rosie was shot to pieces. She had dashed out of the lounge after shoving a piece of burnt birthday cake at Dr Tom and Nate was sure she had been crying. She had reappeared about ten minutes later looking bright and breezy, but Nate knew her. She was in bits and he knew how she felt.

'Me and Rosie are going to do the washing up,' Lily announced suddenly, propelling Rosie into the kitchen.

Which Nate took to mean that Rosie and Lily were about to have a conflab. They certainly weren't washing up because there was a dishwasher available and Nate had done most of the tidying up earlier.

Nate glanced at Emmie chatting away happily to Dr Tom, suddenly guiltily remembering the night in the casino. Ever since that night, he hadn't been able to act normally around Rosie. He hated having secrets from her. Even though relations were dire between them, Nate wasn't used to holding back information – even if it was information that painted him in a bad light. He had always been so honest with Rosie. She knew the good, the bad and the ugly about him. And even though he dreaded having to admit that he had been stupid and weak, Nate would prefer to have everything out in the open.

'Who wants to play Find Daddy slash Jamie in the garden?' Jamie cried, buoyed up by beer and cake.

'Me, me!' the kids shouted, rushing out into the garden after him.

Nate had no idea where Jamie was planning to hide; under the trampoline for a kip, perhaps, but apart from that, he'd be lucky to find anywhere that great to tuck himself away.

'Thank you for letting me come over,' Dr Tom said, smiling widely at Nate. 'I know it's not protocol as such but Emmie was insistent and I felt bad saying no.'

'That's OK,' Nate said, wondering why he felt so antagonistic towards Dr Tom. He seemed like a nice enough guy. 'Shall we sit in the garden? Catch the last of the sunshine?'

'Sounds good,' Dr Tom said. 'Can I bring my cup of tea?'

'Yeah, sure.'

Nate noticed that Dr Tom was wearing jeans without rips in them today. Perhaps he only wore those to be 'down with the kids'. Nate silently reprimanded himself. Childishness was not the way forward. Dr Tom was the best counsellor Emmie had ever had. All the other ones had made her cry or made her feel bad. Which was the last thing she needed.

'Emmie's a great kid,' Dr Tom commented, watching her chasing Jamie around a big, pink slide, while Jamie shrieked like a girl.

'The best,' Nate agreed.

'She loves you both very much,' Dr Tom added. He drank some tea. 'You and Rosie. She talks about you – both of you – in most of her sessions.'

'That's nice,' Nate said. He looked down at his bare knees, enjoying the feel of the late afternoon sunshine on his skin. 'I'm not sure Emmie has much in the way of positive stuff to say about us right now. We're… going through a… a bad patch.' Nate's words sounded hollow, even to him.

'Why do you think that is?'

Nate drummed his fingers on the table. He was going to need another beer if Dr Tom was going to try and analyse him.

'I think it's because we have a daughter who has an inoperable brain tumour.' Nate felt ashamed of himself as soon as he had thrown the sentence out.

'Yes. That's always going to cause stress and anxiety,' Dr Tom said, not batting an eyelid. 'But you've been dealing with that since Emmie was very young. And although I completely understand that such an ordeal takes its toll, I wonder if something else is going on for you two. I'm not prying,' he added, placing his ankle across his knee as he relaxed into his chair. 'Please tell me to butt out if you want to.'

Nate sorely wanted to tell Dr Tom to butt out. But at the same time, there was something very calming about his demeanour, something very non-threatening about the easy way he chatted about fairly contentious circumstances. And Nate was a little sick of keeping everything to himself. He chatted to Gill a bit and to Jamie when they met up for drinks, but that was about it. He was bottling everything up and it didn't feel great.

'I don't really know when it all started to go wrong,' Nate said honestly. 'Me and Rosie – we've always had such a great connection. It doesn't look like it now, I know, but we really did have that special thing that people talk about. The chemistry, the humour, the love.' He realised his voice had gone hoarse and he coughed self-consciously. 'I genuinely don't know how we've ended up here. And it's not Emmie. Her illness has brought me and Rosie closer together, if anything. Well, it did initially, anyway.'

Nate stopped suddenly. Did he have verbal diarrhoea or what? Where had all that come from?

'Actually, that's quite a common thing,' Dr Tom commented. 'The bringing closer together idea, then it causing issues and pushing couples apart. Not Emmie herself, of course. But just the sheer stress of her diagnosis. And how long she's been undergoing treatment. It's incredibly wearing for parents, especially when it's on-going.'

Nate shrugged. 'Yes, you have a point there. We used to talk to parents during chemo who had a specific set of sessions and then it would all be over.' He scratched his chin. 'I envied them, you know? Envied them the fact that they had an end in sight. A manageable one. This many sessions, followed by an op, followed by normality. I yearn for normality, yet I can't even remember what it feels like.'

Dr Tom nodded and drained his mug. 'You are dealing with one of the most challenging situations any parent can find themselves in. You're living in a very real, very difficult situation that threatens to explode and blow up in your face at any second. That's extreme stress. That's like… throwing yourself out of a plane on a daily basis.'

It was. Nate appreciated Dr Tom's ability to understand exactly how horrible this situation was. Wanting to live each day in normality – but also with all the love you could cram into it, just in case the unthinkable happened.

Nate glanced at Emmie and his heart contracted. He couldn't imagine life without her. That was the thing. He couldn't imagine the pain of losing her. He did imagine it at times and he hated himself for it. He had no idea why he would do that to himself either. Realising he had a counsellor sitting next to him, Nate decided to ask.

'I obsess about Emmie dying sometimes,' he confessed jerkily. 'It's like… it's like it's my worst nightmare, but I can't help myself from doing it.'

'Again, it's a very natural thing to do in the circum-stances.' Dr Tom leant forward, putting his elbows on his knees. 'The last thing you want to even contemplate is Emmie not being around anymore. And yet it creeps into your mind constantly, I'm sure. I think it's probably a form of self-sabotage, tormenting yourself this way, but it's also likely that you've adopted it as a defence mechanism.'

'A what?'

'You're mentally preparing,' Dr Tom explained. 'Just in case. You don't want to think about it, because it's the worst thing you can possibly focus on, but equally, you don't want the rug to be pulled out from under you. You want to know how that would feel, even though the thought of it is hideous to you.'

Nate turned to Dr Tom. 'Yes,' he said earnestly. 'That's it. I even think about her funeral, for God's sakes. Her funeral, Dr Tom. I mean, why on earth would I want to dwell on such a dreadful thing?'

Dr Tom gave him a sympathetic smile. 'As I said, you just don't want to be caught out. It's so horrific and unimaginable, your mind – or rather, your psyche – is struggling to find a way to cope.'

It made sense and Nate felt a sudden rush of relief, like water being released out of a barrel. It was something he couldn't even bring himself to admit to Rosie, the fact that he thought about Emmie's funeral. Nate had been appalled at himself the first time it had happened. He had roused himself out a prolonged daydream which had involved him reading out a bloody eulogy like some sort of bumbling idiot, experiencing all the emotions he thought he might feel if they were unlucky enough to lose Emmie.

And it hadn't only happened once. Nate had found himself literally obsessing over Emmie's funeral. Planning the details in minute detail. Experiencing the emotions over and over again. More than once at work, he had had to dash off and have a massive sob in the toilet because he had suddenly found himself overcome at his desk.

'At least I'm not mad,' Nate managed, putting his hands behind his head as he let out a breath. 'I honestly thought I'd lost the plot, thinking horrendous things like that.'

'Not at all.' Dr Tom squinted and checked his pockets. 'Left my prescription sunnies at home. It's honestly very normal. Have you discussed this with Rosie?'

'God no!' Nate shook his head emphatically. 'No way. I have no idea how I would even broach that subject. How could I possibly tell Rosie that I was thinking such a thing? That I think about it more often than even I care to admit to myself?'

'Have you had counselling?'

'Some.' Nate felt defensive. 'I didn't enjoy it. It felt clinical. Not like this.'

'Well, thanks,' Dr Tom said. 'But that's the thing. If you're not able to discuss thoughts you see as heinous with your partner, talking to someone else often helps because you can freely discuss those thoughts in a safe environment.'

'To be honest, I'd rather I was able to talk to Rosie about all of it,' Nate admitted. 'Truly. It's helpful talking to you like this, but I would far rather I could be honest with Rosie. I hate keeping things from her.'

'Are there other things you haven't told her about?' Dr Tom settled back in his chair again.

Nate contemplated Dr Tom. Should he tell him about the gambling? He didn't even know this guy, but he felt compelled to share private information with him. Nate supposed that made Dr Tom good at his job.

'Mostly just my feelings about Emmie. Life without her, that kind of thing,' Nate said, instantly feeling like a fraud. He bit the bullet. Who was Dr Tom to him? 'Well, that and the fact that I gambled again the other day. For the first time in years.'

Dr Tom toyed with his empty mug. 'Right. I assume that's an issue between yourself and Rosie?'

'Yeah. It was. Years ago, of course. But I promised her. I promised her I'd never ever do it again, because I spent some savings I'd put aside for us to do our house up back then. It was my money, but it was for our future.' Nate paused, remembering how rotten he had felt when he had done that to Rosie. 'It was a wake up call. I told her I wouldn't ever lapse again. And then I did. Last week.'

'Shit happens,' Dr Tom said unexpectedly. 'Which sounds flippant, but I actually mean that. Shit does happen. People do bad things. People lapse and make mistakes. The thing about doing that kind of thing is admitting that you've done it. Realising what's behind it. Moving forward.'

Wasn't that the truth? Nate totally understood what Dr Tom was saying. But it was easier said than done. If things were normal between him and Rosie, he wouldn't have gambled in the first place. And that was a fact. Nate hadn't even thought about gambling in years. But if for some strange reason he had and everything was as it had been between him and Rosie, Nate knew he would have come straight home and he would have been honest about it. There was no way he would have made such a huge mistake and kept it to himself, because that wasn't how their relationship had worked. In the past, at any rate.

'So I think this is what might have happened,' Dr Tom said, watching the kids tearing around the garden. Jamie had long since given up and was currently curled up beneath the oak tree in the corner. 'I think that you and Rosie worked really well together in the early days. You shared your fears and your anxieties over Emmie. And then, perhaps, as time went on, you both started to feel the strain. You started to lose hope and positivity. You both feared the worst happening to Emmie and to yourselves. Which is all completely natural.'

Nate listened, spellbound.

Dr Tom cleared his throat. 'You started to hold those thoughts back. Both of you. Instead of sharing them, you kept them hidden, because you didn't want to voice any sense of negativity or hopelessness. You both wanted to stay strong – for Emmie. Admitting how scared you both were, felt like a weakness, despite this being an unbearable situation. It's a vulnerability of sorts, in your minds, perhaps. Disloyalty to Emmie in some ways, because you're doing everything you can to reassure and support her.'

Nate felt a rush of tears hit the back of his eyes. God. He could bawl his eyes out right now. Dr Tom was holding his heart in his hands and giving it a squeeze, even if it was with the best of intentions. But Nate knew he needed to hear all of this. And Gill and Jamie, as lovely as they were, didn't have this kind of insight.

'Go on,' he mumbled, knowing he was on the very edge of his limits.

'So you have both shut down to a degree,' Dr Tom explained kindly. 'You've stopped being open with one another, because your innermost thoughts are too frightening to voice. Especially to each other. Rosie has probably had similar thoughts about Emmie dying. Or her fears manifest themselves in other ways she feels would sound terrible to you as Emmie's dad. And this has caused a rift. A block in communication. Where you were once happy to openly confide in one another about Emmie, you have both retreated within. Does any of that make sense?'

'All of it,' Nate nodded. 'All of it. And it makes me feel bloody, fucking desolate. I get it, but I hate that this has happened to us, that we're some kind of cliché. I thought we were different. I thought what we had was special.'

Dr Tom let out a heavy sigh. 'From what Emmie tells me, you *are* special. Your relationship *is* different. And for the record, it's not about being a cliché in any way. It's about being human.'

'How do we come back from this?' Nate asked, rubbing at his damp eyes. 'Can we come back from this?'

'I think you can,' Dr Tom said. 'I think you're going to need some help, but I think you can do it.'

'Help? What kind of help?'

'I think it will come in a fairly unique form,' Dr Tom smiled. 'And that's all I'm at liberty to say right now. But you have an amazing daughter. She thinks the world of both of you.'

Nate stood up. He needed to step away, collect his thoughts. 'Can I get you a beer?' he said. 'Another cup of tea?'

'Tea would be lovely, thanks.' Dr Tom stood up as well. 'I'll just have a quick chat with Emmie and I'll be off.'

'Stay as long as you like,' Nate said, patting him on the shoulder. 'You've been a great help. Thank you. Sorry for crying like a big girl's blouse.'

Dr Tom grinned. 'I can't even get out of a beanbag,' he said randomly. 'We all have shit to deal with.'

Nate laughed and headed indoors. He had this sudden urge to find Rosie and hug her. Tell her everything. Surely they could heal this rift between them? Heading into the kitchen, Nate found it empty, so he re-filled the kettle and switched it on. Rosie had left her phone on the side so out of habit, he picked it up on the way to finding her. Glancing down at it, he realised that someone had messaged her on Facebook. The message was on her screen, even though it was locked. It was from someone called 'Jonny Barista'. Nate couldn't help himself; he read it. And when he did, his blood ran cold. It said: 'Can't stop thinking about that night. And that kiss. Come and see me at work x'.

Nate thought he might throw up. He hadn't thought Rosie capable of doing anything like this. She had kissed another guy. She had put her mouth on someone else's mouth and she had kissed that person. Nate felt his insides ripping in two. He felt raw, shocked, angry. He didn't know whether to hurl Rosie's phone at the wall and holler in her face or to slide down the kitchen cabinet and cry his eyes out again.

He wanted to feel numb. Why didn't he feel numb? Nate didn't want to feel any more pain. But this was him and Rosie dying. This was what he had once thought was the most perfect relationship in the world turning into something tainted. Dr Tom was wrong; they were a cliché. They had both become people they had probably never imagined they could be.

Nate glanced out of the window. If it wasn't for Emmie, he would get his passport and fuck off, anywhere, take the first free seat on a flight. But he couldn't do that. He had to be here for his daughter, because she needed him. Rosie clearly didn't, but Nate was pretty sure Emmie did. What was he supposed to do now? How could he even look at Rosie? Sit opposite her at the breakfast table? Go to Emmie's appointments?

'Nate.'

He turned and found Rosie standing in front of him.

'I can't even look at you,' he said before he could stop himself.

'I can't even look at *you*,' Rosie replied with equal force.

Nate stared at her.

Rosie stared back unwaveringly. 'So where does that leave us?' she said.

'Absolutely nowhere,' Nate said wretchedly. 'It leaves us precisely nowhere, Rosie.' He knew the empty, dead-ened expression in her eyes mirrored his own.

What now?

Emmie

'Have you had a good day?' Dr Tom asked, throwing himself down opposite Emmie.

Emmie hesitated then nodded. She was sitting on the grass by the trampoline. The grass was making her legs itch but the coolness of the shade felt nice.

'Where's your Uncle Jamie gone?'

Emmie giggled. 'I think he burnt his forehead. He's gone inside for another sleep.'

'Oh dear. He's funny though, isn't he?'

'Sometimes. Thank you for my present,' Emmie added.

'Ulterior motive,' Dr Tom smiled. 'A pen to go with the diary. That way, I can make sure you do your homework for me.'

Emmie hugged her knees. 'I haven't done the last bit, whatever that was. Something about my feelings about something or other.'

Dr Tom pulled a face. 'Something about my feelings about something or other? I think it was quite an important question I was asking you, Emmie.'

'Yes, but it's not important to me,' she said impatiently. She flushed slightly. 'Sorry. It's just that it's not top of my list. I'm not worried about anything to do with me.'

Dr Tom stretched his legs out. 'You're still worried about your parents?'

Emmie looked over towards the house. 'Yes. They can't even talk to each other. It's been a bit horrible today.'

Dr Tom said nothing.

Having been to many counsellors in the past, Emmie knew that not replying was a way for Dr Tom to make her speak. But she didn't mind when it was him.

'I came downstairs last night and my mum was decorating that cake on her own and my dad was blowing up balloons. They were in separate rooms, not talking. It's like they hate each other.' Emmie dropped her head to her knees miserably.

'I don't think they hate each other,' Dr Tom said gently. 'I think they have… disconnected. That's all.'

'Can they re-connect, then, do you think?' Emmie asked, lifting her head to look at Dr Tom pleadingly.

Dr Tom thought for a moment then nodded. 'I think they can, yes. I think anything is possible.' He sat up. 'That thing we were thinking of doing for them? I think we should organise that as soon as possible.'

'Really?' Emmie felt excited. 'Aunt Lily has helped me with it and we think we've sorted the timeline.'

'Great. A spy in the making. We might just need her help to get this all up and running.' Dr Tom looked over his shoulder. Lily was just coming out into the garden with a tray.

'I'll get her,' Emmie said, scrambling to her feet. 'Aunt Lily, Dr Tom needs to speak to you.'

'What about?' Aunt Lily said, setting the tray she was carrying down on the garden table. 'I've got snacks and juice for you lot. Uncle Jamie is snoring on the sofa.' She rolled her eyes. 'Silly… sausage.'

Emmie had a feeling Aunt Lily had been about to say something else. 'I'm not hungry. This is about the thing to do with mum and dad. We need you to be a spy. Kind of.'

'A spy? How thrilling. Right.' Aunt Lily called Emmie's cousins over. 'Maya, George — one snack each and no bouncing around for five minutes afterwards.'

'Five minutes!' they whined as Aunt Lily allowed Emmie to tug her by the hand over to Dr Tom.

Dr Tom brushed grass from his hands and smiled. 'So you're in on this secret mission we're working on?'

Aunt Lily sat down on the grass and tucked her skirt around her knees. 'For my sins, yes.' She met Dr Tom's eyes. 'I think we should crack on with this as soon as possible.'

'I agree,' he said.

'This is great!' Emmie said. 'I wasn't sure if we should do this or not, but if you both think we should...'

'Oh we definitely should,' Aunt Lily said quickly.

'It's a great idea,' Dr Tom said.

He spoke more casually, but Emmie noticed that he seemed keen to agree with Aunt Lily.

'What's the plan?' Dr Tom asked.

Emmie outlined the idea, with her Aunt Lily providing the occasional detail.

Dr Tom listened thoughtfully. 'That bar your Dad worked in, it still exists?'

Aunt Lily picked her phone up and tapped the screen. She showed it to Dr Tom. 'It does. It's not called the Lone Wolf anymore, it's called Shoreditch Escape, but it's still there.'

'Great.' Dr Tom looked pleased. 'I was worried our first port of call might not be a real place anymore. So I guess the important thing is to work around their work situations. Saturdays and Sundays will probably be best.'

'I can look after Emmie on those days,' Aunt Lily offered.

'Oh.' Emmie's face fell. 'I mean, thank you, Aunt Lily. But I was hoping me and Dr Tom might be able to watch them from afar a bit. Not all the time, but maybe the first few. Can we?' She turned to Dr Tom.

He grinned. 'Luckily for you, I don't have a life outside of my work, so yes. We can do that. For the first few. We might need to leave them to it after that though.'

Emmie nodded. 'I just want to make sure they actually do it, you know?'

Maya and George nipped past and dived into the trampoline.

Aunt Lily scowled in their general direction. 'Little so and so's. I told them five minutes.' She turned to Emmie. 'So. How are you planning to get them to do that? To get on board with all of this?'

Dr Tom cupped a hand around his eyes. 'Do you have any suggestions?'

Aunt Lily hesitated.

Emmie frowned.

'Come on, Emmie!' Maya yelled. 'Come and bounce!'

'No thanks,' Emmie called. She ignored her cousins. 'About Mum and Dad. I was just going to ask them.' She felt Aunt Lily's eyes immediately focused on her, shortly joined by Dr Tom's. 'What? Why are you looking at me like that?'

'Oh nothing,' Aunt Lily said, sounding deliberately airy. 'It's just… they might not be up for traipsing around London revisiting their first dates and stuff for all we know.'

Dr Tom cocked his head at Emmie. 'Your Aunt Lily has a point, Emmie. I think you need to prepare yourself just in case this doesn't work out how we've planned it. I'm sure you can be very convincing, but…'

Emmie got up. 'Leave it with me. I know I can get them to do this.'

Aunt Lily looked concerned. Her lovely green eyes softened as she fixed Emmie with a sympathetic gaze. 'What are you going to say?'

Emmie's mouth twisted as she regarded them both. 'I've never done this before. But you both look freaked out. So I'm going to get out the… the…'

'The big guns?' Dr Tom offered.

'Yes.' Emmie pulled a face. She wasn't sure she understood that; she just knew she meant that she was going to have to do something drastic.

Aunt Lily looked puzzled. 'What do you mean?'

'I going to remind them that I have cancer,' Emmie said earnestly. 'I want them to do it because I'm dying of cancer. And I don't feel bad about it, because it's for their own good. That's bad, isn't it?' she said, suddenly feeling terrible.

Aunt Lily gaped. 'Gosh, Emmie.'

'Is that… fair?' Dr Tom asked.

Emmie's eyes narrowed. She could tell that Dr Tom was saying that because he was going along with Aunt Lily, not because it was what he believed. It was something she liked about him; that she could read his face so well.

'Probably not,' Emmie acknowledged. She still felt bad. 'But I think I'm doing it.'

Turning on her heel, she left Aunt Lily and Dr Tom on the grass and headed inside the house. It was silent apart from the odd grunting snore from Uncle Jamie on the couch in the lounge. Emmie had no idea where her parents were or why the house was so quiet, but she made for the kitchen. And found her parents facing one another. The air felt tense and weird and Emmie didn't like it one bit.

'What's the matter?' she asked.

Rosie started a bit, as if she'd been in a trance or something. 'Emmie. I didn't know you were there. Are you OK?'

Emmie stared at her. Her mum looked weird. Her face was all pale and pinched and she was clenching her fists.

'I've only just got here.'

'Sorry, we're just...'

Emmie glanced at her dad. He also looked odd. Like he was about to cry. Or maybe punch a wall or something. He looked angry and upset, like he didn't know which one he was feeling more than the other.

'Will you both do something for me?'

Rosie gave her a watery smile. 'Of course, Emmie. Anything for the birthday girl.'

'Not because it's my birthday.' Emmie chewed her lip. 'More because I'm... sick.'

Nate let out a sound. 'What does that mean, hun? We know you're sick.'

'Yes. I know.' Emmie scuffed her trainer toe on the floor. Why hadn't she planned this speech better? 'OK. So what I need you to do is go on a treasure hunt.'

Her parents looked at her as if she was talking Japanese.

Emmie forged ahead. 'It's a treasure hunt for... for both of you. So you'd go to the place you first met, that type of thing. The... the zoo.'

Nate gripped the edge of the kitchen work top with his hands. 'To what end, Emmie? What's the point of this?'

Emmie suddenly wanted to cry. Her dad looked weary and sick of life and her mum... Her mum just looked totally miserable and as if she wanted to run away and be anywhere but here.

'Just... can you do it for me?' Emmie said, bursting into tears. 'Because I want you to? Because I love you and I want you to do this for me? Just in case I... just...'

'Emmie.' Rosie rushed over and put her arms around her. 'Of course we'll do it. Nate, we'll do it. Won't we?'

There was a pause and then he said 'Yes.'

'I'm sorry,' Emmie said tearfully into her mum's shoulder. She was. She felt terrible now.

'Ssssh. What for?'

'For saying I want you to do it because I'm sick. That's not nice.'

Rosie stroked Emmie's hair. 'Shhh. It's OK, sweetheart. You didn't need to say that, because we'd do it anyway. Because we love you.'

Emmie nodded. Why had she said that? It was horrible of her.

Nate put his hand on Emmie's back. 'Your mum's right. We love you. We'll do it.'

Emmie was scared. Her dad sounded awful. Her mum looked awful. Was this even going to work? Emmie rested her head on Rosie's shoulder again. She had a headache. But that was just because she was worrying so much about her parents. And she wasn't going to say a word about it either, because her parents clearly had enough to deal with. It wasn't one of those kinds of headaches anyway. This was a worry headache. Because Emmie simply didn't know if this was going to work. If her parents were going to be alright. And they had to be alright. Emmie didn't want anything more than that. Apart from someone being able to magically remove her tumour, Emmie would give anything for them to be better, to be back to how they had once been.

But they had agreed, Emmie reminded herself. They had both said yes and they were going on the treasure hunt. Emmie let out a shuddering breath. This was it. It was time to get her parents back together.

Rosie and Nate

'Are you ready?'

Nate glanced at Rosie. 'Yes, I think so.' He patted his pockets. 'Keys, wallet, phone. I'm good.'

'Me too.' Rosie hoisted her bag onto her shoulder. 'Shall we make a move?'

'Let's.'

Rosie paused in the hallway. Emmie was on a playdate with her cousins; Lily had collected her this morning. Lily had promised to call if anything happened and Rosie trusted her. She could get through her Pilates classes without too much stress and anxiety because they lasted for an hour and she was only at a local gym or hall so she could get home immediately if need be. But this was different. This was her and Nate going up to London. All afternoon. Together.

And that was the real issue, Rosie thought as she silently followed Nate out of the house. It was spending the whole day with Nate when she didn't feel that she could even be in the same room with him without screaming at him.

Since Emmie's birthday lunch two weeks ago, Rosie and Nate had barely spoken. Rosie felt such a deep sense of resentment towards Nate about the gambling, she knew she couldn't just play nicely and have casual conversations.

There was so much she wanted to say, but at the same time, there was so much rage and bitterness bubbling away inside her, Rosie knew she would lose it if she even so much as started talking to Nate about it. It was – and she was – too sensitive, too volatile.

God. Why were they even doing this, Rosie thought to herself as they walked to the station? For Emmie, obviously, because this 'treasure hunt' – whatever it was – was clearly important to her. But apart from that, this felt like a charade. Rosie felt fake and disingenuous. As though she and Nate were just playing along with something for Emmie's sake, when really, they wanted to be anywhere else but here, with each other.

'So. A treasure hunt,' Nate said, feeling the need to fill the silence. He wasn't sure why he felt that way. He was so incredibly hurt about what he had found out about Rosie the other week, he was finding it hard to walk alongside her, let alone make polite conversation.

What on earth was he doing here? Nate admonished himself. Emmie. This was all for Emmie. Otherwise, Nate wouldn't dream of being around Rosie right now. What was the point? They were both so incredibly broken, Nate thought, feeling desperate.

'A treasure hunt,' Rosie repeated flatly, not looking up from the ground. 'Yes. I have no idea what Emmie has planned for us.'

'Me neither.'

Nate swallowed and thrust his hands into his pockets. He had spent the last fortnight mulling over how he felt about Rosie and what she had done. Nate felt shocked. It was something he hadn't ever expected to happen. Not from an egotistical point of view – and Nate had questioned himself greatly over this but he knew it wasn't that – it was simply that he hadn't once contemplated either of them cheating. Their marriage had always been rock solid. He and Rosie had always had such an intense, physical, almost chemical attraction for one another, that coupled with how deep their love was – Nate hadn't seen this coming. Even throughout Emmie's diagnosis and treatment, he had always thought that the level of respect he and Rosie had for one another, the closeness and the way they communicated could get them through anything.

Nate paid for their train tickets at the station. He realised things had been terrible between himself and Rosie for a while. But he hadn't ever thought Rosie capable of doing what she'd done. Nate handed Rosie her ticket, feeling his entire body tense defensively towards her. God, it hurt. The thought of her kissing someone else was killing him.

Nate thought about Emmie for a second. He must love her very, very much. Because she was the only reason he was standing here on a train platform with Rosie.

'Right. So we've bought tickets to London Liverpool Street, as per Emmie's instructions,' Nate said. He slipped his sunglasses on, hoping they hid the pain he was sure must show in his eyes. 'What next?'

Rosie checked the chunky, pink envelope Emmie had given her before excitedly skipping off with Lily. 'She says we can open the next bit when we get to London.'

'Right.'

Rosie felt her chest tighten. Nate had checked out. He didn't want to be here any more than she did. Which hurt her terribly. She had reason to feel that way, with Nate's gambling slip, but why on earth would he be acting the way he was towards her? Unless…

Rosie stole a discreet glance at Nate. Could he know about Jonny? Jonny had sent her some silly message some weeks back, but Rosie was fairly certain she had kept her phone with her at all times. She felt her cheeks flush guiltily. God, what a mess.

'Coffee?' Nate asked.

'No thanks,' Rosie replied.

'I'm going to grab one. I need to wake up myself up a bit.'

'Sure.' Rosie cringed. What on earth did they sound like? A couple of people who didn't know each other very well. Who were too damaged by life to properly connect. Rosie let out a jerky sigh. She felt quite tearful. But she hoped to God she wasn't going to disgrace herself and break down in front of Nate. That was the last thing she wanted to do.

'The train is here,' Nate said unnecessarily.

He sipped his coffee and gritted his teeth. An entire day. He and Rosie had to get through an entire day together. 'After you,' he said, stepping back to let Rosie onto the train. He caught a waft of her perfume as she climbed into the carriage and it unnerved him. Apart from the occasional foray into something else because she thought she should, Rosie had worn the same perfume for years and the warm, woody scent suited her. It had always, always reminded Nate of Rosie whenever he smelt it. In a shop, on another woman walking past. He climbed into the train after her and steeled himself. She had kissed another man. Nate instantly felt sick and he dumped his coffee in the bin.

'No good?' Rosie asked, surprised. Nate was addicted to coffee.

'It was fine. I didn't want it,' he answered shortly. He wished he could listen to some music. Or read a paper. Sitting opposite Rosie in such close proximity like this was agony.

'Here's a newspaper,' Rosie said, reading his mind. 'Feel free. I'm going to check my phone. Lily said she was sending over some stuff about some days out for the kids.'

Nate took the paper and gratefully absorbed himself in it. He was still very aware of Rosie on the other side of the sheets, but he did his best to focus on the sensational headlines and tawdry news updates.

Rosie checked her phone lethargically, willing the train ride to be over. She had no idea what Emmie had in store for them, but she hoped to God it didn't involve too much sitting around in silence. She hadn't been this close to Nate in months, Rosie thought to herself. Even in bed, it didn't feel as if they were especially close, as they came to bed at separate times and strategically laid on their respective edges. Dinners together were sporadic due to Nate's working hours and he never had breakfast with her and Emmie before he left the house, preferring to grab a coffee and something to eat on the way.

'We're nearly there,' Nate said, setting the newspaper aside. 'Should we open the next envelope?'

'OK.' Rosie put her phone away and took out the envelope. She pulled out the envelope marked with a large '2' in the centre. Opening it, she frowned. 'Apparently we need to go to Shoreditch. We can open envelope three on the way.'

Nate started. Shoreditch. How weird. He had so many links to that area of London.

'Oh well,' he said. 'Not too far away then.'

'No,' Rosie agreed, perplexed. She had no idea what Emmie was playing at, but she wasn't sure she liked it. Not when things were this tense and awkward with Nate.

Arriving at Liverpool Street station, they left the train and walked down the platform together. Rosie was immediately hit by a memory. Of herself and Nate meeting after work, having a few too many glasses of wine. Kissing, talking in murmurs, touching. Charging through Liverpool Street station later hand in hand, tipsy and laughing their heads off as they desperately ran to jump on the infamous 'Vomit Comet' – the last train back to Essex. Full of commuters who mostly reeked of booze as they munched away on fast food, talking raucously about their evenings out.

'Cab, tube or walk?' Nate asked, breaking Rosie's reverie.

'Ummm…'

'It's as broad as it is long.' Nate shrugged. 'All take roughly ten to fifteen minutes. Cab is probably the quickest, depending on traffic.'

Rosie stole a glance at Nate. He had always had an oddly encyclopaedic brain when it came to London. Even when it came to areas he wasn't familiar with, he had an uncanny way of knowing exactly how long a journey would take using various different forms of transport. Rosie quickly made a decision.

'Cab, perhaps?'

Nate met her eyes. He understood her choice; Rosie had selected the quickest form of transport so they didn't need to spend more agonising moments walking along side by side in silence. Or be thrown against each other on the tube – something they used to revel in. Feeling queasy despite not having had any breakfast, Nate led the way to the taxi rank. Rosie ripped open Emmie's third envelope as they got in and gave the taxi driver the address.

'Where are we off to?' Nate asked, not sure he even cared.

'Somewhere called "The Shoreditch Escape",' Rosie said.

Nate looked out of the window. He didn't have a clue what that was and he was beginning to feel rather irritated with Emmie. She might be their kid and she might be sick, but this was beginning to resemble a farce and Nate had better things to do.

'I haven't been up here for ages,' Rosie murmured. Aside from Nate's frostiness, she was rather enjoying being back in London. She had so many positive memories of the place from when she worked in banking. Drinks after work, clubbing, business meetings in swanky bars. It had been hard work, but it had been fun.

And Shoreditch was far more hip and trendy than it used to be, Rosie decided, watching the bars, restaurants and hotels shoot past the window of the cab.

'Here we are,' called the cab driver. 'Oh, I remember this place. They've done it up and it's now a bar-spa or whatever they call it. But it used to be a right spit and sawdust drinking hole, though it did cocktails and all that fancy stuff as well. Damn. What was it called again?'

'The Lone Wolf,' Nate mumbled, climbing out of the cab in shock. He paid the driver and, out of sheer habit, moved to help Rosie out, but she avoided his hand. Nate recoiled, but did his best to hide it.

'Oh my God,' Rosie said as she looked up. 'It's that bar you used to work in. I mean, it's not, but it's in the same place.'

'Yep.'

Nate squinted up at it. What the hell had Emmie sent them here for?

'I guess we should go in,' Rosie said. She looked inside Emmie's envelope. 'There aren't any more instructions. Oh. Apart from that she wants us to order some drinks. And food if we're hungry.'

Nate led the way, pushing open the vast, glass door that made the place look super-trendy and modern. God, how strange to be back here. Even though the place had been renovated, the architects had obviously decided that some of the original features were cool and worth keeping. Such as the immense, ornate mirror behind the bar. A section of the wooden-topped bar itself, seamlessly blended with a hunk of shiny marble. The saloon-style doors that led to the toilets. They had been tarted up with metallic gloss, but the idea was the same. And somehow, the odd blend of old and new worked.

The Shoreditch Escape was achingly cool, very on trend and rather eclectic, with what looked like a high-end, unisex spa attached to the back of the bar area. It was also empty as it was around 11am and apart from a few dirty coffee cups on the side, not too many people had ventured in yet.

Nate wandered around, taking it all in. His very first job. He had been a bartender. A spinner of cocktail shakers and an all-round cocky bastard. He had loved working in this place, impressing the women with his Tom Cruise-esque cocktail gimmicks and his cheesy banter. There was a whole team of them who used to work here together on various different shifts. Dodgy hours that probably weren't legal, but they didn't care. They had an Irish boss who had looked after them when it came to free drinks and the odd overly long break and they had had a whale of a time.

Nate had finally left to join the police force and he had missed the bar greatly. He and his bar pals had kept in touch for a while, but one by one, they had all dropped off, doing their own thing, starting families and suchlike.

Nate ran his hand along the edge of the original part of the bar. He had been one lucky sod with the women who came in here. His cocktail skills, the male banter, the winks – all of it had worked in his favour. Not that he whored himself around, even back then. He had been all about the flirting and the fun, all about the lads he hung out with. Sure, he had had the odd moment and there had been one or two girls he had been very interested in, on and off. And then Rosie had walked in and from that point, he had only been concerned with impressing her. Jolted, Nate picked up a bar menu and tried to focus on it, shocked at how colourful the memories were. He could actually recall exactly how he had felt when she had walked through the door. Even if the door had been different, Nate just knew how he had felt.

Rosie wandered to the bar, smiling inwardly as she watched Nate soaking up the atmosphere and drawing up memories of the job he had always talked about fondly. And even though the bar looked very different to how it had looked back then, there were enough original features to bring on a sharp recollection.

She remembered the night she had first met Nate. She had strolled in with a male friend from work, turning her nose up at the scruffy little bar she had been taken to. Heading over to the bar, she had been rendered speechless by the sight of Nate, hurling bottles and shakers to a colleague as they re-enacted the entire sequence from the film *Cocktail*. Nate had been showing off for all he was worth, but he had dropped a bottle when he caught sight of her. Rosie had blushed and giggled, but she had loved it. Nate's hair had been longer, but he looked more or less how he did now. Gorgeous. Hot. Sexy. Very alpha.

'What can I get you?' the girl behind the bar asked Rosie.

'She'll have a…' Nate glanced at Rosie and raised an eyebrow. 'A margarita, if it's not too early for one? Heavy on the tequila, white, of course. Salted rim. Splash of olive water, even though that's not what you should have in a margarita.'

Rosie smiled. He remembered. Too much Sex in the City had made her have fancy, bizarre taste in cocktails.

'How about a Red Cap?' the bar girl suggested. 'Hibiscus float on a classic margarita base. No olive water. But definitely a salted rim.'

'Sounds amazing,' Rosie said. 'He'll have whatever bottled beer you have, even though he'll pretend that he loves a White Russian.'

Nate laughed before he could stop himself. Of course. He'd pretended he liked White Russians when they had first met as he thought it made him sound sophisticated. What a knobhead. Mind you, he didn't mind them these days. Coffee in any form was always good. But back then, he had said it to show off.

'Can I order some bar snacks as well?' Nate showed the menu to Rosie but she waved a hand to show that she would share whatever he ordered and took a seat at a nearby table.

She heard him order some very modern-sounding snacks. Crackling strips with spiced apple dip. Ox cheek nuggets with chilli jam. Devils on horseback. Cheese and olive straws with truffle oil.

Nate would be in heaven with all of that, Rosie thought. Upmarket bar snacks would appeal to the foodie in him. Rosie felt strange. Detached, but connected. No. Like her old self. That was it. She felt like herself again. The way she had been before…

Rosie stopped herself. She wanted to hold onto that good feeling. It felt buzzy and positive. And that was familiar, yet somehow also usually out of reach.

'God. How totally random to be back here,' Nate said, sitting down opposite Rosie. He put her fancy cocktail down. 'That smells pretty good. If a bit poofy.'

Rosie sipped it. 'It's divine. If a bit poofy.' She looked around. 'I like what they've done with the place.'

'It's amazing. Cocktails and a massage. Who would have thought it?'

Nate sipped his beer. He couldn't explain how he felt. Happy. Uplifted. Light. Carefree. It was as though they'd gone back in time, despite the modern surroundings. There was a rush of memories weaving themselves around him. Loud music. Lad banter. Flirtation. Rosie. So many feelings about Rosie.

Rosie checked Nate out from under her eyelashes. Seeing him back here… it brought it all back. The way she had felt when she met him. The giddy happiness, the innocent desire and the thrilling expectation. It was like a… like a memory firework going off inside her. Rosie felt as though she was in a bubble and even if it only lasted for a short while, she was holding onto it. She resolutely pushed any bad thoughts away, looking up as the food started coming out.

'Wow. That all smells incredible.'

'It does.' Nate took one of the small plates they'd been given and filled it with a selection of snacks before handing it to Rosie. 'Get your chops around that, gorgeous.'

Rosie blinked at the endearment and took the plate. She hadn't been called that by Nate in a very long time. But she liked it.

Nate started tucking in. The food was delicious. His beer tasted amazing. It was like being on holiday, where, for some reason, glorious sunshine combined with the evocative scent of suntan lotion made even simple meals of bread, garlic prawns and cheap wine taste great.

'This is so good,' Nate managed, with his mouth full.

'Love the ox cheeks,' Rosie said, knowing she had chilli jam on her chin.

'Me too.' Nate handed her a napkin, but only because he knew he should be a gent. He had always loved the way Rosie ate with gusto. She enjoyed her food and wasn't apologetic about it. She worked out and ate healthily most of the time so she could afford to indulge when she wanted to.

'Do you remember one of the chats we had in here?' Nate asked. 'About how we wanted to change our lives and do completely different jobs?'

Rosie dabbed her messy chin. 'I do. Took me longer than it took you though.'

'Yes, but you left your job to be an amazing mum.' Nate met Rosie's eyes and held them briefly. He felt disloyal to Emmie, but just for a few moments, he wanted this to be about him and Rosie. 'I was banging on the about the police force back then. But not doing anything about it.'

'You were having far too good a time here,' Rosie commented. 'Banter with the boys, flirting with all the girls.' She smiled.

Nate licked his fingers. 'Indeed. Some more than others, mind.'

Rosie felt her stomach shift. This was freaking her out. How was being back in this bar that didn't even look the way it had back then making her feel this way? She wasn't deluding herself that she was in the past and that she and Nate had just met. But she felt some of that right now. Some of that old, lovely feeling. Of newness. Attraction. Passion. New beginnings.

Nate finished his beer. 'Another?' he said.

Rosie nodded and held up her glass. 'Same again, please.'

The bar was starting to fill up. Some people were clearly regulars as they were greeted by name by the bar staff, others were tourists or first-time visitors. She and Nate were obviously somewhere in between; not tourists as such, but by no means on first name terms.

Nate and Rosie found themselves people-watching, something they had always done together when they were dating. And beyond. Rosie remembered them ending up in a gay bar by accident and spending many a hilarious hour over drinks working out who was gay, who was straight and – with a mutual sense of non-political correct-ness – who might possibly be a ladyboy. She reminded

Nate of this and when he laughed, she mentioned a a time in France when Rosie had been pregnant with Emmie, in a café full of couples with kids, and she and Nate had spent hours analysing everyone around them.

Rosie realised that right now, all this memory-based chatter was an avoidance. A way to talk non-stop without alighting on any subject which might be contentious. Which might burst the bubble.

Nate watched Rosie as she sipped her cocktail. Another thing he loved about her was that despite having a dirty mind and a dirty sense of humour, Rosie was a real lady. She had a delicate way of holding her cocktail glass, of holding herself. Messy with food, granted, but hey. That was all part of her charm.

'One more for the road?' Nate said, checking his watch. He was aware that he was stalling. That he didn't want this to end. That whilst ensconced in this bar, he and Rosie were safe. They were oddly protected from reality. Nate had done a good job of not thinking about anything negative whilst they had been drinking and chatting. Thoughts had sprung up and he had squashed them down. He knew it was temporary, but he was going with it.

Rosie hesitated. They should get back soon. Anxiety over Emmie was beginning to surface the way it always did, though she hadn't heard from Lily and her phone was in her pocket on vibrate. But maybe…

'Just one more,' she agreed. Her cheeks felt flushed and she was warm on the inside too. When Nate made his way through the now very full bar, Rosie felt the way she had in the early days when they were dating. Proud to be with him. Excited. Happy. Hopeful. Even if it was false hope. That was how she felt.

'This has been really nice,' Nate said, sitting down with their drinks. 'Being back here.'

With you, he thought to himself silently. Why hadn't he said that out loud? Because it was too risky, he realised. Too much.

Rosie met his eyes. 'Yes,' she said. She felt almost shy. As if they were starting over. Was that even possible? With everything that had happened? Maybe. Rosie didn't know if it was the hibiscus margaritas or what, but she felt as though something might – just might – have shifted.

They both drank and chatted about the spa at the back of the bar, discussing what treatments they would have and how they might compare with some spectacular treatments they had had in Koh Samui years ago. About a couple who spent ten minutes bickering at the bar about who should cook dinner that night. For real. And they chatted about food… About Nate's natural obsession with French cuisine that came from his heritage and Rosie's late-in-life passion for sushi. Innocent, safe conversations. That felt good.

Nate wondered at Emmie. Had she thought that sending them here would reignite something? Maybe she was right, Nate thought, glancing at Rosie. She was so beautiful. How could he have forgotten how beautiful she was?

'We should go,' Rosie said, checking her phone. 'Emmie seems fine, but you know…'

'Of course.'

Nate shrugged his arms into his jacket. Then helped Rosie into hers. He caught another waft of her gorgeous perfume as she flicked her hair out from her collar. Nate wanted to kiss her. Put his arms around her. But he was afraid of her reaction. What if she pushed him away?

Rosie felt Nate pause and she almost leant against him. She wanted to feel his arm around her again. Feel him close.

The moment was broken by the bickering couple arriving at their table.

'Mind if we jump in your grave?' asked the man.

'Help yourselves,' Nate said, stepping out of the way.

'Thank you,' said the woman. 'Ooh, they had food, Tim. Perhaps we should do that and not worry about dinner later...'

'That's because you don't want to cook,' Tim huffed.

Rosie and Nate left them to it and headed to the door. They stepped outside into the sunshine and, without discussing it, started to walk back to the station. Rosie wanted to grab Nate's hand. But she couldn't. She didn't know what would happen if she did. If it was right to do it. It used to feel so natural and it made her feel sad to think that it was such an alien, uncomfortable thing between them now.

'There's a train in fifteen minutes,' Nate said, checking the app on his phone. 'We should make that easily.' He was starting to feel that lovely feeling slipping away and he hated it. He could feel Rosie tensing up beside him the further they were from the bar.

'Great,' murmured Rosie. No, she thought. *No.* It felt good back there. It felt like hope again. Like there was a chance. And now it felt as though it was fading.

Why was that, she thought in a panic? She wanted it back. As they walked along together but not together,

Rosie noticed a dirty flyer on the ground. It was for Gamblers Anonymous. Jesus. What were the odds? Suddenly, all that fury rushed back to the surface. Nate was gambling again. And Rosie wasn't sure she could forgive him for that.

Nate felt rather than saw Rosie shut down. Something shifted in her demeanour. He couldn't put his finger on it but her body language was screaming that she had disconnected. Whatever magic had been lit up in that bar in Shoreditch had been doused out by something... maybe just that she was back in the present again.

Nate felt his own black cloud descend once more. The feeling that was like dark, heavy grief. Then they passed a coffee shop. Brilliant. Jonny Barista. Seconds after Rosie, Nate also disconnected.

And that was the end of the first part of Emmie's treasure hunt.

Emmie

'What do you think?' Emmie asked worriedly.

Dr Tom frowned.

Aunt Lily frowned.

'It's not good, is it?'

Dr Tom and Aunt Lily looked at one another.

Emmie lost patience. 'Oh just say something!'

They were standing in the sunshine on the corner of Liverpool Street Station outside McDonald's. They were going to wait for a later train to make sure they weren't seen. But Emmie wanted to know what her aunt thought. And what Dr Tom thought. Because she wanted so badly for today to have been a success.

Aunt Lily rubbed her nose. 'I think it looked good when they left the bar.'

'Yes,' Dr Tom agreed.

'They looked the way they used to,' Aunt Lily mused. 'Happy, connected. Sizzling chemistry.'

'They look fantastic together,' Dr Tom said, nodding. 'They're both attractive people and they had that... "thing" when they left the bar.'

Emmie sighed. What were they warbling on about? She knew her parents looked happy when they left the bar. She didn't know what Dr Tom meant by 'that thing'. She assumed it was good, even if she didn't understand it.

But what about now? Emmie was worried about now.

She, Dr Tom and Aunt Lily had taken up position in a coffee shop opposite the bar and they had watched everything from there. Well, they had watched for a while, at any rate, and then Dr Tom and Aunt Lily had chatted about other things. Emmie couldn't take her eyes off her parents, however. Even though they were in the bar for ages. They looked happy. They were talking. They had some food. And lots of drinks. Emmie wasn't sure how many drinks, but they had definitely had a few.

'They actually had a bit of a moment before they were leaving,' Aunt Lily said. 'Did you see that, Dr Tom?'

'The bit with the jacket?' Dr Tom took his glasses off and polished them on the edge of his t-shirt. 'Yes, I did.'

Aunt Lily grinned. 'I thought he was going for it.'

'I thought *she* might.'

Lily grinned. 'I think it could have gone either way.'

'Please.' Emmie was feeling close to tears. 'I don't even understand what you mean. I don't know about "actual things" and "that thing". Did it work? Do they love each other again?'

'Oh, Em. I'm sorry.' Aunt Lily put her arm around Emmie's shoulders. 'We're not deliberately talking in riddles here. We're just talking about chemistry and stuff.'

Dr Tom looked contrite. 'Sorry, Emmie. We got a bit carried away talking about the bit in the bar there. But it was really positive.'

'And then when we got here?'

They had jumped into a taxi from the bar to beat her parents back to the station. Then they had waited out of sight by the entrance they would be walking past. Emmie had watched them earnestly. But she hadn't felt good watching them this time, though she didn't understand why.

'When we got back here, I would say that maybe something had shifted,' Lily said carefully.

'Shifted?' Emmie was beginning to feel extremely frustrated.

Dr Tom gestured to a nearby wall and they all sat down.

'OK. So this is what I think,' he started. He paused and appeared to be collecting his thoughts.

Emmie tried not to punch his arm to get him to speak quicker. But she wanted to.

'I think that in the bar, your parents re-connected. I think being in that bar again, where your dad worked and where they first met, made them recall that big moment.'

'OK…' Emmie understood that. She thought that too.

'I think they remembered. And I think they enjoyed being in that memory.' Dr Tom glanced at Emmie. 'Does that make sense? It was kind of like being away from reality.'

From me, Emmie thought to herself. I am reality. Me and my cancer are their reality. That was what they had enjoyed being away from. Not because they didn't love each other. But because her illness had torn them apart and made them hate one another.

Emmie had learnt not to voice these thoughts in front of Dr Tom any longer. He was lovely, but he would only see it as a reason to 'validate' her and make her feel that this wasn't her fault. But Emmie knew that it was. She had accepted it a long time ago.

'Yes,' she said. 'Go on.'

'So they connected. They were talking. Cautiously, but they looked happy.'

'They got some food and they had three drinks,' Aunt Lily cut in. 'Which was a really good sign. They didn't just have one drink and leave. Which they could have done,' she added.

'For sure,' Dr Tom said.

'And then…' Emmie didn't even bother to hide her impatience.

'And then something happened,' Aunt Lily said, frowning again. 'On that walk home. Something changed.'

Dr Tom placed his hands on his knees. 'It can be anything in these situations. A comment that came out the wrong way. Something that triggered thoughts of what's going on at home. Something broke the connection, that's all that happened.'

'But that's bad.' Tears sprang into Emmie's eyes. 'That's really bad.'

Aunt Lily took Emmie's hand. 'Sweetheart. Don't be downhearted! It's early days.'

'Day one of the treasure hunt,' Dr Tom chimed in. 'Your Aunt Lily is right, Emmie. Slow down. You can't expect everything to be mended in one hit. I think they have some stuff going on and it could take time to get things back on track.'

I might not have time, Emmie thought to herself desperately. That's what her Aunt Lily and Dr Tom didn't understand. They knew she could have limited time – of course they did. They knew she was sick and they knew there was no cure for what she had. But they didn't have the same sense of urgency. They couldn't have. Because it wasn't their fault that this had happened. And with the best will in the world, they couldn't possibly want her parents to get back together more than Emmie did.

Her shoulders hunched up as she tried to stop her shuddering sobs. This wasn't the way she had mapped it out in her head. This wasn't how it was meant to go. OK, so maybe she had been a bit silly expecting it to all slot into place on day one. But she had hoped for more. More of the way her parents had been at the bar in Shoreditch. Emmie couldn't understand how things could have gone so wrong between there and the train station. What was wrong with grown ups?

'Can I make a suggestion?' Aunt Lily said, twisting her mouth up as she eyed Emmie.

Emmie shrugged. She wasn't sure she wanted to hear it. She had started the day buoyantly and she now felt as though all her hopes had been completely dashed.

'Perhaps we shouldn't observe your mum and dad for the next couple of dates. It's possible that the first couple might not be that successful.'

Lily exchanged a glance with Dr Tom over the top of Emmie's head. Emmie didn't see it but she heard the apprehension in her Aunt's voice.

'I think that's a great idea,' Dr Tom said warmly. 'This has been fun in many ways, but maybe we have to let them get on with it. And trust that they will work things out for themselves. But us observing them like this... it could just be upsetting. If it doesn't work out how we hope in the exact timeframe we have in mind.'

Emmie gulped and wiped her nose on the sleeve of her cardigan. Her mum hated her doing that. 'You mean that I'll get upset,' she said astutely. 'You're worried that it will affect me and probably my health or something.'

'Smartypants,' Aunt Lily said. 'But yes. Something like that.' She squeezed Emmie's hand. 'This is a beautiful thing that you're doing here, Emmie. It really is. But your mum and dad… they're human beings. We don't know what they're going to do or how they're going to react. We want them to act a certain way, but we can't guarantee that they will. All we can do is point them down this memory lane and hope they do the work themselves.'

'And if they don't?' Emmie lifted her tear-stained face to her aunt. 'What then?'

'Then we'll come up with Plan B,' Aunt Lily said confidently. 'But we won't need to do that. Plan A will work just fine. Let's just leave them to it for this next step at least.'

'And what is the next step?' Dr Tom asked. 'I forget now.'

Dr Tom wasn't prone to being forgetful, but Emmie humoured him. She pulled a list out of her pocket. 'They went to the cinema on their second date. They watched *Love Actually*.'

'Might be a bit tricky,' Aunt Lily said thoughtfully. 'Unless we can find a cinema showing it somewhere. Or convince somewhere to do it for us.'

'Maybe we don't need to do that,' Dr Tom said, cupping his chin. 'Maybe we need to pare back this time. Go simple.'

'What do you mean?' Emmie felt a flash of excitement again. Maybe this could work after all.

'I'll tell you on the train,' Dr Tom said, standing up. 'But I think we need to take a different tack this time…'

'Sounds good to me,' Aunt Lily said. 'Come on, Emmie. Let's go home before your parents work out that you were in London today and not with Maya and George. God knows how I'll bribe them to keep their mouths shut as well…'

Emmie followed them eagerly. All wasn't lost. She could make this work. Please let me make this work, she thought to herself. One last wish. Just one. This.

Rosie and Nate

'Let's finish with the classic Pilates move, the Saw,' Rosie said to her class. 'Legs wide apart. Shoulders back. Let's get that alignment in place and our core engaged.' She demonstrated the move once slowly and deliberately.

'And so it's like this… turn, breathe out as you try to stretch your little finger across your little toe. And back to the centre with the arms wide – remember your core – breathe in to prepare and breathe out to the other side, really reaching into that stretch with the palm straight… little finger to little toe…'

Rosie completed her class, feeling the way she always did; invigorated yet relaxed. As though she had done something good for herself and for her class. She needed her Pilates classes at the moment. They kept her balanced and allowed her to think of something other than what was going on at home.

Things had been so strained since she and Nate had gone up to London together. Rosie couldn't help feeling deeply downhearted about it because it had started so well. For a few hours, they had been Rosie and Nate again. Not Rosie and Nate, the parents – and more specifically, the parents of a sick child – but just Rosie and Nate. Two individuals and also a couple, who were neither affected nor defined by what had happened to them.

Rosie collected up her things and hoisted her bag onto her shoulder. 'Good work, class,' she called to the few who were standing around chatting. 'See you next week.' Remembering that her car was at the garage having its suspension looked at, Rosie realised she had a long walk home. In the late afternoon sunshine, mind, but still. A friend from the gym had given her a lift in, but she hadn't arranged one home. She would call Lily but she had had her two and Emmie this afternoon for a sleepover playdate. The walk could do her good, in any case. Some fresh air and some space.

Thank God for Lily, Rosie thought. She had always been supportive, but recently, she had been truly fantastic at taking Emmie for a few hours here and there, giving Rosie a break. Rosie hated admitted that she needed a break, but sometimes she did. Not because of Emmie – she wasn't undergoing treatment right now and seemed in good health – but because of the terrible state she and Nate were in. Lately, Rosie simply felt the need for some space. And especially since the trip to London two weeks ago.

Of course she would spend all night annoying the hell out of Lily by phoning every few hours to check on Emmie. And phoning Emmie a few times. Old habits died hard, as the saying went. Even when Emmie seemed healthy and strong, Rosie didn't stop worrying about her.

'Are you OK?'

Rosie started. Amy, the receptionist, was talking to her. 'Oh yes. Thank you. I'm fine. All the better after my class! Are you OK?'

Amy nodded. 'Me? I'm fine. All good.' She hesitated. 'Are you sure you're OK, Rosie? You look… upset.'

'Do I?' Rosie swallowed. She had thought she was hiding it quite well. The thing was, it was sweet of Amy to ask, but Rosie didn't want to go into how anxious and upset she felt inside. 'I'm just tired,' she assured Amy brightly. 'Need some sleep!'

Rosie pasted on the smile she used when she needed to reassure kindly, well-meant people that she was surviving and not falling apart. Rosie had always told herself never to tire of people checking in on her. They only did it because they cared and she was grateful for that.

Stepping outside into the sunshine, Rosie thought about Nate. She had felt such a connection with him that day in London. Being in that bar… it had felt good between them again. That lovely, connected, sexy, heady vibe came back. All too briefly, but it had jolted Rosie because that time in the bar had proved that it was still there. That bar in Shoreditch had brought back so many memories. Rosie remembered the idiotic smile she had felt spreading across her face as she had recalled meeting Nate for the first time. And sitting with him, drinking cocktails, eating snacks and people-watching that day… it had been so perfect for a while.

And then that dreadful walk home. Rosie grimaced. It had felt as though every single step they had taken, had taken them away from the magic of the bar. Back to reality. Seeing the Gamblers Anonymous flyer on the ground had been the final straw. Rosie had no idea what had caused Nate to shut down, but she had felt him do it. And it had hurt. After such a lovely interlude, it had hurt.

Rosie's phone buzzed. She took it out and glanced at it. It was a text from Emmie. There was a photo attached to it. Rosie opened it and read it. It said:

'Treasure Hunt – Part Two. You are cordially invited to Movie Night. Please go home and look for further instructions.'

Rosie's heart sank a little. She had thought Emmie had given up on this 'Treasure Hunt' idea. She must have seen how tense things were between her parents since the trip to London. Why on earth would she carry on flogging a dead horse? And how was it even a treasure hunt anyway, Rosie thought to herself? What bloody treasure was there to find?

Rosie let out a heavy sigh as she pocketed her phone and strolled home. Poor Emmie. She had tried to do a lovely thing by sending her and Nate into London like that. Perhaps she had hoped they would rekindle something. Remember the good old days. They had, of course, but the walk home… the train ride home… it had all proved that even if there was still chemistry there, it wasn't sustainable. Whatever Nate and Rosie had once had – they had lost it. They had been through too much.

Rosie felt tears springing into her eyes and she was furious with herself. She couldn't seem to stop crying lately. She had cried copious amounts over Emmie since her diagnosis, but Rosie recognised this as a very different kind of grief. She was grieving for herself and Nate. For what seemed to have died. And she had cried more in the fortnight since the afternoon in London than she had in a long time.

Rosie wandered through the high street, not even noticing people or shops or noise. She knew she was heading in the right direction, but she wasn't remotely interested in the journey. Which was why, when she felt a warm hand on her bare arm, she nearly leapt out of her skin.

'Whoah, steady on there!'

Rosie turned and found herself coming face to face with Jonny, the barista.

'Are you OK?' Jonny looked concerned.

Rosie swallowed. Jonny still had his hand on her arm. She realised she was outside the coffee shop she and Lily always went to. Not because she had any intent on bumping into Jonny, but because it was on her way home. There were people sitting at the chairs and tables outside, drinking coffee, munching on muffins, chatting. They all suddenly swam into view as Rosie collected herself and focused on what was going on around her.

'You're not alright, are you?' Jonny removed his hand and put his fingers under her chin instead. He tipped her face upwards. 'You're sobbing your heart out.'

Rosie's lip trembled. 'Don't,' she whispered. 'Don't be nice. I – I can't take it.'

Jonny led her to a sunny table at the edge of the outside area. 'Sit here,' he said gently. 'I'll get you a coffee.'

Rosie slumped down into the chair and let her gym bag slip off her shoulder. She felt a wave of despair. What was she doing allowing Jonny Barista to get her a coffee? She had kissed this man – this boy – and here she was, taking a seat where he worked and allowing him to fetch her a drink.

Rosie put her elbows on the table and her face in her hands. Was she trying to avoid going home? Was she dreading what clues Emmie might have left; what her expectations were for this silly treasure hunt? Rosie wasn't sure what she felt or what she was doing. Maybe it was just because Jonny was being so sweet.

He returned swiftly, carrying two cups of coffee and some pastries. He placed them on the table and sat down opposite her. He'd taken his apron off and if Rosie wasn't mistaken, he had brushed his unruly hair into place.

'So what's going on?' Jonny asked. 'I'm on a break, so I can talk. Please talk to me,' he said, meeting her eyes.

Rosie sipped her coffee. She wasn't sure what to say. How could she tell Jonny that she was heartbroken because her marriage was most likely over? Or how guilty she felt that Emmie had tried to get her parents back on track and they had royally messed it up? How on earth could Rosie explain to a young boy with little life experience that she was just so incredibly tired? Of what they had been through with Emmie. Of the way things were disintegrating irretrievably between herself and Nate.

'It's not your little girl, is it?' Jonny asked kindly. 'She's OK, I hope?'

Rosie rubbed her eyes. 'Emmie's fine,' she said. 'It's… I'm just…'

'Feeling a bit low?' Jonny leant forward. 'I get that. You're having a tough time.'

Rosie gave him a watery smile. He was a nice kid. Very caring. He meant well. Rosie blushed, remembering their drunken kiss. But looking at him in the cold light of day, she felt very clear. Jonny wasn't Nate. He had just been in the right – or wrong, depending on how you looked at it – place at the right/wrong time. She had been vulnerable and Jonny had been there. But he wasn't Nate. He wasn't significant in Rosie's life. All that really mattered was Nate and their marriage, but Rosie didn't have a clue how to claw it back.

'I sent you a message,' Jonny was saying.

Rosie glanced at him. 'I'm married,' she said.

'I know that.' He looked away and frowned. 'I mean, sorry. Did I get you into trouble?'

'It's not that. I just mean that I'm married. And even though I'm… even though things are…' Rosie stopped, not even sure how to describe what was going on. 'It's not right,' she added. 'You and me. It's not a thing. It's not going anywhere. I can't see you again.'

Jonny nodded slowly. 'I guessed as much. When I didn't hear back from you. And you've obviously been avoiding coming here as well.'

'I haven't, I've just been…' Rosie's voice tailed away. She probably had been avoiding the coffee shop. She hadn't wanted to encourage Jonny. Hadn't wanted him to think there was more to the drunken kiss than there had been. It had been a mistake. A silly moment. Never to be repeated.

'It's OK,' Jonny told her. He reached out and put his hand over hers. 'I know you're having a tough time. I wasn't trying to take advantage of you, I promise. I just… I just like you, I guess.'

Rosie shook her head, smiling sadly. She believed him. And in different circumstances, she was sure she would be flattered. But she was – very unfortunately, considering the fact that Nate no longer seemed to feel the same – in love with her husband. Even if Nate had fallen out of love with her, Rosie still loved him. She hated him for the gambling, but she did still love him. The afternoon in London had proved that.

Not that such a fact could save them, Rosie thought desperately. It was too late for that. With this realisation, she burst into noisy sobs. She didn't even notice when Jonny Barista got up from his chair and came around the table to hug her. Rosie welcomed the contact, but in that moment, she didn't care who was giving her sympathy. She just badly needed a hug.

-

Pausing at the traffic lights outside the coffee shop having stopped by the gym to pick up her so they could go home together and see what Emmie had planned for them, Nate couldn't believe his eyes. There was Rosie. She was cuddling the kid from the coffee shop. The kid she had kissed some weeks back. In the street in front of everyone. What the hell?

Receiving a *bib* from the car behind him to get a move on, Nate pulled away and felt his insides burst into flames. That was it. He was done. Done trying to make things work with Rosie. After the day in London, he had felt guilty. Guilty because they had let Emmie down. Guilty because he had allowed what he hoped was a silly indiscretion that Rosie had had to ruin the fantastic vibe they had re-kindled between them that day. He had received a text from Emmie inviting them to some movie night thing she had planned and Nate had come to collect his wife from work, knowing that her car was in the garage. And now look. Rosie was back at the coffee shop, no doubt deliberately stopping by to see someone she had kissed.

How long had it been going on? Nate tightened his grip on the steering wheel as he continued towards home.

Was it more than a kiss? Christ. Was it a full-blown affair? He had been ready to forgive Rosie. To blame it on the stress of what was going on with Emmie and because their marriage was shot to pieces. But an affair? Canoodling in the street? No fucking way.

Nate pulled up outside his house. He thought for a second. He felt bad for Emmie because she clearly had something important planned for tonight. Nate hadn't particularly pondered Emmie's cryptic clue but whatever it was, it was going to have to wait. Because Nate had been prepared to give Rosie another chance. Until he had driven past and seen some bloody kid draped all over her in the high street.

No. Enough. He and Rosie were done. Nate couldn't do this anymore. Rosie could do what the hell she liked, but as far as he was concerned, there was a casino with his name written all over it. And the fact that he would rather spend the night talking to a croupier he hadn't even clapped eyes on before than his own wife told Nate everything he needed to know.

Sorry, Emmie, he thought. Sorry, sweetheart. It's too late for us.

With a heart full of dark, heavy regret, Nate drove off, with self-destruction as the main header on his to do list.

–

Rosie tiredly put her key in the door and let herself in. She hadn't stayed much longer at the coffee house. Enough to make absolutely sure Jonny Barista understood that she wasn't available or interested, but that was it. She had left him to go back to work and she had headed home.

'Nate,' she called as she went from room to room. But he wasn't there. The house was quiet and still. Rosie hated it when the house felt like this. It always sent her mind spiralling because she imagined that this was how the house would feel if Emmie was no longer with them.

Her heart contracted painfully. Why did she do that to herself? There was no point in thinking that way, but for some reason those thoughts would burst into Rosie's head unexpectedly and they would often linger. Thoughts of the horror of receiving even worse news (if such a thing existed), thoughts of Emmie dying. Her funeral. How empty the house would feel without her. It was hideous, but not something she could avoid. Rosie wouldn't dream of discussing such things with Nate. Imagine how sick and twisted she would sound, contemplating things that neither of them wanted to even think of. No, all of that stuff was best kept to herself.

Rosie frowned. Surely Nate had received the same invitation from Emmie? She called his mobile a few times but it went straight to voicemail. She called Lily and checked on Emmie. Emmie wanted to chat.

'Hey, mum.'

'Hey, sweetheart.' Rosie smiled. She loved hearing Emmie's voice on the phone. It sounded so innocent and sweet, despite her having recently turned eleven.

'Did you get my invitation?'

Emmie sounded excited.

'Yes, yes. I've just got home.' Rosie looked around. Had she missed a clue? 'I'm not sure what to do next.'

'There's a clue by the kettle,' Emmie said. She sounded a bit disappointed. 'I thought that would be the first place you would go when you got in.'

'Top work!' Rosie said, heading to the kitchen. 'It normally is. I… went to the loo and got distracted.'

'What about dad?'

'He's…' Rosie hesitated. 'He's delayed at work. He'll be here shortly.'

'Oh really?' Emmie sounded confused. 'He called to say he was going to collect you from the gym.'

'Did he?' Rosie started to open the envelope. 'How strange. I must have missed him.'

'OK. I need to go. Have fun!' Emmie signed off.

Lily came on the phone. 'Where's Nate?'

'Not a clue,' Rosie said. 'I didn't see him at the gym.'

'Weird. OK, well, hopefully he'll turn up soon. I'll leave you to it.' Lily paused as if she was going to say something, but she clearly thought better of it. 'Speak soon, Rosie.'

Rosie put her phone down and opened the envelope. It contained a clue which led her to the lounge. Thinking she should maybe carry on so that when Nate arrived, she would have set everything up, Rosie went ahead. She went around the house following the cute little clues Emmie had left, only to find herself back in the lounge. She found a note on the DVD player that said 'Play Me' along with a whole tray full of cinema-style snacks and soft drinks.

Rosie smiled. This was adorable. Emmie had gone to so much trouble. If only Nate were here. She decided to wait for him for a while, so she watched something on TV and flicked through a magazine for a while. She called Nate's phone a few more times but didn't leave any messages. Finally, out of curiosity, Rosie played the DVD.

'Oh, Emmie.' Rosie put her hand over her mouth. It was *Love Actually*. The film Nate had taken her to see on their second date. The penny suddenly dropped. Emmie was recreating their dates. She had somehow found out how her parents had met and she had put them in the same bar. Tonight, she had reconstructed the cinema night Rosie and Nate had enjoyed, watching a Richard Curtis film that had resulted in some serious cuddling in the cinema, a knee-trembling kiss outside and some extremely inappropriate behaviour in Nate's car. Rosie still blushed when she thought of that – it wasn't her usual style, but the chemistry between her and Nate had been absolutely electric back then.

And for most of their marriage, Rosie acknowledged achingly. She had been told by so many other couples that she and Nate had something everyone wanted... that special something, that heat, that intensity. They had always fancied the pants off of one another, as well as being deeply in love. And Rosie hadn't ever taken it for granted. It was only when she realised that the incredible thing between them seemed to have died that she realised how much she had loved and cherished it.

With an effort, Rosie returned her mind to what Emmie had put together for tonight. And she might not know it, but that second date had, in Rosie's head, secured Nate's place in her heart. Not because of the heat between them in the car. Or because it had heralded the promise of another exciting date. No. What had done it for Rosie had been the way Nate had cheered in the right places during the film, but mostly the fact that he had wept like a girl (his words) throughout the latter part. He had tried hard not to, but he had been teary at the part where

Andrew Lincoln awkwardly confronts his love for his best mate's girlfriend Keira Knightley. He had ended up with tears streaming down his face when Emma Thompson had cried on the bed to Joni Mitchell when she realised her husband had bought the necklace for someone else. And as for the part where Laura Linney had put her brother before the very gorgeous love of her life, Karl... well. Nate had been a snivelling, snotty mess, apologising profusely, accepting a handful of tissues from Rosie as he noisily blew his nose into them.

And Rosie had fallen head over heels in love with him in that moment. With this sexy, headstrong, confident alpha male who had just been reduced to tears by a truly slushy, romantic film that had shamelessly tugged at his heartstrings. It had been a defining moment for Rosie – a second date, no less, though she had spent the next three or four dates playing it ridiculously cool and hadn't let on for a second that her mind had been made up weeks previously. Emmie might not have known all that critical detail, but Rosie thought it was extremely sweet that she was trying to get them to re-live those early days.

Rosie checked her watch. Nate was hideously late. God only knew where he had got to. But Rosie had a real urge to watch the film. She watched it every Christmas when she wrapped presents and drank Baileys, but it had become part of her routine. This time would be different. This time she would watch it and remember that second date.

Rosie made a decision. She wouldn't touch the cinema snacks because she'd eaten earlier and she wasn't really hungry, but she would watch a bit of the film. She could always quickly switch it off when Nate turned up and they could watch it from the beginning again.

A few hours later, Rosie woke up. She had watched the film and she must have fallen asleep on the sofa afterwards. The house was still quiet. Unless Nate had crept upstairs to bed?

Rosie left the film and the snacks on the coffee table in the lounge and headed upstairs to bed. She did what she always did if Emmie was absent; she went into her room and hugged her pillow for a second. She inhaled the scent of her then put the pillow back.

Thank god Emmie wasn't losing her hair anymore. It had been awful finding Emmie's hair everywhere. Not just on her pillow, but all over the house. Rosie felt as though she had spent roughly two years on and off hoovering non-stop. Hoovering up hair that seemed to shed on every conceivable surface and cleaning, spraying antiseptic spray on all the work tops and floors. Wiping everything down with antibacterial wipes because of Emmie's low blood cell count. Rosie had been on high alert with regard to germs. Like some kind of neat freak sergeant major on acid.

Rosie sat down on Emmie's bed. Her daughter was amazing. She had been through so much. And now she seemed hell-bent on doing something for her parents. Rosie's breath caught in her throat. How lucky she and Nate were to have Emmie. It hadn't been easy since her diagnosis and it was like living on a knife edge now that she had decided to refuse treatment. But what a fantastic kid she was! Selfless. Beautiful. Caring.

Rosie returned to the bedroom she shared with Nate. What a shame he hadn't made it home yet. Because however bad things had been since the afternoon in London, Rosie was sure that Nate might have melted a bit at what Emmie had done. Their daughter was amazing. She obviously wanted her parents to remember how they used to feel. On a whim, Rosie nipped back downstairs again. OK, so she wasn't over the moon about Nate's gambling. She hoped it was a one-off, maybe, and not something he was planning to repeat. But Rosie wanted him to know what Emmie had done and how it had made her feel. What she had remembered about their second date.

Grabbing a piece of paper, Rosie scribbled on it *Date No. 2. All those tears. This is when I fell bonkers in love with you.* She hesitated then added *No one kisses the way you do x.* Leaving the note under the DVD box, Rosie hurried upstairs to bed before she could change her mind and put the note in the bin. She had no idea if they could recapture any of what they had had before. She just knew that for some reason, what she had just written… she needed to write it.

–

Nate moodily contemplated his drink. He knew he should go home, but he wasn't ready yet.

'So. Have I convinced you yet?'

Nate turned to Gill. 'I don't know. I heard what you said about the coffee kid. And maybe you're right. But they were hugging. In the bloody street.'

Gill sighed. 'And I think he was being a mate. Placating her. Sympathising. I do not believe that Rosie is having an affair with some silly boy from a coffee shop.'

But instead of heading to the nearest casino, he had called Gill. And she had left Sexy Kev eating a vast Chinese take-away to come out to meet Nate in the pub around the corner from her house. Nate had never appreciated his partner more than he did tonight.

'I don't believe it, Nate,' Gill repeated.

'Can you believe she kissed him? Because she did. She fucking kissed him.'

'If she did, she was drunk,' Gill said reasonably. 'And she didn't mean to.' She put a hand on Nate's arm. 'Nate. I know you're not egotistical. I know this isn't about your hurt pride. It's because you love Rosie so much. Yes?'

Nate's mouth twisted painfully at Gill's words, but she was right. No, he hadn't ever expected this to happen. Not to them. Not to him and Rosie. Because – and perhaps he was being egotistical here – they were stupidly in love. They had that layered thing that ranged from pure, erotic sexual chemistry right through to the basic kind of love that incorporated hair-holding during vomiting, worrying about whether or not that person had put their seat belt on when they went to work that day and cooking dinner when shattered to the point of exhaustion just because the other person had had a shit day.

But more importantly, what was killing Nate was that he hated that he and Rosie had ended up here. In a situation where even though Rosie might have been drunk and vulnerable, she had crossed a line Nate had never once contemplated crossing himself. But maybe he could forgive her. If it was just that. A stupid kiss when her defences were down. But a full-blown affair? No way.

'Nate, listen.' Gill leant forward. 'You did well not to gamble tonight. I know you were close. But you should be at home. Emmie obviously had something planned for you two. And I know it was bad timing driving past the coffee shop like that.' She sighed. 'But this is Rosie. You love her. And you both love Emmie. Things have been terrible between you for so long now. This has to stop. You both have to stop.'

Nate nodded. He knew Gill was right. He and Rosie had to sort this out somehow. Find some way of getting along again.

Gill started to put her jacket on. 'And forgive me for this, Nate. But you owe it to Emmie. You owe it to her to at very least try. She's trying to help you. She wants her parents to be happy.'

Nate put his jacket on as well. He had no idea if he and Rosie could get things back on track. He didn't know if they could find their way back after everything they had been through. But that wasn't going to happen if he gambled himself stupid, or if he sat in the pub drinking the night away.

'Gill, you're a superstar.' He dropped a kiss on Gill's head. 'What would I do without you?'

'End up in a gutter, penniless and maudlin,' she replied caustically. 'Only joking. You'll be fine. Just… go home.'

'Apologise to Sexy Kev for me.'

'I always do,' Gill grinned. 'Get outta here, Johnson. I'll see you tomorrow at work.'

'OK. And thank you,' Nate said. 'You really are the best.'

'Oh do stop it. I'll start thinking you have the hots for me.' Gill waved him away. 'Be gone.'

Nate hailed a taxi. He'd have to pick his car up tomorrow but he'd had too much to drink to be able to drive home tonight. The house was in darkness when he arrived. Apart from the lamp in the lounge, which he assumed Rosie must have left on.

When he went in to turn it off, he found the coffee table littered with coloured rectangles of paper. They were covered in Emmie's handwriting and Nate worked out that Rosie had left them in the order she had found them so he could see how Emmie had sent her all over the house. The thought of Emmie planning this made him smile.

Nate picked up the DVD box. *Love Actually*. He shook his head. His and Rosie's second date had been to see this film. He blinked. Emmie was trying to get them back together. The 'treasure hunt' was about them. The 'treasure' was their relationship.

Nate sat down on the sofa with a heavy thud. The little monkey. But what a fabulous kid she was. He put the DVD box on the table and realised that there was another piece of paper there. One in Rosie's handwriting. He read it and felt an actual jolt in his heart. He didn't think he had ever needed to hear – or rather, read – something as much as he had needed that.

Maybe Gill was right. Maybe the thing between Rosie and the coffee boy was nothing. Maybe it didn't matter. The problem was, Nate didn't know if it was too late for him and Rosie. He had no idea. They had been through so much pain and they had lost their way completely. He wanted so much to believe that there was a way back. But there might not be.

Nate wished he hadn't seen Rosie at the coffee shop. He wished he'd picked her up at the gym and that they'd come home together and watched the film. But Nate wished for many things that seemed to be slipping through his fingers. He had to try harder to hold onto the things that mattered to him. He had to find a way.

Nate put the DVD on. He loved this film. And he had loved watching it for the first time with Rosie. So he watched and he remembered and he sobbed like a complete idiot throughout the entire film.

Emmie

'Hey, why are you looking so upset?' Cara caught up with Emmie in the hallway at school.

Emmie shrugged. 'Just this thing with my mum and dad.'

Cara slipped her arm through Emmie's. 'OK. Let's go and find somewhere to have lunch and we can talk about it.'

They found a table in the corner of the main school hall away from the chatter and got their lunch things out. Emmie left hers unwrapped on the table. She was too miserable to eat right now.

'I'm starving,' Cara said, tearing the clingfilm off her roll. 'I've had double P.E.' She munched for a second, then paused for air. 'OK, shoot. What's the latest?'

Emmie fiddled with her packet of sandwiches. 'So you know I organised that movie night for my parents?'

Cara nodded.

'It went really badly.'

'What, worse than the thing in London?' Cara was fully up to date on that one.

Emmie nodded glumly. 'Far worse.'

'Oh no! You need to eat something,' Cara said, gesturing to Emmie's lunch. 'You know your mum goes nuts if you don't eat properly.'

Emmie half-heartedly opened her sandwiches. Cara was right; her mum did go crazy if she didn't eat properly. And she followed this whole 'anti-cancer' diet thing to the letter. Emmie ate an awful lot of fruit and veggies. Way more than any of her friends. And most of the time, she was happy to do so. But today, she felt sick with worry.

'So what happened with movie night?' Cara prompted. She unwrapped Emmie's sandwich for her and handed it over.

'My dad didn't turn up.'

Cara looked shocked. 'But... you sent him an invitation on his phone, didn't you?'

'Yes. He definitely received it. He went to pick mum up from work but missed her and then he went off somewhere else.'

'Where did he go?'

Emmie ate some of her sandwich. It was no good; she felt as if she had sawdust in her mouth.

'I don't know.' She pushed her food away miserably. 'Maybe to a casino.'

Cara looked unconvinced. 'No. I don't reckon he did that. Maybe he went to see a friend or something?' She opened a bag of crisps and made her way through those.

'He was gone for hours apparently.'

'How do you know all this?'

'My mum told my aunt and she passed the info on. My mum watched the DVD on her own and felt all warm and fuzzy. I think she left my dad a note and he came in later. I don't know if he watched the film though.'

Cara finished her lunch and put everything away. 'You'd better bin that if you don't want your mum to have a go at you.'

'I'll do it later.' Emmie gathered it all up. Maybe she would get her appetite back in a while.

'Have you spoken to Dr Tom about it?'

'I'm seeing him next week.' Emmie got up. 'But maybe I should just give up on this whole thing with my parents.'

Cara grabbed her arm. 'Stop. Why would you want to give up?'

Emmie hung her head. 'Because it's not working. I don't think they want to patch things up. I think they're over. And nothing I can do is going to fix them.'

'You can't say that!' Cara hurried to catch up with Emmie. 'Just because it hasn't worked yet, you can't throw the towel in so soon. We have a whole plan mapped out. We've worked so hard on it.'

Emmie continued to stride through the school at high speed. She was pretty sure she had P.E. next, so she was heading to the changing rooms. 'I know that, Cara. But what's the point? Like I say, they don't want it to work. They got on fine in London and then by the time they left that bar, they looked as though they wanted to kill one another again. And last night was a total flop. My dad didn't even bother to turn up. Does that sound like a success? No. That's two fails.'

'Wait.' Cara yanked Emmie's arm. 'Listen. Listen to me!'

Emmie looked at her, surprised. Cara was extremely chilled most of the time. She was almost shouting, which was very out of character. People were staring.

'OK, OK. There's no need to shout at me. Take a chill pill.'

'Don't tell me to take a chill pill!' Cara looked angry. 'Look, one of the great things about you is that you're tough. Tougher than anyone I know. You never whine about what's happening to you and you never give up. Never.'

'Actually I do.' Emmie was feeling rage stirring inside her as well. She stormed into the girls' changing rooms. 'I *do* give up! I gave up on my cancer treatment.'

'Yes, because it wasn't working!'

'Exactly!' Emmie was shouting now and she could feel her cheeks flushing. 'It wasn't working, Cara. And neither is this. That's why I want to leave it now.'

Cara looked upset. 'You stopped your treatment because it was making you feel bad and because it wasn't making any difference to the cancer. You don't know that this treasure hunt thing isn't working, Em. All we know is that the first couple of dates didn't go as we'd planned.'

Emmie felt like bursting into tears. Or hitting something. Not Cara, just… something. She felt so wound up but she slumped down onto a nearby bench. No one understood. Not her Aunt Lily, not Cara – not even Dr Tom. Emmie put a hand on the side of her head, not because it hurt, but because it was where she felt all her angst. She didn't know how much time she had left. If she had five years, fair enough. But what if she had five months… or worse still, five weeks? There simply wasn't enough time for this not to work. And Emmie couldn't bear the thought of spending the rest of her life – however long it might last – with her parents at each other's throats.

Emmie leant over and put her hands over her face. She was fine about dying. She knew she was going to at some point and she knew her odds of lasting more than a few years were slim. But she wasn't fine about dying when she had destroyed her parents' marriage. Because that wasn't what she wanted to leave behind. Emmie felt so horribly guilty about her mum and dad.

'Oh, Em.' Cara sounded close to tears. 'I don't know what to say to you. Or what to do. But I hate seeing you like this. Please.'

The bell rang to signal that lunch was over and both of them jumped at the shrill sound it made.

Emmie sat up jerkily and took a breath. 'Sorry, Cara. Sorry.'

She tried hard to get control of herself. This is what she struggled with. Not in the early days of her diagnosis, because she had been too young. And for much of her treatment, she had just got on with it, not knowing any different. It was only when Emmie got older that the words 'brave' and 'tough' were bandied about. She understood that such words were said in admiration, but Emmie felt under pressure to be strong all the time. That being anything less than that would cause harm in some way. Emmie felt that not being brave would be seen as weak. That moaning about her situation, not believing she would get well again, giving up – these things would be seen as failure. And Emmie didn't want to let anyone down.

Emmie felt exhausted with it all sometimes. Because no one liked seeing her fall apart. Everyone loved her strength… being tough, as Cara called it. But Emmie couldn't always be tough. She was just a girl. She was eleven. Sometimes she just wanted to curl up and cry her eyes out. But everyone hated seeing her that way. No one seemed to be able to cope when she broke down. The only person who seemed OK with it was Dr Tom.

Emmie wished she could talk to Dr Tom right now. Cara was her best friend and she loved her, but Dr Tom was so calm and, what was the word? Unflappable? That. Calm. Reassuring. Nothing Emmie did was unacceptable or out of bounds. Emmie suspected that even if she told Dr Tom she was scared of dying or that she wished she would die sooner, he wouldn't react badly.

Emmie picked up her P.E. bag. She rarely wanted to be excused from a lesson, but she wouldn't mind going home right now. She just didn't feel up to it.

'Why don't we just see if we can get your parents on the next date?' Cara said, wiping her eyes. She took a seat next to Emmie. 'The zoo one? If your dad ducks out or it all goes tits up, then fine. We ditch this idea and we… and we think of something else. Plan B.'

Why did everyone keep talking about a Plan B? Emmie put her bag down and pushed her hair out of her eyes. She didn't have a Plan B. This was it. This was Plan A, B, C and Z. She didn't have anything else. If this didn't work, Emmie was fairly certain she wouldn't be able to come up with anything better.

Cara sniffed. 'The zoo date was a good one, remember? Your Aunt Lily said they talked about having you. Maybe that will bring them closer together, the memory of that.'

'See, that's what I'm worried about, Cara. What if it doesn't.'

'Doesn't what?'

The changing room was starting to fill up.

'Bring them closer together.' Emmie bit her lip. 'I think it might do the opposite.'

'I don't get that.' Cara's brow knitted together. 'I mean, I know we can't predict what they're going to do, but they love you. I don't see how this could make them feel bad.'

Emmie suppressed an aggravated sigh. This was what she found so hard at times, that people close to her were so relentlessly positive. She was a positive person herself, but Emmie had learnt to be realistic too. She had to be. She had grown-up things to accept, like life not lasting forever. Or that life – for her – genuinely was going to be short.

Why didn't anyone understand that from what Emmie could see, everything had been fine until she had come along? Well, not her, but her illness. That was what had made things so hard for her parents. That was what had caused all the pain and tension.

'OK,' she said finally. Everyone was getting changed around her. Emmie needed to decide if she wanted to do the lesson or not. She hardly ever dropped out of a class (everyone always got so worried about her, it wasn't worth it), but she really didn't know if she felt up to doing P.E. today.

'OK, what?' Cara gave Emmie a hopeful glance.

'OK, let's do the zoo thing. I'll speak to Dr Tom and he can help me set it up. Maybe the zoo and the dinner together. Or just the zoo. Whatever.'

Cara grinned. 'Yay. That's great. I just don't think we should give up yet, OK?' She gave Emmie a hug. 'I'll do whatever I can to help you, I promise.'

'Thanks.' Emmie nodded. 'I'll be OK. Go to your lesson, you'll be late.'

'Speak later,' Cara said, realising she was already was.

Emmie took a deep breath. And started to get changed. She didn't want to draw attention to herself. She didn't want her parents to worry. She was shattered, but it was only netball. She wouldn't push herself too much and then no one would be asking her questions and getting anxious. She wouldn't be sent to hospital to have her bloods checked. Because she didn't need anything checked. Emmie felt fine; this was about her parents. She would call Dr Tom when she got out of school and she would get the zoo date organised. And if that didn't work, Emmie didn't know what on earth to do next.

Rosie and Nate

Rosie looked at herself in the mirror. She looked OK. She was wearing a cream silk shirt she thought Nate would like with dark jeans, brown wedge-heeled sandals and a brown leather jacket. She might be a bit warm, but she didn't care. She wanted to feel good today.

'Are you ready?' Nate called up the stairs.

'Nearly,' Rosie called back.

She felt embarrassed about leaving that soppy note for Nate on *Love Actually* night. It had felt right at the time, but now Rosie felt foolish. Nate hadn't said a word about it. She had thought he was going to when he came in from dinner a few nights ago; there was a look in his eyes she couldn't read, but even if he had been about to mention the silly note, he had thought better of it. Rosie couldn't decide if she was relieved or upset about that.

'Should we take some food with us?' she called down the stairs.

'Nah. I'm full from brunch,' Nate called back. 'We'll grab something in London.'

Rosie wouldn't call bacon sandwiches brunch, but if Nate was happy with that, great. They had actually eaten them separately as Nate had eaten his before dropping Emmie off and Rosie had munched on hers as she got ready. She picked up the clue Emmie had left them before heading off to see Dr Tom. It was a picture of Noah's Ark which had been superimposed onto a photo of London. It had made Rosie smile. Even if she hadn't known that Emmie had recreated date three, she would have guessed that she meant London Zoo.

Rosie grabbed her handbag and checked herself in the mirror one last time. She wasn't sure how she felt about going to London Zoo with Nate. Things didn't seem quite as tense between them as they had been, she supposed. Which was strange because obviously the movie night had been a total flop. Rosie still had no idea where Nate had gone that night or why he had taken off the way he had. All she knew was that he had deliberately chosen to stay away. But somehow things seemed to have shifted. Just a fraction and it was almost imperceptible, but Rosie had sensed it.

Was it because he hadn't turned up? Because he had chosen not to connect with her over something romantic and intimate that Rosie knew would have helped click a few things back into place, perhaps. And she felt sad about it, sadder than she had felt before they had started this whole treasure hunt thing. Because beforehand, everything had been guesswork. Missing the film felt deliberate. Rosie didn't know for sure, but it felt deliberate and that made her feel confused and hurt. Why would Nate do that?

She headed downstairs. At least Emmie was in safe hands today. And if anything should happen, she was exactly where she needed to be, so Rosie knew she would feel more chilled out today. Lily was a fantastic carer, but in a worst case scenario, there was nowhere better than the hospital for Emmie.

'You look lovely,' Nate said as he watched her walk down the stairs. He meant it. Rosie looked amazing. Quite like her old self. She had colour in her cheeks and she looked fairly relaxed. Maybe a little wary. But Nate understood that. Rosie always worried about Emmie when she was due to spend time away from her but aside from that, Rosie had no idea why he hadn't turned up to watch the film with her the other week.

Nate wondered how to broach that subject. He wanted to tell Rosie what had happened, but he might have to own up to the whole gambling thing then as well and he wasn't sure Rosie deserved that. Or could handle it on top of everything else. And he wanted to mention that note she had left him. Nate's hand closed around it. He had carried it in his pocket ever since.

'So Emmie is with Dr Tom all day?' he asked, as he gathered up his keys and wallet.

'Yes. She has some big assessment, apparently.'

'Wonder what that's all about.' Nate gestured to the door and they left the house together. 'But I guess it means that she's in the right place. I mean if...'

Rosie gave him a half-smile. 'I know. I thought the same thing. Silly, isn't it? She's been fine for such a long time but still...'

'Yes.' Nate nodded. He didn't need to say any more. He and Rosie both understood this aspect of Emmie's condition in a way that no one else could.

Nate relaxed. Rosie seemed more like her old self and that made him feel at ease too. He'd had a huge pep talk from Gill last night who was absolutely convinced that apart from a silly kiss, Rosie wouldn't dream of having an affair. Nate wasn't sure what to believe yet, but he was doing his best to feel positive.

'So, the zoo,' Rosie said as they climbed on the train. Weirdly, the journey to the station seemed to have gone quickly this time. Last time, when they had gone to Shoreditch, every aspect of the journey had grated on her nerves and it had felt like it had lasted an eternity. This time, things seemed to be flowing more. Even the train was perfectly on time.

'The zoo,' Nate said. He sat opposite Rosie, but this time, felt no need to stare at a newspaper. 'We haven't actually been there since that day.'

'I know. How weird is that? We had such a lovely time.'

'We did.'

Nate smiled. He had already been in love with Rosie by the time they had visited the zoo. He had only been in love with one girl before Rosie had burst into his life, but it had taken him a few months to have any serious feelings towards her. Not that it particularly mattered, of course. Gill said it had taken her around six months to even find Sexy Kev fanciable. In fact, she hadn't even liked him for a while. Said he wasn't her cup of tea. Then somehow, he had turned it around and now, as Nate well knew, Gill wouldn't dream of looking at anyone else. So it wasn't the timing that mattered. But Nate couldn't help it; he had always thought that the passion and intense love he had felt for Rosie so early on was a sign that they had found something special.

'Emmie just messaged,' Rosie said, looking at her phone. 'I think she's worried about us.'

Nate sat back and stole a surreptitious glance at Rosie as she and Emmie messaged back and forth. The thought of Emmie worrying about them distressed him greatly. The kid had enough to think about; she didn't need to be stressing about her parents. And that was why Nate was going to make sure he did whatever Emmie asked them to do from now on. He had made a huge effort at home to be more relaxed and approachable, because he felt so incredibly guilty about missing movie night. Especially when he could see that Rosie had turned up and carried on with the night that Emmie had planned.

No more letting anyone down, Nate told himself firmly. This was about Emmie. Even if he and Rosie could be friends and could get along in that way, it would be better for Emmie. Nate wasn't sure about anything else – too much water under the bridge perhaps. But he was prepared to do whatever it took to make Emmie happy.

'Is she OK?'

Rosie nodded. 'She said that Dr Tom is doing this big quiz with her. Sounds like it's mostly fun, but she reckons he's slipping in some "psychological stuff", as she calls it, every now and again.'

'I like Dr Tom,' Nate commented. 'Even if he does wear dodgy jeans.'

'Dodgy jeans.' Rosie grinned at him. 'You'd never wear dodgy jeans, would you?'

Nate opened his mouth then closed it again. 'Oh man! I had some jeans like that, didn't I?'

'You certainly did. When you worked at the bar and then some years later, if I'm not mistaken.'

Nate shook his head. 'Guilty as charged. Bloody hell. I must have blocked those from my mind, because they were so terrible.'

'Aah well. We've all been guilty of the odd fashion faux pas,' Rosie commented, enjoying watching Nate squirm.

'I can't remember you making any,' he said, folding his arms. 'You've always looked pretty perfect.'

'Perfect. Ha!' Rosie scoffed. 'As if.' Nate wasn't telling the truth; she had worn some shocking outfits. And they both knew that. But Rosie understood that Nate was trying to be charming. She looked out of the window, feeling herself blush slightly. When he went back to his old self, she immediately found him irresistible. It was the sullen, disconnected side of Nate that she found difficult. And that had caused the same thing to happen to her; she had disconnected.

Or had she disconnected first? Rosie had no idea, but it probably wasn't fair to blame Nate. She was sure they had both pulled back at various times; it was pointless trying to pinpoint which one of them had done it first.

They made friendly chit chat as they travelled from Liverpool Street to Moorgate and then onto Camden. They arrived at London Zoo, finding it sunny and crowded.

Everyone called it ZSL now, Rosie noted. Which stood for the Zoological Society of London, by all accounts. Rosie was still going to call it London Zoo, however, as it had been when they first visited.

'Has Emmie sent us anything about the order we're supposed to do things in?' Nate asked as they queued up and bought their tickets. 'We probably could have done this bit online. But it's quite fun being sent on a treasure hunt, isn't it?'

'It is,' Rosie agreed. 'She did say we need to open this when we get here.' She held up an envelope.

'Go on then.' Nate slipped his sunglasses on. 'What is our daughter telling us to do next?'

Rosie liked seeing the amusement in his green eyes. They looked clearer today, the way they did when he was happy. He didn't believe the colour of his eyes was affected by his mood, but it most definitely was.

Rosie ripped the envelope open and pulled out a card. She laughed and showed Nate. The card simply said 'Have fun!' and instructed them to open one final envelope whenever they finished at the zoo.

'She's so cute,' Nate said. He gave Rosie a zoo guide. 'You've always been better at organising stuff than me. Where to first?'

'Gorilla Kingdom?' she suggested.

'Cool. Who doesn't love massive, great scary gorillas?'

Rosie laughed. She had forgotten that Nate was a big girl's blouse when it came to animals. And spiders.

'They have something called "In With the Spiders",' she told him slyly as they headed towards the Gorilla section.

Nate shuddered and stopped walking. 'What? No way. I don't want to see spiders. Did we do that last time?'

'No, we didn't do it last time,' Rosie giggled, as she pulled playfully at his arm. She saw him glance down at her hand as if jolted by her touch. 'Sorry,' she said, letting go.

'Don't be,' Nate said gruffly.

They both started walking at the same time and awkwardly bumped into one another.

'Sorry,' they both said together. They both laughed.

'OK, the word "sorry" is banned for the rest of the day,' Nate said. 'Agreed?'

'Agreed.' Rosie smiled then looked away.

They started walking again.

'So, why didn't we do the spider thing last time?' Nate said, clearly still recovering from the concept of such a thing. 'Was it even here?'

'I don't know,' Rosie chuckled. She consulted the brochure. 'It's the UK's first ever walk-through exhibition. Aah. It was unveiled in 2015. So that explains why we didn't do it when we came.'

'No, that's because we're intelligent people who don't see any kind of benefit to walking through something that has spiders dangling from the ceiling,' Nate retorted, looking positively green around the gills. 'What on earth possessed them to create such a hideous...'

Avoiding the spider enclosure, Rosie and Nate moved around the zoo with thousands of other people, admiring the animals. Each time they stopped at an enclosure, Rosie read from the brochure, much to Nate's delight, because he was a person who loved knowing all the details.

'England's biggest penguin pool. Really?' he said, while they watched one of the twice daily live feeds. 'Whoah.' Nate ducked as a bird swooped past his head. 'I felt that graze my buzz-cut.'

Rosie laughed. 'It says in here that Humboldt penguins,' she pointed them out, 'that's those ones over there, they apparently love preening themselves. They get oil from this gland thing in their tails and put it all over their feathers. Like hair gel.' She nudged Nate. 'That was definitely you back in the day.'

'I had a proper quiff,' Nate reminisced. 'I miss my quiff. When did I get rid of that?' A few seconds later, his face fell. 'Oh God. Sorry, Rosie. I forgot I shaved it off when Emmie…'

'That's OK,' said Rosie. 'It's probably good that you forgot.'

'Do you think?' Nate felt awful. What a stupid thing to say. 'I'm surprised I forgot, to be honest. It was a pretty big moment.'

'We've had loads of those.' Rosie nodded her head towards the penguins. 'See that? They swallow the head first because they never chew their food.'

'Another thing I have in common with them,' Nate said, still worried he had upset Rosie. He touched her hand that was resting on the fence in front of them. 'I don't want you to think that the night Emmie started to lose her hair isn't etched on my heart. Because it is. It was a stupid, flippant remark.'

Rosie looked down at his hand on top of hers and swallowed, realising how much she had missed Nate's touch. How much she loved it.

'I'm not upset,' she said, turning her head to meet his eyes. 'Honestly I'm not. There are things I forget too. Things I would never have imagined I could possibly erase from my mind. And then they pop into my head when I least expect it because something else triggers it. And I find myself feeling surprised.'

Rosie hadn't ever voiced this out loud before – which was strange in itself – but it was true. She wasn't just saying it to make Nate feel better; it was something she had noticed recently.

'I've never told anyone that,' she said, almost to herself.

'Haven't you?'

Rosie looked at him. Nate was looking at her weirdly. She felt defensive.

'No. Is that wrong?'

'It's not wrong, no. I didn't mean that. I mean… It's just…' Nate's voice petered out. 'God, I do that too.' He hadn't taken his hand from hers and he didn't want to. He knew he should, but it felt natural there. He decided to leave it there for as long as he could get away with.

'You do it too?'

'Well, not on purpose,' Nate explained. 'I mean, I'm not deliberately blocking things. Not like my ripped jeans.' He smiled then felt sober again. 'I mean, things just seem to have slipped my memory for some reason. Maybe because they're too difficult to think about, who knows. But like you, I find them rushing into my mind at the weirdest times. Even…' Nate decided he might as well be totally honest. 'Even challenging memories about Emmie's treatment. Gill asked me something about Emmie's chemo the other week… about how we used to pass the time. And I remembered that we all used to stare at one another, do you remember? Like we were watching each other on TV.'

Rosie nodded. 'God, yes. The Chemo Room. Wow. Now that's a memory I think I've deliberately put out of my mind. I… I honestly don't like thinking of any of that stuff Emmie went through. I can't bear it.'

Nate squeezed her hand. Not because he was trying to do anything other than show Rosie that he was being sympathetic. 'I know. It was all horrific. Watching her go through that when she was just a kid…' His voice broke. 'I wasn't sure I could deal with it. Thank God you were there, Rose.'

Rosie felt a sob in her throat. She had felt the same. There was no way she could have got through Emmie's treatment without Nate.

'I don't actually know what was scarier,' Nate said, quickly rubbing his eyes in case he'd disgraced himself. 'Emmie going through all that treatment or her deciding she didn't want it anymore.'

Rosie bit her trembling lip. 'Yes,' she nodded. 'Yes.' Nate was right. Chemo, the operations, radiotherapy... all of it was terrifying and sickening to watch, let alone to go through. But when Emmie had decided she had had enough after a particularly harrowing time in hospital... Rosie had been utterly petrified. Especially when Emmie's consultants and surgical team had agreed. Because whilst there was still treatment, there had been hope. But as soon as that had ceased, the rug had been pulled out from under them and Rosie and Nate had been forced to deal with the fact that Emmie's future had an inevitable, early end. That was the certainty. The only part they didn't know, which was actually the most agonising part of all, was how long Emmie had.

And it had changed things between them from that point, Rosie realised. Living without any kind of hope at all had created a heightened level of tension, perhaps. It had put her and Nate on edge to the point where even the slightest irritation with each other had been magnified. Because when there had been treatment, there had been a plan. A structure. Something to get through because it might change the diagnosis or at best, give Emmie more time. Without any treatment on the horizon, they had been left with nothing. No hope, no plan and nothing to detract from the fact that Emmie was dying.

Rosie stared at Nate. She hadn't even realised this until now. She hadn't ever dwelt on the shift that had occurred when Emmie and her team had decided that enough was enough – and how it had affected herself and Nate. Because looking back, that was the point when everything had folded in on itself and they had stopped talking and connecting and being who they had once been.

Nate finally removed his hand. 'Let's move on,' he said. 'Not from this chat, but from the penguins. I'm over them.'

'Me too,' said Rosie, feeling emotional. 'Lions, maybe?'

'Excellent,' Nate said. 'Emmie loves lions. Let's get some photos for her.'

They strolled towards the lions. Nate was desperate to take Rosie's hand, but he wasn't sure if he should. They'd hardly had any real contact for a year or so now. Which shocked the hell out of him.

'Why haven't we ever said that stuff before?' Nate asked. 'Feeling that way about Emmie's treatment. About forgetting some of the horrible stuff we thought we could never forget.'

'I have no idea.' Rosie didn't want to say that they probably hadn't talked about any of this because for the longest time, they hadn't really been talking about anything much. 'But I think it's good that we're doing it now. I – I just thought about when Emmie decided to stop her treatment.'

Nate glanced at her. 'What about it?'

Rosie tried to explain. 'I feel as though a light went out when Emmie decided to stop. It was like hope and optimism had been extinguished, you know? We had some small hope of change and improvement and then suddenly, it was as though we had no choice. Just… a horrible ending.'

'Yes.' Nate thought about that. 'Yes, you're right. That's so true, Rose. I think I felt the same. Just… completely devoid of hope. As though we are waiting, almost. For the most horrible thing we could imagine.'

Rosie nodded, relieved. Nate felt the same and even that felt good. They paused at the Land of the Lions. Nate took a series of photos on his phone to show Emmie later.

'The zoo's newest exhibit,' Rosie read from the brochure. 'This is an Indian-themed exhibition which apparently has a train station, a temple and a guard hut. It's an interactive adventure thing.'

'Is it?' Nate looked so-so about the idea of that. 'Do you fancy it?'

'Not really.' Rosie would rather talk properly to Nate. 'We could check out the tigers and the aquarium and then we're more or less done.'

They strolled along together in silence for a while, then started talking. Haltingly at first, then with more animation. Nate felt himself grinning. This felt like the old days.

Arriving at the tigers, Nate turned to Rosie and smiled. 'I bloody love tigers. They're so beautiful.'

Rosie couldn't help smiling back. She felt more relaxed with him than she had in a long time. 'You wanted a tattoo of a tiger once, do you remember?'

'God yes! On my butt.'

'Shame to ruin such a great butt.' Rosie stopped. And went bright red.

Nate laughed. 'Thanks. But I think we know who has the great butt around here.'

Rosie went even redder. They looked at the tigers some more then moved on to the aquarium.

'I remember this,' Rosie said. 'We spent ages in the Coral Reef.'

'Because of the seahorses,' Nate added. He gave her a sideways glance. 'You wanted a tattoo of a seahorse once. Do you remember?'

Rosie clapped a hand to her mouth. 'Did I want it on my butt?'

'I think you did.'

'God. We did make some good decisions sometimes then.'

Nate led the way to the Amazonian Fish area. 'Yikes. Look at those. Red-bellied piranha.'

Rosie consulted her brochure. 'They have razor-sharp teeth and apparently, they are very timid and shy. They swim in shoals not to hunt, but for their own protection.' She looked up and found Nate staring at her.

She touched her hair. 'What? Does my hair look funny?' Nate used to joke that her hair looked crap all the time because he actually thought it was one of her best features.

'Yes, Rosie. That's exactly why I'm looking at you like that. Because your hair looks funny.'

She held his gaze until he went on.

'What I was actually thinking about was decisions. Good decisions we've made.'

'Not to have tattoos on our butts?' Rosie offered.

'That, yes.' Nate reached out and deliberately took her hand this time. 'But also, Emmie. Having Emmie was a good decision.'

'Of course it was.'

Rosie frowned. What did Nate mean by that? She stood still for a moment and then she understood. It had been right here in this aquarium that she and Nate had decided they wanted children together. On their third date. Their friends had laughed at them for getting ahead of themselves. But they had known. They had just known they were right for each other and they had known what they wanted.

'It was here,' Rosie whispered, close to tears. 'It was here that we decided we would have children.'

Nate nodded and tightened his grip on her hand. 'And I just wanted to say that whatever we've been through, I haven't regretted it. The decision we made here.' He looked down for a second. 'I wasn't expecting what we've been through and I know you weren't either. Who would? But even though it's the hardest thing we've ever been through, I don't regret Emmie.'

'Neither do I,' Rosie said.

She burst into tears and Nate immediately pulled her into his arms.

'It's OK,' he murmured into her hair. 'It's OK. Neither of us saw it coming, what happened with Emmie.'

'We were so innocent,' Rosie sniffed into his shoulder. 'Were we naïve?' she asked, lifting her head.

Nate smoothed her hair away from her face. 'No way,' he said. 'No way. Why were we naïve? We just wanted a kid together. We were so in love and we wanted a baby. We didn't know she was going to get sick.'

Rosie couldn't stop crying and she fell into Nate's arms again. 'I love her so much, Nate. I can't… can't bear the thought of losing her.'

'Me neither, Rose. I can't even contemplate it.'

He wrapped his arms around her and held her, not caring if people were staring at them. He and Rosie were above any of that with everything they'd been through. They were used to stares in the Chemo Room and they were used to gossip and pointing as they walked down the street with Emmie wearing a bright, pink wig. None of that stuff fazed them anymore.

Nate pulled back from Rosie finally. 'Wow,' he said, taking a breath. 'Where did all that come from?'

'Being here again, I guess,' Rosie said, fishing some tissues out of her bag. 'God, it's like *Love Actually* all over again.'

'I know.' Nate hesitated, but he wasn't sure the time was right to talk about her note. 'Listen, shall we make a move?'

Rosie nodded and they made their way to the nearby exit. She felt exhausted and ready to head home. She was glad she was wearing her leather jacket as it was quite chilly now that the sun was disappearing behind the skyline of London. They didn't talk much as they headed back to Liverpool Street, but it was a comfortable silence. And this time they sat side by side on the train, not opposite one another.

They had bonded, Rosie realised. Over wanting to have Emmie in the first place, of all things. She suddenly remembered something.

'We didn't open Emmie's other envelope.'

'Aah, crap. Open it now,' Nate said. 'She'll be quizzing us when we pick her up.'

Rosie pulled it out and read what was inside. 'She's written "If the date goes well, feel free to move onto date four... dinner out. Aunt Lily will pick me up."'

Nate smiled. 'The sneaky little monkey. She's properly pulling our strings at the moment.'

'I know.' Rosie tucked the note away. 'Should we go out for dinner?' she asked tentatively. 'Emmie has asked us to text her so she knows who will be picking her up.'

Nate shrugged and Rosie felt a stab of disappointment.

'Sorry, what I should have said,' Nate said quickly, 'was that I think we've had an emotional day together. I'd love to have dinner with you another time, but how about a take-away tonight?'

'That does actually sound good,' Rosie agreed. 'Take-away tonight it is.'

'And dinner another time?' Nate prompted.

'Dinner another time.'

They fell silent for the rest of the train ride home, but Rosie felt more relaxed than she had in a long time. Maybe she and Nate could be friends. She didn't know if anything else could be salvaged after everything that had happened, but friends... that would be nice.

When they picked Emmie up from Dr Tom, she looked gutted.

'Did it go badly then?'

'Not at all,' laughed Nate. 'Why would you think that?'

'Well, you're not having dinner together, are you?'

'Not tonight, no,' Rosie said. 'But another time.' She and Nate exchanged a glance and both of them felt Emmie's excitement from the back of the car.

Rosie frowned. She didn't want Emmie to get her hopes up. Or actually, did it matter? They both just wanted the best for Emmie – they wanted her to feel comfortable and secure.

'How did it go with Dr Tom?' she asked.

'It was fun,' Emmie said. 'It was more or less a quiz. I'm seeing him again soon to get the results.'

'Before you tell us about it, what take-away would you like?' Nate said.

'Pizza please,' Emmie said happily. 'So these questions of Dr Tom's were mostly about…'

As Emmie chatted away nineteen to the dozen about her afternoon, Rosie and Nate glanced at one another.

This afternoon had felt good, Rosie thought. But she was worried that there were many more things she and Nate hadn't talked about yet. What about his gambling? What about Jonny? She turned away guiltily. She didn't want to get into a negative headspace again now that they were home like last time. Because today had been a breakthrough of sorts. And Rosie didn't want to let go of that.

By contrast, Nate was feeling on top of the world. He and Rosie had really talked today. They had opened up with one another about things they had felt scared about with Emmie. Why hadn't they done that sooner, Nate thought to himself? If only they'd been able to talk more, maybe this gaping hole wouldn't have formed between them. Perhaps that was mostly down to him, as Nate knew that Rosie was far better at communicating than he was.

Either way, Nate felt as if they had opened a door today. Like Emmie's ongoing condition, he had no idea what was behind it, but he felt better knowing that a door that had felt very firmly shut for a long time now might – just might – be slightly ajar.

If only he hadn't gambled again, Nate thought uncomfortably. If he and Rosie were going to start being honest with one another again, he knew he was going to have to confess to that at some point. And when would be the right time for that?

And Rosie had secrets of her own to confront, Nate remembered. But today had been a start. A move in the right direction. A possible new beginning, oddly forged over an old, sentimental memory.

Emmie. Where this had all begun.

Emmie

'So. How do you think it went on the zoo date?'

Emmie regarded Dr Tom. He was very nosy about everything, but she liked that about him. And they were in this together. As ever, Emmie was grateful that she could speak freely to him about everything and not feel as though she was upsetting anyone. Dr Tom was very… whatever the word was that meant that he sat on the fence a lot.

He also looked rather strange today, Emmie decided. He was trialling some contact lenses so he wasn't wearing his glasses and he was blinking way more than he usually did. His eyes were all red as well. Emmie didn't like to tell him that he suited glasses and looked totally weird without them, because although she meant it nicely, he might not take it that way.

They were sitting in his office, but Dr Tom had wisely chosen to sit in his big chair rather than one of the beanbags. He had all the windows open because it was such a lovely, sunny day and the other thing that was different was that there was a big, pink jar on his desk. Emmie wondered if the jar was something to do with her.

'I think it went quite well,' she informed him. She shuffled her body into a comfy space in her beanbag. 'They didn't go for dinner, but we all had pizza together.'

'Maybe they were too tired to go to dinner,' Dr Tom observed. 'After their trip to London.'

Emmie didn't comment on that. Grown ups always went on about being tired, but she couldn't see what was so tiring for them if she was honest. Emmie had experienced such extreme fatigue after chemo once or twice that she had tried to crawl upstairs to bed. Her dad had carried her in the end, but she had literally had no energy to even move.

'Did they talk about the zoo?' Dr Tom asked.

'Not really. They had taken pictures of the lions and tigers to show me. I like big cats,' she added, in case Dr Tom thought that was odd.

'So do I. I like panthers best, but you don't see many of those around.'

Emmie smiled. Dr Tom was so unusual. Of course he liked panthers.

'Do you feel more upbeat about your treasure hunt?' Dr Tom gathered some paperwork together and pretended to read it.

The reason Emmie thought he was pretending was because she knew Dr Tom was very organised. She was pretty sure he read all of his paperwork before she even came into the room.

'More upbeat?'

'You were quite down after the first couple of dates. They didn't go as you'd hoped.'

Emmie considered the artwork on Dr Tom's wall. Counsellors always had interesting artwork in their offices, in her experience. She wasn't sure what it was about studying people that made counsellors want to buy weird pictures, but she liked looking at them. Dr Tom had one with big, colourful swirls on it, with mini, copper-coloured leaf shapes printed in all the gaps.

'No they didn't,' Emmie said, answering his question. 'I mean, the second one was a disaster. My dad didn't even turn up.'

'Do we know why?'

She shook her head.

Dr Tom put his paperwork down and leant on his desk. 'Well, it sounds like the zoo date made some progress at any rate. You said your parents seemed more friendly with one another. They were talking more. Is that continuing?'

'I think so.' Emmie thought for a second. 'They're not spending loads of time together or anything, but Dad is still working quite long hours. But when they're both in the house together, it feels better, if you know what I mean.'

'A better atmosphere?' Dr Tom suggested.

'Yes. That.'

'So, before we move onto the evaluation we did the other day, what's the next move? What can I help you with?'

Emmie took a leaflet out of her pocket and got off the beanbag. 'Aunt Lily has made a booking here for them to go to dinner.'

Dr Tom took the leaflet. 'Wow, this place looks amazing. Was this really their fourth date?'

Emmie shook her head. 'No, actually. Dinner at some Italian restaurant was their fourth date and then they had several dates after that having drinks, more cinema, lunch, that kind of thing. This is where they got engaged.'

'Aah. OK. I thought it was a bit much for a fourth date.' Dr Tom gave the leaflet back. 'So hang on, are we

combining the fourth date of dinner with the engagement?'

'Yes.' Emmie tucked the leaflet back into her school
bag. 'I want to keep them guessing a bit. I don't want
them thinking it's just going to be us replicating every
single date they had. Aunt Lily reckons the engagement
packed a powerful punch – do that sound right?'

Dr Tom smiled. 'Yes.'

'So we're going straight to that.'

'Good call. Any particular reason for hurrying to the
engagement apart from that?'

Emmie settled into her beanbag again, feeling
confused. What did Dr Tom mean?

'I'm just wondering if you're feeling a sense of urgency
about this.' Dr Tom rubbed his eyes. 'I'm really not liking
these contact lenses. Scratchy.'

'Your eyes look really sore,' Emmie commented.
'Maybe you should put your glasses back on?'

'I was trying not to look geeky.' Dr Tom started to
laugh as if he found himself ridiculous.

'You *are* geeky,' Emmie told him kindly. 'Glasses look
good on you.'

Dr Tom thought that one over. 'Thank you. I think.
Anyway, I was asking you if you feel a sense of urgency
about getting your parents back together.'

'I know. I didn't really understand what you meant.'

'Remember to always say that to me,' Dr Tom said.
'And then I can try to explain myself better. I guess what
I'm getting at is this: are you worried that time will run
out before you can move to all the stuff which "packs a
powerful punch" as such?'

'Well. Yes, kind of. But I'm always worried about time running out.' Emmie felt confused.

Dr Tom laced his fingers. 'Do you feel well in yourself, Emmie?'

'You're the one with scratchy eyes,' she pointed out.

'Good point, well made. But that's not really what I mean.' Dr Tom got up and gingerly made his way over to the beanbags. 'Life in my own hands here... ooooh.' He managed to settle into one without too much hassle and made sure he had Emmie's attention. 'Would you tell me if you didn't feel well? If this... lovely treasure hunt you're arranging for your parents got too much for you?'

Emmie stretched her legs out. She felt well in herself. She didn't feel overly tired. She hadn't had any issues with her vision since the last times a few months back. Of course she worried that she might die at any second, but that was no different to normal. Although Emmie did admit that she felt as though other people didn't understand that she wanted to rush to the end, because they didn't have big tumours in their heads. Arranging the treasure hunt for her parents made her feel less anxious than doing nothing at all. Because even though she now realised that her expectations had been way too high in the beginning, doing something to try and get them to fall in love all over again was better than standing by and watching them fall apart.

Emmie told Dr Tom these thoughts as a series of bullet points.

He inclined his head. 'Excellent. I'm very clear about all of that now, thank you. So let's talk about your evaluation. Oh, lord.' He looked over towards his desk.

'Did you leave your paperwork there?' Emmie asked. Seeing the answer etched on his vexed face, she got out of her beanbag expertly and collected it up.

'No peeking,' Dr Tom said playfully.

Emmie handed the paperwork over without looking. Why did she need to peek? She remembered answering Dr Tom's questions. There hadn't been anything too weird about them.

'Thank you. So let's start with that whole section about dying.' Dr Tom grinned at Emmie. 'Is that alright?'

'Yep. You're all obsessed with it. Go on. What do you want to know that you didn't ask me the other day? And haven't we talked about this endlessly?'

Dr Tom nodded. 'We have a bit. But when we talked the other day specifically, I picked up on the fact that no one has really talked to you about your funeral. Whenever that may be. You mentioned it several times the other day, even though I wasn't asking you about it especially.'

'That's right.' Emmie played with the end of her hair. She enjoyed touching her hair, especially now that it was a good length again.

'Are you worried about it? Do you think people are too scared to discuss it with you?'

'That's two questions. Hang on.' Emmie thought. 'Yes, I'm worried about it. And no, I don't know if they are too scared as such. They just all get upset.'

'Who gets upset?'

'Well, Mum and Dad, obviously. I talked about it once a few years back and my mum started crying and my dad came and hugged me and told me I didn't need to think about that just yet. Then I mentioned it again earlier this year and the same thing happened.' She shrugged. 'It's not something they like talking about.'

'Of course. That's understandable. What about your Aunt Lily? She seems like a very down to earth lady.'

'She is,' Emmie agreed. 'But she doesn't like talking about me dying either. Nor does Cara. I thought she might be a good person to talk to about this, but she got all hysterical about it a few months ago and her mum had to come and calm her down.' She sighed.

Dr Tom let out a sympathetic sound. 'They all love you very much and they can't bear the thought of you not being there anymore. Are you talking about it more for any reason?'

Emmie started to plait her hair. 'Not really. I mean, after I asked to stop having the chemo and my team agreed, I suppose I've been thinking about it a bit more. Which is funny because the chemo used to make me feel like I was dying. And now I'm not having it, I feel better again. Like there's nothing wrong with me.'

Catching sight of Dr Tom's expression, Emmie rolled her eyes. 'I know I have a big brain tumour, Dr Tom. I'm just saying that I feel much better now that I'm not having chemo anymore. That's normal, right?'

'I wasn't suggesting that you were deluded for one second,' Dr Tom said. 'I just find you very mature for your age. And I enjoy your observations about your illness and about life in general.'

Emmie smiled. She liked Dr Tom.

'So I was wondering if you might want to tell me about your funeral?' Dr Tom said. 'I should mention at this juncture that I have checked with your parents and they were understandably worried but they want you to have a safe place to talk.'

Emmie was surprised. She didn't know Dr Tom had contacted her parents. She realised he was talking again.

'And this isn't because I think you need to think about it at any great length… it's a bit doomy, isn't it? Funerals are never a barrel of laughs if we're being frank about it. But the thing is, as much I would miss you if you leave any time soon, I'm not going to cry. Even if you tell me you'd like them to play a song by Justin Bieber. Apart from the fact that he's not my bag AT ALL.'

Emmie burst out laughing. Justin Bieber? At her funeral?

'Crazier things have happened,' Dr Tom advised her seriously. 'Have you thought about music? Are, er… Little Mix more your thing?'

If Dr Tom carried on like this, Emmie wasn't going to be able to stop giggling. It was enough watching him squirming around in his beanbag with bright red eyes like he had conjunctivitis.

'I haven't really thought about music,' Emmie confessed. 'Every time I talk to someone about it they start sobbing, so I haven't got that far. I should think about it actually. Otherwise they might just put Justin Bieber on thinking I like him. I'm not a 'Belieber', Dr Tom.'

'I'm not even going to pretend I know what that means.' Dr Tom looked perturbed.

'But I don't want to be cremated,' Emmie said suddenly. 'That's the one where those funny curtains come across and you go off to some horrible furnace, right?'

'Kind of.'

'I saw that in a James Bond film.' Emmie shuddered. 'I don't like the idea of that.'

'Fair enough. I'm not keen either.' Dr Tom touched his eyes. 'Ouch. I really want to take these out. So the other thing that came up in your evaluation was all the guilt you seem to be carrying around.'

Emmie had heard that expression before. It sounded as though guilt was a big, heavy weight she had on her shoulders that she was literally 'carrying' around. Which was probably a good way to think about it, because it did feel like something she didn't want to feel, but it was just *there*.

'Someone told me once that guilt is a man-made emotion,' Dr Tom was saying. 'Which sounds odd, but if you think about it, it's true. We can't often help it, but it's something we choose to feel.'

Emmie frowned. Now Dr Tom was being silly. As if she would choose to feel this way.

'But either way, I thought we could do this thing.' Dr Tom pointed to the pink jar on his desk. 'Could you get that please, Emmie? And the Post-It notes next to it?'

Emmie got up and collected the jar and Post-It notes, which were also pink. 'What's it for?'

'It's a Guilt Jar. I'd like you to write down anything you feel guilty about and put it in the jar.'

'Then what?'

'Don't get ahead of yourself,' Dr Tom chided her. 'Here, take my pen. And go for it. I won't be seeing any of the things you're writing, so just be honest.'

Emmie sat down on the beanbag and thought about her task. What did she feel guilty about? OK, so first of all, she felt guilty about her parents. For putting them through such a hard time. Emmie wrote that down on a Post-It note and stuffed it into the jar. And she felt guilty because she knew Cara would really miss her when she died. Emmie wrote that down. The same thing applied to her cousins. Another Post-It note. And her Aunt Lily and Uncle Jamie.

Emmie had another long think. She felt guilty about… about stopping her treatment, even though her doctors agreed with her, because she didn't want to let anyone down. Another note in the jar. She felt guilty about making everyone sad all the time. About her parents' marriage falling apart because of her. About making other people feel uncomfortable because she had something no one liked talking about. Once Emmie started, she found that she couldn't stop.

Dr Tom said nothing, sitting quietly while she stuffed the jar full of paper. When she'd finished, he checked with her that she was done. She nodded.

'Wow. Emmie. Look at that.'

Emmie peered into the jar. It was almost full to the brim.

'You really have been carrying a lot of guilt around.'

Emmie looked at Dr Tom. His eyes, even though they were red, were full of compassion. Emmie suddenly felt like crying.

'Is that bad?' she asked.

'Bad?' Dr Tom handed her the lid and almost fell off the beanbag. 'Of course it's not bad. If anything, it's sad. Sad that you feel this way. Because none of this is your fault.'

Emmie screwed the lid on. 'What do we do with it now?' she asked, realising her voice sounded tearful as well.

'We can bury it, we can put it in the bin. We can smash it, we can keep it here.' Dr Tom put the jar on the floor between them. 'It's up to you. What would feel good?'

Emmie swallowed and stared at the jar. 'I think I want to smash it,' she decided.

'OK.' Dr Tom rolled off the beanbag. 'Holy moly. I'm still pants at that.'

Emmie couldn't help laughing. She helped Dr Tom up.

'Where are we going to smash it?'

'I'm not sure. I haven't really thought this through.' Dr Tom frowned. 'I know. How about we find a bin outside and throw the jar into it?'

'Yes!' Emmie felt all fired up then realised something. 'Won't that only work if the bin is empty?'

'Oh man. Maybe.' Dr Tom picked the jar up. 'Let's just find somewhere to smash it. And I'll take the blame.'

They hurried out of his office into the sunshine. They walked around the side of the hospital, looking for a suitably empty bin or a corner to hurl the jar in. But Emmie worried about the glass going everywhere. Dr Tom eyed some huge bins that were full to the brim around the back of the hospital. Then lifted his eyes.

'I have an idea,' he said. Emptying a dustbin full of rubbish into one of the larger bins, he positioned it behind them, glancing upwards over and over again as he did so. Emmie had no idea what he was doing, but she trusted him.

'Come on,' said Dr Tom, looking excited. 'How good is your aim?'

'Not bad,' Emmie panted as she followed him back into the hospital and up some stairs. 'I'm pretty good at basketball.'

'Fantastic.' Dr Tom led her out onto the roof. 'It's OK. It's the smoking area. Not that I smoke, obviously,' he added swiftly.

Emmie smiled. She couldn't picture Dr Tom doing anything naughty. This was probably extremely daring for him. He took her to the railings at the edge of the roof.

'See, perfectly safe. Now. Can you see the bin we moved?'

Emmie looked. 'Yep.'

'Can you get the jar in there from here?'

'I can try.' Emmie held it over the edge. She felt stupidly happy about doing this.

'After three. One, two… three!'

Emmie hurled the jar down with all her might. It landed squarely in the bin and smashed in an explosion of pink glass and pink paper.

'Yay!!!!!'

Emmie jumped up and down.

'Yay!' Dr Tom high-fived her and missed.

Emmie shrieked with laughter. 'Dr Tom, you really are a geek.' She stopped and a sob escaped. 'Oh.'

Dr Tom gave her shoulder a squeeze. 'A bit emotional, right?'

She nodded. 'Why?'

'Because that's lots of grown-up feelings you've been holding. And you're a kid. You've been through more than your young soul and body should have.'

Dr Tom's voice was so gentle, Emmie felt all weird and scared for a second.

'And now you've let go of all that guilt. You might feel some or all of it again, but I hope you feel a bit lighter for hurling that jar down there.'

'I do.' Emmie rubbed her eyes. 'Now my eyes hurt. Holy moly.'

Dr Tom grinned. 'Are you making fun of me again?'

'No way. I love saying "holy moly".' She looked at him. 'But just so I don't feel guilty for not saying this, you look better in glasses. Fact.'

'OK. I'll be geeky again. Thanks.'

'Dr Tom, do you think I can make my parents fall in love again?'

He stared at her. 'I don't think we can make anyone do anything, Emmie. But I think if two people really loved each other in the first place, they can find their way back again somehow.'

'They really did love each other before me,' Emmie said earnestly.

Dr Tom's lip curled strangely then he leant back on the railings. 'They loved each other after you too. So let's trust. Trust that we've put them on the right path and that they will find one another again.'

Emmie stood next to him and mirrored his lean. 'And something by Adele at my funeral maybe… Because she has a beautiful voice.'

'Adele I've heard of,' Dr Tom said approvingly. 'Great choice. For whenever you need it. Hopefully not for a very long time.'

Emmie rested her head on Dr Tom's arm for a second. She had no words.

Dr Tom cleared his throat. 'You're very welcome, Emmie,' he said, looking straight ahead. 'Very welcome indeed.'

Rosie and Nate

Nate checked his tie in a nearby mirror. It wasn't the same one, but as far as he could remember, it was close. Either way, he felt good in a sharp, navy suit, a crisp white shirt and a navy tie with pink in it. It almost what Nate might have chosen for himself.

He wandered back to the bar. He rather liked the fact that he had arrived first today; it felt like the old days. Like a proper date. Emmie had sent him on a merry old dance around the office at work (aided and abetted by Gill and no doubt Lily, Nate now realised), with clues that hinted at the venue he was to arrive at, culminating in him discovering a suit bag containing the clothes he was wearing now.

Nate had found the whole thing highly amusing. His own kid had sorted out date night and an outfit. Not on her own, naturally, but still. She had researched it and she had re-created it to the best of her ability. Emmie had done well.

And how strange, being back here, Nate thought as he took a good look around. Freyton Manor. A beautiful fifteenth-century manor house crammed full of genuine, period pieces. It was glamorous, unashamedly high-end and deliciously cosy. It was more suited to winter with its log fires and huge, comfy armchairs and window seats, but it was still beautiful in the summer.

The manor house wasn't far from where they lived – a twenty-minute cab ride away, but it felt as though they were in the middle of nowhere because it was set in such wonderful countryside. The manor had beautiful gardens and a lake and a few acres that stretched out for miles at the back of the property.

Once again, Nate marvelled at his daughter. Obviously she'd had help – Lily, Dr Tom perhaps, but still. This was her idea. She was behind this whole, romantic thing and that both impressed and floored Nate. It impressed him because she was eleven and she had proved herself to be incredibly resourceful and doggedly determined. It floored him because Emmie must be desperately sad and worried to be trying so hard with this.

Nate wished he could reassure Emmie and make her feel secure. She had so much on her plate; the last thing she needed was to be agonising about her parents not getting on. Poor Emmie. How distressed she must have felt about the way her parents were behaving. Nate wished she'd voiced her feelings, although he wasn't sure what difference it would have made if he was honest. It was seeing Dr Tom that seemed to have opened Emmie up and Nate was grateful that Emmie had been matched to him. Dr Tom was one hell of a guy, let alone what a fantastic counsellor he was.

Nate checked his watch and wondered if Rosie was definitely coming. She'd told him she was, but then, he had planned to attend the movie night. Nate hoped Rosie turned up and believing that she would, he ordered a good bottle of red wine for them both and took a seat at a table by the fireplace. Despite the summery date, the fire was on now that it was getting dark and it was warm and inviting. A waitress brought the wine and two vast, shiny wine glasses to the table.

Nate had the weirdest feeling Rosie had just walked into the room, even though he had his back to the door. They had both experienced this when they were dating and beyond; an innate ability to sense one another's presence before the visual swam into view. Jamie used to sneer at this, but Nate had proved himself right repeatedly and even Jamie had had to admit that he and Rosie had some weird connection that way.

He turned in his seat. Wow. She looked incredible. Stunning. She was literally taking his breath away. She was wearing a snug-fitting, wine-coloured dress that coated her curves, but covered her from neck to knee. It was classy and sexy and Nate was speechless.

'Hey,' she said, as she reached the table. 'You look good.'

'You took the words right out of my mouth,' Nate managed, standing up and making sure Rosie could take her seat. 'You look absolutely beautiful, Rose. That's a new dress. There's no way I wouldn't remember it.'

'Thank you. Yes, it's new.'

'Did Emmie choose that for you too? Or rather, Lily?'

'Lily helped, yes.'

Rosie felt absurdly flattered by Nate's compliments. She'd gone to a lot of trouble to look and feel good tonight – hair washed and blow-dried at a salon, nails and toenails done in shellac. Lily had helped with her make up as she was brilliant at shading eyeshadow and Rosie was terrible at it. She was even wearing incredible new underwear, also wine-coloured. Not because Nate was going to see it. No way. That wasn't a thought that Rosie was even considering. But because Lily always went on about matching underwear and how good it felt, so Rosie had decided to give it a try. And she had to admit, she felt great. She had borrowed Lily's Louboutins, too, and they made her walk differently.

Rosie felt confident and desirable. She just wasn't sure how Nate saw her these days.

'Wine?' Nate held the bottle up.

'Yes please.' Rosie looked around. 'It feels so strange being back here. But isn't it gorgeous? I'd forgotten how lovely it is here.'

'And it's only down the road as well.'

Rosie chinked glasses with Nate. This is where Nate had proposed. They had actually come here for lunch and Rosie hadn't known Nate had even thought about proposing. They had talked about having children at the zoo, but Rosie hadn't been sure if Nate was into marriage. He never really mentioned it and she was old-fashioned; if he didn't want to ask her, she wasn't going to try and make him do it.

Rosie glanced down at her hand. The ring Nate had chosen hadn't been what she might have expected, but it was spectacular. Unusual, delicate and set in white gold. She smiled. She had been so happy then.

Nate watched Rosie. He loved the way he could read her face when she was unguarded like this; she was re-living that moment where he had been down on one knee next to the table, presenting her with that ring. He had felt sick, his steak had nearly made a reappearance and he had got cramp in his calf, but it had all felt right. Nate had known without a shadow of a doubt that he was doing the right thing.

'Are you ready to come to your table now?'

They looked up to find a smiling waitress next to them. Nate raised his eyebrows at Rosie and she nodded. They followed the waitress into the main dining room and Rosie was sure Nate had brushed his fingers against hers. It was ridiculous. She felt like they had only just met again. Her stomach was fizzing like crazy.

Nate glanced at Rosie. He had tested the waters by brushing his fingers against hers and she hadn't flinched or pulled away.

'The same table too,' Nate said. 'Of course.'

'The same table?' the waitress asked.

'We got engaged here,' Rosie explained. 'Some years back but we sat right here, by the window.' She touched the heavy curtain. 'This wasn't here because it was lunch, but still.'

'How lovely!' The waitress went all gooey-eyed. 'That's so romantic, that you're back here! I'll mention it to the chef and for now, I'll leave you the menus and I'll be back shortly to take your order.' She efficiently ran through the specials with them before leaving them to it.

'I think it's a good job we didn't tell her our daughter arranged this for us,' Nate said to Rosie. 'I think that might have finished her off.'

'Ha, probably,' she agreed, opening the menu. 'Wow. This looks so good. I think they've upped the ante since we came here last.'

Nate nodded. The menu looked incredible. After an in-depth discussion, they chose some red prawns in a coconut sauce and a mushroom risotto to share as starters and some steaks to follow. Different cuts of meat with different sauces but some delicious-sounding sides they both wanted to try.

Munching on a warm, home-baked roll, Rosie felt herself relax. Even though it wasn't so much now, food had become a real issue for the entire family after Emmie had started her treatment. She hadn't talked to Nate about it before; it was just something they had presumably both accepted about the situation.

'Do you remember the way Emmie used to react about food?' Nate asked, handing Rosie some chilled butter.

'I was just thinking that. She used to associate hospital food with being ill.'

'Not just the food, the hospital itself,' Nate reminded her. 'Do you remember how she used to almost vomit when we drove past it, or even another hospital?'

Rosie sipped her wine. 'She couldn't even bear us eating in front of her in hospital because it made her feel sick. It brought back all the feelings she had about her cancer and the chemo.'

'Yes.' Nate nodded. 'It was really tough. She'd only eat a few things. Mostly sweet, which isn't her at all now.'

'It affected the way we ate as well though, didn't it? We used to eat in private at home. We barely ate in hospital. We used to find ways to drive all round the houses to avoid driving in front of hospitals to delay the nausea.' Rosie gazed at Nate. 'Not her fault at all. Just another part of her illness.'

Nate sat back. He and Rosie hadn't ever talked about these aspects of Emmie's illness. He wasn't sure why they hadn't – it was almost as if they had soldiered on, trying so hard to be strong for Emmie and brush the weirdness and disruption under the carpet. Because they hadn't wanted Emmie to feel bad about the impact her treatment was having on all of them. Because it wasn't her fault.

'We didn't eat in front of Emmie much and I used to clean around the clock,' Rosie mused. 'Hoovering, spraying away germs, washing bedclothes and trying not to cry because Emmie had shed her hair all over them.'

Nate reached across the table and took Rosie's hand tentatively. She squeezed it and he held on tighter.

'We both worked out more whenever we could spare the time,' he observed. 'I'm not even sure why.'

'I spoke to Lily about that once. It's a control thing, I think. Something we could control when we couldn't control anything else?'

Nate felt surprised but if he thought about it, it made sense. 'Yes, I get that.'

Rosie paused as the waitress returned to top their glasses up, smiling mistily at them holding hands across the table.

'You make such a good-looking couple,' the waitress said. 'The chef was so excited that you two got engaged here.'

Rosie and Nate chatted with the waitress briefly, relieved when she finally went away.

Rosie took a breath. 'I… I know that I became very paranoid when we were going through the first bout of Emmie's treatment.'

Nate waited. This was the first time they'd spoken like this in ages.

'I became paranoid about germs. About leaving Emmie alone. About making sure Emmie didn't overhear me on the phone talking about her illness. About anyone negative being around her. Or us.' Rosie stopped. 'I was in a state of high alert.'

Nate linked his fingers through hers. God, it felt good. Intimate. Right. He re-focused with an effort. 'I think we both were. Just… in different ways.' He moved back as their starters arrived and reluctantly let go of Rosie's hand.

'Those prawns smell so good.' Rosie inhaled, but she didn't lose Nate's gaze. 'You were saying,' she prompted when they were alone again.

'My paranoia?' Nate helped Rosie to some prawns.

Rosie had always loved the way he did that.

'My paranoia wasn't so much about the germs, but I knew you were taking care of that one.' Nate sampled the risotto. 'That's excellent. Truffle oil. I was also paranoid about Emmie being left on her own. About appearing strong in front of her. I was terrified I might break down in front in of her,' Nate said, trying to make sure he explained himself properly. 'And as her father, I didn't want her to see me as weak. As not being able to cope with what was happening.'

Rosie did remember Nate holding onto his tears way better than she had. Sometimes she hadn't been able to help herself because she had been so distraught, and on occasion, she would find herself gathering Emmie up and sobbing onto her heart-breakingly sparse hair. But Nate had been super-strong. At least in public. Rosie knew he had cried alone many times. She had wanted to comfort him, but he had often pushed her away. The rejection had hurt her. Why couldn't they share their pain?

'I… please don't hate me for saying this,' Rosie said, loath to spoil the moment. 'But I really wanted to put my arms around you when you were crying. I wanted to cry with you. You shutting me out… it really upset me.'

Nate took a gulp of wine. 'The thing is, Rose, I didn't want you to think I was crumbling either. I wanted to be strong for both of you. But you know what I'm like. *Love Actually* makes me weep. Emmie being ill? It destroyed me. I thought it was the least I could do to appear strong and tough for both the women in my life.'

Rosie felt tears approaching and she rushed to force them back. 'I wouldn't have thought you were weak for crying. You're only human, Nate!' She dabbed at her eyes with her napkin. 'I wanted to cry with you. I felt so alone.'

'God.' Nate shoved the prawns out of the way and took Rosie's hand again. 'I'm so sorry, Rose. I felt alone too. What an idiot. I thought I was doing the right thing. I didn't want either of you to think I was a big girl's blouse.'

Nate shook his head. 'I'm a prick. And a big girl's blouse.'

'Only one of those things,' Rosie corrected him. She took her hand back. 'Let me sort my face out.' She got a mirror out and checked her mascara. 'And I do understand what you were trying to do.'

'There were so many times I couldn't sleep,' Nate said suddenly. 'I told you I was like you, that I was so exhausted I just passed out. But I often didn't.'

Rosie stared at him. Why on earth had Nate kept that to himself?

'I didn't want you worrying about me,' Nate shrugged. 'It's not a big deal. I would just go downstairs and watch terrible TV. Read a book. I read lots of books.'

Rosie pushed her knife and fork together. 'Wow. Nate. This is weird. I feel as though we were having a completely separate experience and keeping it from one another.'

'Well, I think I was doing that more than you, but I get what you mean.' Nate waited until the waitress – who was intuitive enough to know that this wasn't a good time for chatting – had removed their plates.

'Listen. I think we were both so focused on making sure that Emmie felt OK, we weren't focusing too much on what we were doing. All that stuff,' Nate waved a hand, 'the cleaning, the hoovering. That was still all for Emmie. Me crying alone and not wanting you to know or to come and hug me – that was for Emmie. We've made mistakes, but I honestly believe we both did it for the right reasons.'

Rosie was still reeling from Nate's revelations. She agreed with what he was saying, but she wished they hadn't done it. 'We've made mistakes,' she said. 'And I get all the reasons why we did it. Emmie is our priority and always has been.' Rosie let out a breath. 'But what about us? What did we do to us?'

Nate stared at her. She was right. Rosie was spot on. What had they done to themselves, their couple, by prioritising Emmie over absolutely everything? But what else could they do? Emmie was their kid. She had cancer. She had to come first.

Did Rosie hate him for putting Emmie first? Surely not. Rosie had done the same thing. Nate barely noticed as their steaks were put down in front of them.

Rosie looked at the steak, not sure she could stomach it. It was amazing that they were finally being honest with each other, but hearing all of this; it was a little too much to take.

'Nate. I'm so pleased we're being honest with one another. But… is there more?'

'More?'

'Other stuff you haven't told me? Anything else that I don't know?' Rosie rubbed her hands together nervously. Her fingers felt freezing cold all of a sudden. 'I don't even mind what it is. If you told me you did something during Emmie's treatment, but you felt you couldn't say it, you can. Is there anything you need to tell me?'

Nate found he'd been chewing the same piece of steak for ages. He swallowed it eventually and sighed. He didn't have anything else to tell. Not about Emmie's illness or about the way he might have behaved during her treatment. But he did have something he should get off his chest. He didn't want to, but he should.

'I have something to tell you actually. But it has nothing to do with Emmie's illness. This is just me being a complete twat.' He took a deep breath. 'A month or so ago, I gambled,' he said flatly. 'I went to a casino and I gambled. Not for long. I played roulette and for a while, it felt like relief. Like… an alcoholic giving into a craving. And then I felt sick.'

Rosie stared at him in shock. She knew about the gambling and that was the last thing she had expected Nate to come out with.

'Did it happen again? The night we were due to watch the film?'

'Nearly,' Nate admitted. 'But I phoned Gill instead and she took me out for a drink and told me off.'

Rosie couldn't help smiling. 'I love Gill. OK. So it was just that one time?'

'Just that one time. And I was… on the edge. I was feeling horrible about us.' Nate decided he had nothing to lose by telling Rosie the full truth.

'I… I knew about you gambling again,' she confessed. 'I found a chip from a casino in the kitchen.'

'You did?' Nate was flabbergasted. 'Why didn't you say something?'

Rosie pushed her hair out of her eyes. 'I couldn't. I wanted to, but I couldn't bring myself to confront you about it. We weren't even talking. I wasn't sure how to broach the subject and I… I didn't like you very much for a while.'

Nate accepted that. It was understandable. He was shocked that she knew and hadn't said anything, but at the same time, he was moved that she hadn't seen it as a deal breaker.

'And the night of the film?' Rosie was perplexed, remembering that he hadn't turned up that night and she still didn't know why. 'Why didn't you come?'

Nate regarded her. This wasn't a tit for tat, by any means. But if they were being honest, they both had to be honest. And there were things he had to know. Even if he was dreading the answers. He had to know the extent of Rosie's indiscretion. And he wanted her to tell him herself without him having to tell her that he already knew.

'Do you mind if I ask you the same question before I answer that? As in… do you have anything you need to tell me about?'

Rosie's mouth had gone dry. Oh God. Jonny Barista. She was going to have to tell Nate. She didn't want to. She really didn't want to. They were moving closer and this was going to kill it dead. Oh God.

Rosie felt sick. What was she supposed to do? She wanted to be honest and Nate deserved that. He had told her about his gambling. He had opened his heart about how he had felt during the worst time with Emmie and he had made himself vulnerable. So Rosie was going to have to be brave. She was going to have to tell Nate what she had done. Who she had become. There was no way he would forgive her. No way on earth.

'Oh, Nate.'

'Just say it.'

Rosie was crying. She couldn't help it. She was just about to tell the man she loved that she had kissed someone else. It was hideous and she only had herself to blame.

Nate waited, feeling tormented.

'I kissed someone else,' Rosie blurted out. She covered her face with her hands because she felt so ashamed.

'Who?' Nate said, because he wanted her to say it.

'Some kid at the coffee shop.' Rosie gulped. 'Nate, I am so sorry. So, so sorry. I was drunk, I was horrifically sad. They're not excuses,' she added in a rush. 'They're not, I promise. Nothing excuses what I did.'

Nate bit the bullet. 'Was it just a kiss?' He held his breath.

'Yes!' Rosie looked appalled. 'It was just a stupid kiss. Nothing more.'

'Have you seen him since?'

'No.' Rosie shook her head. 'I've avoided the coffee shop ever since.'

Nate dropped his eyes. Shit. She'd just lied.

'No, wait.' Rosie held her hand up. 'He came up to me as I walked past there once. I was crying. He got me a cup of coffee. I think I cried on him.'

Nate felt a weight shift from his shoulders. Thank God.

'Hang on.' Rosie brushed her tears away and studied him. 'You knew.'

He nodded. 'I did. I saw something on your phone. And I drove past you when that kid was hugging you that day.'

'Oh no.' Rosie felt terrible. 'Nate.'

'That was the night we were supposed to be watching the film. That's why I didn't turn up. It's why I nearly hit the casino again.' Nate took Rosie's hand again. 'Because I couldn't… I can't bear the thought of you with someone else.'

Rosie couldn't help it; she was weeping again.

'Can I get you anything else?' the waitress asked tentatively.

'Just the bill and a taxi if you wouldn't mind,' Nate answered. 'I think we need to go home.'

'Sure.' The waitress hesitated. 'Forgive me, but I hope you manage to sort everything out. You look as though you really love each other, whatever else has gone on.'

'Thank you,' said Nate.

'Do you forgive me?' Rosie asked. She knew her voice sounded choked but she couldn't help it. 'I understand if you don't. I'll hate it, but I wouldn't blame you.'

Nate nodded. 'Yes. I do forgive you. It was just a kiss, I can let it go. Because I know I have to take some responsibility for my part in this too. It's not just about you doing that. I gambled again and I promised you I wouldn't do it ever again.'

Rosie felt so relieved, she thought she might be sick.

'We've made mistakes,' Nate said honestly. 'But we've also been through something that most people won't ever have to experience. Thank God. Because you and I know that as much as we love Emmie, we wouldn't wish the cancer on anyone else. And she's the best kid in the world.'

'Agreed.'

'So we fucked up a bit.'

'Yes. I guess we did.'

'Let's go,' Nate said, buttoning his own coat.

They were stopped as they were about to leave the restaurant by the waitress who thrust a box at them.

'The chef made you a special dessert and he wanted you to have it,' she said. 'Because of your engagement here.'

'Thank you,' Rosie said, taking the box.

In the taxi, she turned to Nate. 'What's happened to us?' she whispered. 'Who are we?

'We're people who have a very, very sick child,' Nate said, pulling Rosie's head into his shoulder. 'That's who we are.'

Rosie nodded and clung onto him. When they arrived home, Nate helped her out of the taxi. Inside the house, Lily was babysitting and she was doing her best to looked relaxed, but her face was pinched and she was clearly on edge.

'How was your night?' she asked brightly.

Nate looked at Rosie. 'How would we describe it?'

'Emotional,' she stated.

'Cathartic,' he added.

Lily looked at them, not sure what to make of that. 'And is that… good?'

'Very,' Rosie said, sitting on the sofa. 'How was Emmie?'

'Bouncing off the walls like a frog on acid,' Lily replied promptly. 'A tad over-excited, let's say. What's in the box?'

'Oh.' Rosie handed it to Lily. 'That's dessert. Have that, for your troubles.'

Lily opened the top and peered into it. 'Er… no. I think you two should have that. Listen, I'm shooting off now, but I'm glad you had a good night.'

Rosie saw her out and they hugged at the door.

'You OK?' Lily mouthed.

Rosie nodded. 'Think so,' she mouthed back.

'Did you kiss?' Lily whispered.

'No. It wasn't like that. We talked. About everything.' Rosie leant her head against the door. 'It was good. I don't know what it means, but we talked.'

Lily kissed her cheek. 'I'm glad. That's something.' She waved and walked to her car.

'Did you see this?' Nate pointed to the dessert box.

Rosie peered into it. The chef had somehow found out the date of their engagement and he had piped it in icing across a chocolate flan. And he had decorated it with red hearts.

'That's… kitsch. But totally cute.'

'Yeah.'

'I think I need to go to bed,' Rosie said. She avoided Nate's eyes. It was too soon for anything like that. She didn't even know if they could get back to that place.

Nate yawned. 'I'll be up in five. Just need to check my work phone in case Gill has messaged me.'

Rosie nodded. That meant Nate would probably put the TV on and fall asleep in front of it. But she couldn't expect miracles. She left him to it and headed upstairs. In bed fifteen minutes later in a t-shirt after checking on Emmie four times, she heard Nate come in. He pottered around in the bathroom for a few minutes, checked on Emmie, then climbed into bed.

Expecting him to sleep on the edge of the bed again, Rosie said 'Thank you for dinner. Night.' She suddenly felt his arms snake around her and she tensed for a second, then relaxed against him. She hadn't felt Nate around her like this in months.

Nate kissed Rosie's shoulder. There was so much more he wanted to do. But for now, perhaps this was enough. This was more than enough. He and Rosie were wrapped around one another. And they were holding hands.

Rosie felt Nate's hand in hers and she held on tight. Even if this was all they could be, it was something. It wasn't everything, not by a long shot. But it was something.

Emmie

'So they seemed really happy when they got home?' Emmie could hardly contain herself.

Aunt Lily glanced at Dr Tom and then looked back at Emmie. 'I mean, I think so, yes. They weren't kissing or holding hands or anything. But they seemed... close. Closer. Better.'

Emmie frowned. Aunt Lily sounded cautious and Emmie wasn't sure why. It all sounded positive. The fact that they were happy and chatty when they got home was huge. The fact that they had seemed calmer and more normal with one another for the past two weeks since was amazing. Emmie understood that it didn't mean that everything was back on track just yet, but she wasn't sure why they had to be this low-key either.

'What do you think, Dr Tom?'

'I think it all sounds very encouraging.' Dr Tom smiled.

Emmie considered him. Dr Tom was wearing his glasses again which meant that he looked more like himself, but at the same time, it made him a little harder to read. When he'd been wearing the contact lenses, his eyes had been completely exposed. If rather red and squinty.

'I think it sounds brilliant!' Cara said excitedly. She shot Emmie a look as if to say 'why are the grown-ups being so weird about it?'

Emmie smiled. Good old Cara. She could always be relied upon to be upbeat about everything. Well, apart from Emmie dying at some point, but she was only human. Emmie didn't hold that against her. She'd probably hate it if Cara wasn't there anymore, if she thought about it hard enough, but luckily it wasn't something she needed to worry about.

Today with Dr Tom was unusual in that he had asked her to bring her Aunt Lily and Cara along to her Tuesday afternoon session at his office. He said he wanted to speak to the people she was close to and get a grasp of what they were dealing with in relation to her illness. Emmie found it a bit strange, but she trusted Dr Tom. If he thought it could be useful to talk to the people around her – and Emmie suspected he might try and get them talking in the special way that he had – good for him. So far, they had only talked about the treasure hunt, however. But it was fun, the way all Dr Tom's sessions were. Emmie and Cara were snuggled up in two beanbags whilst the two grown-ups were on Dr Tom's terrible grey chairs.

Aunt Lily had been amazing since she and Dr Tom had taken on this project, Emmie thought, watching her chatting away. And she got on well with Dr Tom anyway so she had left Maya and George back at the house. But Emmie was impressed that Cara had given up her gymnastics class to come here. Cara rarely missed a class, let alone one involving her favourite sport, so Emmie took it as a sign of how tight their friendship was that Cara had made the effort. Although Emmie suspected that Cara had been dying to meet Dr Tom for a while. She kept flicking her hair at him, which was a bit off-putting.

'So what's the plan for the next part of the treasure hunt?' Cara asked Dr Tom with a charming smile Emmie had never seen before. 'I know we skipped a few dates to get to the engagement, so what do we do now?'

Dr Tom turned to Emmie, seemingly unfazed by Cara's attentiveness. 'You're the boss. What next?'

Emmie fished her notebook out of her school bag. 'Well, me and Aunt Lily have been through what Aunt Lily remembers about mum and dad's dates.' She consulted her notes. 'We know they visited various bars and restaurants over the months that followed the engagement. They saw a few plays together, went to the cinema. Had lots of cosy dates at home.'

Lily nodded. 'They were inseparable after the engagement. I couldn't get hold of Rosie when she was with Nate because she was so besotted with him and vice versa. So they spent every second together.' She smiled. 'It was cute. They had fallen head over heels for one another and they spent the year before their wedding completely loved up and in each other's company.'

'Did they socialise much?' Dr Tom asked. 'Not having met that special someone myself yet, I find this interesting.'

'From a scientific point of view?' Aunt Lily asked him, looking amused.

'Sort of,' said Dr Tom.

Emmie wondered why Dr Tom had gone rather pink.

Aunt Lily laughed, but not unkindly. 'Well, I'm not sure Rosie and Nate are a fair benchmark, if I'm honest. I mean, me and Jamie hung out quite a bit when we were dating, but we weren't like those two.'

'In what way?'

Dr Tom was going all detective today, Emmie decided. She wasn't sure why he was asking so many questions about her mum and dad, but she knew that he must have his reasons. And actually, Dr Tom was nosy at the best of times, which was one of the things Emmie liked the most about him anyway. He said he found her interesting, but she felt the same about him.

Emmie shot Cara a frown in an attempt to get her to stop making gooey eyes at Dr Tom, but it didn't make any difference. Emmie sighed and realised Aunt Lily was mid-explanation about her parents. She tuned back in to listen.

'Me and Jamie are what I would describe as an average couple,' Aunt Lily was saying. 'We… get along. We're good friends. We, umm… grab a few moments when we can.'

Aunt Lily gave Dr Tom a funny look at this point and Cara started to giggle.

'And there was me thinking I was being all diplomatic,' Aunt Lily huffed. 'OK, well. I see myself and Jamie as normal. I love hanging out with him and we do all sorts of stuff together with the kids. You've met him, Dr Tom; he's a funny guy.'

'He is,' Dr Tom agreed. 'But you see yourselves differently as a couple than Emmie's parents.'

'Yes,' Aunt Lily said simply. 'They were so in love, they wanted to be around one another constantly. In answer to your earlier question, yes, they did socialise. They weren't that insular. They went out with friends – both his and hers – and we did stuff as a foursome too. But they've always had a special connection. I'll be honest, I did see a glimmer of that a fortnight ago after their date.'

'Excellent,' Dr Tom said approvingly. 'So Emmie, what do you think? Is it worth us re-creating these dates they had in between their engagement and their wedding?'

Emmie shook her head. 'I don't think so.' She pointed to her notebook. 'This might sound weird, but I wondered if we should skip to the wedding.'

'How romantic,' Cara gushed, staring at Dr Tom as though she was imagining them walking down the aisle together.

Emmie rolled her eyes. She had never seen Cara act this way before, not even over Jack Ramsden in Year 12 – and everyone fancied him because he looked like one of the Beckham boys.

'Are they ready for that?' Aunt Lily looked concerned. 'It might be a bit much to move right on to the wedding.'

'I don't know,' Emmie admitted.

She was being truthful; she didn't know. She just knew that for some reason, the next step needed to be significant. Emmie knew she was probably getting ahead of herself, but she couldn't shake off the feeling that she was meant to.

'That said, maybe they're ripe for us to really go in for the emotional stuff,' Aunt Lily said, sounding more confident.

Cara nodded. 'I think it's a lovely idea. Although... we're not going to try and make them get married again, are we?'

Emmie turned to Aunt Lily, who looked shocked.

'God no, 'Aunt Lily said. 'That definitely is too much.'

'So?' Dr Tom raised his eyebrows.

'I think we should... send them to the venue,' Aunt Lily suggested. 'They went back there for their first wedding anniversary too. Apparently that was – oh I'm not even going to pretend that I'm talking about something else – apparently, it was a very special night for them.' She paused. 'I've just remembered something, too. Rosie arranged for Nate to go into the kitchen at this place as the food is off the hook. He got really into cooking after that. I wonder if I can speak to them and see if they can do something like that again.'

Dr Tom smiled. 'Well, this sounds like a lovely, romantic thing to do. Maybe they should stay overnight there together?'

'They'll never leave me on my own,' Emmie fretted. 'It's too far away. It's in Oxford, I think. Isn't it? Mum will panic that she won't reach me in time if something goes wrong. I mean, I feel fine, but I know what she's like.'

'Good point,' Dr Tom nodded. He pushed his glasses back into place. 'Your mum won't be able to relax if she's worried about you.'

Aunt Lily put her finger to her mouth. Emmie smiled; her mum did the exact same thing when she was thinking.

'How about... you and I stay somewhere nearby?' Aunt Lily said. Her eyes lit up triumphantly. 'Rosie – your mum – can't argue with that. And it would be fun for us, wouldn't it, Emmie?'

Emmie grinned. Aunt Lily was being so amazing at the moment. She always had been a lovely aunt, but recently, she had been incredible. She stepped in to help constantly so this treasure hunt could take place and she always found a way around a problem. It made Emmie want to cry a bit, but in a good way.

Dr Tom looked absurdly pleased. 'Fantastic idea! Do you need me to do anything?'

Aunt Lily shook her head. 'No, I'll sort it. Emmie, can you come up with some clues for them?'

Cara sat up eagerly. 'Can I help with that too?'

Emmie nodded, feeling bad for thinking Cara was being silly around Dr Tom as soon as her best friend slipped her arm through hers. Emmie felt very lucky today.

Dr Tom consulted his notes again – or as Emmie thought, pretended to. 'I wonder if I could speak to your Aunt Lily alone for a moment or two? Just a little idea I have, but it's a surprise.'

Emmie shrugged. 'Cool. I can show Cara where we sit sometimes. Under that big oak tree?'

'Perfect.' Dr Tom saw them out and closed the door behind him.

'This way,' Emmie said, showing Cara the way to the double doors at the back of the hospital. 'Me and Dr Tom sit under here sometimes when we get bored of his office.'

'He has funny paintings.'

'He's a funny guy,' Emmie said, giving her a sideways glance.

'He's *hot*,' Cara said, going all girly. 'Don't tell me you haven't noticed!'

Emmie gave her a stern glance. 'He's my counsellor. I don't look at him that way.'

'Well.' Cara flapped a hand in front of her face. 'I wouldn't be able to help it if I were you.'

Emmie didn't like to say that Dr Tom normally talked to her about far more serious issues. Fancying him was the last thing on her mind.

'What do you think they're talking about?' Cara asked as they strolled out into the sunshine with their arms linked.

'Me,' Emmie said wryly. 'And that's not me being big-headed, I promise. But Dr Tom always wants to talk about me. I think he finds me one of his very best case studies.' She threw herself onto the grass beneath the huge oak tree. 'Isn't this a nice spot? It's lovely and shady.'

Cara's expression had suddenly become rather serious. In fact, Emmie wasn't sure if her friend was about to cry.

'Hey. What's wrong?'

'I don't know.' Cara looked down at the grass and tugged at some of it. 'I think it's because we're here. At the hospital. It reminds me that you're sick.' Her voice broke slightly. 'I don't mean I ever forget that, Em. But this brings it back.'

Emmie wrapped her arms around her knees. She knew what Cara meant. It was the worst thing about seeing Dr Tom. Now that she had made the decision to stop her treatment, Emmie hated being anywhere near a hospital. Hospitals made her feel sick and they brought back dreadful memories. Not that it had been a terrible experience in every way because the staff at any of the hospitals she had attended had been awesome. So kind and caring. The treatment had probably gone as smoothly as it could when it was as intensive and harsh as some of hers had been.

But Emmie couldn't help the way she felt when she came back here. The smell of the disinfectant. The smell of the food. She shuddered. She had to work hard not to feel sick or be sick when she entered the building. But

Emmie felt bad that Cara was sad because she was only here as a favour.

'Sorry,' she said out loud.

'It's not your fault.' Cara gave her a watery smile. 'I wanted to come. Dr Tom is great and it was nice chatting about your parents and stuff. I just hate thinking about you being sick. And now that you're done with the chemo and your hair is all lovely again... I don't know. I guess I sometimes let myself think we're going to be friends forever.'

'We *will* be friends forever!' Emmie said. 'Cara, you're my best friend. No one has been there for me the way you have. I feel fine, I promise you. Please don't worry.'

Cara started to cry, frantically brushing her tears away. 'Sorry, Em. Honestly, it's just being back here. I try not to think about it and most of the time it's alright. It's just this hospital.'

Emmie put her arm around Cara. She did worry about Cara and how she might react if – when – the worst came. She had gone through a phase of trying to get Cara to make friends with some other girls so that she wasn't lonely when Emmie had gone. But Cara had seen through it straight away and she had been pretty angry. So Emmie had stopped doing it. Because it wasn't up to her who Cara was friends with. She wanted her to be alright, but she knew she just had to leave things as they were. Emmie had a feeling that Darcy, a girl in their class, would be the perfect new best friend for Cara if she needed to be, but Emmie didn't dare suggest it.

'We've got ages together,' Emmie said, trying not to cry as well. 'We're going to go to concerts together. We're going to go shopping together and buy clothes. We're going to – we're going to double date,' she added.

Cara laughed, but only a bit. 'I hope so. I don't want to be best friends with anyone else. I hate the fact that this has happened to you.'

'Yeah, me too.'

'Hey, you two.'

Emmie looked up. It was Aunt Lily and Dr Tom.

'Good chat?' Emmie asked, feeling concerned. Aunt Lily looked like she'd been crying.

Dr Tom put his hands in his pockets. 'Great chat. Thanks for being patient.'

Aunt Lily looked at Cara. 'Are you OK, honey?'

Cara nodded and wiped her eyes.

Aunt Lily crouched down next to them. 'I have an idea. Why don't we pick some pizzas up and take them back to yours, Emmie?'

'Sounds good,' she said, getting up and brushing herself down.

Aunt Lily helped Cara up. 'See you at my car in a minute,' she called to Emmie.

Emmie looked at Dr Tom. 'Aunt Lily looked like she'd been crying.'

'It's my speciality,' Dr Tom said jokily. 'Making women cry.'

Emmie looked at him. 'I'm really glad you're my counsellor, Dr Tom.'

'Me too.' He leant back on his heels as though thinking about something. 'Hmm. OK. I have some homework for you. I wonder if you could write something about all the important people in your life. What they mean to you and so on. Your parents, Aunt Lily. Cara. Your cousins. Could you do that for me?'

Emmie smiled. 'But that's nice homework, Dr Tom. Are you sure you want me to do that?'

'Very sure. So I'll see you next week, OK? The homework, could you do it by then?'

'Holy moly,' she moaned. 'You're worse than my teachers.'

'Slave driver,' Dr Tom agreed. 'Bye, Emmie.'

'Bye, slave driver,' she said with a grin. 'Stay away from beanbags.'

'Ho, I will do,' he said. 'Laters,' he added, waving his hand as he walked off.

He's such a geek, Emmie sighed to herself affectionately as she headed to the car park.

Rosie and Nate

Rosie zipped her suitcase up. It had been a long time since she had been away anywhere nice. She had stayed at many a hotel near a hospital and she was an expert at mastering broken sleep in unknown beds. But Emmie had been with her every time.

Rosie sat down on the bed. She still didn't know where she and Nate were going; all she knew was that Lily and Emmie were staying in a hotel nearby. But she couldn't help feeling edgy about it. She trusted Lily with her life, of course. But babysitting was one thing; overnight was another. Rosie had no idea why that would be any different if she was honest; it was only a few more hours. She wouldn't have contemplated it during the worst times of Emmie's illness, but she supposed it should be OK now.

Her phone rang; it was Lily.

'Stressing about me and Emmie staying somewhere overnight?'

'Yes, psychic twin.' Rosie smiled into her phone. 'I'm trying not to, but I'm only human, OK?'

'OK. But we're literally five minutes down the road,' Lily told her. 'Closer than my house is to yours, in fact.'

'Right. It's fine. Can I know where I'm going yet?'

Lily started singing 'No, because it's a sur-pr-iiiiiise,' before Rosie interrupted her. 'Stop that, Lil. You know I got the singing gene.'

'I know. Nails on a blackboard. You should find your final clue downstairs, I think. By your keys…'

'Am I meeting Nate there or am I…?' Rosie stared at her phone. Lily had gone.

Rosie sighed and checked out how she looked. She was wearing a pretty summer dress – white, sprigged with cherries – and some bright red sling-backs. That would be terrible for driving in if she was due to drive anywhere, she realised. And she had only packed a pair of flat gladiator sandals and a pair of dressy heels for dinner – if dinner was involved.

Collecting her suitcase and her handbag, Rosie went downstairs. She stopped by the stand in the hallway that had all the keys on it. She couldn't see a note on it anywhere. Then she saw it tucked in the mirror on the other wall. A card, tucked behind it. It had a couple in wedding dress in front of it. A guy in a suit, a woman in a big, white dress. Inside, it said 'Happy memories! The big day – and one year on. Your carriage awaits.'

Wow. She and Nate were going back to their wedding venue. Rosie looked out of the window and frowned. She couldn't see a car, but within seconds, Nate's car pulled up. She smiled. Nate wouldn't mind driving to Oxford – not even on a Saturday afternoon. And at least she didn't have to change her heels.

'Do you know where we're going?' she asked Nate as she got into the car, her luggage safely stowed in the boot. He looked gorgeous. And smelt amazing.

'Nope.' He grinned. 'Because Jamie told me it was a sur-priiiiise.' He sang the last bit tunelessly.

'They're all in it together,' Rosie said, handing him the card.

'Wow.' Nate looked at it then gave her a sideways glance. 'Our wedding venue.'

'Yes.'

'And our first wedding anniversary venue.' Nate put his sunglasses on and gave her that smile he always used to give her when he was thinking something dirty.

'Yes.'

Rosie felt herself blushing. That had been one hell of a weekend. So incredibly romantic and sexy, she could barely think about it.

'And there was me thinking Emmie and Dr Tom had decided to send us on one of the dates we had after we got engaged,' Nate said, setting off. 'Like… us curled up on the sofa together watching some TV series. Or watching one of those high-brow plays I used to pretend I liked after we got engaged.'

'Oh stop it. You loved those plays.'

'I didn't *love* those plays. I loved that you loved them. And I wanted you to think I was intelligent.'

'Oh man…'

'Ha.'

They bickered all the way to Oxford, but there weren't any undertones – no making a dig or avoiding a difficult subject.

Rosie couldn't remember the last time that had happened. She felt so relaxed with Nate again. She knew they still had huge steps to take. Enormous. But even this felt like a step in the right direction. Rosie glanced at

Nate, who looked calm. He loved driving. Rosie was glad they had managed to keep things on an even keel since the dinner at their engagement venue. They had slept close to one another every single night since and Rosie had loved that. Nothing else had happened and she felt bad for even hoping that something might. Because sleeping around each other was a huge thing after sleeping on the edge of opposite sides of the bed for the past few years.

Speaking of which, Rosie felt weirdly sleepy all of a sudden. But not in the exhausted way she used to feel over Emmie and her treatment. This was more like a contented sleepiness. Rosie knew she shouldn't fall asleep right now because she and Nate were chatting like they did in the old days and she wanted to carry on doing it. She promptly fell asleep.

Nate noticed that Rosie had dropped off and he smiled to himself. She always used to do that on longish car journeys. She would be talking away nineteen to the dozen and then she'd fall into a slumber, curled up in her seat like a child, her seat belt coiled around her. Rosie was the only person he knew who had been able to fall asleep standing up on trains and in uncomfortable, economy aeroplane seats practically from the second they got on board.

Nate realised with a sense of shock that he was happy. Happy reminiscing and happy in the present. Happiness wasn't an emotion he had felt connected to for a while. He had been aware of feeling that way in the past, he very much knew it existed. He had been blessed with immense happiness before Emmie had got sick. But since then, he had only felt very short bursts of it. Bursts at some good news about Emmie's health, though the good part of the news had always been short-lived. Beautiful moments with Emmie, even after her diagnosis, that had been magical. But that magic had been marred by the terrifying fear that each wonderful milestone might be the last. Bursts of happiness with Rosie that were mere moments, but even those had been riddled with guilt, because they were dealing with something so hideous, it seeped into everything.

But Nate felt good today. Happy. And he was going to allow himself to feel it. Just for a while.

'We're here,' he said loudly, to wake Rosie up.

'Oh no! I fell asleep.'

'That's OK. It was a good drive.'

Rosie looked up at the hotel. This was where she and Nate had got married. It was stunning. A gorgeous, small hotel which was actually very modern, but beautifully done. There were only twenty rooms, all of them individually designed, and the whole feel was exclusive, cosy and luxurious.

Rosie quickly made a call to check on Emmie.

'Do you love being back at the hotel?' Emmie asked.

Rosie could hear how thrilled she was. 'We do, sweetheart,' she said. 'It's the most wonderful surprise. You are so clever. Here, Daddy wants a word.'

Nate took the phone. 'Who's a superstar? What a fantastic thing to arrange, Em. We're so happy to be here.'

Rosie could hear Emmie laughing and chattering down the phone. Nate chatted for a couple more minutes then passed the phone back.

'We're going in now, baby,' Rosie said. 'I'll speak to you later, OK?'

She finished the call and they got out of the car and went into reception. It was almost all white and silver with attractive staff wearing pale grey jackets.

'Mr and Mrs Johnson? Welcome. We have your room ready.'

Check-in was seamless and efficient. They were shown to a different room to the one they had stayed in previously, which they both loved. In some ways it would have been nice to re-visit the other room they had stayed in after their wedding and for their first anniversary, but there was something refreshing about a new room that had no memories attached to it.

It contained a vast bed, covered in a pristine white-covered duvet and piled up with super-soft faux fur cushions in greys and taupes. The bed looked perfect to snuggle in. The furniture was white and shiny, teamed with a silver-grey carpet and heavy grey drapes that looked as though they would shut out every ounce of morning light. The bathroom had a stand-alone bath that had big, shiny taps and looked deep enough to stand almost waist-deep in water, and his and hers sinks with high-end toiletries and warm, white towels.

'They've arranged a cooking lesson for us this afternoon,' Nate called from the other room.

'For both of us?'

Nate nodded as Rosie joined him. 'Do you want to go?'

'Of course. I mean, I'm terrible in the kitchen, but I can watch you waving a knife around quite happily.'

'It's good to be back here with you.'

Rosie nodded. 'Ditto.' She looked out towards the gardens. 'I remember that view. I had my make-up done facing a window just like this and I remember having such butterflies thinking about seeing you downstairs for the ceremony.'

'Charming,' Nate pouted. 'I was a hundred percent certain I was doing the right thing. I was mucking about with Jamie drinking champagne, all excited that you were due to come downstairs at any second. *I* didn't have butterflies,' he added, nudging her.

'Oh I knew I was doing the right thing,' Rosie retorted. 'I just felt nervous. About what you would think of my dress. How I'd look in the photos. That kind of rubbish.'

'What?' Nate looked astonished. 'You know I think you're beautiful in everything. In nothing, for that matter.'

Rosie grinned. And her stomach flipped over.

Nate came over to the window. 'I can't believe you were worrying about stuff like that. I thought you were perfect from the second I met you.'

'No one's perfect. And I'm definitely not.' Rosie inclined her head.

'You're perfect to me. And I really mean that.'

Rosie was annoyed to find herself feeling emotional. It was just that she hadn't heard Nate say anything like that in a long time. But it was lovely to hear. She found herself turning into him and she thought he was leaning into her.

Was he going to kiss her? The butterflies Rosie had had on her wedding day weren't a patch on the ones she had now. He was. Nate was going to kiss her.

Nate was sure this was the right moment. He had been wanting to do this ever since their lovely dinner together, but he hadn't wanted to frighten Rosie off. And he didn't want her thinking this was just about sex, because it wasn't.

It was about their history together and the amazingly special thing they had had. That they still had. Nate put his hand on Rosie's waist.

There was a knock at the door and suddenly, the moment had gone.

'Come in,' Nate called.

The door opened and a pretty girl in the hotel's grey jacket and skirt came in. 'They're ready for you in the kitchen,' she said. 'I hope you've had a chance to settle in; it's just that the chef has a tight schedule for dinner tonight.'

'No, that's great. Thank you.'

Nate could have happily missed the cookery lesson, but he didn't want to disappoint Emmie who would no doubt want to hear all about it.

'If you'd like to follow me down?' The girl politely waited for them.

Rosie quickly changed her heels for the gladiator sandals as she wanted to wear flats and she and Nate headed down to the kitchen. The inside of the hotel was as striking as they remembered: stylish carpets, unique *objets d'art* and huge windows like archways that showed off views of the carefully-tended kitchen gardens and a small lake covered by a weeping willow.

Nate remembered their wedding day very clearly. It had been a fresh summer's day – not searingly hot, but warm enough and not a drop of rain in sight. A slight breeze. It had been a small affair with very close family and friends for the ceremony and a wonderful wedding breakfast. Everyone had stayed over and they had had breakfast together before Rosie and Nate had headed off on their honeymoon.

'Our wedding was so fantastic,' Rosie said to Nate as they hurried after the girl who was showing them the way. Rosie wasn't sure if Nate was thinking about it, but she was. She felt a stab of pain, thinking of the elegant, low-backed champagne silk dress with spaghetti straps that was boxed up in the loft. Would Emmie ever wear it?

Yes, Rosie decided. She would. Emmie was going to be with them for years. She wouldn't allow herself to think any other way.

'It was the best day ever,' Nate said, grabbing her hand.

Rosie smiled at him and they walked hand in hand into the huge, busy kitchen. Within seconds, they had been put into crisp, white aprons with over-sized chef hats.

'Hello, I'm Jasper.' The head chef introduced himself. He was bald, six foot six and he wore a scowl. He directed them over to a worktop covered in marble. 'We're going to be making chocolate truffles today. And we haven't got much time so I'll explain everything once and then we'll get on. OK?'

'Yes, Chef.' Nate pulled a scared face behind his back at Rosie.

She giggled and knew she was going to struggle to keep a straight face.

They were shown briskly through the process of truffle-making which involved rolling a very rich-looking ganache into balls before rolling them in a variety of coatings: tiny shards of glassy, salted caramel, dust that was apparently coconut and lemongrass and crushed cacao nibs with lavender.

'We'll put them into these presentation boxes and you can take them with you. Alright?'

'Alright,' Rosie said, shoving Nate who hadn't answered.

'Alright,' he said on cue.

'Good.' Jasper strode off and left them to it while the rest of the staff got on with the dinner prep.

Making the truffles was easy, messy and fun.

'Well, I had hoped we might be learning how to make a cheese soufflé or a stuffed chicken ballottine, but hey.' Nate rolled a ball of ganache in the coconut dust.

Rosie hushed him. 'Shhhh! Massive Head Chef Jasper will come and tell us off.'

'He's one scary dude,' Nate said, daringly popping his finished truffle into his mouth because Jasper wasn't looking.

'How are we going to have enough of these to put them in the special presentation box?' Rosie said, laughing as Nate made her eat some ganache from the bowl by waving his finger in front of her face.

'We won't. And he'll probably sack us. Ooooh! At least we won't have to peel potatoes later.'

'Stop it.' Rosie swiftly made a few truffles and put them in the box. She licked her fingers. 'God, that's gorgeous. Is this what your lesson was like when we came for our anniversary?'

'Definitely not. I learnt how to cook steak properly and we made *gratin dauphinois*.' Nate wiped his chocolatey hands on his apron. 'And the chef back them didn't look like a serial killer. This one needs a piece of my mind...'

'How are you getting on?'

Nate jumped out of his skin, realising Jasper was behind them. 'Er, very well, thank you, Chef. We've made lots of truffles, Chef.'

'Good. Make some more.' Jasper stalked away again.

'*Very well, thank you, Chef, we've made lots, Chef,*' Rosie mimicked. 'Wow, you really told him, Nate. I bet he's shaking in his boots.'

'Yeah, yeah,' Nate said sheepishly, before coming up behind her and smearing ganache all over her face.

'Nate! You're really not taking this seriously...' Rosie started laughing. She had chocolate all over her face. And Nate was looking at her the way he used to look at her. And it felt amazing. She felt him snake an arm around her waist and then he suddenly pulled her in for a kiss. 'That's very...'

'Chocolatey. I know.' Nate kissed her again. 'But also bloody sexy.'

'Yes. Sexy. Yes.'

Rosie put her arms around Nate's neck and kissed him back. It had been years. Years since they had kissed like this. Why had they stopped this? Even with all the stress, why had they stopped this?

'I've missed this,' Nate whispered against her mouth. 'And I've missed you.'

'Me too,' Rosie said. She clasped the back of his neck. 'Do it again.'

They kissed endlessly, their hands in each other's hair, moving to roam all over each other's bodies. They kissed with their eyes open, with their eyes closed. Whichever way they did it, it felt natural and right and lovely. They were barely aware of the clatter of saucepans, the swish of water and the chop-chop-chop of knives on boards. When they finally pulled apart, they realised Chef Jasper was standing over them with his arms folded.

'Do you want to finish the truffle-making?' he asked them sternly.

'Out,' Jasper said flatly, pointing comically towards the door.

They didn't argue; they left the kitchen. And they went back to their room. And for the first time in a very long time, they showered together. And spent four hours straight in bed. They called Emmie again quickly, barely made it down to dinner on time, then they headed back to the room and carried on.

'This has been amazing,' Rosie said, curling into Nate's shoulder.

He wrapped his arm around her and kissed the top of her head. 'It has. I'm sorry we fell apart, Rose. My feelings for you haven't changed one bit, I promise.'

'Nor mine. It's just…'

'The illness,' Nate said. 'I know. I refuse to say it was down to Emmie, because it's not her. It's the fact that she got sick.'

'That's such a good way of looking at it,' Rosie said, stroking his neck. 'I hate thinking it's because of Emmie's because she is such an angel. It's not her.'

Nate shook his head. 'No. Emmie has made everything better. She did when she arrived and look, she still is now.'

'I know.' Rosie got choked up and buried her head deeper into Nate's shoulder.

'No,' Nate said. 'No, Rose. No crying. Not tonight. This is so perfect. Emmie is safe with Lily and she's two minutes down the road if she needs us. Let's let tonight be about us. Please? I think that's what Emmie wants too.'

'OK,' Rosie whispered. 'Tonight is about us.'

'And some other nights will be too,' Nate said, turning and putting his hand on her thigh. 'We have to learn to be us again, Rose. Emmie's parents, yes, with everything that comes with that, but we need to be us too. Nate and Rosie. A couple who used to love each other very much. Who still love each other very much.'

'I'm absolutely crazy about you,' Rosie told Nate. 'I think I just forgot for a while. Because my head was too full of other stuff.'

'Same here.' Nate pulled the duvet over their heads. 'Now do stop talking and pretend we just got married.'

'Oh that was a very… naughty… night,' Rosie giggled. 'Although not as bad as our anniversary…'

Nate groaned. 'Stop talking, woman… Do that tomorrow…'

–

'Now, *that* – is a breakfast,' Nate said, surveying his plate. It was piled high with smoked salmon, scrambled eggs, crispy bacon and toast.

'You've worked up an appetite,' Rosie said, eyeing her own plate which featured a pile of streaky bacon, sausages and hash browns.

'Here, you'll need half a bottle of ketchup with that,' Nate said, knowing Rosie's taste well.

'Thanks.' Rosie looked up and started beaming. 'Emmie!'

'What?' Nate turned and held his arms out. 'Hey! What are you doing here?'

Lily followed Emmie in, looking sheepish. 'I'm so sorry,' she said. 'Emmie was desperate to come and see you, so I hope it's alright. I wasn't even sure you two would be down for breakfast, ahem…'

'Well. We have to eat,' Nate said, giving her a wink.

Rosie shook her head. 'Of course we're having breakfast. Sit here, Ems. Have some of my bacon.'

Nate politely asked the waiting staff if they could have a couple more chairs at their table and they were brought over. A waitress brought up some extra plates and cutlery and got them some more coffee and orange juice.

Emmie started tucking in. 'It's nice,' she said, looking around. 'No wonder you got married here.'

'Right?' Nate nodded. 'The Head Chef is a bit weird though…' He told her all about the truffle-making and Emmie giggled.

'So, this isn't the end of the treasure hunt,' Emmie told them, with a mouthful of bacon. 'Because you look really happy, but I don't want you to forget and get unhappy again. So I'll be sending you on some more dates, if that's OK.'

'That's definitely OK,' Nate said, smiling at Rosie across the table.

'We'd love that,' Rosie agreed. She knew they didn't need it, not now. But if it kept Emmie happy, who were they to tell her she couldn't do it?

'Oh, you both look like you used to,' Lily grinned.

'How's that?' Nate asked, laughing.

'Perfect,' Lily said, sitting back. 'You look perfect together. And I couldn't be happier for you both.'

Rosie and Nate stared at one another. Thank God they'd found their way back. Their eyes slid to Emmie who was busy swilling orange juice and munching on toast. All thanks to Emmie. Who probably thought she was the one who had blown them apart in the first place. But she wasn't. They had accidentally fallen apart. And it was Emmie who had put them back together again.

Her, Nate and Emmie, thought Rosie. The three of them. Perfect together.

Emmie – Two Months Later

Emmie was lying in bed. She had done her homework. Cara had come over for dinner and they'd made Rice Krispie chicken together and they'd eaten it with ketchup and some potato wedges.

Emmie pulled her diary towards her. She'd done her homework for Dr Tom as well. He wanted her to write down all of her feelings about her illness so she could 'release' them and feel peaceful about it. Or something. Emmie loved Dr Tom's thinking and she thought it was possible that she did feel better about it now she'd written it down. And she was surprised to find that she wasn't as angry these days. Maybe because things were so much better with her parents.

Emmie smiled to herself. She had sent them on another three dates so far, all with treasure hunt clues. They had been to the cinema, out for brunch and crazy golf – not because they'd been before, but because Emmie knew her dad would love it. They seemed really happy again. They still bickered. Her dad still sometimes worked late and that irked her mum. But they were OK. They were back on track. And that was all she had ever wanted.

Emmie had talked about their next date with Dr Tom, but they had agreed just one more. And then her parents could do whatever they wanted to do. Emmie knew it was out of insecurity that she had carried on. They had seemed so happy at their wedding hotel, but Emmie had been terrified that it had just all been in the moment and that it wouldn't last. And the thought of that was too horrible to contemplate.

Emmie stretched. She felt tired quite a lot recently. And her vision had been a bit blurry again. Only on and off; she had barely noticed it. She was due for a check-up again soon, but Emmie felt so good apart from those couple of things that she was sure she was fine. Emmie wondered what she needed to get ready for school tomorrow, but she couldn't seem to grasp hold of her thoughts. She had P.E. And Maths. And maybe Geography. No – History. Where did she have History? Did she have History? Or Maths?

Emmie felt a pain in her head. Not sharp, not unbearable, just a pain. It came and then it went. Emmie breathed. It was OK. But no, it had come back. She felt oddly at peace, though. Calm. Contented. Everything in her life was how she wanted it to be. She was happy at school. Cara was a wonderful friend. Her family were ace. Dr Tom was geeky but fab. And her parents were back together. She had got them back together and they were going to be alright.

Emmie cried out because the pain in her head had increased. It became sharp and definitely unbearable. Emmie realised she should try and call for help, but the words wouldn't form.

So this is it, Emmie thought to herself, feeling a cold realisation flood through her. *This is it. This is the moment when I go.* It was a shock but at the same time, Emmie had been expecting this for years so it felt familiar in an odd way. She braced herself because she wasn't sure she wanted to do this. Could she stop it?

Emmie wanted to stay for a bit longer. She wanted to say goodbye to everyone. She wanted to see Cara again. Aunt Lily and Uncle Jamie. And her cousins. Dr Tom. Her mum and dad. Emmie wanted to see her mum and dad. Just one last time. She was going to miss them so much and she wanted to say sorry because she knew they would miss her terribly. They had worked so hard at keeping her alive, at making her short life incredibly happy.

But Emmie knew it was OK for her to go now. Unexpectedly, a small tear trickled down her cheek. Emmie knew everyone would feel sad, but she didn't have any choice in this; she never had. And now her head felt excruciatingly painful. As though it was swollen and about to burst.

And then, just as quickly, the pain had gone. And a few seconds later, so had Emmie.

The Funeral

Rosie stood next to Nate staring at the wooden cross that bore Emmie's name and significant dates. This felt like an appalling nightmare, but at the same time, it was hideously real. Their baby had gone. They were alone by Emmie's grave and Rosie couldn't seem to bring herself to leave. Yet part of her wanted to be as far away from here as she could possibly be. It was a brilliant sunny day in August and Rosie knew she would hate this month forever more.

Nate couldn't speak. All he could do was stand next to Rosie. The funeral had been arranged by Lily, who seemed to have all the info about Emmie's requests. It was at a place in Essex not too far from where they lived, where there was a huge burial area. It wasn't religious or with an attachment to any church as such, but it was lovely and open and Emmie had chosen a biodegradable, wicker coffin. Nate didn't even know Emmie knew about biodegradable coffins.

The ceremony had been beautiful. There had been a huge crowd of people present. Nate's parents had flown in from France. Rosie and Lily's parents were there. Loads of kids from Emmie's school. George and Maya. Dr Tom and some of the staff from the hospital. Gill and Sexy Kev and half the office at the station had turned up on Nate's behalf. Rosie's colleagues from the gym and many of her Pilates devotees, too.

Jamie had read from one of Emmie's favourite books and Dr Tom had delivered such a moving speech, he had only just managed to finish it without breaking down. The music had been an Adele song and a couple of others that Emmie had apparently chosen. Nate didn't ever want to hear those songs again, but he knew that at some point, they would probably bring him comfort.

Nate didn't know what to say to Rosie. And Rosie didn't know what to say to him. Everything since Emmie had been diagnosed had been about Emmie. And now she had gone. They had never known how long she might have, but they had all hoped it would be longer than this. That she would experience more of life. That selfishly, they would be able to enjoy her for years and years to come. Their gorgeous, bright, huge-hearted girl.

Nate didn't know how he would breathe again. He felt as though he had had something trapped in his throat since the night Emmie had died. It felt as though his heart had exploded and a piece was lodged right there, where he was meant to breathe. And what about him and Rosie? They were broken. Not like before, where they had drifted apart and there was a yawning gap between them. Right now, they had been broken beyond recognition. They had been shattered into fragments because a huge part of their lives had been taken away from them. The beam of sunshine that had complemented their relationship had diminished. And Nate couldn't stand the pain.

Rosie felt empty. As though the life had been sucked out of her. Which was stupid, because it wasn't her life that had been sucked away, it was Emmie's. Yet there was a hole inside her that Rosie knew would never, ever feel full again. Their poor baby. Why hadn't she had longer? Rosie felt rage building inside her. They all knew that Emmie's tumour was a ticking time bomb. They all knew that it could expand at any second and that Emmie would have no defence. But she had been well for such a long time. She had lived life like any other kid her age and it had felt as though Emmie might just survive this. It was ridiculous, but the shock of losing Emmie had damned near knocked Rosie sideways and she hated herself for letting herself get into a headspace where she thought they were safe.

'Are you both OK?' It was Lily.

Rosie turned into her arms. She saw Nate do the same with Jamie.

'I'm here for you,' Lily said, crying on Rosie's shoulder. 'I'm being useless at the moment, but I promise you I will be strong and together soon and we'll get through this.'

Rosie nodded.

'I'm lost for words,' Jamie said to Nate hoarsely. 'And you know that never happens to me. She was a little diamond.'

Nate rubbed his eyes. He had no words either. No words to describe his beautiful, talented, special girl.

'Jamie, let's go. We'll see you back at the house,' said Lily. 'Take your time. We'll deal with everything.'

Rosie and Nate stood silently again.

'I'm so sorry for intruding, but I just wanted to come and give you both a hug.'

It was Dr Tom. Rosie let him hug her. He felt strong and comforting.

'I'm so terribly sorry,' Dr Tom murmured.

'She told you about her funeral then,' Rosie said, pulling away and sniffing into a tissue.

Dr Tom had a man hug with Nate then turned back to Rosie.

'Yes. Is that OK? About her funeral?' Dr Tom looked worried. 'Lily got in touch and I passed on the info.'

'Of course it's OK,' Rosie nodded. 'I could never bring myself to talk to Emmie about it. Neither could Nate. It made it too real. And now it is.' Her face crumpled.

'Understandable, Rosie. I wanted to ask if you'd read Emmie's diary yet? The one I gave her?'

Rosie shook her head. She hadn't touched anything in Emmie's room. She didn't know if she could go in there for a while yet.

Dr Tom touched his glasses. 'I asked Emmie to write about the people who meant something to her in it. And I asked her if she was OK with people reading about themselves in the event of this… this heart-breaking end. She was more than happy for you all to know her thoughts. She wrote something so honest and funny and sweet about me, it made me cry weeks ago when she wrote it.'

Rosie bit her lip and looked at her shoes. She didn't know when she would be able to do that, but at some point, she was sure it would be lovely.

'Do you think she knew?' Nate asked suddenly.

'Knew what?' Dr Tom turned to Nate.

'That she didn't have much longer left,' Nate managed. 'I just wonder if that's why she was so keen to get us back together. Why it became her… her life's mission. Her last wish.' He choked on the words.

Dr Tom pushed his hands into his pockets. 'Well. I don't know if she sensed it, but I have seen this in terminal patients before.'

'Seen what?' Rosie said. She could barely take in what Dr Tom was saying, but she knew he was saying something important.

'There is sometimes a sense of urgency at the end. The need to tie up loose ends. And then they feel safe to go. Don't get me wrong; Emmie had no control over what happened to her. This isn't like a natural situation where a person in hospital will often wait until relatives have left and then they go. It's just an innate sense of needing to get things done. But no, I don't think she had any idea of it at all. I just did whatever I could to help her with her loose ends.'

'She thought the world of you,' Rosie murmured.

'And I, I thought the world of her too. She was… enchanting and funny and clever.' Dr Tom faltered. 'Her positive outlook and her braveness were just a few of her lovely qualities.'

'How do we move forward, Dr Tom?' Nate asked, out of the blue. 'Me and Rosie… we don't know what to do.'

Rosie swallowed. She loved Nate so much. But the pain of being around him right now was too much to cope with. His intense, jagged grief mirrored her own, but Rosie couldn't stand being in her own grief right now, let alone witnessing and feeling Nate's so deeply.

'Do whatever you have to do to survive,' Dr Tom advised immediately. 'This is the most terrible thing for both of you. Heartache on a grand scale. If you can be together and help one another, do so. If you need to be apart, be apart. Not forever, please. That would be an incredible waste. You are both such great people who have just recently found one another again. It was Emmie's legacy to get you back together. You love each other as much as you loved her. Heal and then you can re-build your lives together. It will take time, I'm sure. But Emmie believed in you. And so do I.'

Rosie felt tears streaming down her face. She couldn't look at Nate, but she knew he would be crying right now. It felt so horribly cruel. She and Nate had been brought back together by their child and now she had gone and their hearts were crushed.

'I'll leave you to it,' said Dr Tom kindly. 'But please know that it was my greatest privilege to work with and to know Emmie. She will always have a special place in my heart and I'm not meant to let any of my patients in there.' He smiled with great sadness. 'But she crept in and stayed there and I will miss her.'

He left and Rosie began to cry again. The pain was excruciating.

'I think I need to go somewhere,' she said to Nate. She was scared to say it out loud, but she felt she should speak up.

'Go where?' Nate felt hollow. He had been thinking the same himself, but stupidly, it hurt that Rosie had voiced the same thing.

Rosie shook her head vaguely. 'A Pilates retreat, perhaps? Something like that. Abroad. Away from here. But I'll only do it if you need to go too. I won't leave you alone.'

Nate cleared his throat and rubbed his eyes again. 'I don't know. I thought maybe I'd go on a cooking tour.

Near my parents' place in France. But not if you need me here. I won't leave you alone either.'

'Maybe we need some… some time apart,' Rosie stammered. She stared straight ahead, knowing that if she looked at Nate, she would be on her knees. 'And it's not because I don't love you. It's because I love you so much, in fact.'

'Yes. That's how I feel,' Nate agreed slowly, his voice sounding strange. 'You're the only person who knows how I feel, the only person who understands. But I feel so… raw. I feel like I'm bleeding and you're bleeding and I need to heal myself. But I can't when you're bleeding too. Does any of that make sense?'

Rosie clasped her hands together. 'All of it. All of it makes sense. I just hate myself for having to be away from you. But I know I can't be around you right now. It hurts too much.'

'I miss her, Rose. I miss her.' Nate started to weep. 'The world seems dark without her.'

'Like it's lost its sparkle.' Rosie wanted to hold Nate. She wanted to hold him so badly. Her face was wet and her whole body ached from the wracking sobs that had torn her apart for days. 'We will come back together, won't we, Nate? We will find each other again?'

Nate stared at her. 'We have to, Rose. We have to. Not just for Emmie, but for us. Because we've been in this together. Right from the start. Before Emmie. And she showed us that. I have… loved you for the longest time, Rose. You're the only person I want. Now that we've lost Emmie, you are the only person.'

Nate wanted to fiercely hug Rosie. He wanted to crush her to him and take her pain away. But he was useless and smashed up and no good for anything right now.

Rosie wiped her eyes. 'And you, are the only person for me too. But I have to try and deal with losing her, Nate. And I can't be around you to do that. Everything about you reminds me of Emmie.'

Nate said nothing. He couldn't be near Rosie either. He knew one of them had to leave first and he knew it should be him. Rosie deserved some time here alone with Emmie because she was her mum.

Nate walked away. His heart was heavy and the pain was intense, but it was the only thing he could do.

And then Rosie did the only thing she could do. Her shoulders rounded and slumped and she bent her head and cried. For herself and Nate – but most of all, for the brave little girl whose eleven years of life had filled their hearts with both tragedy and joy. And who had now left behind a bleeding wound Rosie wasn't sure she and Nate knew how to stem.

Three Months Later

Nate threw down his keys and made himself a cup of coffee. It was Friday night and the house still felt stagnant and empty. But Nate was learning to be here and not hate it now. He strolled into the conservatory and switched on the little heater they used in there when it got chilly. It was November and the garden reflected that. Some of the trees were stripped bare, others were still adorned with gold and red leaves. Nate had moved Emmie's trampoline to the near corner of the house because looking at it made him cry.

Nate wrapped his hands around his coffee cup to warm them up. Three months. It had been three months. He had only taken a month off work in the end and he had spent most of it with his parents in Normandy. He had attended a few classes at local restaurants learning classic French cooking but apart from that, he had allowed himself to be looked after by his mother who had treated him like a child, cooking and cleaning up after him. Nate had taken plenty of long walks that allowed him brief moments of solitude for thinking and crying ridiculous amounts and he had visited lots of historic areas he now had no memory of.

Nate sipped his coffee. He missed Emmie. He missed Rosie. Nothing in his life felt the same. And he was pretty sure it wouldn't ever be again. Nate leant back in his chair. Now that he was home, Gill had assumed his mother's role, bringing him casseroles and doing a quick tidy-up of the house whenever she popped in. Nate was certain Sexy Kev must want to strangle him by now, but he appreciated Gill's friendship and support.

Lily and Jamie had been fantastic, Nate mused. Lily phoned every day and Jamie had come over with packs of beer and take-away curries, refusing to take no for an answer. And he didn't bat an eyelid when Nate abruptly burst into tears because something on the TV or in conversation had set him off or quite simply just because certain things reminded him unbearably of Emmie.

Nate had been scared that he wouldn't be able to go near his niece and nephew, that seeing them would be too painful. Children, not surprisingly, reminded him poignantly of Emmie and what he had lost. But he had found George and Maya to be a huge comfort. Cuddles with their warm, little bodies made him emotional, but Nate was grateful for their affection and love. Dr Tom had been in touch too. He hadn't over-stepped the mark but he had checked in now and again. It meant a lot.

Nate still hadn't been into Emmie's bedroom. Well, he'd been in and he had sat on the bed, but he hadn't been able to stay for long, because the smell of her still lingered in the room and every single item belonged to and reminded him of Emmie. Nate had gone into the bedroom one more time to put all the sympathy cards he'd taken down in there. He couldn't stand looking at them anymore, but if – when – Rosie came back, Nate knew she would want to see the cards and read all the beautiful messages people had written.

Rosie. Nate got up and walked to the window. She had left shortly after Emmie's funeral and she had gone to a Pilates retreat in Koh Samui. Nate had been surprised to find that she had been in constant contact and he often re-read her messages and listened to her voice mails again. And she sent long letters and trinkets for him to take to Emmie's grave which he dutifully deposited each week into a box he had put there especially. Rosie didn't often phone, but Nate didn't mind that. He messaged her back, telling her his news and his whereabouts. He openly mentioned that he visited Emmie's grave every Friday night before the weekend and he didn't hold back about anything he was feeling.

Nate had the feeling some people didn't understand what Rosie had done, how she could leave him alone at a time like this. Not Lily and Jamie or anyone close, but Nate sensed disapproval and condemnation from others – neighbours, a few of the guys at work. His mother.

But Nate didn't blame Rosie. Not one bit. He had needed the month away – from here and from Rosie. If he hadn't worked in the police force, he would have taken longer, but maybe work had helped him. At the same time, Nate also felt he needed the space away from Rosie at home. It had helped him come to terms with things better – being alone with his thoughts and not having to bolster Rosie up as well. It would have been too much.

Nate had no personal wish to be in Thailand doing yoga or Pilates or meditation. But he and Rosie were different. And people – those who weren't close to the situation – couldn't possibly understand. Nate and Rosie had lived on the edge for around eight years since Emmie's diagnosis. They had experienced extreme highs and lows and they had always teetered on the brink of possible, impending grief. And now that grief had hit them. And it was all-consuming. It was heart-breaking. It was like a dense, dark fog that coated them and invaded their insides and made everything feel agonising and hopeless. It was far worse than either of them had imagined. And as Dr Tom had advised, Nate and Rosie were doing what they needed to do to survive. And to hell with anyone who didn't understand or approve.

Would he like to know when Rosie was coming home? Of course he would. Nate finished his coffee. But he trusted her. She would be back when she was ready to come back. Nate had no idea what would happen when she did, but he would tackle that when he needed to. Since they had lost Emmie, he had learnt to deal with each day as it came. He didn't think ahead too far and he did his best not to worry about how he would respond or react to anything.

Nate glanced at his watch. He should get going. He was visiting Emmie's grave and absurdly, since he wasn't sure if she knew or not, he hated being late. Nate threw on his thick overcoat and grabbed his keys. It was only a short drive there and he always collected some fresh flowers on the way. Pink roses usually, sometimes orange ones. Anything he thought she would find pretty. Today he had a mini Christmas tree in a pot that was covered in fake snow, because he knew she would love that.

When he arrived at the burial ground, Nate cleared away anything from the week before. He left a glass dolphin Rosie had sent through the post in the box and he propped the mini Christmas tree up by Emmie's cross. He took a deep breath. He had started to accept what had happened recently. He hated it, but he wasn't as angry. He was learning to appreciate the time he and Rosie had had with Emmie, rather than being furious that they hadn't had more.

Nate felt a familiar prickle across his back and he straightened. Rosie. *Rosie.*

'Nate.'

He turned. She looked tanned. Slim. Terribly sad. Remorseful. She wore a camel-coloured overcoat tied at the waist with chocolate brown boots and a brown scarf knotted around her neck.

Nate's heart reacted immediately to seeing her. It was racing and out of control. He had never been so pleased to see anyone in his life.

'Oh my God, Nate. I've missed you so much.' Rosie ran into his arms.

Nate held her. So tightly he thought he was probably hurting her a bit. But he couldn't help it. He didn't want to ever let her go again.

'I'm so sorry,' she mumbled into his shoulder. She felt so incredibly guilty that she had been away for so long. 'I love you so much, but the pain… Emmie…'

'I know, Rose. I know.'

Nate didn't need Rosie to explain. No words were needed. Other people might not understand but he did. He took her face in his hands and he kissed her. Tenderly. Then with more passion. Then he stopped and looked at her.

Rosie drank him in. She had spent the past month in Thailand wanting to jump on a plane and come home. But something kept stopping her. She didn't want to come back before she was ready. She didn't want to put that on

Nate. Rosie wanted to come home when she knew she had healed as much as she could heal.

'When did you get back?'

'Just now. I dumped everything at Lily's and borrowed her car to come straight here.'

'I'm so happy to see you.' Nate pulled her close and kissed her forehead. He was crying again and he didn't care.

Rosie was crying too. 'I wanted to come home a month ago, but I was too emotional still.'

'A month ago I'm not sure I could have coped with you coming home either.'

'Really?' Rosie felt a rush of relief. 'I've been so worried about you.'

Nate smoothed her hair away from her face. 'Same here. And no one else could possibly understand apart from us. But we had to do what we had to do to survive, right?'

Rosie turned to face Emmie's cross and Nate slid his arms around her waist. 'I used to obsess about Emmie's funeral. I don't think I ever told you that because it was so morbid. But I did. I hated myself for doing it, but I couldn't help myself.'

'I used to do that too,' Nate admitted. 'Like you, I used to wonder why the hell I was doing that to myself. But it just used to swim into my head.' He kissed her neck. 'Do you think we might have been OK if we'd talked more? About stuff like this?'

'I don't know. I don't think it matters.'

Rosie suddenly felt paranoid with Nate's arms around her waist. Because she had news to tell him and if he moved his arms a little lower, he would instantly know.

Big news. She had barely been able to believe it herself because she was in her early forties and her periods had been erratic for the past few years. But it was official. She had found out two days after she had booked her flight home and she had checked no less than ten times. She had even checked at Lily's house before coming here, just in case tests in Thailand weren't 100% accurate.

Rosie didn't know how to tell Nate, how he would react. She glanced at Emmie's grave. Would Emmie have minded – did she mind now? They hadn't done it on purpose. Rosie had no wish to replace Emmie, not ever. But this had happened, it was happening and even though it had been a tremendous shock, Rosie now realised she wanted it to. She was terrified about this new baby. Absolutely petrified. But somehow, she was going to have to find some courage from somewhere so she could do this.

I miss you, my darling, Rosie told Emmie silently. *And I will be back to see you, I promise. But for now, I need to be with Daddy and I need to tell him the news about this miracle baby that would have been your brother or sister.*

Rosie felt choked up. How Emmie would have loved to have been a big sister. But it wasn't meant to be. Emmie had had all the time she was allowed to have.

'You need to tell me all your news from Thailand,' Nate said. 'The bits you haven't already told me, at any rate.'

Rosie looked at him. Knowing Nate as she did, she knew she was in for some tears when she updated him about what she hadn't yet told him about Thailand. But Rosie was certain they would be happy tears, even though there was still work to be done still between them. And as much as they had loved Emmie, maybe it was finally time for Rosie and Nate to move forward together. With Emmie in their hearts and a new baby in their lives.

'Let's go home,' Rosie said to Nate.

Nate nodded. 'That's the best thing I've heard all day.'

Thinking Nate might have spoken too soon, Rosie broke into a smile. With their arms around one another, she and Nate took their first new steps forward together.